H (2) B/ JP

FOOL'S GOLD

GILLIAN GODDEN

B

Boldwood

First published in Great Britain in 2021 by Boldwood Books Ltd.

Cover Photography: depositphotos and istock

A CIP catalogue record for this book is available from the British Library.

Paperback ISBN 978-1-80280-056-2

Large Print ISBN 978-1-80280-057-9

Hardback ISBN 978-1-80280-055-5

Ebook ISBN 978-1-80280-058-6

Kindle ISBN 978-1-80280-059-3

Audio CD ISBN 978-1-80280-050-0

MP3 CD ISBN 978-1-80280-051-7

Digital audio download ISBN 978-1-80280-053-1

Boldwood Books Ltd
23 Bowerdean Street
London SW6 3TN
www.boldwoodbooks.com

1

REFLECTION

Isn't it strange how your life can change just as quickly as flicking a switch? One moment in time can change your whole future. Sometimes for the good or the bad – you really don't know until you follow the path put in front of you. Looking out of the window as the train sped past trees and houses, a feeling of foreboding gripped Julie. Suddenly she felt sick. What was she doing? Especially with a man she hardly knew. An ex-con with fingers in more pies than a baker. Thinking about her life and the difficulties in it, Julie felt she didn't have many regrets. There was no point. A lot of her lifestyle was her own doing, but she'd never been given a chance to be anything else. Was this the crossroads to a brighter future or just another mistake in her life? It had already been filled with sadness and dead ends. In addition, she had done her fair share of evil deeds to survive and realised she had rarely done anything for herself. It had always been for the good of someone else. Was this her chance to make something good for herself?

A few days ago, in her bedsit in Liverpool, it had all seemed so feasible. Making love and spending time with Ralph Gold seemed like the only thing in the world that mattered. No sooner had he proposed than he turned on his heel, made his excuses about business and left. He had told her to sort things out in Liverpool and join him as soon as possible in London.

The sound of a baby crying broke into her thoughts and, turning around, she could see a young woman embarrassed and apologising to the people around her. The more the baby cried as she held it to her shoulder and patted its back to soothe it, the more she apologised.

It seemed everyone had turned towards the woman, making the situation even worse. The elderly couple opposite Julie were tutting and looking annoyed as they tried to read their paper. Instantly, she thought of her small nephew, Josh. How she wished she could hear him cry like that.

Julie had had to leave him behind at the hospital with only her old neighbour Gertie to visit him and the nurses to watch over him in his incubator full of wires and tubes to help him breathe. He had another chest infection. No one had expected him to survive. However, he had proved to be a fighter against all the odds and, whatever problems he would face in the future, Julie just knew the little boy would show the same spirit he had demonstrated since birth.

It was a foregone conclusion that he would have some form of mental health problems. Josh had been born a heroin addict due to her own sister Frankie's addiction, although no one would know to what extent he had been affected until he was older.

Although she had agreed to meet Ralph in London, she sorely wished she had not. She had not thought it through properly. As the train stopped at each station, she felt the sudden impulse to get off and leave this promise of a bright future behind her. After all, promises were like piecrusts. They were meant to be broken.

For Christ's sake, Julie, she mentally scolded herself, *you look desperate and foolish and you always swore you would never let any man make a fool of you.* Looking up at the elderly couple facing her and the strange stares they gave her and each other, Julie realised she must have been thinking aloud. She felt she was going crazy, and now she was talking to herself in public!

Craning her neck to look over at the woman again, it saddened her. Frankie, her sister, should be sitting like that, holding her baby to her bosom and nursing it. Instead, she had lived an awful life surrounded by drugs and prostitution and, after giving birth to Josh, she had died. It all seemed so long ago and yet it was just a matter of a few months.

Josh would now be in Julie's care. She would look after him the way she had tried her best to look after Frankie. Neither of them had anyone else. Julie's mother was still alive, but currently serving a prison sentence for murder so was in no position to look after a baby.

'Do you want a cup of tea from the buffet bar or something?' she shouted across the other passengers' heads. Pleased to see the woman half smile as she looked up at her, Julie smiled back reassuringly. There was no point in asking; that poor woman was in dire need of a cup of something. Preferably laced with gin. 'Don't worry about this lot, love, they have obviously just arrived from Mars and never heard a baby cry before. God help their own kids!'

Ignoring the other passengers' stares, Julie got up and stumbled her way through the aisle of the train to the buffet carriage. Ordering two cups of tea and a chocolate bar, she opened her purse and saw that she only had twenty pounds in it. Ralph had given her the money for the train ticket and, stupidly, for the first time in her life, blinded by excitement, she had forgotten to ask for more. More to the point, he had not offered any more.

She had given Gertie a few pounds towards her bus fare to go and see Josh, and had bought a new top to look her best for when Ralph met her at the station. The money in her purse was all she had left in the world. Maybe, she mused. Although she knew Ralph was a man of his word, she was nervous. Prostitution was a past life. She had done what she had needed to, to survive. But now she had found a good, honest man and he deserved the best. Doubting herself, Julie knew they were worlds apart, but she was determined to make him proud of her and not regret his decision. He deserved the best and that was what she would give him, putting her seedy past behind her. This was a fresh start with a man she loved and who loved her. Who could ask for anything else?

Disappointment and doubts hung in the air like a cloud over her peroxide-blonde hair. Ralph had only been out of prison a few days when he had come to visit her and had proposed, but now she wondered if he had really meant it. Had it just been freedom talking? All his plans just pent-up desires he been thinking about in his cell? She could always go back to prostitution, she decided while waiting for the woman behind the counter to stop talking to her colleague and eventually pour the tea.

It was an honest trade and never went out of fashion. But just thinking about going back to that life made Julie feel like crying. Her hands felt sweaty as the train moved closer and closer to London. Had this all been some stupid pipe dream? Businessmen didn't marry women like herself. They were mistresses and someone to use when you felt the urge. For the first time in years, she felt frightened and worried. She hated weakness. She'd learnt from experience that showing your weaknesses gave other people control over you. She had always been the strong one and looked after everyone else. Now she wished she had someone to look after her. There was no one to turn to for help. Maybe that was why she wanted to believe Ralph Gold and all of his promises of their future together. She was tired of the life she was living and realised she was going nowhere fast. Moreover, there was little Josh. She would make damned sure whatever happened that he would always know where the next meal was coming from. She would pet and spoil him and make his childhood memorable for all the right reasons.

Picking up the two cardboard cups of tea, the jewelled fingers on her hand sparkled. Ralph had given the rings to her when he had proposed. Well, that was another option. If they were real, she would have something to pawn. They looked genuine enough but now she was not so sure. With her mind racing in all directions with every negative thought bouncing around in her head, she tried reasoning with herself. She liked Ralph Gold and she had trusted and believed his plans for their future. He was a quiet man who noticed everything but said nothing. He was a closed book. Even his facial expressions didn't portray what he was thinking. For all of his money, he showed little bravado. He was a thinker and, surely, a man like that would not make rash proposals to women. The overly hot tea nearly burnt her mouth as she took a sip. It had not helped that the train had jolted and she had taken a bigger sip of the hot liquid than intended.

'For God's sake, do British Rail try and kill all of their customers? Put some bloody cold water in these, will you, and be grateful I'm not suing you.'

'You can always put your complaint in writing.'

'Well, maybe I will, you snotty cow, standing there gossiping with your mate. I wonder what British Rail would think about you ignoring your customers!' Snapping and glaring at the woman behind the counter, she waited until the woman poured some cold water into the cups and steadied herself as she walked back to her seat. She wanted to lash out at someone. Anyone. She knew she had made a fool of herself believing Ralph. Anyway, it served that snotty cow right.

She took a cup over to the woman with the baby, who by now seemed to be getting quieter in the care of its mother's soothing voice and with the motion of the train settling it. 'Here take this, and this. Sorry, there is no brandy in it.' Looking down at the baby and handing over the chocolate bar to the woman, Julie smiled as the grateful, tired woman held her free hand out for the cup.

'How much do I owe you, erm...?' the flustered woman with the baby asked Julie while trying to reach for her bag.

Julie shook her head. 'Julie. And no, you don't owe me anything, love. What is it?'

'It's a boy. Steven. Thank you, Julie.' For the first time on the journey, Julie saw a faint smile on the woman's face.

Looking at the healthy baby before her stabbed her heart. Josh should be sitting on his mum's lap like that, annoying people with his cries. Walking away from this happy scene of mother and child, Julie squeezed herself back into the seat opposite the elderly couple. Their sideways glance at each other as she sat down made her blood boil. 'What are you two nosy bastards staring at?'

Not answering, they turned their heads and looked out of the window, ignoring her comment. They treated her as if she was something they had just wiped off their shoes.

Tentatively taking another sip of the tea, Julie started the mental conversation in her mind again while looking out of the window at the houses in the distance, replaying the last week in her head. Why had she fallen for this man's charming fantasy? Deep down she knew why. It was simple: because Ralph Gold was the only man who had ever treated her like a lady. She had never known anyone like him. He was an unpretentious man. The calming Irish side of him put her at ease and his sense of humour matched her own. The mixture of the deep green eyes of his mother and the black hair from his Jewish father made him look distinctive. He, too, had been a survivor and now, through protection rackets and his connections with organised crime, he had become a very rich businessman. Although he was a quietly spoken man, she knew he didn't suffer fools gladly and business was business. Ralph Gold was a man to be reckoned with.

Even though they had met a couple of times by chance, the timing hadn't been quite right for them. And when they had at last met properly, while she had been an escort and he was a client, they had clicked straight away. None of her past had bothered Ralph. He had quoted sayings from the Bible when she had shown concerns. Possibly his Catholic mother's words: 'Julie,' he had said, 'judge not, that ye be not judged.' Ralph knew that to survive in this world you had to use whatever means you had. He had his own stories of how he'd started out, bare-knuckle fighting for a few pounds. Even though he was older than her, the chemistry between them had been right. Instinctively they both knew they had found their soul-mate. He had shown her respect. And their lovemaking – yes, she admitted to herself, it was lovemaking – was a two-way street. It wasn't self-gratification for an hour. She had never felt like this before, and didn't like the feeling of not being in control of the situation.

Raising her cup to her mouth, Julie noticed the woman opposite her admiring the rings on her fingers. Purposely, Julie laid her hand on the table in front of her to give the woman a better look. Getting the reaction she wanted and raising her eyes to her, Julie smiled. She could feel the sarcasm already dripping from her mouth. 'Nice aren't they?' Waving her fingers around to let the light from the window make them glisten and sparkle, she paused for effect. 'It's a shame the jeweller's were shut when he bought yours.'

'That's my wife you're talking to. Stop being so rude.' The man jumped in quickly to prevent his wife from further embarrassment.

'You said it, honey. She is your wife and that is your problem. Better luck next time.' Julie's red, glossy lips portrayed a wide grin. She was ready for a fight. She wanted one. All the pent-up tension inside of her felt like poison that needed to pour out of her. A boil that needed lancing.

'Don't, Rodney, she's not worth it. She's not our sort of person. Look how she's dressed in that short skirt and low top.'

Feeling angry at the snub and comments, Julie's face flushed. 'Well, he likes my low top, dear. At least everything is pointing north. Your tits went south years ago.' But as she looked at her reflection in the window, she couldn't help feeling that maybe they had a point. She looked like exactly what she was: a tart. Now her self-esteem dropped even lower. She thought she had been clever, snapping at this couple, ready for battle, but in fact it was them who had won the war.

The announcement from the train driver almost made her blood run cold. She couldn't change her clothes now; it was too late.

'Ladies and gentlemen, we are now approaching King's Cross station.'

Everyone jumped from their seats, started collecting their bags from the overhead luggage rails, and made their way to the centre aisle. Watching them all, Julie remained in her seat. She didn't know what lay ahead of her. She felt nervous as the train came to a halt and people started getting off. She desperately needed a cigarette.

'Thank you for your kindness, Julie.' A voice broke into her thoughts; she turned and saw the woman with the baby, who had now decided to go to sleep.

'No problem, darling. Take care.'

Suddenly, Julie didn't want to get off. What was the point? But, realising she was the only person left in the carriage and the train staff were walking down the aisle with rubbish bags collecting all the empty crisp packets and sweet wrappers left by the passengers, she stood up and walked towards the luggage compartment near the doors and picked up her holdalls. It wasn't much to show for a lifetime. Two bloody holdalls! They contained everything she had in the world.

Making her way along the platform amongst all the passengers, some waiting to get on the train and others making their way to the exit, Julie followed the crowd and tried find her way out. 'What time is the next train to Liverpool?' she asked one of the guards standing at the gates. His answer that it would only be a couple of hours made her feel better. Time enough to sell these rings and go home.

Walking out of the dark station and shielding her eyes from the sunlight, she heard someone shout. Looking around, she heard her name.

'Are you Julie?' A young man sitting on the bonnet of an expensive car smoking a cigarette pointed at her.

'My name is Julie,' she stammered. 'Who are you?' Puzzled, she stood rooted to the spot.

'Are you Ralph's Julie from Liverpool?'

'I suppose so,' Julie felt herself blush, not quite knowing what to say.

Flicking his cigarette on the floor, he walked over to her and held his hand out for her bags. 'I fought I'd missed you. Everyone else came out ages ago.'

'Look, sonny, I asked you who you were. Now before you run off with my bags, do you want to answer me?'

'Didn't Ralph tell you? I'm here to pick you up. I drive for him sometimes. You don't fink he'd let you catch the bus to the hotel, do you?' His smile was warm and friendly as he opened the boot of the car and reached out for her bags again.

His attempts to sound posh with his cockney accent made Julie smile as she handed over her bags to him. Taking out a handkerchief, he opened the back door and made a point of dusting it before she got in. Finding this all very funny, and getting in the car, relief washed over her. Ralph hadn't forgotten about her at all. Whether he was going to marry her or not, he still wanted to see her!

The heavy London traffic slowed down the journey to the hotel. 'Well, you know my name, so what is yours?' Trying to sound more confident than she felt, she decided to make small talk. This way she might get some information about what Ralph had said about her.

'Christopher, but everyone calls me Chris.' He seemed friendly and chirpy enough with his easy cockney manner.

'Do you have a spare cigarette, Chris?' She knew that he did because she'd seen him smoking outside of the train station. He handed her his cigarette packet and lighter over his shoulder while he kept his eyes on the road. 'Is it okay if I smoke in here? I'll open the window.'

'Yes, course, I'll open the back window for you. They're electric, you know,' he boasted proudly as he pressed the button to open the window.

'How come Ralph didn't come and meet me, then?'

'Dunno, Julie. You don't mind me calling you Julie, do you?' He paused.

'That's my name. Do you mind me calling you Chris?' Julie laughed. He was obviously very nervous.

'Dunno why Ralph couldn't come. Busy, I suppose. He just rang me and told me to go to King's Cross station and meet a blonde woman called Julie. When I asked him how I would recognise you, he laughed and said, "Oh, you will know her when you see her, Chris. But keep your hands to yourself – she bites."' They both burst out laughing, then Chris shouted out of the window to some driver who had just cut across him.

Inhaling on her long-awaited cigarette, she blew the smoke out of the window and looked at all the people rushing around on the pavements, going about their daily routines. Fleetingly, Julie remembered the last time she had been in London. She'd not been the usual tourist. She had come on a mission to commit murder and even the score on an old friend. These were very different circumstances.

Remembering Donna and her fateful ending stabbed at Julie's heart. They had been friends, good friends, and had worked at Carrie Smeltzer's brothel together. It still made Julie wince when she thought about how it could have so easily been herself that had been murdered by that sadist client. He had handcuffed Donna to the bed face down and not even realised while he was having sex with her that he was pushing her face into the pillows, suffocating her. When Julie had heard his screams of panic and run upstairs, she hadn't known what had shocked her more – the fact that he had killed Donna, or the fact that he was a police officer who enjoyed going to swinger parties with his wife.

The brothel where they had worked had hosted the party, but the girls who worked there were strictly off-limits unless paid. And Inspector Connor was a sadistic man who had paid Donna for sex. This had been her fateful ending.

When Julie had wanted to telephone the police, Carrie had been afraid of the scandal and had succumbed to Connor's pleadings. His wife, who was also in the police force, had instructed Julie and Carrie to leave the house, so that they could dispose of the evidence and Donna's body. Julie's stomach had turned. It had been three against one. No matter how many times she had tried to convince Carrie to call the police to this murder scene, she had been ignored. She didn't stand a chance. Who would believe some prostitute against the might of the police force? It had made Julie feel sick when, days later, there were reports about a woman's body being found in the river, and it had broken her heart.

Through Ralph Gold she had been given the chance for long-awaited vengeance, when the same police officer who had killed Donna had also been investigating Ralph. With the help of Ralph's Mafia connections, she had been given the opportunity to go to the hotel room where Connor was protecting a witness and had shot him. She felt justice had been served but it would never bring Donna back. Even now the thought of Donna brought a tear to her eye. But Julie's actions had brought closure and wherever Donna was now, hopefully this had given her peace.

Chris pulled into the hotel, right at the front doors. 'That guy at the front will find a parking space for us while I settle you in.' Getting out, Chris opened the back door for her. She'd worked many hotels in the past as an escort, but nothing in this league. It felt intimidating and she looked down at her clothing again and pulled her coat around her.

'I'm not sure if Ralph will be back yet so let's get you signed in.' Throwing the car keys to the waiting valet standing on the steps, Chris picked up the holdalls and opened the doors for Julie.

'Gold is the name.' Standing there straightening his tie, Chris flaunted his importance.

'Mrs Gold, how lovely to meet you at last. Your husband said you would be joining him today. He's not back yet but he left this for you and there is champagne and strawberries in your room.' Turning to a pigeonhole behind reception, the receptionist took out an envelope and handed it to Julie with her best-rehearsed smile. 'If you need anything, just ring down and we'll arrange it for you.'

'Do you want me to carry your bags upstairs?'

Coughing behind them to get their attention, a porter reached down for Julie's bags. 'I will take it from here, sir.'

'No, Chris, I'm okay. Thank you. Oh, here are your cigarettes. Sorry.'

'Keep 'em. I've got more in the car. Just one thing.' His cheeks flushed with embarrassment as he looked down and kicked the highly polished reception desk, much to the annoyance of the receptionist. 'Don't suppose you would put a good word in with Ralph about being his permanent driver, would you? I've looked after you, haven't I? I know he likes to drive himself and just uses a driver now and again, but he's a good bloke, your Ralph,' he said, looking sheepish and younger than his years.

Julie nodded. 'Rest assured, I will mention it to Ralph about how well you have looked after me. Thank you.'

Reaching over for the pen and paper on the desk, he wrote down his telephone number. 'Just in case you need it, eh?'

Taking the paper from him, Julie put it in her handbag. 'Thanks. I daresay I'm going to need someone to carry my bags and drive me around.' She winked and watched the smile appear on his face again.

'You make sure you look after her proper, like, or Mr Gold will hear about it. And he will have somefing to say to you,' Chris warned, wagging his finger at the receptionist, which did not impress her much. She looked him up and down with distaste at his dropped vowels.

After a quick ride in the lift, Julie waited while the porter opened the bedroom door for her. Once inside, she looked around at the lavish surroundings of the hotel room, trying her best to hide her shock from the porter. This wasn't a hotel room – it was a full suite and looked like an apartment. She never knew hotels had rooms like this, and she had worked in a lot of them. It was somewhere a pop star or a famous movie star would stay. There was a dining room and a lounge area complete with large sofas, a television and thick rugs laid on the floor. Julie had never seen anything like it before. This was another world.

The bedroom was en-suite with bath and shower, but there was also a spare toilet down the corridor. She could have fitted her small bedsit into this place five times over. Smiling to herself, Julie realised the closest she had come to one of these posh showers before, with its glass surrounding, was when she walked in the rain.

Breaking into her thoughts, the porter spoke. 'Would you like me to pour some champagne for you, madam?' Walking across to the silver tray that rested on the well-stocked mahogany bar, he took out the bottle of champagne and popped the cork. Once he had poured her drink, he put the bottle into a large silver bucket full of ice. This was pure luxury.

For once, Julie was being treated like a very special lady. She'd always accepted peoples' opinions of her as a part of life, but Ralph Gold was changing all of that. She was starting to be given respect and treated accordingly. He was a very special man and she realised how lucky she was. It wasn't the money. There was always someone with money. But you couldn't buy what she felt for Ralph at this moment in time and it was impossible to describe it. In an instant, he had turned her life around. The past was well and truly behind her. She was going to be Mrs Ralph Gold and he would never doubt his decision to marry her; she would make sure of that. She felt like a queen and couldn't stop smiling.

Wanting to laugh, Julie took the glass from the porter. She had been called 'madam' before but not in this context! Noticing he was hovering around plumping pillows and checking the curtains, it dawned on Julie that he was waiting for his tip.

Taking out five pounds from her bag, grudgingly she handed it over. Her money was dwindling fast, but she couldn't look like a cheapskate and just give him fifty pence. Although he didn't look impressed, he took it anyway and left.

For the first time all day, she could relax. Kicking her shoes off and taking another drink of her champagne, she walked over to the windows and looked out. She hadn't expected to be here in London drinking champagne. During her nerve-wracking journey, this was the last thing she had thought about. Opening the balcony windows and letting the cool breeze in, she stepped out to look at London in all of its glory. In the distance she could see the top of St Paul's Cathedral. The skyline was full of other famous buildings. Leaning on the barrier, she sipped her champagne and looked down. Cars of all shapes and sizes were coming to the hotel and the hustle and bustle of the valets meeting them interested her. And the well-known shops in the distance seemed to be full of people carrying their designer shopping bags. She had always enjoyed people watching, and this was the perfect place to do it.

Feeling the stress leaving her body, she looked around. The excitement building up inside of her made her feel like a kid at Christmas. She wanted to pinch herself. Surely this couldn't be true? The theatre billboards in the distance took her attention. Smiling to herself, she craned her neck to look at all the famous names of plays she had only heard about. This was living!

Taking stock of London and the hundreds of people going about their business, Julie made a mental note to herself. She was going to take London by storm. She would make London *her* place. She would wear all of those fancy designer clothes and reinvent herself. Gone was the old Julie. This was a fresh start with a new life and she was determined to grasp it with both hands. Walking back into the lounge, she filled her glass again and thought about Ralph. She didn't know when to expect him, but remembering that the hotel staff had called her Mrs Gold made her smile.

So that was Ralph's game, was it? Spinning a respectable line to the reception staff that he was expecting his wife. Looking over at the large four-poster bed, it looked inviting. This had seemed like the longest day in her life and now the adrenalin was wearing off, she felt tired. Maybe she would have a nap before Ralph turned up. Walking into the bathroom, she spied all the wonderful soaps and scented oils left by the hotel. Deciding to have a bath first, she walked over and turned the large gold taps. As the bath began to fill, she poured in the bottle of bubble bath. It was a nice feeling running a hot bath without having to put money into the meter and waiting for the water to boil in the immersion tank as she had at her bedsit. Watching the liquid burst into a scented foam on the water made her feel better already.

Walking into the bedroom again, she poured herself another glass of champagne and then saw the envelope the receptionist had given her earlier. She had forgotten all about it. Opening it, she saw that it was full of money. She couldn't believe her eyes. Taking it all out, she displayed it like a fan and kissed it. Then she saw a piece of paper fall out. Picking it up, she saw that it was a note from Ralph.

I do hope you're reading this, Julie, because if you are that means you are here. I did wonder if you had got cold feet and changed your mind. I hope not. I have a little business to do but I will be back as soon as possible and maybe we could have dinner? In the meantime, go shopping, enjoy yourself and welcome to London, my love. And for the record, I do love you, Julie.

Ralph x

Looking at the note again, she smiled. A wave of relief washed over her. It seemed she wasn't the only one who'd had doubts. Even when she had called him to tell him what train she would be on, he still hadn't been sure if she'd meant it. It seemed they'd both had their doubts once leaving the warmth of each other's arms and the cold light of day had crept in. A wide grin crossed her face and her eyes lit up at the wad of cash in her hand. Walking into the bathroom, she turned off the taps and pulled the plug out, watching all those scented soap suds float away. Sod the bath. This was London: Oxford Street and streets full of shops. Stuffing the money in her handbag, she slipped on her shoes and coat.

'Look out, London, Julie's here!' She laughed aloud and slammed the door behind her.

2

STOOL PIGEON

Walking down the small side street in the East End of London, Ralph retraced his steps. It was only a few years ago that he had been down this way. However, he remembered the owner of one particular pub very well. Charlie Jenkins was an egotistical, self-important pimp and publican, too caught up in his own affairs to give a damn about anyone else, and that was just the way Ralph wanted it. He was just what Ralph and his Italian business partner, Carlos, needed to cover their tracks.

Ralph remembered the first time he had met Charlie, during his very first stay in London. Ralph had gone to the East End in expectation of something; he wasn't sure of what. The myths and reputation that surrounded the place seemed like one of London's biggest tourist attractions, apart from Buckingham Palace.

It had started to rain and so he had gone into the first pub he saw for cover. The small pub on the corner with its blacked-out windows and peeling paint hadn't looked inviting, but it served a purpose. On opening the door, the blast of music that greeted him was almost deafening.

The noise from the customers' laughter and cheers had made

him turn his head in the direction of their shouts. In the far corner, he spotted a makeshift triangular stage surrounded by all walks of life. Dancing on it provocatively was a half-naked woman shaking her breasts towards the crowd, making them cheer and clap even louder. He'd never expected this. Now he understood the blacked-out windows. This was very different from Ireland and the pubs he'd visited there.

Pushing his way through the crowd, Ralph walked up to the bar. He leant forward and cupped his hand around his mouth. 'Whisky,' he shouted to make himself heard over the music. The busty barmaid, who looked flustered and rushed off her feet, quickly turned to the optics behind the bar and held a glass under the whisky bottle. Without saying a word, she held her hand out for the money. Handing it over, he shouted again, 'Is there any chance of a clean glass?', pointing out the faint lipstick mark still on the rim of his glass from its predecessor to make his point.

Picking up a soiled tea towel, she took the glass and wiped the rim. 'That's as good as you're going to get here, mate.'

Smiling at her and shrugging, he raised his glass to her and took a sip of the whisky, which warmed him. The barmaid's permed, blonde hair with its black roots hypnotised him. It was stationary as she moved her head from side to side, pulling pints for thirsty customers. There must have been a whole can of hair lacquer on it.

'Hello, mate. You're a long way from home.' A short, stocky man tapped him on the shoulder, clearly wanting to make his presence known.

'Am I?' Raising one eyebrow and taking another sip of his whisky, Ralph took stock of the stranger in a suit standing there as if Ralph should know who he was. He noticed two men also in suits standing a few feet behind him. It was clear they were this man's minders or henchmen. Either way, these young men stood there trying to intimidate Ralph.

'Well, me and my boys here haven't seen you in here before.' Jerking his thumb behind him to make their presence known and to point out he wasn't alone should Ralph give him trouble, he gave a jolly laugh. 'Irish, isn't it? That accent of yours?'

'You're right, considering I have hardly said anything and you can hear me above the music. Yes, I'm from Ireland.' Staying calm and with his eyes firmly focused on the men standing behind this man, Ralph smiled and held out his hand. 'Ralph is the name, sir. And what is yours, might I ask?'

The three of them laughed as though he had said something funny.

Holding out his hand, the man shook Ralph's. 'Charlie Jenkins. That's my name. And this is my place. You must be a very long way from home, Ralph, if you've never heard of me.' Again he turned to the men behind him for confirmation of his importance. Status seemed to mean everything to Charlie Jenkins and those two behind him just agreed with everything he said to appease him.

Beckoning the barmaid over, he made a big show of his authority. 'Whisky and leave the bottle,' he barked at her. During the proffered drinks, which Ralph knew were to loosen his tongue, a barrage of questions was thrown at him. It was more like a Spanish Inquisition about where he lived and why he was here. Most of all, the underlying question was why he had chosen to come into this pub.

Ralph was puzzled; a publican who didn't like new faces? It didn't make sense. Unless of course he had something to be paranoid about. Ralph came to the conclusion that Charlie, with all his front and wide boy ways, was frightened of something or someone. As though he was expecting trouble from strangers.

'Do you normally ask so many questions about the men who frequent your pub to admire your lovely ladies?' Ralph nodded to the overweight stripper in the far corner. Christ, this place was sleazy. She looked older than his mother did. Ralph had answered all of his questions calmly, telling him everything about himself but nothing at the same time. 'I was in the area and with the rain coming down, your pub found me,' he remarked.

Throwing his arms open wide, embracing his empire, and spilling some of his whisky from his glass on the threadbare, faded carpet, Charlie beamed with pride. 'This is my place, Irish Ralph. I know most of the punters in here and they know me as the Bossman. You want something, I'm the man to come to. With me and my boys here keeping the East End safe, your granny is able to walk home late at night with her bingo winnings. Nothing happens on my turf.' Charlie was becoming louder and a little worse for wear after consuming so much of his own whisky, while Ralph had sipped sparingly at his own. This was all bravado and Ralph wasn't impressed.

Listening as Charlie boasted about his status in the East End and how feared he was, each time turning to his men to confirm what he was saying, Ralph had almost laughed aloud. In the space of a couple of hours, Charlie had told Ralph everything about himself. Well, almost; he hadn't mentioned the colour of his underwear.

So, this drunk, overweight fool was known as the Bossman in local parts. Charlie Jenkins was a minor crook who hired young boys to do his fighting for him. This rundown pub, with its overweight strippers and faded carpets, was his empire! What a joke.

Charlie enjoyed throwing his weight around, expecting everyone to tremble in his wake. He was a sleazy laughing-stock. Nevertheless, he was entertaining, Ralph had to admit that. It almost reminded Ralph of his friend back home, Paddy. A few drinks down his throat loosened Paddy's tongue as he tried to impress people, and Charlie Jenkins was no different. They had parted company with a shake of hands like old friends.

That had been a few years ago now, when Ralph hadn't been sure if he had enough money to pay the hotel bill and he thought Don Carlos had duped him. Of course, he had been wrong. Time and an ever-growing bank account had proved that. When Carlos had suggested they needed a fall guy for their money-laundering at an old West End nightclub they had recently acquired, Charlie Jenkins, a big fish in a small pond, had instantly popped into Ralph's head.

After doing his homework and dropping Charlie's name amongst his new-found friends and police commissioners, Ralph had also found out that not only was Charlie known to the police, he was also one of their regular informers. This high and mighty man with his gangster profile regularly tipped off the police with information about rival gangs on the south of the river. This was the angle Ralph and Carlos liked. It was insurance. If the other gangs ever found out that it was Charlie who had put their friends behind bars, his life wouldn't be worth living.

Today was a very different visit to Charlie's pub. Ralph knew that whatever deal he offered, Charlie he would agree to it. The stakes were high and the offer on the table was more than Charlie could ever imagine. Smiling to himself as he approached the rundown pub with its once red, peeling paint, Ralph knew the Bossman would agree to his offer without a second thought. Life was strange, Ralph mused to himself. His chance meeting with Charlie had been an accident and now he would be a godsend.

On entering, Ralph noticed that nothing had changed. Inside was still black apart from the few disco lights in the far corner lighting up the triangular stage. As was the first time he went in, there were men laughing and shouting at the aging stripper, overly made up and overweight.

Some women, obviously prostitutes, wearing very short dresses to go with their stockings and suspenders, were sitting at tables crowded with half empty glasses and overflowing ashtrays, hoping someone would join them. At least the darkness of the pub hid the dismal decoration. Pushing his way to the bar, Ralph looked around for his target. Ordering a drink and scanning the room, he didn't have long to wait. Hearing laughter coming from a far-off corner booth, Ralph cocked his head to one side and followed the merriment.

There he was. Charlie Jenkins in all of his glory, surrounded by a group of men, holding court. Picking up his drink, Ralph walked slowly over to the booth. 'Hello, Mr Jenkins. Nice to see you again. Can I get you a drink?' As Ralph approached the crowd and spoke directly to Charlie, the laughter stopped. Everyone looked up at Ralph, puzzled and curious, not knowing who he was. Seeing no recognition in Charlie's eyes, Ralph prompted him. 'It's been a long time since I was in these parts and my Irish accent isn't as strong as it used to be. But the last time you made me very welcome in your establishment.' Still nothing, although Ralph did notice how Charlie looked at the suit he was wearing.

'Should I remember you, mate? This is a private party and I know a lot of people.'

'I just remember you saying that night that if there was ever anything someone wanted, you were the man to come to.' Turning on the charm and flattering someone like Charlie was the key. Showing him the respect he thought he deserved was Ralph's way in. 'Sorry to bother you, Mr Jenkins.' Shrugging and turning around, Ralph slowly walked back to the bar, knowing he was about to hook the fish.

'Wait! Yeah, yeah, I remember you. The Irishman. We had a few drinks together,' Charlie shouted. Ralph turned around. Ralph had a feeling that Charlie didn't have a clue who he was but didn't want to look foolish in front of friends.

'Thanks for that, Mr Jenkins.' Keeping it on a formal basis,

Ralph held out his hand to shake Charlie's, making a big show of how happy he was that Charlie was giving him the time of day.

'Of course I remember you... Oy, you lot, get my friend here a drink.' Charlie waved his arms around, giving orders, while moving up in the corner booth so that Ralph could sit beside him.

'Is there somewhere we could talk more privately?' Looking directly at him, Ralph waited as Charlie looked around at the men sitting at his table suspiciously, then back at him.

'We can have a drink here. Here, let me introduce the lads.'

'I did say in private, Mr Jenkins.' Ralph's calm, authoritative voice stopped them all talking again.

'You tooled up, mate? Got something you want to give me in the office, eh?' Charlie was laughing but when he noticed that Ralph didn't smile, he quickly stopped.

'Yes, sure. This had better be good,' Charlie warned as he stood up and straightened his tie. He didn't want to lose face but he could see that Ralph was deadly serious. Given his dress code and his manner, he knew this man wasn't looking for cheap thrills.

Following Charlie's lead into the back room, which was even worse than the front of house, Ralph looked around. This man's so-called office was a dump, considering he portrayed himself as the boss of the manor.

His desk was nothing more than one of the pub's old wooden tables, which still had the stained rings of the beer glasses embedded in the wood. Newspapers were scattered everywhere, mainly the horse-racing pages, along with half-empty take-away boxes. The whole place stank to high heaven. Not exactly the image of a self-made man making a fortune. This made the offer he was going to make to Charlie seem like a dream come true. Leave this dump and go to the West End? There was no comparison.

Satisfied with his choice, Ralph waited while Charlie picked up a few newspapers off a wooden chair and invited him to sit down. This was exactly what Ralph wanted. A fool chasing fool's gold. Charlie would take the carrot Ralph was about to dangle in front of him if it enriched his reputation. He would also take the meagre offering Ralph was prepared to pay. More to the point, he would take all the blame.

'So what can I do for you, erm...? Sorry, your name escapes me again.'

'Let's leave names aside for now. I'm sure it will come back to you.'

'Okay, let's have it. What do you want? You're not the police because I have never seen one wearing a suit like that.' Looking down at his own suit, Charlie brushed away the cigarette ash that had fallen on his lapel.

'Neither have I, Charlie. Neither have I.' Ralph smiled. 'I have a club over in the West End. It needs someone with knowledge of how things work, with a reputation like yours to look after it.'

'The West End? You are asking me to be a manager in a club? That's a bloody insult. You want a bar boy? Do you know who you're talking to?!' His arrogance and anger rising, Charlie's sneering face flushed.

'I do, or I wouldn't be here.'

'If your club is in the West End, mister, you can get a manager anywhere. They would bite your hands off.' Taking in Ralph's appearance and relaxed, calm manner, Charlie was curious. Reaching down and opening a drawer, he took out two glasses and a whisky bottle and held up the bottle to Ralph.

Ralph nodded to accept the drink. Charlie poured and Ralph carried on, knowing that he had now captured his interest.

'I said someone with your knowledge and reputation. Someone with his eyes open and his mouth shut. What you do and earn from the club is irrelevant.' Ralph shrugged and sat back on his chair. He could see Charlie's brain was trying to get to grips with what he was saying.

'What exactly are you going to be using this club for?'

'A bit of this and that.'

'Are we talking drugs?'

'We're talking money-laundering, maybe. But if it's too much for you, I'm sorry to have wasted your valuable time.' Standing up, Ralph held out his hand to shake Charlie's. The greed in Charlie's eyes was apparent. He was already weighing up the odds and running his tongue over his lips to moisten them.

Charlie picked up his drink and took a gulp. 'Sit down, sit down. It's just a lot to take in all at once. Give me a minute before you walk, eh? Nothing's too big for me. You know that or you wouldn't be here. My boys and I can handle anything. So what's in it for me?'

Sitting down again, Ralph smiled. This really was cat and mouse. 'As I say, I have a club in the West End. It hasn't been used for some time but you could put your name above the door and run it however you see fit. All profits would be yours. I won't interfere.'

'So why don't you do it?'

'I'm no publican, Charlie. You know how things are run and you know how to turn a blind eye. This could be very lucrative for you. In fact, very lucrative for us both.' Nodding and smiling at him, Ralph waited.

'Yes, and I'm also the fall guy with my name above the door.' Gulping back his drink in one, Charlie started to pour himself another, proffering the bottle to Ralph.

'No thanks, I think it's time I left. Maybe I have said too much.' Ralph realised it was now time to play his insurance card, just to keep Charlie in check. 'We both know that you have friends in high places. Especially the police force.' Pausing, Ralph waited for his words to sink into Charlie's brain.

'What do you mean by that? You saying I'm some sort of grass or something?' Suddenly, Charlie reached into his jacket pocket and took out a gun, pointing it at Ralph. 'It's a shame you didn't get that suit in red, Mr Whatever-your-name-is. No one calls Charlie Jenkins a grass. Do you fucking hear me, you Irish prat!'

Holding his hands up in submission, Ralph realised he had touched a raw nerve. This man had more to fear than Ralph had first thought. 'I never said that, Mr Jenkins, but it is understood that a clever, prosperous man as yourself always knows someone who knows someone else. That is good business. No offence meant.' Looking into the barrel of the gun pointed at him, Ralph wanted to knock it out of his hands and punch him hard, but now wasn't the time or the place. 'I'll leave you in peace now. My apologies. Here is my number if you change your mind.'

Ralph gave Charlie an untraceable number of a telephone and answering machine left in an old council house that had been deserted by its tenants. Then he put his hands in his trouser pockets and crossed his fingers as he turned to leave, hoping he wouldn't end up with a bullet in his back. This nervous, trigger-happy fool was capable of anything, especially after a few drinks.

Pushing his way through the crowd, Ralph stopped at the table with Charlie's men still sitting there, and nodded. 'Evening, gentlemen.' Each one of them looked at him with surprise, looked over their shoulders to where Charlie's office was, and then back at Ralph. These clever gangster boys. Not one of them had thought to frisk him in case he had a weapon. Already, it proved to him just how amateur they were. No one was ever allowed in Don Carlos's rooms without being searched first. It was standard procedure.

Hook, line and sinker, thought Ralph as he looked down at the faces of these so-called mobsters. It had been easier than he had thought and he knew Charlie would ring the telephone number he had given him as soon as he left the office. Satisfied with the outcome, Ralph congratulated himself on one of his better brainwaves. That council flat was a brilliant smokescreen and one that would come in handy many times in the future.

Stepping outside, Ralph inhaled the fresh air. Now his business was done and he would go and have dinner with Julie. He wasn't sure if she was in London or not, but it was a nice thought after what he'd just been through. Waving his hand out for a black taxi, Ralph laughed to himself. He wasn't sure what was worse: looking down the barrel of a gun or Julie's wrath at being so late after her arrival... At least she made him laugh and she smelt and looked decidedly better than this dump!

3

HARSH TRUTHS

'Good evening, Mr Gold. Your wife has arrived safely. I just thought you would like to know.'

'Thank you.' Although calm on the outside, inside Ralph was jumping for joy. She was here! The lift didn't go up fast enough and, at last, he was swinging the hotel room door open and stepping inside. The first thing he did was nearly trip over – Julie had indeed been shopping. There were bags and clothing sprawled all over the bed and the floor.

Turning from the mirror as she heard the door open, Julie beamed. 'Ralph, you're a sight for sore eyes. How are you, darling? Do you think this skirt suits me...? Damn it. I'm not ready yet.'

Almost breathless and trying to compose himself, he discarded a coat hanger with a bra on it that had caught on his shoe.

'Not ready? I've been gone for hours. I'm glad you came, Julie.' Flustered and excited, Ralph walked towards her. Shaking his head, he couldn't believe it. Their meetings were never as he imagined they would be. It wasn't like this in the movies where the romantic couple always ran to each other across meadows and crowded streets. But not him and Julie. He had nearly fallen over a coat hanger attached to his foot!

Although, he reasoned as he watched her happily parading her new clothes to him, at least she wasn't angry with him. She wasn't some nagging woman complaining that he hadn't met her at the station and left her alone for so long. This was his Julie and this was the height of their romance.

Julie was standing half-naked in front of the long mirror admiring her new clothes, taking off a blouse she had bought and getting ready to try on another one. Looking around at Ralph, her happy smile brought a smile to his face. 'Is that a gun in your pocket, Ralph Gold, or are you pleased to see me?'

Cocking his head to one side and grinning, Ralph put his arm behind him and put his hand in the waistband of his trousers, pulling out a gun; he put it on the dresser at the side of him. Then he pulled down the zip of his trousers. 'Both, I would say.' The eruption of laughter as they both jumped on the bed amongst Julie's multitude of clothes flying in the air made for a happy reunion.

* * *

'Well, that was all very nice, Ralph. However, I'm hungry now. Let's get showered and go to the restaurant.'

Lying back on his arms as he rested on the bedhead, Ralph felt disappointed. He wanted Julie to himself tonight. 'We could always order room service and stay here?'

'No! Not with all these new clothes I've bought. Or rather, you bought. Come on, move your lovely arse and get dressed. Anyway...' Her voice echoed from the bathroom as she ran the shower. 'This is no different to my bedsit. A room at the top of a building – it just has better carpets and room service.'

Ralph couldn't help laughing to himself. Here she was in one of London's finest hotels with every amenity and she had just compared it to her top-floor bedsit. Pulling back the cover, he got out of bed, walked to the bathroom, and opened the sliding door to the shower. The steam from the shower blocked his view a little, and he waited until the mist cleared and watched as the water rained down on Julie's head and body. Wiping away the water from her eyes, she looked up at Ralph standing there.

'Well, are you coming in, then, or are you just going to watch?'

* * *

'So, we've had our fun, we're eating dinner and now it's down to business.' As he put down his knife and fork, Julie noticed this was Ralph's serious face. She had started to pick up on some of Ralph's little habits over the time she had known him.

'What is it?' Putting down her own knife and fork, she sat back on her chair and folded her arms. This was what she had been dreading. The cold light of day. He had obviously been thinking.

'Firstly, we need to sort out little Josh and get him transferred to London. You're going to have to sort that out. So that's your job for tomorrow.'

Puzzled, Julie looked across the table in the dimly lit hotel restaurant. This was not the conversation she had expected. 'You want to do that for Josh?' Her mouth felt dry and she reached for her glass of wine. She suddenly felt humble. Ralph was an unusual man. She felt so relieved that he was including Josh in their plans. Some men would have discarded him, especially with the problems he had. It's not as though he was her own child. Some men didn't want women with 'baggage', but once again Ralph had astonished her; his kindness and sincerity seemed to know no boundaries.

'Yes, of course! You do come out with some silly things sometimes.' Now it was his turn to look surprised. As much as they had shared a bed and each other's bodies, it seemed they were still skirting around each other. 'I have an early meeting in the morning with Carlos, so I will be pretty much tied up all day. You sort out Josh. And we're going to need to start looking at houses. We can't stay here forever, not now we have a family to look after. So that's another job for you. Find some brochures or something.' Ralph waved his hand in the air dismissively. He had something to say and he wanted to get it off his chest.

Feeling herself blush slightly and sitting quietly, Julie let him finish his speech. She felt nervous and her hands felt sweaty. Ralph seemed to be railroading her with all of his plans. 'I do hope you're not one of those control freaks.' She smiled. She didn't want to sound ungrateful, but she needed to get her point over. 'I've always been independent. I appreciate what you're saying and I know you mean well, but please give me time to take it all in. I would like to discuss "our" plans. Not just yours.'

Ralph stopped short. He hadn't meant this to sound overbearing, like he was taking over. That wasn't what he meant at all. Reaching for her hand, he squeezed it. 'I'm sorry, Julie.' His voice was almost a hushed whisper. Now he was the one that was blushing slightly. Julie was right, of course. He knew that. She was a woman with a mind of her own, unlike his first wife. Irene had relied on Ralph for everything and it had become tiresome, which was why he loved Julie so much. 'I know I sound a bit much. I'm just so pleased that you're here. My head is spinning with all of the things we're going to do together. You're right, of course. I should discuss things more with you. Respect breeds respect... forgive me?' Raising one eyebrow, he cocked his head to one side and smiled.

A broad grin crossed Julie's face and she nodded and squeezed his hand. She had made her point and she couldn't be happier that he felt this way. 'What else have you got in mind, Mr Gold?'

'You're also going to need a bank account. I don't like leaving money on the side for you, it doesn't feel right. If you know what I mean.' Now Ralph looked down and brushed a piece of imaginary dust from his napkin on his knee. He didn't want to mention how he'd first met Julie and that he'd once paid her for her services.

'How do I get a bank account? You need an address for that and I don't have any identification!' Julie looked at him. 'All my money is in cash and that's how I pay for everything. Bloody hell, Ralph, even the rent for my bedsit was in cash with no identification needed. If you couldn't pay, you were thrown out. Actually, that reminds me,' she mused, pursing her lips. 'I paid a deposit up front for that place. I want my money back. A bank account, eh?' She had never been able to open one before without a man setting it up and there had never been anyone close to her to help. At least these days it was possible. Thank goodness for women's rights, with independent women handling their own finances. How the world had changed.

'There you are, then. You do have an address. Use that one for now. If you have a bank account you can apply for a credit card. Actually, until we get that sorted I can just add you to mine. That might be easier for now.' Ralph held his hand up to stop her butting in. 'And while you're doing all that, you also need to sort a date and a place for our wedding.' Ralph's face softened and he held his hand over the table to hold hers.

'You really mean it, don't you?' Julie felt her eyes brim with tears. In her whole life, no one had ever cared for her. Not really cared. Not like Ralph Gold. She had always been the one in charge, looking after everyone else, and it felt a little scary. Usually when someone was nice to you it was because they wanted something from you. But all Ralph Gold wanted was Julie to be herself. No airs and graces, just Julie. It seemed incredible. The very idea that someone had her back for a change felt good. Sniffing hard and shaking her head to fight back the tears, she forced a laugh. 'Blimey, how long is this meeting you're having? You want me to do a lot in one day!'

'You will manage somehow. I know you will.' He couldn't help but grin.

'Damned right I will. But to open a bank account, I need some money.'

'What? You've spent what I gave you already?' He couldn't hide the surprise in his voice.

'Well, nearly. And all that running around. Taxis and stuff. You know what I mean. For God's sake, Ralph, I'm not going to ask you every time I need money for a tampon or something!' Raising her voice to hide her embarrassment, she shifted in her chair. Suddenly she felt uncomfortable asking Ralph for money. He wasn't a customer; he was her fiancé. They were a couple. Normally, she wouldn't have thought twice about bartering for more money, but this felt different. Was this housekeeping money? She almost laughed to herself. Now she did sound crazy. She wanted to be Ralph's equal, someone he would respect. As far as Ralph was concerned, her gold digger days were over.

'No, sorry, Julie. You're right. I will give you all the money you need. But we do need to talk properly. There are many things we need to talk about. Not now, but soon. Now finish your dinner because there is a dessert trolley over there and I know you love desserts.'

'I thought you were dessert.' She winked and smiled at him. 'But what is it that you want to talk to me about? What's on your mind? What do you want to know?'

Ignoring her saucy comments. Ralph picked up his drink and took a sip. 'This is not a conversation we should be having here. Not in public. Later, when were alone.'

'Well, at least give me an idea. Come on, what is it? I'm losing my appetite,' she snapped, back on the defensive. All her doubts came flooding back. This was too good to be true and she had let her guard down and believed everything he had said. She felt herself tremble slightly and suddenly the delicious food made her feel sick. What was it he wanted to know? Everyone had their skeletons; he knew she was no virgin with a snow-white background. So what was troubling him? She didn't want to think about it.

'Okay, for starters: will your mother be coming to the wedding?' Raising his eyebrows and spreading his hands out, he waited for an answer.

Now he had taken her totally off guard. All kinds of worries about her past had quickly gone through her mind, but not this.

'Will yours?' was her only answer. Why was Ralph asking questions about her mother when he seemed to already know the answers? Did he want her to confirm what he already knew about her mother's whereabouts? To see if she would tell him a bare-faced lie? He was testing her, she felt sure of it. Trust and loyalty meant a lot to Ralph and it seemed to her he needed to know if he could trust her to be honest with him. Without trust, no relationship stood any kind of chance.

'I doubt it. You know mine is very ill and doesn't even know what day of the week it is.'

Julie knew it saddened Ralph to think of his mother, who was being cared for back home in Ireland.

Pausing in silence for a moment, Julie looked around at the restaurant full of people. This was not the place, but it was definitely time to clear the air before they went any further together.

Taking her napkin off her knee and putting it on the table, she stood up. 'Come on, let's go back to our room and talk. But, be warned, you might not like everything you hear. But then there are plenty of skeletons in your closet too. You're a closed book, Mr Gold, and I intend to read every bloody page.' Walking ahead of him to the lift, she pressed the button and waited for Ralph to catch her up.

There were other people in the lift and so for the next few minutes they both stood in an eerie silence as the lift doors opened and closed, letting people in and out. Finally, they arrived at the top floor and made their way silently to their room.

'Before you start, pour me a drink. I'm going to the loo.'

Letting out a sigh, Ralph picked up the decanter and poured them both a drink. He felt quite deflated after the afternoon they'd had together.

When Julie returned, her face was flushed and her anger was rising. She pointed a long red fingernail in Ralph's face. 'Don't you glare at me, Ralph Gold. And stop rolling your eyes at the bloody ceiling. It's so annoying!'

'I'm not angry. I just think we need to clear the air. You are so suspicious of me. You don't trust me and I want to know why.'

Taking her drink from him, Julie sat on the edge of the bed and kicked her shoes off. 'My mother won't be coming to our wedding because she's in prison. However, you already know that, don't you? A man like you with the people you know will have done your homework on me. She is in prison for murder, manslaughter, whatever. But she is innocent.' Her voice was low, as if all the fight had suddenly left her as she thought about her mother. She looked tired and fed up. Sitting beside her, Ralph put his hand over her shoulder and pulled her closer towards him.

'Everyone is innocent in prison. Didn't you know that?' His voice was no louder than a whisper and he spoke as though he was comforting a child. This was not the time for recriminations. He should never have broached the subject.

'But she truly is. I write to her and send her money so she always has some extra in case she needs anything. But she never writes back. She wanted a better life for Frankie and me. Something better than she ever had, and I have made her a promise that I will do my best to make that happen.'

'What makes you so sure she is innocent? If that is the case, we could appeal and get a retrial.' Ralph was puzzled at Julie's insistence of her mother's innocence. Although maybe she just wanted to believe it. *Some people prefer denial to the truth*, he mused to himself. Julie snuggled closer into his arm. The scent of him and the muscled arm holding her closely like a protective blanket made her feel safe.

Looking down at the carpet and idly following the pattern with her toes, Julie confessed. 'I know, because I murdered my stepfather.' Nervously, she glanced at Ralph, waiting for his reaction. There wasn't one. Trying to continue, a lump rose in her throat, and her voice trembled as she spoke. 'It wasn't my mum who did it. I jumped to the wrong conclusion and thought he was messing with Frankie, but he wasn't. And even though he was a lazy drunk who had an allergy to work, he didn't deserve it. Frankie lied, so that I wouldn't leave her and go on holiday without her.' Raising her head fully, Julie looked into Ralph's eyes. There wasn't a flicker of emotion in them as he silently listened to Julie's outburst. Warningly, pointing her finger at him, Julie snapped, 'Don't say a word against her. I think Frankie has paid for her sins, don't you? But after I killed him, I pissed off to Spain and Mum was left to take all the blame. We both know the truth, but we don't mention it.' Brushing away the tear that had fallen on her cheek, she felt Ralph take a breath. This was judgement day. Would he turn his back on her now?

Shocked and surprised, Ralph pushed her back to face her properly. 'Is that the truth? Say it again.'

'Yes, it's true! I paid my penance, though. The time we spent in Spain was terrible.' As though lost in a world of her own, Julie's eyes glazed over as she replayed all of the horror she had witnessed.

The whole story came spilling out. Of how she and Frankie had been kidnapped by people traffickers, and how they'd made their way back to Liverpool by boat, never to be the same people again. It was like a poison in her veins that she needed to get rid of. Closure. That was what this confessional was.

Ralph winced and cringed inside at her story. Now so many things made sense. Even down to how she had spent all the money he had given her. His life had been almost paradise in comparison. He wanted to pet her and love her. Keep her warm and safe. Although while she talked he felt sad and guilty, fighting his own demons.

Because before Julie, Ralph had been married. He had never loved his wife the way he had come to love Julie in the short time he had known her. More than he could ever have imagined. But he was plagued with guilt over the death of his wife and their son, Shaun, who he missed terribly.

He would put all of those thoughts in a little box at the back of his brain. He did not like to dwell on it. His life had changed so much, he hardly recognised himself these days.

'Are you going to tell your mum we're getting married?' Julie asked tentatively. The picture she had just painted of herself wasn't exactly glamorous.

'I don't know. I don't want to go back to Ireland. There is nothing for me there now.'

'Don't be ridiculous. Apart from your mum, there is all that property you own and that scruffy bastard Paddy is the landlord!' Sitting up straight again and taking charge of the situation, Julie stuck out her chin. 'When we get married, half of that property is mine and that vain lowlife Paddy can get his hands off it.'

'Why do you dislike him so much? You hardly know him.'

'I know and have seen enough. People like him are two a penny. Parasites living off other people's charity.'

'You're entitled to your opinion, but sometimes Paddy comes in handy, although, believe me, I have my reasons not to trust him either. Don't you see, neither of us are innocent? I have my own family's blood on my hands too. My pride and stupidity killed my wife and child. I wouldn't help Paddy's political friends and losing my family was the price I paid.'

Feeling almost relieved that he wasn't turning his back on her, Julie started to cry. These were tears for the past and the present. She had never been able to relax and let herself grieve. Strong Julie never cried. She had all the answers. But now, she had opened her heart to Ralph. He had stripped her to the bone and this was the Julie he wanted.

Both of them had shared their innermost thoughts. This was the start of a new beginning for them both. Now they could move on.

They both felt drained as they talked and shared the darkest things about them that no one else would ever know. This was the beginning of trust.

Julie held out her little finger towards him and smiled. He entwined his own around hers. 'We're much the same, you and me. We're both guilty of hurting those we love. There is just no way back. So let's go forward, eh?'

Wrapping his arms around her, Ralph held her tightly. He would always look after Julie and keep her safe – no matter what.

Raising her head up from his chest, Julie smiled. 'So. Do you want dessert now?' Laughter filled the room as they embraced and kissed. This was a new Julie and Ralph. Suddenly she felt closer to him than she had anyone else. Their masks had slipped and their bond was stronger. Emotions were high as they held each other close. This was a bond that could never be broken.

4

FUTURE PLANS

Yawning, Julie half opened her eyes. 'It's the middle of the night. Where the bloody hell are you going?' Lying in bed, flat on her stomach, Julie turned her head sideways and rubbed her eyes, while pulling the covers up higher to shield them from the light peering through the curtains.

'It's not the middle of the night. It's 7.30 in the morning. I tried not to wake you. I have a breakfast meeting with Don Carlos. Go back to sleep.'

'Who has a meeting at this time of the morning?'

'Businessmen do. Go back to sleep and don't forget all the things you have to do today. I've written a list. It's on the dresser.'

'Shit, you're making more noise trying to be quiet than if you just hurried up and got dressed normally.'

'Okay, okay, I'm leaving. See you later.' Quietly trying to close the door behind him, he decided to make a run for it as Julie threw a pillow at the door.

'Will you bugger off!'

Turning on her back, she looked at the clock. Christ, she couldn't remember being up so early since she was a kid. Sometimes she was only just coming home after working the hotels. Lighting a cigarette, Julie reached for the telephone, called reception and ordered breakfast. Getting out of bed, she opened her handbag and found the piece of paper Chris, her driver, had given her. Deciding she would need his help for the day, she dialled the number. Then she called the hospital to find out how Josh was doing. While she was on the telephone, she also asked the nurse how she would go about getting Josh moved to London to a private hospital.

The nurse was very helpful. Apparently, they knew many private hospitals in London, but it would be up to the consultant to decide if Josh could be moved. 'I'll call you later this afternoon, then. Tell him I want Josh near me and as I am moving to London, it's only natural. Will you put a list of hospitals together so I can contact them?' The nurse was even more helpful than Julie could have imagined and told Julie she would telephone around the hospitals herself to see if they had a space for Josh.

Ralph had left a wad of cash for her on the bedside table and so she decided to get up and shower while waiting for her breakfast. That was one job underway. Now to get to work on the rest. Chris had been thrilled she had called and promised her he would take her wherever she needed to go.

* * *

'He's waiting for you in the office, Ralph. Good to see you, my friend.'

Ralph shook hands with yet another one of Don Carlos's 'soldiers', as they were known. Then he was shown into another room off the hotel suite, which Don Carlos used as an office. Carlos was talking on the phone but he beckoned Ralph in.

'Well, it's very nice doing business with you, Pablo. We will speak soon. Bye. Come in, Ralph. You're just in time; breakfast is on its way.' As always, Ralph was greeted with a hug. He had got used to the Italian way of doing things now and didn't find it odd at all. It had never occurred to him to hug his friends back in Ireland. It just was not the 'done thing'.

Raising his eyebrows, Ralph looked at Carlos. 'Pablo? Is that who I think it is? I've only heard of one man called Pablo and he's a Colombian.'

'The very same. The drug baron himself. We have a little business together.'

Ignoring any further questions, Don Carlos led the way to the dining table, rubbing his hands at the trolley of food in front of them. 'Let's eat, boys. Sit down. *Sedetevi*, all of you sit down.' Once Don Carlos had given them all permission to sit in his presence, the atmosphere seemed more relaxed. 'Did you know, Ralph, the hotel the Arab prince is staying at has a helipad on the roof?'

'No, why should I know that?' Ralph was as puzzled as the rest of the men, who sat themselves around the large dining table and started filling their plates with food from the heated trolley.

'That means he will fly by helicopter to the hotel and it will be at his disposal the whole time he is here.' Carlos was bubbling over with excitement at this news.

'Okay, now you've lost me. What does that have to do with us?' Everyone around the table busied themselves pouring coffee and eating. Sausages, eggs and bacon with all the extras were passed around the table.

'That is our escape. That is how we get away from the hotel once we have stolen the jewels. This will be the biggest jewel heist of the century.'

'I thought we were going to steal the jewels from the museum?'

'Change of plan, especially now we have this new information,' one of them commented while biting his toast, much to Carlos's annoyance.

'Shut up, Simon, this is my revelation and I am going to tell Ralph about it,' snapped Carlos. Then as always, he slipped into Italian. Whenever he was angry or excited, his native tongue came out. '*Stai zitto e mangia.*'

'Okay, Don Carlos. I will shut up and eat. I was only helping.'

Sweeping back his black hair with his hands, Carlos paced the floor. 'This is excellent news. It means we can steal those jewels and be in the air in minutes.' Punching the air with excitement, Carlos paced the room as everyone looked on.

'The jewels, boys... you don't really think the real jewels are going to be in a bank vault and transported to the museum. No way – every one of those precious bambinos will be closely guarded in the safe in the prince's rooms. The penthouse suite will be at the very top of the hotel with just the helipad above him.' Carlos kissed his finger and blew into the air.

'Okay, but what about the other stuff? The paintings and sculptures?' Not wanting to burst his bubble, Ralph felt he had to ask.

'I'm not interested in them. You could never sell the paintings and the sculptures are probably fake anyway. For now, boys, concentrate on the jewellery. Just the jewellery. He will have had fakes made. The real ones will not be on display. He is saving the real ones for the private auction. His insurance would insist on it.'

'How do you know all of this?' Everyone seemed to stop eating and looked up at Carlos.

'Because, you stupidos, I have done my homework. Two years this has been in the planning. I have informers in the right places.'

Ralph looked around the room at everyone eating and drinking. Each one of them were immaculately dressed in their dark suits even though it was early morning. Carlos could not stand untidiness. Everything had to be immaculate. He had a bathroom cupboard full of bars of soap in their packets. He would open one, wash his hands and then put it in the bin. And although Ralph noticed this, he would never dare to comment. It was one of those idiosyncrasies that Ralph had never come across before. God knows what the maid thought when she came to clean the room and saw wastebaskets full of bars of soaps.

'Just where do I come in all of this, Don Carlos?' Taking a drink of his coffee, Ralph looked down at the table.

'You're going to be the diversion, Ralph. You blow the vault the fake stones are in. The truth about the whereabouts of the real stones will be a closely guarded secret. Believe me. There will be so many police heading for that place, no one will pay attention to us.'

Swallowing hard, Ralph felt like he was supposed to be the spokesman. 'And who is going to fly this helicopter?'

'I am. Didn't I tell you I could fly? I have a pilot's licence.'

Surprised at this revelation, Ralph nodded. 'So you won't need Julie's help after all?' Ralph was secretly pleased at this. He hadn't liked the idea of putting Julie in danger, but Carlos seemed to insist on it. She was meant to be their inside man during the jewel heist.

'Yes, of course we need Julie. She is a clever woman who thinks on her feet. I have something special in mind for her. All her talents will come in handy.'

Narrowing his eyebrows, Ralph looked at Don Carlos. The room went silent and everyone stopped chewing.

'What do you mean by "talents"? Are you implying her former profession?'

The burst of laughter that erupted from Carlos eased the situation. 'For God's sake, no! I think it is too early in the morning for you to think straight. When we have finished eating and drinking our coffee, I will explain properly that this job is not one job, but three in one.'

Stunned at this revelation, they all looked around the table at each other.

Now he had dropped the bombshell, Don Carlos ignored their looks and turned to fill his plate as though nothing had happened. 'By the way, did Julie arrive safely? You didn't say.'

'Yes, she did,' Ralph answered slowly. It was clear that Carlos did not want to discuss his plans any more. That was the end of the conversation, but he had given them all a lot to think about. Carlos seemed to be thinking ahead for his own gratification. He didn't need the money and yet something about Carlos's plans involving Julie unnerved Ralph. Carlos was already holding Julie to ransom to do his bidding. He knew she had killed Inspector Connor and he was prepared to use it against her. Carlos was usually a rational man – a little crazy at times – but this whole plan seemed like a can of worms just waiting to be opened. Just what would be the outcome, he wasn't sure.

5

TRUE LIES

Ralph had sent three of his street soldiers to meet Charlie Jenkins at the club and offer him the keys to manage the place so he could launder his money through it. The three men feared Ralph and did his bidding, and that was all that interested Ralph. He preferred to call them 'employees', but the outcome was the same. He paid them well to follow orders and they knew the results if they didn't. Many times they had witnessed Ralph's wrath and they were glad they weren't on the other end of it. They were not the brightest of muscle he could employ, but they weren't hired for their brains. They had worked for Ralph for a while now and were his eyes and ears on the streets, while he preferred to remain anonymous and respectable.

'Oh God, this is him, I can feel it. Look at the state of that car; it has more spare parts than an organ donor clinic. Right, lads, we've got our orders. Let's just show him around and give him the keys.' Standing on the corner of the high street outside of the club, Johnny, Mick and Norman watched as the blue Volvo swerved up the pavement like a tank. Just inches away from them.

Sticking his thumb out to the driver, Norman nodded in the direction of the back of the club where they could park. Slowly, the window opened. Norman could see two men in the back of the car and two in the front. 'Round there, mate. You can't park here – the traffic wardens will give you a ticket.'

Nodding, the driver did as he was told and went around the back.

'How many of them are they, Norman?'

'Four. I presume the older one in the back is the person we're supposed to meet, that Charlie Jenkins. But he's come mob-handed, suited and booted, and God knows who else is tailing his car.'

'What's he got to be so paranoid about? We're only giving him a set of keys. Come on, let's get this over with.' Flicking his cigarette into the air, Johnny straightened his tie, turned and walked around the back to meet Charlie Jenkins and his boys.

The three of them waited on tenterhooks as the back window opened. 'Who are you? You aren't the person I agreed to meet.'

Johnny looked over the car bonnet at his two friends and nodded. He had guessed right. The older man shouting out of the window at them was indeed the man they were there to meet.

'He couldn't come, Mr Jenkins,' interrupted Mick. 'We've come to meet you instead.'

Butting in, Johnny stepped forward and dangled the keys he was holding in front of the open window. Then he walked to the back door, started searching on the keyring for the right key, and unlocked the door to the club.

'After you, gentlemen.' Pushing the door wide open, Johnny waited for them all to get out of the car. Johnny was a middle-aged man with a thin, unpleasant face and his dark hair was slicked back with a huge quiff at the front like some old fifties Teddy-boy fashion. They all wore dark suits as instructed, but Johnny had bought a cheap suit and pocketed the rest of the money Ralph had given them to buy a decent suit with, so his didn't fit well. His surliness showed in his face.

Young Mick had been sent along more for company than muscle. His youth and boyish smile made a pleasant comparison to Johnny's sneer.

Moving his head from side to side, trying to see in the doorway, Charlie Jenkins looked up at Norman. 'It looks bloody dark in there. How do I know this isn't a trap or something? You go first, mate.'

'There's no trap, Mr Jenkins. Look, I'll go first and see if I can find the light switch.' Eager to help, Mick stepped forward and walked into the club, disappearing for a few minutes, and then suddenly the whole place lit up. Walking out and rubbing the dust off his hands, Mick nodded and smiled. 'See, that looks better, doesn't it?'

Charlie and his men followed the others' lead and walked into the club. It was dusty and there were cobwebs everywhere. It hadn't been used in a long time. It was like some ghost ship where everything had just been left and closed up. There were glasses on the bar with dregs of beer left in them and all the glass-fronted fridges behind the bar were still fully stocked with all kinds of bottles of lagers. However, even in its sorry state, it was much better than Charlie was used to.

'All right, lads, check it out.' Trying hard not to show how impressed he was, Charlie couldn't believe his eyes. He felt like the cat who'd just had the cream. Here he was in the West End of London and he'd been handed the keys to a club by a bunch of suckers!

Standing in the doorway while his men walked around the club, Charlie lit a cigar and surveyed his good fortune. 'Put some more fucking lights on, will you? I want to see my property!' Exhaling on his cigar and blowing a cloud of smoke into the air, he looked across at Johnny, who was standing idly and looking bored at the end of the bar. 'So, are you going to hand over those keys or what?'

'Sure, catch.' Johnny threw the keys into the air towards Charlie, showing nothing but distaste in his manner. He was being cocky and rude, even though Ralph had warned the three of them to be on their best behaviour and give Charlie Jenkins respect.

Showing his annoyance, Charlie caught them with one hand and waited while his men re-appeared from their search of the place. 'Everything's okay here, Charlie. There's no one else around.' Their curiosity was roused as they all looked around at each other. It looked like someone had just shut the door and walked out. The cash register was still open and although there were no notes in it, it still had loose change in it from the cash float. It smelt musty and the eerie silence made it worse. Their voices echoed around the room. Everyone stood around, not knowing what to say or do next.

'I don't do business with monkeys, boys. Only the organ grinder, so where's the guy that invited me here?'

'You deal with me now. I'll put everything we need into place. You just concentrate on your club. Congratulations.' Pausing, Johnny narrowed his eyes. 'I take it you do want the club? If so, someone will be in touch.'

'Look, just who the fuck are you, mate? Show some bloody respect, will you? It's your boss that needs me... he came looking for me, so don't you forget it, you prick.' With a nod of his head at his men, Charlie pointed at Johnny.

Instantly, Norman stepped forward and tried calming the situation. 'Guys, guys. Let's not get excited, eh? Mick, look behind the bar and find some whisky. You look like a whisky man to me, Mr Jenkins.' Johnny seemed to be going out of his way to annoy Charlie, but whether he liked him or not, they weren't being paid to have an opinion.

Charlie put his hand up to stop his men. Already they had taken knuckle-dusters out of their jacket pockets and were putting them on, punching their fists into the palms of their hands to make them fit better.

'I don't mind a drop of whisky. Sure, why not.'

All seven of them stood in the middle of the club, on their guard, none of them daring to take their eyes off each other.

'I can't guarantee the state of the glasses, but the whisky looks good.' Mick's chirpy manner seemed to ease things as he put some glasses on the bar and started to pour the whisky, handing over the glasses to Charlie's men.

'Here, make sure Mr Jenkins get the big glass.' Mick smarmed his way around the men, more out of nervousness than the instructions Ralph had given them. He was not a fighter. His nickname was Fingers and he was a pickpocket. A thief. He'd been in and out of detention centres since he was a kid, but knuckle-dusters and a group of hard men looking for a fight just wasn't his scene. He glared across at Johnny. At this moment in time, he hated him. No one apart from Ralph knew they were there. They could be killed and left inside the place and no one would know.

Gulping down his drink in one, Charlie felt better. Clapping his hands together and rubbing them in a businesslike manner, Charlie walked around this ghost club. The whisky had softened his mood and relaxed him. Now he felt in charge again. After leaving his message on the answerphone for Ralph to contact him, he still hadn't felt 100 per cent sure about the situation. It all seemed very mysterious – who gave away a nightclub in a prime location?

Ralph had been very careful with his words when he'd returned his call. He had let Charlie do most of the talking and then had finally given Charlie the time and date to meet at the club and the address. Charlie had been intrigued, but he was also in turmoil. He had decided to come purely out of curiosity, but now he was glad he had. Everything that mad Irishman had promised him seemed to be on the level.

'Well, this dusty shithole needs a good clean-up and some decorating and I'm not paying for it.' Sliding his fingers along the dusty bar, Charlie decided to try another approach. He had tried to find out more about Ralph, but there were no leads to who he was or what he did. 'That Irish bloke, Ralph. I take it he's your boss?' Charlie spied them all curiously as they nodded in unison. 'So, just exactly who is he? Where's his manor?'

'That's his business, not ours, and definitely not yours. If you aren't happy with the arrangement, let's all leave now.' Johnny held out his hands for the keys.

'Will you get out of my fucking face, you long streak of piss. Simon, show this prick who's boss around here, will you? He needs teaching some respect.'

Walking over, Simon pushed Johnny and grabbed him by the jacket while pulling back one arm to throw a punch.

Reaching into his pocket, Johnny pulled out a gun and pointed it at him. 'Throw that punch, mister, and I'll decorate this club with you. You want it decorating, well, that's just fine by me.'

Looking back at Charlie, Simon put his hands in the air and stepped backwards. The relaxed mood had now taken a different turn. Mick and Norman looked at Johnny. 'Put that bloody gun away, Johnny. What do you think you're doing? We're all on the same side here. We haven't come for a fight!'

'You know, sonny, I've got one of those as well.' Reaching towards his jacket pocket, Charlie was about to reach for his own gun, when Johnny stopped him.

'Same side, are we? Don't even think about it, mate.'

'Do you always come tooled up for a friendly meeting when you're acting as estate agents for your mystery boss?'

'I always carry my friend here, especially when I think some chancer like him might want to take a swing at me.' Sarcasm dripped from Johnny's mouth. He'd taken an instant dislike to Charlie and his men, even though Ralph had told them he was an egotistical arsehole and to ignore him.

'Stop it! Stop it now!' Norman walked over to Johnny and pushed him, trying to knock the gun out of his hand. The atmosphere was explosive and Norman was worried that someone was going to get hurt. 'Ralph will have your balls on a plate, Johnny; put the fucking gun away, you fool!'

'Take your friend's advice, mate, because my patience is running low. In fact, get out! All of you get the fuck out of my club. I'll sort this place out without your boss. I don't need three monkeys like you hanging around. Now piss off.'

Pulling on Johnny's arm, Mick steered him to the door. He knew this had gone too far and now there was bad blood between them. 'Come on, Johnny, Mr Jenkins is right. We've done our job. Let's go.'

'Hey, you,' Charlie shouted as Johnny begrudgingly walked towards the door. 'I never forget a face and yours is firmly in my head. Don't you ever come here again or it will be the last thing you ever do.'

Pushing Johnny out of the door before he could answer Charlie, or worse, fire that bloody gun of his, Mick almost dragged him to the car.

'Take your hands off me, you little prick – he was threatening me. I've met lowlifes like him before. Why is he getting that club free? Why wasn't I asked to run the place? What makes him so special?'

Looking across at each other as they bundled Johnny into the car, Norman and Mick both now realised what Johnny's grievance was. He was jealous and angry because Ralph hadn't offered him the club. It had nothing to do with Charlie and his men; it was about himself and feeling that Ralph owed him something.

Mick drove the car and couldn't get away fast enough.

'You do realise, Johnny, Ralph will go crazy if that Charlie says anything about this – and I've got a feeling he will. We don't know why Ralph wants Charlie to have that place, but that's his choice and he will have his reasons, you know he will,' Norman said angrily.

Pulling away his arm from Norman and straightening his jacket, a red-faced, angry Johnny put his gun back in his pocket. He was too worked up to think about what Ralph would say. 'Oh, shut the fuck up. I don't remember you saying anything in there while that fat bastard was throwing his weight around. I don't take orders off arseholes like him. And before you butt in, at least we've showed that Charlie that Ralph is serious and not to be messed with. We've done him a favour.'

Mick looked into the rear-view mirror at Norman. There was nothing more to be said. They were all going to be on the end of Ralph's anger if this deal went wrong. They had all witnessed Ralph's wrath. He had once coldly put his hand around a man's windpipe, held him against the wall and squeezed, watching his lips go blue as he went limp into semi-consciousness. He had done this without showing his anger and still taking a sip of his coffee. Then he had calmly taken his hand off the man's throat, letting him drop to the floor gasping for breath. They had all looked on in horror, not knowing what to say. That had all been because he had challenged Ralph and called him a fool about a business decision. Their quiet, friendly boss who always asked about their families and looked after them financially was the very devil himself and didn't suffer loose tongues and fools gladly.

Suddenly Johnny's bravado left him as Mick turned in to the car park at Ralph's hotel, where Ralph had instructed them to go directly after their meeting with Charlie. Now they were all dreading it. Ralph would want good news, and all they could give him was a 'maybe' as to whether Charlie Jenkins would take the club or not. On the face of it, it looked like he had accepted Ralph's offer, but Johnny had firmly rocked the boat.

* * *

'Ralph, that snotty receptionist is on the telephone – someone called Norman is waiting for you downstairs.'

'Thanks, Julie.' Ralph smiled, picking up his jacket up and putting it on. 'I'll be back in a minute.' He had been on tenterhooks waiting for them. Sitting in his hotel suite, he had flicked channel after channel on the television to pass the time, not really watching anything.

The hotel restaurant was full of people having lunch, but the bar was less busy. 'This way, boys. Let's have a drink.' Waiting while they gave the barman their order, Ralph looked around. 'There's an empty table over there,' Ralph said before walking away. The three men followed his lead and sat down. 'I take it by the look on your faces that things didn't go to plan?'

Norman spoke up first; he wasn't going to take the blame for this. 'I think he liked the place, Mr Gold. Although he did mention that it might need a lick of paint and he wouldn't be paying for it.' At least that brought a smile to Ralph's face.

'That's easily sorted. What I want to know is what is it you're not telling me?' Ralph took a sip of his orange juice and, over the rim of his glass, he watched the three of them fidgeting and casting sideways glances at each other, carefully calculating which one of them was going to speak up first. He saw Mick lower his head and rub his hands nervously on his trousers. Instantly Ralph realised that whatever had gone wrong had nothing to do with him.

'It was Johnny, Mr Gold,' Norman blurted out.

'Thanks for that, you fucking grass.' Johnny glared at him and sat there sulkily.

'Please don't swear and cause a scene in the hotel, Johnny, they don't like it. I sent you as the oldest, thinking older is wiser but obviously not, eh?'

Blushing slightly at Ralph's reprimand, Johnny automatically looked around him to see if anyone had heard him swear.

'That Charlie turned up with three minders, just like you said he would. He was being a bit cocky and clever and Johnny just lost it and took his gun out. He pointed it at one of the minders who was going to take a swing at him.'

Nodding his head to Mick, Ralph smiled to reassure him. 'Thanks, Mick, I appreciate your honesty. I don't like my employees arguing with each other. You're supposed to be a team, Johnny – why didn't you tell me?'

'I thought I was doing you a favour, Ralph. I knew they would go tooled up with guns, and I was right that Charlie had a gun on him. That's the sort of bloke Charlie Jenkins is. All wind and piss. I showed him that you're in charge; he was mouthing off about you.' Trying to defend himself and make Ralph appreciate that his actions had been in Ralph's best interest, Johnny told Ralph what had been said and done.

A frown crossed Ralph's brow. He was puzzled; Johnny seemed to know a lot about Charlie Jenkins, and it was strange that even though he had pulled a gun, Johnny had come out of the fracas unscathed. But according to them all, they had never met Charlie before. Ralph was beginning to wonder if Johnny knew more than he was letting on and he looked across at the barman as he tried to gather his thoughts. Something about Johnny's story didn't quite add up.

'Well, we'll just have to wait and see, won't we? I'm sure Mr Jenkins will let me know what his plans are. Why don't you all take the rest of the day off? It sounds like you've had a stressful morning.' Ralph stood up, shook each of their hands in turn and walked towards the lift. Ralph remained his usual calm self, although inside his blood was boiling. This was supposed to be a sealed deal. Charlie Jenkins had taken the bait after a lot of cajoling on his behalf and now it seemed a stupid fool who worked for him had scuppered all of his and Carlos's plans. What the hell would Carlos say? He'd trusted Ralph to sort this and now he'd let him down. Ralph felt like a dead man walking. Carlos didn't like failure. He needed to sort this and fast.

* * *

'Bloody hell, what's up with you? You've got a face like a slapped arse!' Looking up from the sofa, Julie knew something was wrong.

'What makes you say that?' Walking over to the decanter, Ralph poured himself a drink.

'Well, honey, if it had gone well, you would have come in and suggested a shopping trip. Instead, you slam the door, go for a piss and pour yourself a drink. You rarely drink in the day. So come on, tell Aunty Julie what's wrong.' Patting a seat beside her on the sofa and putting her magazine down, she started the conversation. 'Did old man Jenkins accept your offer and take the keys?'

'If you want something doing, do it your bloody self. Those silly bastards have screwed it all up.'

'Jenkins will take the club. His vanity will see to that. You've been setting this meeting up for the last three weeks. He's left more messages on that answerphone than it can cope with. He's desperate. I went to that shithole of a pub of his last week and he won't be able to resist getting out of that place.'

'You did what? Why did you do that? You know sometimes, Julie, I wish I didn't tell you anything!'

'Oh, shut up and have another drink. I am your eyes and ears, Mr Gold. We're partners, remember? And I wanted to see that place for myself.'

'And what if they recognise you in the future?'

'Christ's sake, you wouldn't recognise your own mother in that place, it's so dark.' Laughing aloud, Julie lit two cigarettes and handed him one, which he gladly took.

Raising one eyebrow and inhaling on her cigarette, Julie blew the smoke towards him. 'Well, well, Ralph. However did I get through life without you?' Her dramatic coyness suppressed a sardonic smile. 'A wig, some bad clothing and a lot of make-up and I looked just like one of the tarts in the place. No one took any notice of me. Don't you get it? Those men don't see your faces. Their eyes are embedded in your cleavage; they don't even look up.'

Ignoring her remark, curiosity quickly got the better of him. 'Why did you go there?'

'I wanted to see what kind of man he was. The kind of man you're doing business with. You see, I can go into places you can't without a good excuse. He lets the prostitutes use the toilets for sex and takes a commission. Women speak to women, and your Charlie is a lowlife bully who takes one hell of a commission for protection. Some of those shopkeepers are working half of the week just to pay him. He waves a gun in their face or has them beaten up. He doesn't look after them; he bullies them until they pay him. He'll take your club, if only to get away from the enemies he's made. And believe me, there are a lot.'

Ralph sat there gobsmacked. Julie really had been busy. 'Well, a thought has just occurred to me, if you wish to don your wig and make-up once more…' Still troubled by Johnny's remark about Charlie Jenkins, another idea crossed Ralph's mind.

'I'm listening, go on.' Now it was Julie's turn to be curious.

'Do you remember Johnny? He was with me the day you picked

me up for lunch after you had been to see Josh settled in at the new hospital.' Ralph waited. It had been nearly a month since Josh had been brought to London and Julie had been busy sorting out their lives. Suddenly he saw her eyes light up.

'Do you mean that skinny weasel with a bad attitude to match his bad suit? The bad Elvis lookalike?'

'Well, I suppose that's one way to describe him. Not exactly complimentary but yes, he has a quiff like Elvis.'

'Ooh, creepy, weird guy. Yes, I remember him. Why, what's he done?'

'He made a comment today that makes me think he knows our Mr Jenkins more than he led us to believe. If you're game, I'd like you to go to Charlie's pub and see if Johnny's there. I figure he'll go there if my instincts are right.'

Slapping him on the back and smiling, Julie stood up and reached for her lipstick, which was always on standby. 'I'll be back in just a minute. Sit tight.'

Ralph waited for fifteen minutes before Julie reappeared in their room.

'Close your eyes.' Walking around and standing in front of the sofa, Julie counted down: 'One –two –three. Okay, open up.'

Stunned, Ralph sat there, his jaw almost on his chest. Before him stood a woman he hardly recognised. She had red, permed hair. Bright red lips. Lots of bright blue eyeshadow. The dress, if you could call it a dress, was a silver sequinned, elasticated, strapless dress that just about covered her bottom. It was obscene.

'What the hell do you look like? Bloody hell, you look like a clown! I don't know what to say.' Letting out a huge sigh, Ralph sat back on the sofa and ran his hands through his mane of black hair.

'I look like a tart on the pull, Ralph – get over it and pick your jaw up. Would you recognise me?'

Daring to look up at her again, he shook his head and stammered, 'No, I erm, I don't believe I would. I don't know what to say.' He was flabbergasted at the change in Julie's appearance.

'Good – get my long coat. I have to walk through reception.'

'You can't walk through the hotel looking like that.'

'I'll put the collar up. Come on, you won't relax until you find out. Now scoot, get my coat. You can't come with me; I'll get a cab.'

'No. I'm coming with you. You're not going alone.'

'Fair enough, but follow behind. We aren't together, especially if the manager of this hotel decides to have me arrested. I don't think they like my sort giving their hotels a bad reputation.' Letting out a loud cackle, Julie put her arms into her long overcoat, which Ralph was holding for her, and opened the door.

Ralph watched her get out of the lift and march towards the doors in reception. He looked on as the duty manager ran and shouted after her, wanting to know who she was. She was causing a stir amongst the residents as they looked on with disgust. 'Look, just fuck off will you. Don't worry, I won't be back!' she shouted as she pushed the huge glass doors open to leave.

Asking the valet to bring his car around, Ralph drove to the pub and parked at the top of the street. Suddenly he realised that this was madness. Julie was impulsive and hot-headed. Neither of them had thought this through properly.

After an hour and a chain of cigarettes, Julie came out of the pub, laughing and talking to a couple of men. One man had his hand on her bottom and was rubbing it provocatively. Ralph's blood was boiling. He was tempted to get out of the car and beat the man to a pulp. Ralph stopped short when he noticed Julie looking around. She was clearly looking for him. Looking past their heads as the men said goodbye and kissed her on the cheek, Julie spied Ralph's car, then she turned and flung her arms around a man on the pub's step under the porch light and kissed him on the cheek.

It was getting dark, and Ralph wiped the windscreen with his hand to get a better view and moved closer. Christ, he'd been right and Julie had brought Johnny out in full view for Ralph to see for himself. Smiling and shaking his head, Ralph watched as Julie flaunted her wares and waved to the men before walking away. She was amazing. Judas! She'd just hugged and kissed the man she had betrayed.

6

REVENGE

Knocking on the door of Johnny's flat, Ralph wanted answers but he also wanted revenge.

'Ralph? What are you doing here?' Pulling his bathrobe tighter around him to cover his nakedness, Johnny stood at the front door, furtively looking around the dark night air to see if Ralph was alone.

'Waiting for someone? You look very on edge. It is a shame that porch light doesn't work, isn't it?'

'Well, it did last night.' Johnny held his hand out to the broken plastic covering. 'Bloody kids or something, thinking they're funny. Wait until I get my hands on them. Look, they've even stolen the light bulb. They would steal your false teeth around here if you smiled for too long.'

'I'm sure you can get it fixed. And don't go smiling at anyone you don't know, and then you'll keep your teeth.' A sardonic smile crossed Ralph's face.

Before knocking on the door, Ralph had already reached up, broken the plastic covering, and smashed the lightbulb inside it. He didn't want anyone seeing him here. 'Mind if I come in?' Pushing his way past Johnny, Ralph walked into the hall and waited.

Johnny for once seemed at a loss for words. Instinctively he knew this meant trouble.

'It's not convenient, Ralph. I'm not alone.' Johnny nodded his head up the staircase to prove his point.

'A woman? That's okay, I'll wait five minutes until you get rid of her. Kitchen through here, is it?' A stern-faced Ralph marched past him and stood in the kitchen, making a point of looking at his watch.

Johnny's face paled and, turning, he walked up the stairs and shouted to whoever was up there. Ralph looked up at the ceiling and listened to the muffled voices and the anger of a woman; he soon heard footsteps down the stairs. 'I'm sorry, babes, it's work. I have business to see to. Another time, eh?'

'You can fuck off!' she screamed. 'How dare you just throw me out? Who the fuck is in there anyway?'

Barring her way from the kitchen, Johnny led her towards the front door. 'Later, baby! We'll talk later; this is business. Please, baby,' Johnny pleaded. With that, Ralph heard a slam of the door and waited for Johnny to walk into the kitchen. 'Sorry about that, Ralph. Women, eh? You can't live with them and you can't live without them.' His flippant manner didn't change the look on Ralph's face.

Ralph smiled, before going in for the kill. 'I want the truth, Johnny. How do you know Charlie Jenkins? Do not lie to me, because I know you do. I've seen you coming out of his pub.'

Cornered like a rat, Johnny tried appeasing Ralph and smiling. Ralph's calm exterior, as he leant his back against the worktop, portrayed a man burning up with anger inside.

'What are you going to do?'

'Just answer the question.' Poker-faced, Ralph waited.

His voice shook as he blurted out excuse after excuse. 'I know about him. And when you told us to meet him, I knew he would want a bit more information than you'd given him. It was worth money, Ralph.' Johnny started to tremble and sweat.

'You see, you're not clever at all. A man like Charlie doesn't let you insult him in front of his boys. You point a gun at him and not one of his men attack you, or even put a bullet in your leg? Not very believable. Even I know Charlie is trigger-happy. Well, I need him, but I do not need you, Johnny. Men like you are two a penny.'

'I could run the club for you, though; why give it to him?' Tears rolled down Johnny's face as he fell to his knees in fear. 'I'm sorry – no harm done. He never found anything out about you and anyway, what is there to tell? We don't know anything. You never tell any of us anything!' Screaming at Ralph and holding his arms around himself to stop them from shaking, Johnny knew he was on dangerous ground. 'For God's sake, Ralph. I've been loyal to you. I deserve another chance.'

Ralph nodded his head and smiled. He was bored with the pleadings of this man. 'At least have the courage of your conviction. Well, like I say. At this moment in time, I need Charlie. What I don't need is you.' Taking his hand out of his pocket, Ralph pointed his gun and pulled the trigger. It was a direct hit and Johnny fell into a crumpled heap on the floor as the blood poured out of his head. Walking over to his lifeless body on the floor, Ralph kicked him with his foot.

Turning all the lights off and all the gas rings on the hob on, Ralph opened the door ajar and looked out. There was no one around, so he calmly lifted the latch, making sure the door was unlocked, and closed the front door behind him, walking away from the devastation inside.

Leaving the latch on the door up meant it could be opened easily, knowing someone would go in and switch the lights on. That would ignite the gas. The whole place would go up in smoke, Johnny's body included.

Ralph walked further up the street and stood behind a hedge, waiting. He'd heard Johnny tell his girlfriend to come back in half an hour and by the time she did, the house would be in darkness and full of gas. The first thing she would do would be to switch the hall light on. Ralph felt sorry for her, but there were always casualties and he wasn't sure if Johnny had mentioned his name. The good thing about this was that Johnny had had an argument with Charlie and his boys. When Mick and Norman found out about Johnny's death, word would soon spread and Charlie and his boys would be questioned before anyone else. Maybe Johnny had done him a favour after all. Now Ralph was sure Charlie would want to lie low and move on for a while. And the new nightclub was the perfect escape.

Pulling the collar on his overcoat up further against the cold night air, he heard the sound of high-heeled shoes approaching. Ralph's instincts were right; Johnny's girlfriend walked up the path to the house and, fumbling for her keys in her bag, took them out and attempted opening the door. Realising it was open, she pushed it further and shouted out for Johnny. As predicted, Ralph saw the lights go on and the instant explosion that followed.

The house had been filling with gas for over half an hour; the front door erupted into flames and almost flew into the air as a ball of fire burst through the house. The noise of shattering windows and more explosions told Ralph it was time to leave.

* * *

'Did you kill him?' Walking into the hotel suite, Ralph saw Julie's hand raise from the back of the sofa, chinking the ice in her glass in the lamp-lit room. Shocked by her remark, he started unbuttoning his coat. 'Well?' Julie raised her head and looked over the back of the sofa towards him.

'You shouldn't ask questions like that; people don't always like the answer. Anyway, I thought you would be asleep by now.' Walking over to the dresser, Ralph poured himself a drink and held up the decanter towards Julie. 'Top-up?'

'No, I just poured one. Don't be coy with me. Did you get rid of that son of a bitch?'

'Yes. Satisfied now?'

Lounging on the sofa in her black, satin negligée, drink in hand, Julie patted the seat beside her. 'You don't really think I could go to bed and sleep, do you? It's 3 a.m. – what took you so long?' Reaching over, she kissed him. 'You're cold; come here.' Kissing his cold hands, she put one under each of her armpits to warm them. 'My mother used to do this when I was a kid.'

He smiled and leant in to kiss her. All his cares and woes seemed to fly out of the window with Julie by his side.

'I've been thinking, Ralph love. You need an office. A place of business. You can't do business from the hotel with all kinds of men walking in asking for you. We'll look for a place tomorrow.' Looking up at the clock on the mantle, she smiled. 'Or should I say today.'

'Don Carlos does his business from the hotel. What's the problem?'

Seeing a frown cross his brow, Julie stroked it away with her hand. 'Don Carlos doesn't live there. He has a home in Italy and the only men that visit him are his council of the same men that more or less live in the hotel. He doesn't have strangers popping in from all walks of life. People may remember that Johnny was in the hotel with his friends talking to you. We must detach ourselves as Don Carlos does. Let the men who work for you carry the messages.'

Although he was tired, he realised she was right. Don Carlos's hotel suite was like a fortress and was strictly invitation only. Maybe

Julie had a point, but he was used to doing things himself. He liked keeping his darkest secrets to himself. He had learnt from the good old days that the only person you could trust was yourself. 'Let's go to bed; I have an early meeting.' Loosening his tie, Ralph stood up and walked to the bathroom.

Satisfied, Julie put her drink down and walked into the bedroom. She had sown the seeds and she knew Ralph would act upon them. Like all men, he just needed a nudge in the right direction. Thankfully, she had spent the evening looking through brochures of office blocks for sale and to let. She had seen the perfect one and tomorrow she would take Ralph to see it.

Showered and refreshed, Ralph walked into the bedroom.

'What is this meeting you're having today?' Now Julie was curious.

'It is the meeting we're both having with Don Carlos about the robbery. It seems we're good to go.' Throwing back the duvet to get into bed, he smiled. Just now and again, it was good to have some news Julie didn't already know about. She seemed to know everything, even before it happened!

'Oh, is that all?' She yawned with disinterest. 'I thought it was something important!' With that, she let out a laugh and cuddled up closer to him, knowing she had just burst his balloon.

'You know, you're always making plans. But in all of this time, there is one plan you still haven't made and that's our wedding. When are you going to set a date?'

'When I can be certain that we're not going to be exchanging letters from Strangeways or waving from a prison cell at each other. Let's get the job done for Carlos and then I promise I'll set the date for the wedding. Now go to sleep; I'm not going anywhere.' Lying in the crook of Ralph's arm, Julie was glad of the darkness. She wanted to marry Ralph, but she didn't want to be a widow or vice versa. All of these plans that were to be discussed with Carlos seemed like a huge mountain to climb. Anything could happen to either of them. Now was not the time to plan for the future. For once in her life, she had found a soulmate and yet she could so easily be robbed of him. Entwining her fingers in the hairs on Ralph's chest comforted her as she felt his chest rise and fall as he drifted off to sleep. She felt afraid and moved closer to him, holding him tightly and never wanting to let him go.

7

THE PLAN

'God, what is this, King Arthur's Round Table?' Even though Ralph had warned Julie to be polite, she couldn't help herself. 'What is this place?'

'It's the conference room. There will be lots of people here this morning. Far too many for the suite. Show some respect; Don Carlos is connected to some of the biggest family names in organised crime. Some of those other family members will be here this morning too.'

'Don't worry; I know this is an important meeting. But don't you find it just a little intimidating?' Standing to the side and watching groups of suited men walk past them into the conference room with its enormous, highly polished table surrounded by what seemed like a hundred chairs, Julie suddenly felt nervous.

Looking towards the wooden double doors at the other side of the room, they waited for the door to open and Don Carlos to walk in. Even Julie had to admit to herself he seemed a very authoritative, domineering figure. His black hair and Italian good looks highlighted by his silk suit made for a very handsome man who demanded respect. Very different from the man she had sat with at his hotel and spoken to all those months ago. This was the real Don Carlos, surrounded by all the other gangland families. Someone pulled out a chair for him and once he had sat down, he opened the palms of his hands and nodded, indicating they could all sit too.

Then Don Carlos held up his hand to quiet everyone and spoke. 'Does anyone have anything to say before we start business?'

Looking at the sea of unknown faces sitting around the table, Julie swallowed hard, reached for one of the many bottles of water and glasses on the table, and poured herself a drink. Then she raised her hand and all the men around the table turned to face her. 'What is it you have to say, Julie?' asked Don Carlos, smiling.

Taking a sip, she looked up. 'With respect, Don Carlos, whatever plans you have in mind for me in your scheme of things, I would like it known that Ralph and I are not married yet. Therefore, it isn't a joint payment. I get paid for what I do, separately.'

'We don't discuss money. We all trust each other around this table. But I understand what you are saying. You are your own person and wish to be treated as such. Although I appreciate, as always, your meter is running and you want to know what is in it for you. Goodness me, do you really think I would dare swindle you? You would have the fillings out of my teeth if I smiled too wide.' Carlos laughed to the other men in the room, who also found it amusing. Carlos knew Julie was all about profit. She did nothing without her money upfront. But this time she would have to learn to be patient. This wasn't some client; she was playing with the big boys now.

Giving a weak smile, Julie nodded. She didn't dare look at Ralph, who was further up the table towards Carlos, but she could feel him glaring at her so much her face burnt.

'Firstly, gentlemen and lady,' Carlos acknowledged Julie. 'I know that the jewels our Arab friend is bringing with him will travel with him, not ahead of him as we were previously led to believe. There will be a flight with a metal trunk but it will contain fakes and will come in all of the pomp and glory it deserves from its exhibition in Las Vegas. The media is going wild for a glimpse of the jewels he has at his disposal. Some of the necklaces weigh pounds. Imagine that: five or six pounds of diamonds or rubies all shaped into a necklace and draped around the neck of the lady of your choice. I also know he will be travelling with his assassins. One is his secretary and personal valet, but the others who will be travelling with him as his bodyguards are all assassins. Of course, he will be travelling in his own aeroplane.

'The museum will house all of his paintings and sculptures. I have seen them and here is a collection of catalogues for you all to see.' One by one, a couple of the men standing at the doors of the conference room came forward and handed out the museum catalogues to everyone. 'We don't want the paintings; they are far too bulky.' Don Carlos waved dismissively in the air. 'We will be stealing a couple of the sculptures. We could never sell them but we're going to sell them back to the insurance company.'

'How the hell do we do that without getting caught?' Julie blurted out without thinking. She could have bitten her tongue when everyone looked up and stared at her. 'I'm sorry, Don Carlos,' she stammered, realising her mistake. 'I didn't mean to butt in,' she apologised.

'Not a problem, Julie, and it's a very good question. This kind of thing goes on all of the time. The insurance company do not want to have to pay the full money to their client. Therefore, you can barter with them. They are businessmen, not police officers. No insurance company likes to pay the full money out, isn't that the case?' Everybody nodded and laughed in agreement. Julie wanted to ask more questions, but it seemed Carlos was already ahead of her.

'Our Arab friend will get his sculptures back. The insurance company have only paid half of what they should have, and we get a load of money. Everyone is happy.'

Taking a drink of her water and looking around the room, Julie was intrigued. It all sounded very simple. Surely it couldn't be that easy. She felt hot and sweaty and the bright lights from the chandeliers hanging over the table were giving her a headache.

'Ralph, you and the boys here are going to create a diversion. Only a handful of people know that the Jewels in the museum are fakes – albeit very good ones and probably worth quite a bit of money. The necklaces will be around a porcelain bust in cabinets surrounded by laser security. You are going to blow the museum and the laser security, giving me time to get away with the real stuff. There will be so many police rushing to the museum, they will not give me a second thought.'

There was a knock at the door and everyone went silent. Two huge minders in black suits slowly put their heads around the door and spoke quietly. Then, turning, they wheeled in large trolleys of food and coffee for everyone.

'Aah, refreshments, everyone.' Don Carlos clapped his hands and rubbed them together. 'Shall we all take a bathroom break? Help yourselves to food.' One of Don Carlos's men pulled back his chair as he stood up to leave the room.

Walking across the room towards Julie, Ralph stood beside her. 'Do you want some coffee or something? Are you okay? You look a little pale.'

'Yes, I'm fine. I'm going to powder my nose first.' Standing up, she looked around the room again. All the men now seemed very relaxed and were walking around the room, talking to each other and shaking hands.

Welcoming the coolness of the toilets, Julie looked at herself in the mirror. She looked flushed. It all seemed so surreal and she felt overwhelmed by it all. It was like a scene from a movie, being surrounded by all these powerful men in their expensive suits discussing a major robbery. Running the cold water on her wrists to cool herself down, and applying more lipstick, she felt better. She hadn't expected anything as big as this. Although she knew about the robbery, she hadn't really thought about it. Now, amongst these men, it all seemed real. Mentally, she scolded herself. What the hell had she agreed to? This was not pickpocketing. This was much bigger than she had realised. Offhandedly, she had agreed to it, but now it sounded dangerous with a long prison sentence at the end of it if anything went wrong. And she felt sure there was no such thing as the 'perfect robbery'; that was why the prisons were so full.

Ralph had poured her some coffee and put some sandwiches on a plate for her on the table where she was seated. 'You look better. Come here, I want to introduce you to some friends.' One by one, Ralph introduced her to some of the men in the room. They were all very courteous and polite. The perfect gentlemen, considering they were all killers, embezzlers and racketeers.

Again, she felt she'd taken Ralph, her 'Goldy', for granted. He was at ease with these men and they knew him well. Each one hugged him, pleased to see him. They joked and laughed like old friends together. Dawning realisation crept up on her. For the first time she felt she really was punching above her weight with Ralph. He was a rich man, involved with some of the most powerful people she could imagine. Why would he want her? She didn't even know which knife and fork to use in those posh restaurants. This sharp-suited, handsome man saw something in her that she didn't see in herself and she was glad of that, but she was also nervous. Ralph Gold was an important man and it was time she came to terms with it and realised just who he was. She felt determined that she would match him. She would watch and learn everything there was to know about life in the upper classes. She would be bigger and better than them all. Everyone was a fake, all of their lives were lies, and she was damned sure she was going to be the biggest fake of all.

After a while, the lights dimmed and flickered. 'What's wrong with the lights?'

'That's to let everyone know the break is over. It's time to get back to business. Come on, back to your seat.'

Everyone sat down as before and waited for Don Carlos to continue.

'Right, gentleman, back to business. I will meet our Arab friend and his men at the airport. It will be late afternoon, early evening.' Don Carlos pondered, drumming his fingers on his chin. 'I've monitored each one of his exhibitions and he is making a small fortune. The museum is charging twenty-five pounds a ticket to go in and view these dazzling delights.' He paused and waited for everyone to suck in air and let out a slow whistle.

'His assassins will check the helicopter and then load it with the real jewels and themselves. I will fly them to the helipad at the hotel. Bring in the model.' Don Carlos waved a hand at one of the men standing around the room, who left and swiftly returned holding a large model of the hotel, which he placed in front of Don Carlos. It even had a little helicopter on the top. Whoever had made this model had gone into every detail.

'You can see the helipad here. Just aside from the platform is a lift that leads directly into the penthouse suites.'

Looking around the room, Don Carlos knew by the way they scrambled closer, looking over each other's shoulders to get a better view, that he had captured the interest of his companions. 'Of course, the manager of the hotel and his trusted staff will be expected to meet and greet their honoured guest. You, Alfredo, will be our man in charge. His right-hand man who organises everything and sees that everything runs smoothly. Dressed in your white robes and headdress, you will have travelled ahead to advise them on protocol. Dressed in hotel uniform will be four others and you, Julie.' Looking across the table, Don Carlos nodded at her and smiled. The surprised look on her face when her name was mentioned made it even more satisfying for him. 'Yes, I feel the feminine touch would relax the situation more. You standing there with your hotel uniform on, clipboard in hand to meet and lick arse!' He laughed, encouraging the others to turn and look at her and laugh too. Some even patted her on the back.

'But he'll recognise me.' Her voice wobbled at this revelation. 'He'll be able to give the police a description of me.'

'Julie. You are the master of disguise. My chameleon. I'm sure you can sort your side of things out.' His calm, velvety voice instilled confidence in her. But she knew that Carlos was very good at manipulating people. Nodding, Julie concentrated on the model of the hotel. She felt self-conscious and out of her depth now that her role in all of this was being discussed.

Taking a drink of his water, Don Carlos averted his eyes from Julie. 'I take it I can rely on you, Ralph, to speak to the Jewish bosses. They speak very highly of you.'

'All in hand. We have already met, Don Carlos.'

Swiftly, Julie turned her head to look at Ralph. She didn't know any of this. What Jewish mob? Puzzled, she decided now was not the time to ask... maybe later. Bloody hell, Ralph was a dark horse. She knew he had Jewish connections, but he had never discussed it with her. Ralph was part of the Jewish mob? She wasn't sure if this was an oversight, or if he had just decided not to mention it. There was a lot more to Ralph Gold than met the eye, she was sure of it.

Carlos carried on, 'This is when we ambush them. They will be tired and looking out of the windows, waiting to get out of the helicopter and freshen up. All they will see is a bunch of boring hotel staff. They will ignore you and treat you like dirt. The prince will get out of the helicopter last; the others will carry his battered trunk off the helicopter. That is when you strike. I will still be in the helicopter. You will incapacitate the prince's staff and then load the helicopter with the trunk and I will fly the jewels off to their destination. We will all be in contact with each other; I have earpieces for you all. Any questions?'

'Yes, Don Carlos.' Raising his hand to his mouth and coughing before he spoke again, one of the men at the table spoke up. 'How do we get off the helipad? You will have flown off. God knows what kind of fight those Arabs will put up. We cannot shoot the Arab prince. There will be all kinds of repercussions.' Nervous at stating the obvious, the man looked around at the sea of faces staring at him, knowing they were all thinking the same thing but didn't dare challenge Don Carlos.

'Good question. And my answer is simple. Whatever happens, each of you must go down in the lift and swiftly out of the hotel to the waiting cars.'

'But how do we do that if we're bloodstained or something?'

'You fucking imbecile!' Don Carlos screamed. 'Do I have to think of everything? Shall I tell you how to spend all the fucking money you're earning from your part in this?'

As the man apologised and blushed at Don Carlos's eruption of anger, Julie thought he was going to cry. Angrily, Carlos swept some of the glasses off the table with his hand, making everyone stand aside as glass and water flew across the floor. His face was red, and he started shouting in Italian. Walking around the table, Carlos walked up to the man and slapped him across the face. 'If you do your job properly, you will get out unscathed! I don't want to hear excuses. You are men and should be able to think on your feet. Get him out of here now!'

Two men walked up to this now shaking, quivering man,

pleading his apologies and begging for mercy, and dragged him away, kicking and screaming, into one of the side rooms. Julie looked across at Ralph, but he turned his head and avoided her stare. There was nothing to say.

Like a flick of a switch, Don Carlos swept his black hair back, sat down at the head of the table, and apologised to the rest of them for the disturbance. 'Any more questions?' he calmly asked the bystanders. This time no one spoke. 'Good. We have two weeks to get everything in place. I will keep you updated when we meet again for the last meeting.' Standing, Don Carlos straightened his tie and walked to the door. As an afterthought, he turned around. 'Ralph, I wish to see you in my rooms.'

Everyone started to leave the conference room and Ralph held back.

'Julie...'

'I know, I heard him. He wants to speak to you. I'm exhausted; this meeting has gone on for hours, and I need to go home, take a bath. You come home when you're ready. Personally, I'm pleased to get out of here.'

'I'll see you later and we'll have dinner. Maybe you need this time on your own to gather your thoughts.' Reaching out his hand for hers, Ralph kissed it, hoping to see that smile on her face that assured him everything was okay between them.

'We're good, Ralph. Don't worry, I'm just tired.' Forcing a weak smile, Julie turned and walked out of the door.

She felt like Carlos was risking all of their lives on a whim. Julie felt uneasy about it all, but, she didn't want to show her doubts to Ralph. If she knew anything at all about him, she knew he would be having the same thoughts. They were cut from the same cloth and this whole plan seemed like one big fantasy that would inevitably go wrong, though neither of them wanted to admit it. Exhausted from the meeting, Julie just wanted to get out of there. The whole room, full of cigar smoke, seemed to have an air of doom hanging over it. They were in it up to their necks and there was no backing out now. Swallowing hard, she opened the main doors and walked onto the pavement, breathing in the fresh air to clear her head. Only time would tell.

8

CROSSROADS

Walking into the hotel room alone, Julie felt different. Turning on the bath and watching the bubbles rise, her mind wandered to all kinds of things. Her past life and possibly her future life with Ralph. This was her chance to go forward or backwards. Suddenly she felt terribly alone. Climbing into the bath and letting the warm water envelop her, tears fell down Julie's face as she thought about her mother and sister, Frankie, whose lives had both been wasted. Julie had always cried in the bath, so that the water washed the tears down the plughole and no one ever knew her sorrow. The tears of a clown, Carrie the madam from the brothel where Julie had once worked called it. The smile was always there but it wasn't always real.

Running the shampoo slowly through her hair, Julie noticed how harsh and bleached it was. If she was going to fit in with these fine people, she needed to look the part, she decided. If things were going to change, then she would have to start with herself.

* * *

'Ralph, have a drink and sit down; we have private things to discuss.' Back in his hotel suite, Don Carlos loosened his tie and stretched out on the sofa. There was only a small group of men left now, each of them pouring a drink and lounging around on the sofas. 'Well, that went better than expected, apart from Fabrizio. He is a coward, Ralph. We do not need any loose ends in our plans.'

'What is it you need to see me about, Don Carlos?' Accepting a drink, Ralph took a sip and waited.

'Carlos, please. We are alone now. You know I like everyone to make a last will and testament before our work. Things don't always go as planned. You never know what is going to happen until you get there; this job is worth approximately a hundred million, give or take, but there are bound to be a few bumps and scrapes along the way. That is why I insist you get your house in order before. It saves lots of confusion for the families should the worst happen. Well, you need to adjust yours now you have Julie in your life and, well...' Carlos trailed off.

'You want me to ask Julie to make a will, don't you? I'm not sure I want her involved in all of this. I have reservations.'

'I know you do; it's written all over your face. That is where I come in. I want Julie to not only make a will, but to claim parental guardianship of your son, Josh.'

'My son?' A frown crossed Ralph's brow. For a moment, he was confused – his son had been killed – but then he realised who Carlos meant. Little Josh, Julie's nephew.

'He is to be your son. Who else does he have? Biology means nothing; it is who brings you up and loves you. I would like to give you and Julie peace of mind and sign guardianship of Josh over to my family and myself, should anything happen to you. You know he would always be well cared for. He will soon be out of hospital and then he can be baptised. I could be his godfather.' Carlos's eyes twinkled with amusement at the prospect of being 'the godfather'.

They both burst out laughing, but Ralph knew all Italians took that role very seriously.

'Okay, I can see you are worried. Julie can make her own choice. I will not be offended if she pulls out, *capisce*?'

'Thank you, Carlos, I appreciate that.' Ralph shook the other man's hand. He felt better now Julie had some form of get-out clause. She was his woman; he didn't want her dragging into all of this. It was his job to protect her and look after her. Inside he felt he had let her down, but at least Carlos had recognised this and was prepared to let Julie make up her own mind.

'On another note, how are things going with your friend Charlie Jenkins?'

'Well, he's taken the keys and hasn't sent them back yet, so I think he's taken the bait.'

'Good, we will put an office through the back with a false wall. Our accountants can sit behind that with their cash counters. I want you to put a clock on the wall. A very special clock. This one will have a spyhole in the middle of the face. It will record every move he makes. We will watch him like a hawk and he won't even know it.' Slapping Ralph on the back, Carlos laughed again.

'You don't trust anyone, do you? Sometimes I wonder if you trust me. Or maybe you never have.'

'Do not be sentimental. In my position, I cannot trust anyone, but you and I are friends. Or you wouldn't be here. Yes, I trust you because you have only ever spoken the truth to me, be it good or bad. And for that I respect you.' Reaching forward, Carlos hugged Ralph. 'Now, how are the wedding plans going? I'm surprised Julie hasn't waltzed you up the aisle already!'

'She's dubious. She wants this job over and done with first before she sets a date. Actually, I was going to ask something. It's been on my mind and I wasn't sure how to ask. You have been very good to me over the years, Carlos. Look at me: I'm a different man. I own property and have a bank balance with more zeros on the end of it than I could ever have imagined.'

'Wait, Ralph.' Holding his hand up, Carlos stopped the conversation. 'I think I know where this is going and I think you're wise to ask your oldest friend, Paddy, as your best man. You were young kids together; you share a lot of history. Good and bad. And whilst I would love the honour of being your right-hand man, I am Don Carlos. It is completely out of the question. I can only be the best man if it was a brother or a close Italian family member.' Carlos emphasised the word 'Italian'.

Forlorn, Ralph felt embarrassed. It had been a stupid idea to ask Carlos, but they had become such good friends, sometimes he forgot who the other man was.

'What I would like to be at your wedding – a wedding that I insist on paying for as my present to you...'

Shocked, Ralph shook his head. 'I couldn't let you do that; that's far too generous, especially with Julie's shopping list.'

'I'm not arguing. Anyway, anyone brave enough to marry feisty Julie deserves all the help he can get, *sì*?' But I do want to ask a favour of you.'

'Anything, Carlos. Whatever you want.' A warm feeling crept over Ralph. Their barriers were down. This was simply two friends having a man-to-man conversation.

'What I would like is to be the master of ceremonies at your wedding, with yours and Julie's permission, of course.'

'I would like that very much.' They shook hands and Ralph felt it was time to change the subject. 'Anyway. How are your wedding plans going?'

Carlos was also set to be married soon, but he had said very little about it.

'Everything is in hand there. They will tell me when to turn up.

It will be a good marriage; she will look after my children and it will be very advantageous in business.'

Ralph already knew it was an arranged marriage between the families, but Carlos's indifference to it made it seem like just another business deal. But, if he was happy with that, he wished him well.

'Of course, you will be there, Ralph. Surely I don't have to issue a formal invitation to you?'

'Oh God, Carlos, I wasn't fishing for an invite. Just asking how things were going.'

Apologetically, Carlos put each hand on one of Ralph's shoulders. 'You will come to Italy and be at my wedding. Yes?'

'I'd like that, thank you.'

'Has Julie ever been to Italy? She will like it. Make sure she has a passport.' Politely, Carlos extended the invite to Julie as well. Not all of the men were invited to take their partners. It wasn't a free-for-all and Ralph knew that.

Carlos wanted to see Ralph happily married again. Julie was a real, feisty pain in the arse, but she was funny and good for Ralph and sometimes in life you have to break a few eggs to make an omelette. And Carlos was also aware that it was he who had been responsible for the loss of Ralph's first wife and son – a dark secret that remained buried between them. Carlos believed it had all been for the best, but knew that Ralph wouldn't see it that way. And he knew Ralph must never know.

'Well, you had better go and see if Julie is okay and check up on Charlie Jenkins. I have some business to attend to.' And with that, Ralph was dismissed.

Picking up his coat, Ralph walked to the door. A thought occurred to him and he turned back to Carlos. 'Just out of curiosity. What is a master of ceremonies?'

Shrugging and opening his arms wide to the other men in the

room Carlos burst out laughing. 'It's the best man, without showing any favouritism!'

* * *

Hearing the door, Julie shouted from the bedroom, 'Is that you, Ralph?'

'Were you expecting someone else?' Holding out his arms for her, he could see she was in a better frame of mind. 'Are you okay? You didn't seem yourself earlier, after the meeting.'

'It was a bit in your-face, wasn't it? No one opposes Carlos and he just runs off his plans like a steam train. I'm okay, it was just a little bit more than I expected.' Smiling and giving him a peck on the lips to reassure him, she laughed. 'Maybe I should have done a collection. It was like some upper-class stag night. All those men and little old me was the only woman there. Now there was an opportunity missed.' She winked. 'And I've just spoken to the hospital. Josh has put on weight, and his chest infection has cleared and they think in a couple of weeks he can come home!'

'That's great news. Now we have to buy a house and quickly. I'm glad you've brought Josh up because there's something I need to talk to you about.'

Ralph sat down and told Julie about his conversation with Carlos. As much as she resisted and flew off the handle about this mad scheme of signing Josh over to the family of an Italian mobster, she realised Carlos had a point. Who would look after Josh in her absence? It wasn't just this job; it was in the event of *anything* happening to her.

'So he expects one of us to die during this job, then? He is one crazy bastard, and just who are you to Carlos? I know he thinks highly of you, but there is more to it than that, isn't there?'

Ralph let out a deep sigh; this wasn't a conversation he wanted to have, but he knew he had to tell Julie the truth. 'I'm a captain. It's like a family tree. There are the bosses, such as Carlos. Then there are the "captains", like me, who deal directly with Carlos, and then there are the "soldiers", who get the street guys to be their eyes and ears and report back. That's all there is to it.'

'Well, Captain Ralph. All the nice girls love a sailor, but what is this about the Jewish mob? Where do they come in? Apparently he is relying on you to speak to them.'

'All walks of life have their own culture and "mobs", Julie. I deal a lot with my own family culture and over the years they have learnt to trust me. And in return they get access to Don Carlos.'

'I see. Well, I will agree to sign Carlos's form. As for his job, I will do it, but I have my doubts. And I want him to guarantee that, if I die in the process, the money he is meant to be paying me will go to Josh. Would he honour that?'

Ralph nodded, which seemed to satisfy her. He still had his reservations about her role in the job, but she seemed determined and he knew once she had made her mind up there was no changing it.

'I'd forgotten you were Jewish. Does that mean we have to do special things at your wedding? I don't know a lot about their culture. Or do I have to do an Irish jig because of the Irish in you?'

They both laughed together at the idea of Julie doing Irish folk dance. Thinking about it made Ralph laugh all the more.

'Do whatever you want. As I say, Carlos is footing the bill.'

'Great, then we will have the most expensive wedding he can afford!'

Letting out a laugh, she moved closer to Ralph so that he could put his arm around her.

'Talking of weddings, I have set a date. Two months from today, so we had better get our skates on. Is that okay? Carrie, an old friend of mine, used to say, "Plan for the future, then you have a goal in mind."'

The delighted look on Ralph's face didn't need words. He hugged her tightly and kissed her. 'I know I don't say a lot, and I'm not a man to wear my heart on my sleeve. But I love you, you know that, don't you?'

Putting her hand on his chest, Julie opened his shirt buttons and slid her hand in to stroke the dark hairs there. 'I haven't had much practice either, Ralph, but I love you too. I'm not going to be saying it often, so remember this moment.' Embracing each other, their lips met; nothing else mattered in the world as long as they had each other.

9

A HEAD START

'Chris, London isn't my territory, so where would you find an exclusive apartment for two newly married people?' Julie asked her driver.

'Chelsea. Although the Barbican in the Square Mile is exclusive. All the posh people live there. Mega expensive, though.'

'Good. After you've dropped me off at the train station, I want you to pick three places for me. Get some brochures and ask around and I'll give you a call when I want you to pick me up. Did you look at those units I told you about?'

'The offices, yeah. All sorts in that unit block. Solicitors, insurance places. The empty one at the end was some kind of import and export place that went bankrupt. Is that the one you want? It's lease only, I'm afraid. Grabbing bastards know they can get more money in rent than if you bought it.'

'Well, that's the world over. Ralph has houses for rent in Ireland, some other properties too.'

'Yeah, I know. Been hearing some odd stories about Ireland lately. Not that it's any of my business, of course.' Faltering slightly and looking in the rear-view mirror at Julie, Chris felt he had overstepped the mark. He'd driven her around a lot lately and he liked it, but one word from her and this could all stop.

'No offence taken. Tell me what you've been hearing – just between you and me, of course.' Sitting slightly forward, Julie lit two cigarettes and handed him one. She was intrigued about what was happening in Ireland.

'It's that Paddy and his brother Liam. Right pair of bastards by all accounts. Putting up people's rent and throwing them on the streets when they can't pay. Sorry, Julie, please don't mention this to Ralph; I know Paddy is his mate.'

'How do you know all of this? Who told you?' Seeing how uneasy Chris felt, Julie tried putting him at his ease and encouraged him to talk to her. Of course, it was strictly between them. After all they were friends, weren't they?

'I know a bloke called Billy who works for Ralph in Ireland. He's more mates with my older brother but we keep in touch and I speak to him regular. Billy's from my old stomping ground and then he joined the army. A lot of the blokes who work for Ralph used to be in the army, didn't they?'

Nodding her head, Julie smiled. She didn't know why Ralph employed army men. And he hadn't mentioned that there was trouble with that sleazebag Paddy. She hadn't even known Paddy had a brother. But she made a note to talk to Ralph about it just as soon as she was back. First she had a trip to make back to her old stomping ground –Liverpool.

'Right. I won't be gone long, just a few hours. I want to drop in and see an old friend. I'll call you when I'm getting the train home. Don't forget my jobs now.' Shutting the car door, Julie smiled and waved at him. With just her handbag for luggage, she got on her train, heading home for Liverpool.

After her crying episode in the bath, Julie had called her old friend Swinger Sue, who was a hairdresser and a beautician. She had been a good friend to Julie in the past, and maybe she could help sort out this harsh blonde hair and make it look softer and classier. Well, as classy as she could look. Julie had telephoned her and had been glad when Sue had remembered her. She trusted Sue and she knew she would help her.

Julie didn't want to go to the posh salons in London. Well, not yet anyway; she felt a little embarrassed walking into some posh salon and them telling her that her hair was like straw, then let them try to sell her some overpriced products supposed to work miracles. What a load of bollocks! She was going to someone she trusted to tell her the truth and help her without a ridiculous price tag.

When she arrived, Sue's salon was bigger than Julie had expected. However, she'd realised very early on, in their first meeting at the brothel where Julie had once worked, that Sue wasn't short of money. Sex at the swingers' parties was Sue's idea of fun and the friendship between her and Julie was based firmly on trust; Sue relied on Julie's discretion.

'Julie love.' Sue greeted her like an old friend. As usual, Sue was fully made up and glamorous-looking. She had class and Julie liked that. 'What are you up to these days? Love the expensive clothes.'

'I'm getting married. Yes, me, getting married!' They were sitting alone in the back room having a cup of tea and a discreet catch up. The shop was busy, which meant the staff were too. 'I need to change a little. My hair feels dry, possibly over-bleached. It needs to look classier, not so bleached. I have never had it done professionally. I have to look the part now I am going to be a married woman. What do you think?' Wincing, Julie waited for Sue's professional opinion as she cocked her head from side to side and looked at it from all angles.

Stepping forward, Sue stroked her hair. 'You're right, Julie. It's dry and needs a conditioning treatment. You have lovely shoulder-length hair but I'm afraid the ends are fucked. There are better hair dyes than the old bottles of peroxide. Softer ones that aren't so harsh on the hair. So who is this knight in shining armour, then, who has stolen your heart? Is he a good fuck?' Sue laughed and chinked her mug of tea against Julie's. 'Maybe I should meet him.' Sue winked cheekily.

'It's a guy called Ralph Gold; we met when I was working at the brothel and then later when I was escorting. I'm living with him now at a hotel in London, but we need to buy somewhere because I'm looking after my sister's baby, Josh. He's been in hospital and he's coming home soon. So I need a house, a wedding dress and this bloody hair sorting out!'

A frown appeared on Sue's brow and she stopped laughing. 'Ralph Gold? I've heard of him. Isn't he that rich man who was accused of murder? I think I remember reading something about him in the newspapers.'

'Well, that's one way of putting it. But, yes, that's him.'

'Ooh, he's handsome. Lots of black hair. You've done well for yourself there. Anyway, come and sit at the sinks and let's have a look. I'm going to cut it, you know that, don't you?'

Nodding, Julie accepted her fate and put herself in Sue's capable hands. After all, this was what she'd come here for.

Over Sue's mindless gossiping, Julie looked in the mirror facing her and watched Sue and her scissors. Bit by bit she watched cuttings of her hair fall on the floor and she felt bits of the old Julie falling away too.

'Now, tell me about your wedding plans. What about your dress?'

'I haven't really had time to look around, but I want something big and glamorous. Lots of layers and a tiara.' Julie's enthusiasm returned as she thought about her wedding day.

'Here, take a look through these magazines while I make you even more beautiful.'

Each one Julie pointed out, Sue snubbed. 'No, lots of women have worn them. You're marrying a rich man with money to burn. You can't get married in some old frock and look like just another bride. Come on, Julie, think big.' Sue met Julie's eyes in the mirror before them. 'I see diamanté and rhinestones on the bustier and sewn into the wedding gown. Lots of them and lots of sparkle and at least three layers of netting underskirts. You will look like Cinderella. Satin or something shimmery. Why not have one made? You could do that if you hurry up. There's an old woman who had a bridal and prom dress shop up the road. She could do it. She's retired now, but bloody hell did she turn out some fantastic dresses. All the stones were sewn on by hand. I'll give her a call in a minute and get her to pop in.'

Sue was very enthusiastic and it seemed to be infectious amongst all the other staff and customers, everyone bouncing their ideas around. Feeling happy, Julie laughed with them all. It was the first time she'd had a woman's company in a long time. Frankie, her sister, would have loved this – all the girls together, laughing and joking. They had always been so close. She wished with all her heart that she was here and would be her chief bridesmaid at her wedding. She hadn't realised how much she'd missed her daily catch-ups with Carrie and the girls.

Now just talking with Sue and the other girls here, Julie felt like a bride-to-be and the excitement bubbled inside of her.

'You know, Sue, I've just realised. I don't have anyone to walk me down the aisle. I don't have any family. Maybe it should be just a low-key wedding at a registry office, with a couple of traffic wardens for witnesses.'

'What, with Ralph Gold? You're not going to get away with that. What about your friend Carrie Smeltzer?' Sue winked at her in the mirror. 'I tell you what, once you've exhausted all your options, including any of Ralph's mates he might want to do it, I'll do it, or my husband will.' Her warm smile made Julie feel better; suddenly, she didn't feel so alone any more.

Julie had never had her hair done professionally before and her arse was numb, she'd been sitting in the styling chair for so long. Now she was sitting with cling film around her hair as the dye worked its magic. She looked like an oven-ready meal as they thumbed their way through magazines.

'Here she is. Maggie, come and meet Julie. You're going to make her a dress that will make all other brides cry with jealousy.'

As good as her word, Sue had telephoned the dressmaker and she had come straight away. Making Julie stand up, she measured her. 'My God, you're like an hourglass. Such big tits and a tiny waist.'

Shocked at her statement, Julie looked at Sue.

'We used to be members of the same reading club.' Sue glanced at Julie and, instantly understanding her meaning, Julie nodded. So, Maggie here was also a swinger. That made a lot of sense as to how she and Sue knew each other so well.

After what seemed like hours, Sue nodded with satisfaction. 'There you go, my lovely. All done.'

Standing aside, Sue moved so that Julie could get a better view in the mirror. It was a total transformation. Instead of her overly bleached long hair, she had a neat, neck-length, blonde bob. All the straggly bits had gone. Sue had blow-waved the sides into her face and shaped it. It looked full, thick and glossy.

'Oh my God, Sue, that's beautiful. It looks so shiny. How am I going to keep it blow-waved like this?'

'You live in a hotel! You go down every morning and let them do it. You're going to be Mrs Julie Gold, for fuck's sake. Don't start penny pinching now!'

They all burst out laughing. But Julie was in awe of her reflection. The different blonde tones Sue had put in her hair gave her face much more colour and she looked and felt she looked like someone Ralph could be proud of, befitting her status in his social circle. She felt like crying.

'How much do I owe you?' Julie opened her bag and took out her purse.

'Don't be silly; I've had a wonderful afternoon. It's been a long time since I've had a proper challenge. This is why I became a hairdresser many years ago. To transform people.' Sue laughed.

'I should give you something.'

'You will; you'll have to come back for dress fittings and then you can buy me lunch.'

'That's a definite. And when you come to London for the wedding, I'll pay your hotel bill.' Mentally, Julie decided she would put that on Carlos's bill.

Sue dropped her off at the train station and Julie couldn't stop admiring herself in mirrors and shop windows as she walked past them. Sue had been right, it had been a lovely afternoon, but now she just wanted to get back to Ralph and show him her new look. She would make herself look glamorous and then when he was putty in her hands, she'd quiz him about Paddy's brother.

* * *

'Cor blimey, Julie, I hardly recognised you.' Flicking his cigarette on the floor and stubbing it out with his shoe, Chris was stunned.

'You cheeky bastard.' Julie laughed, lapping up the compliments. 'Are you saying I looked shit before?'

'No, no offence, I didn't mean that. I meant that you look great.' Blushing slightly, Chris opened the car door for her.

'Don't be daft; I'm only joking with you. Believe me, when you piss me off you will know about it. Did you sort them things out for me?'

Now on firmer ground, Chris nodded as he drove out of the car park. 'I spoke to the guy who owns the units. You can go and see it tomorrow morning. And I picked up a couple of brochures for you; they're on the back seat. Some places in Chelsea, the Barbican, oh and the marina. Them flats got a nice view. Got all the numbers and told them you would call to make an appointment.'

'My, you have been busy. Thanks, I appreciate your help.' Sitting back in the car and picking up the brochures, Julie smiled to herself. This was turning out to be a fantastic day. Noticing the price tags on the apartments, she squirmed inside. Maybe these were out of Ralph's budget. They were bloody expensive!

Getting out of the car, Julie opened her handbag and counted out a hundred pounds. 'I know Ralph pays you, but I want you to have this. You've been busy for me today and we all like a bonus.'

'Oh God, no, Julie. Ralph pays good money. I don't expect anything.'

'Take it, Chris. Have a drink on me. And I want you here early tomorrow so we can look at that unit, okay?'

Seeing his boyish smile light up while stuffing his money in his pocket, Julie walked into the hotel. She felt like a million dollars and the admiring looks from the staff told her she looked like a million dollars, too.

Surprised to see Ralph home and relaxing in front of the television for once, she waited for him to take his eyes off the football and look up at her properly.

The look on his face said it all. It was the exact impression she had envisioned on her journey home.

'Julie, you look stunning!' Standing up, he looked on in awe as this even more beautiful woman did a twirl before him.

'You like it, then?'

'Too bloody right. Where have you been all day? Come here, I've missed you.'

As he reached out for her, she stopped him. 'Be warned: you can do whatever you like to me, but do not ruffle my hair!'

'Come here, woman, I want to hold you.'

'Well, if having my hair done brings out the passion in you, I must have it done more often. I've been to Liverpool. A friend of mine has a salon there; she did it for me and she helped me arrange my wedding dress. I'll have to go to Liverpool for a few fittings – that's okay, isn't it?'

Ralph's eyes lit up. At last, Julie was getting the ball rolling and thinking about their wedding day. 'You're having it made in Liverpool? Why not here?' He was curious now. He had presumed Julie would have bought her wedding dress at some expensive bridal shop in London.

'I'm having mine made. Just for me. A one-off, just like me. This is someone I know and trust, plus you're not getting any sneaky peeks.' Stroking his face lovingly, she kicked off her shoes and accepted the drink he offered her.

'That sounds great to me. Get Chris to drive you up there. You don't want to be hanging around train stations.'

'No, it's quicker by train. And what would he do while I'm there having lunch and gossiping with my friends?'

'He'd wait for you. That is what chauffeurs do. They hang around a lot and sleep in the cars.'

'We'll see. But for now, I'm hungry. I'm going to freshen up and change and you can put a clean shirt on. I have a few things to discuss with you.'

'That sounds ominous. What do we need to talk about?'

'Well, to start with, honey...' Julie headed for the bathroom, and then turned. 'You can browse through those brochures from the estate agents' and help choose us a new place to live. Come on, get your skates on!'

* * *

'Well, you've brought me to my favourite restaurant. You look amazing and the champagne is chilled. You have me all softened up now, so what is it you want to talk to me about?'

It had been a lovely evening and full of Julie's idle chatter and jokes. Ralph knew she had something serious on her mind she wanted to discuss.

'Order some brandies first; have a cigar.'

Now he knew he was in trouble. Julie was smiling and flirting and with her new look it was very hard to resist.

'You haven't said anything about the brochures for the apartments. Are they too expensive? Have I gone a little over the top?'

'The houses? Is that what all this is about? No, Julie. Go ahead, buy whatever you want. Believe me, darling, we can afford three times as much. I haven't said anything because I know you will have made your own mind up anyway; you're just asking me out of politeness.' Ralph shrugged and laughed.

'Fair enough. Well, as long as you can afford it, that's what really matters. I do like the look of one of them particularly, in the Barbican. It has its own gardens and stuff. Lots of privacy for Josh and us. Only the people that live there have access to its private grounds. I want you to come with me tomorrow to take a look. Chris will come to pick us up about ten in the morning. There is an office unit I want you to look around, too. It's for lease and I think it will be perfect for your office. Somewhere people can see you without coming to our new home...' Julie emphasised the word 'home'. Once they had left the hotel, she was damn sure she wasn't having all walks of life knocking on her door.

'I get your point. Do I need to come with you or have you already paid the deposit?' Again, Ralph laughed. He loved this woman, but she was a slippery as a snake.

'I'll sort it. Now tell me, who is Liam, Paddy's brother? You've never mentioned him before and I never met him when I was in Ireland.'

Confused, Ralph paused and waited. This was a bolt out of the blue. Inhaling on his cigar and swirling his brandy around in the fishbowl glass, Ralph stared at Julie and gathered his thoughts. She obviously knew something he did not. Cautiously, Ralph toyed with his glass. 'I don't know who's been talking but there isn't a lot to tell. Yes, Paddy has a half-brother. His father liked to sow his wild oats even after marriage. There must be a million brothers and sisters Paddy has scattered over Ireland. He just turned up on the doorstep one day and announced he was Paddy's brother. Millie, Paddy's poor mum, just took it all in her stride and put another plate of stew out.'

'I'd have told him to piss off!'

'You are not an Irish, Catholic woman who accepts her lot in life, Julie. Things were different in her day. The rent was paid, she got her housekeeping money and she turned a blind eye to the rest.'

'Well, rest assured, my eyes are well and truly open. You're a handsome man, Ralph, and you're mine. Don't ever forget that.'

'I like it when you say things like that.' Reaching across the table, Ralph squeezed her hand. 'Don't ever doubt me, Julie. You're my woman.'

Embarrassed, Julie brushed away his hand. 'You are a soppy old bastard at times. Anyway, getting back to the conversation. I think we need to go back to Ireland. Paddy and his brother are causing mayhem with your properties and tenants. All in the name of Ralph Gold.'

'What do you mean?' Sitting up straight, Ralph waited for the rest of the story.

'He's putting up the rents. You're still getting your money, but he's creaming it off the top and Paddy and his brother are running the show. Well, my name will soon be Gold and half of that business will become mine, so we're going to Ireland to sort it out.'

'Whoa! Hold up, how do you know all of this? It might not be true.'

'When was the last time you spoke to that lying sleazebag?'

Thinking about it, Ralph nodded his head. 'It's been a few weeks; I've been a bit neglectful lately. I've had other things on my mind.'

'Well, you need to start focusing again. We have business to sort out and that means all your properties in Ireland. While we're there we will go and see your mum. No arguments, Ralph – we're doing this.' Gulping back her brandy in one, Julie looked across the table defiantly at Ralph.

'Don't look so mad. I'm shocked at what you know but I'm not angry. I've been meaning to go to Ireland anyway. Carlos thinks it would be a good idea if Paddy was my best man at the wedding.' Holding up his hand to stop Julie's outburst, Ralph continued. 'It's the perfect cover for why we are really going.'

Accepting what he said, Julie agreed. 'If that Paddy thinks he's going to show me up at my wedding, you had better warn him. I'm no Irish Catholic woman who accepts her fate. I'll publicly kick him up the arse!'

Throwing his head back, Ralph burst into laughter. 'You are funny when you're angry, Julie.'

'Well, let's hope you never find out just how funny I can be!'

Ralph's laughter was infectious and Julie started laughing at her own joke, but mentally she was already preparing herself for a showdown with Paddy and his brother.

10

TROUBLED TIMES

'Ralph, Ralph, is that you, mate? Sorry to ring you so early at the hotel, but I thought you should know... Johnny is dead. His house blew up. Seems really fucking odd to me, especially after he had that argument with that Jenkins bloke.'

Ralph listened to Norman's distressed voice. He seemed panic-stricken and frightened. He probably thought he was going to be next.

'Norman, what happened? I haven't seen him for a few days. I've been pretty busy organising my wedding.' Ralph winked at Julie.

It was six in the morning and the first lie-in Ralph had had for weeks and now he had Norman on the telephone. Trying to gather his thoughts quickly, he gave the usual sympathy and asked the obvious questions.

'Gas explosion or something. His girlfriend is dead too. Fire brigade are looking into it and even though Johnny was burnt to a crisp, apparently he had a bullet hole in his head! His mother identified his body. Just a charred skeleton. Oh God, what are we going to do?' Ralph could hear Norman crying on the other end of the telephone. He was terrified. 'Shit, Ralph, do you think it's turf war? Have you heard anything from that Jenkins bloke?'

'Not since you visited him, although it is time to get in touch I suppose. I'll call him and see if he knows anything. Norman, calm down. Whatever has happened to Johnny, he brought it on himself. I doubt it was Jenkins. Johnny owed a lot of money. Gambling debts. It could have been anyone.'

'Yes, suppose you're right, but you've got to admit, it's one hell of a coincidence.'

'Calm down and let me look into it. If Jenkins was going to do anything, he would have done it that day, when you were there. He had his gun and the place was empty apart from you lot. Leave it with me, eh?' Once Ralph had appealed to Norman's better judgement, he put down the telephone.

'Trouble at mill?'

'Something like that. I'm awake now so I am going to jump in the shower. Shall I order breakfast?'

Yawning, Julie lay back on the pillows. 'You're not going anywhere until we've seen that unit. That telephone call just proves my point. What if the hotel staff are listening in and they hear big mouth talking about people being murdered? Not exactly the image you want to portray, is it?'

'Why should they listen to a private call?' A frown crossed Ralph's brow.

'Because they have fuck all else to do at this time in the morning and hearing some guy panicking and screaming down the telephone for you would make me curious. Now order breakfast and then tell that receptionist I want to book the hairdresser's for nine. I need to look my best.'

After making the calls, Ralph went to the shower and pondered on what Julie had said. He had to admit it, she made sense. Time to sort his life out and stop living like a bachelor on a wing and a prayer. Julie was good for him; she was a good businesswoman and was wise to the ways of the world. She saw things he didn't.

* * *

'Well, it looks better on the inside than it does on the outside. Much bigger than I expected.' Hands in pockets, Ralph looked around the unit. From the outside, it was just a square unit with metal shutters. On the inside, it was very different and comprised of large office spaces. A main one, behind glass. He would feel like a goldfish in a bowl, but on the other hand, he could see who was hanging around. In addition, it had blinds if he needed privacy. There was an oval reception desk and three small offices for staff. It had its own parking out the front and even a delivery yard. All the usual amenities, toilets and beverage bay. Near the back was a conference room, big enough for ten people at a push. All the office furniture was included in the rent.

Nervously, Julie looked around and waited for Ralph's reaction. It was modern and even the telephone lines were connected.

'They have a caretaker for safety, and there are security cameras.' Again she waited while he walked in every room and looked around.

'Okay, we'll take it.' Ralph looked at the agent and shook his hand. 'Where do I sign?'

Beaming at the thought of his commission, the agent gladly shook Ralph's hand and couldn't put his contract under Ralph's nose quickly enough.

'We can put the sign outside for your business, Mr Gold. What do you want putting on it?'

'Gold Enterprises Ltd.,' Julie butted in. 'Import and export. That's why the yard is so good for deliveries. We also have properties in Ireland to let.'

'Well, here's your keys. We will finish up the paperwork at our offices if that's okay.'

Once back in the car on the way to the agent's office, Chris couldn't help himself. 'Did you like it, Mr Gold? You going to take it?'

'Well, I wouldn't be following him back to his office if I didn't.'

Seeing the hurt look on Chris's face at Ralph's snub, Julie punched Ralph in the arm and gave him a dirty look.

'What?' Rubbing his arm, he looked at her, confused.

Leaning forward discreetly, Julie whispered in Ralph's ear. 'Try to be nice to the poor kid. He's helped me find this place and he's just excited, you prick.'

Prompted into action, Ralph smiled. 'You've done well there, Chris. You too, Julie. It's just what we're looking for.'

'Thanks, Mr Gold. Only the best for you and Julie.' With the smile back on his face, he carried on driving while Julie gave Ralph another dig in the ribs. She liked Chris.

'Sorry,' Ralph mouthed discreetly to Julie.

'I've got a card here, Mr Gold. It's an agency for secretaries and stuff. Thought you might need it.'

Stunned, Ralph sat back in the car. The last thing he wanted was people knowing his business.

'Thanks, Chris, good thinking.' Julie slipped the card into her handbag.

Ralph wasn't sure where all this was going, but he knew Julie had something up her sleeve.

'We have to register you as a limited company. All the posh people do it. If you go bankrupt, the taxman can only take your business off you. Your own assets are your own. I used to have a "regular" friend who was an accountant; he told me all that stuff.' Julie winked.

Knowing exactly what she meant by 'regular' friend, Ralph nodded.

'When we've finished here, Chris, take us to the Barbican. I need to get that sorted.'

'When you make your mind up, you really do, don't you?' Ralph was amazed at the speed Julie was moving. Within a space of three hours, Ralph had offices and a fourth-floor, three-bedroom apartment in the Barbican.

'It's got a lovely balcony with hanging baskets and flowers for Josh to sit out in his pram and see some sunshine. Look out here, Ralph.' Standing outside the patio doors on the balcony, Julie looked around. 'It has its own restaurants and cinema. What do you think? Can you afford it?'

'Definitely.' Ralph smiled and hugged her. He liked Julie's choice. The apartment was nice and private.

Julie was elated at their productive morning. All the wheels were set in motion.

'I have some business of my own to see to, Julie; we'll drop you off first and then Chris can take me to meet Mr Jenkins.'

'Okay, sweetheart. I've got stuff to do too. I'll get the receptionist to book our tickets to Ireland. Then I need to look at furniture and stuff for Josh. I'd really like that nanny-cum-nurse that's been looking after him to come and work for us, too,' she hinted. 'She knows him and he knows her,' Julie mused.

'I daresay if you offer her enough money, she will.' He squeezed her hand, giving her reassurance.

Julie smiled and kissed him on the cheek. 'Thank you.'

'Don't thank me. You are doing it for us. For Josh. Our family.'

Julie could feel the tears brimming in her eyes, and quickly brushed them away with the back of her hand.

'Well, come on then. You have money to earn. You are the

breadwinner. Now let's go.' Holding his hand, Julie walked back to Chris waiting in the car.

Chris drove to Charlie Jenkins' pub. 'You going in there, Mr Gold? There is a lot of talk about the person who owns that place. Police been around here a lot lately. He's bad news. Watch your back, boss.'

Puzzled, Ralph sat in the back seat of the car as Chris rambled on. Now he knew who Julie's source of information was. This young driver was so eager to impress and ingratiate himself, he made a point of befriending anyone who could boost his career.

'Is your mouth always a runaway train?'

'Sorry, Mr Gold. No disrespect.' Once again being put in his place by Ralph, Chris lost his enthusiasm and parked the car without saying anything else. He preferred driving Julie; she was more fun and enjoyed his snippets of information.

Ralph looked around. 'On second thoughts, park in the side street and wait for me; I won't be long.' If the police were hanging around, Ralph didn't want to be seen mixing with Charlie.

'Would you tell Mr Jenkins Ralph is here to see him, please,' Ralph asked the barmaid. Looking around the place made him cringe inside. This place was a real shithole; God knows what Charlie would do to that West End place. Christ, it didn't bear thinking about.

'Ralph, long time no see, mate.' Charlie held out his hand to shake Ralph's. 'I thought you would have been in touch before now. Weren't you afraid I would take the keys and run?' He laughed aloud for everyone to hear.

'No, Charlie. It never crossed my mind.'

The smile dropped from Charlie's face. Ralph's unruffled calmness unnerved him. He couldn't ever remember seeing Ralph Gold laugh.

'Come through to the back; we have business to attend to.'

Heightening his importance, it was more of an announcement to the pub as Charlie bellowed his words to anyone that would listen.

Following Charlie's lead through to his office, Ralph stopped the two men that were permanently on Charlie's heels. They were more like a double act, always there to laugh at Charlie's jokes and act as minders.

'You two wait here; I have business with Charlie. Not you.' The quiet, authoritative words from Ralph made them falter and look at Charlie, who nodded his approval.

'Drink?' Taking out his whisky, Charlie started to pour into two glasses. 'I haven't been in touch because there has been a bit of bother lately. Nothing I couldn't handle, of course. But I decided to wait a while.'

'Trouble? What kind of trouble?' Ralph didn't touch his drink, but waited while Charlie took a sip of his own. It amazed Ralph how this man ever made a profit. God knows he drank more than he sold.

'Ah, it's nothing.' Charlie waved a hand in the air, trying to look in charge of the situation. 'One of those people you sent with the keys ended up dead. Not my business. Right nasty piece he was by all accounts. Don't know why you sent him; nearly changed my mind, I did.'

Knowing this was complete fabrication, Ralph felt smug that his plan had worked. Charlie Jenkins was shitting himself at the idea of being stitched up for something he didn't do. However, as everyone knew Johnny had frequented the pub and ended up dead, it didn't look good for Charlie. Ralph was curious as to what piece of information he had given the police to get them off his back.

'All sorted now? I presume it must be.'

'Yes, it was that south-east mob; I would put money on it. Heard he owed them money and he tried getting it out of me for information about you. But we're mates, Ralph; if I need to know anything about you all I have to do is ask – right?' Raising his eyebrows in expectation, Charlie waited and was assured by Ralph's nod of his head.

So, Charlie had pointed the finger at another gang. This man was a walking time bomb.

'I heard you wanted the place decorating a little if you were to take it. Did you like the club?'

'Nice place, but does need a wash and polish.' Hearing this, Ralph had to take a sip of his drink. He nearly choked at Charlie's joke about cleanliness. 'Not at my expense, though.' Again, he looked at Ralph hopefully. 'So let's get this straight: it will be my name above the door, all the takings are mine and I make all the decisions without any input from you. Is that right?'

'Nearly. All of what you just said, but business associates of mine will be using it to money-launder. So a lot of what goes through your cash registers will go through my accountants. The profits are yours and I think in your capable hands it will do well.' Ralph smiled. 'But I want no interference from you. What do you say?'

'We'll give it a try and see what happens, eh? Cannot say no fairer than that. How soon do you think you can get that place cleaned up?'

'How quickly can you apply for the licence and get your name above the door?'

'Not a problem. I know a few guys; they owe me a favour. We're looking at a couple of days at best.'

Standing up, Ralph held his hand out to Charlie. 'Right then, a couple of days it is. You will be dealing with the accountants and one of my trusted employees from now on, unless you have any problems. You know how to contact me.'

'Don't you want some kind of contract signing or something?' Charlie was surprised at Ralph's flippancy.

'Gentlemen's agreement, Charlie. It's your club. You are the manager. I'm just the sleeping partner. As you say, not my business.'

Ralph knew exactly what Charlie was thinking. He thought Ralph was a real pushover. An idiot that he was going to fleece for every penny. Nothing in writing to prove someone else owned the club. The only problem was Charlie didn't have the deeds, just in case he thought of selling it. And Ralph didn't want his signature on anything. No paper trail. He owned the land the property stood on. What went on inside wasn't his problem, it was the very stupid Charlie Jenkins'.

Back in the car, Ralph sat back in his seat. 'Chris, you seem to know a little about everything. Do you know the south-east mob?'

'Heard of them. Know of them, but don't know them if you know what I mean. They are all Jamaicans, I think. Heavy into prostitution and drug-dealing. They keep to their own side of the river.'

'Where are their meeting places? How do you find them? I presume you know that.'

'Word is there is a pub near the Elephant and Castle where they meet upstairs, but that's as far as I know.' Chris didn't want to say any more. He didn't want to incriminate himself and for Ralph to think badly of him.

'Take me there. I'd like to see for myself.'

The pub was very near the Tube station – handy if they needed a quick getaway – and was like any other in the area, but walking inside was quite a different matter. It was the first time that Ralph had been in a pub solely owned and used by Jamaicans. As he made his way to the bar, people stared at him and nudged each other, as curious about him as he was about them. He didn't have a name to ask for so he felt like he was punching in the dark.

'I was told to come here to ask for the man in charge. The boss in charge of the south-east,' He asked the barmaid. She looked up, put a drink he hadn't asked for on the table and walked away. Two men stood up from their table and joined Ralph, one on either side of him.

'Who you looking for, mister? Nice sharp suit, man.'

Standing his ground, Ralph smiled. 'Well, I'm not entirely sure. I was pointed in this direction when I said I had some business regarding Charlie Jenkins.' He instantly realised he'd struck a nerve as they passed quizzical looks at each other.

'Open your jacket, man.'

Doing as he was told, Ralph spread it wide open. Grabbing the sides of his jacket, they put their hands into the inside pockets and trailed down to his trousers and then nodded to each other. 'You got five minutes, mister. Come with us.'

Ralph liked their style. These men were professionals. They had checked him for weapons, unlike any of Charlie's men. They led Ralph to a staircase through the back; one man went before him and one stood behind him as they climbed the stairs. Not knowing what to expect, even Ralph felt a little uneasy. Upstairs, which seemed like the living quarters above the pub, Ralph was surprised to see it was plain floorboards. There was tables and chairs, but it was all very sparse. A group of men sat huddled around a table in the far corner. They were counting stacks of money.

'Marlon, someone to see you about that scumbag Charlie Jenkins. Fucking Bossman, my arse.' He kicked a wooden chair towards Ralph with his foot. 'Sit down,' he ordered.

One of the men, wearing a black leather cap, turned around, displaying a row full of gold teeth and pointing a gun directly at Ralph. 'What's your business here?'

'My name's Ralph Gold; I have some business I'd like to discuss with you. You know who Charlie Jenkins is. Well, I also want you to know that he is going to be managing a club I'm in possession of.'

'Fuck the long-winded chatter, man. You got five minutes and you have just used up three of them.'

As odd as it seemed, Ralph instantly liked these men. They were straightforward businessmen.

'I thought you might like to know that it was him who suggested to his friends that you had something to do with the recent killing of a guy called Johnny.'

All of them looked at each other, and the other men at the table turned their chairs around to take a better look at the stranger before them. 'And you're telling us this because...?' They waited.

'I just thought you'd like to know.' Ralph shrugged. Everyone in the room was measuring him up. They didn't know what to make of him.

'You're employing him and yet you're grassing him up. Does he know that?'

'He knows he can make money out of me, but as for loyalty I owe him none. I've just left him and, according to him, you had something to do with the killing. Now if he's told me, it makes me wonder who else he's made the assumptions to.' Ralph felt it was better to tell them the truth, because he knew they would find out if he was lying.

A tall man came through from another room. He wore a red silk shirt, with a mountain of gold chains around his neck and wrists. Ralph was instantly drawn to the gold spurs on his black, leather cowboy boots. 'I'm Marlon; this is my turf. What's your business here? What do you want?' He clicked his fingers at one of his men, and a wooden chair was quickly brought forward for him.

'I want you to keep an eye on him for me. Shake things up now and again. Don't let him get complacent. You owe him nothing. Have the police been here regarding his accusations?'

'Why should we trust you? How do we know he hasn't sent you, eh? You must think we're stupid. Get out. You're wasting our time.'

Holding his hands up first, Ralph proceeded, under the watchful eye of the gun still pointing at him, to take out his wallet.

Counting out a thousand pounds, he walked slowly forward and put it on the table. 'A down payment.'

'You wanna keep the fat man on his toes, mister? Did you know Karen, Johnny's woman who was killed, is Jerome over there's half-sister? Whoever killed him, killed her.'

Ralph feigned surprise and sorrow at this information and, as guilty as he might have felt, it was also another trump card against Charlie Jenkins, should he ever feel the need to use it. There was always collateral damage and it couldn't be helped. There was nothing Ralph could do about it now. But this was the kind of insurance he liked and it had just fallen into his lap.

'I heard he had a bullet in his head. Did she?'

'No, she was burnt to a crisp. She caused the explosion by turning the lights on. Now that fat bastard is pointing the finger at us. I'll take your money, mister, and I will shake that fat bastard up and I'll want the same again next month.' Marlon stuffed the money in the back pocket of his jeans.

'I'll pay you as and when I need you. This is all about trust. I've come here in good faith. To meet with you, give you money and information. All I want is a watchful eye over Charlie. I'm sure we can come to some arrangement.' Ralph held out his hand, which seemed to surprise Marlon, who shook it. Then he turned and left.

'Oy, mister,' someone shouted down the stairway. 'What is your name again?'

'Gold. Ralph Gold.' Ralph smiled to himself. Now he had just caused turf war. This would make Charlie Jenkins want to run even faster to the West End. It was a full circle of deceit and hatred.

'Drop me off at the hotel, Chris. Then take Julie shopping and to the hospital. Incidentally, I never came here today and if I ever find out that I did, I will know who told them, won't I?'

'Came where, Mr Gold? Don't know what you mean. We've been looking at flats and office units.'

'Good boy. Now drop me off and get some lunch. Here.' Ralph stuffed a fifty-pound note into Chris's top pocket. 'Now drive.'

After the long day he'd had, being greeted by Julie's warm smile and constant chatter was a welcome change. She was buzzing with excitement with all the things they had bought and was making plans about furnishings. Most men would find it boring, but day-to-day trivial matters were a welcome escape from someone pointing a gun at you. That was what he liked most about Julie. She never questioned him for being late or left alone for hours. She never complained when he had to go out. And he never dreaded going home, knowing that he was walking into a sulky argument. Although, there were times when he wished he didn't leave Julie alone so much. That was when she had time to think and come up with hare-brained schemes. Such as these office units. Life was never dull.

'I've told Chris to come back for you and take us to the hospital.'

'No need, I've been. I've also secured that nurse-cum-nanny. You were right. Money talks and when I said where we would be living, she was well impressed.' Undoing Ralph's tie and pouring him a drink, she sat on his knee. 'I've been thinking, Ralph.'

Ralph suddenly felt an air of foreboding. *Oh God, Julie has been thinking!*

'Your offices are going to be squeaky clean.' Wagging a warning finger in his face, Julie meant business. 'This is your smokescreen for when people ask how you got so bloody rich. No money-laundering or anything through that place. All above board. We are going to do haulage. Okay, maybe not completely kosher – see, I'm learning.' Julie laughed at her own joke. 'But people always want stuff moving around. I've rung that agency for receptionists, by the way. We want an older one with brains, not some young bird filing her nails.'

'Stop, Julie. Take a breath. We only got it today. Nothing is set up and we don't have any orders for anything.'

'You're wrong. We will have orders. You're going to get them. Are you telling me all those men you drink and deal with at the Masons' lodge and rotary clubs won't give you any of their business? Isn't that what you do with your funny handshakes and stuff? Drum up some business and let's get sorted. Oh, by the way, we leave for Ireland tomorrow afternoon.'

Sucking in his breath and listening to her, Ralph was amazed. God, she was like a whirlwind. 'Just how many balls do you juggle in the air at once? Take a breath, slow down.'

'Well, that's another thing I wanted to talk to you about. Why don't we put a crap movie on, order some room service and see just how many balls I can juggle at once?' Her infectious, dirty laugh filled the room.

11

BACK IN TIME

Ralph had telephoned ahead to Billy to pick them up at the airport. It felt strange being back in Ireland. Suddenly, he felt like he didn't belong here any more. It was the past, and his mother had always said, 'Never look back, always go forward.' Billy had become a trusted employee over the last couple of years, and he'd enlisted other men he knew from his army barracks once they had left, to help run things. 'First things first, Billy, let's book into the hotel, get freshened up, and go and see Paddy. You can fill me in on the way about what he's been up to.'

'Really glad you're here, Ralph. It's mayhem. That Paddy couldn't run a piss-up in a brewery. Throwing his weight around everywhere. You do know all the rents have been put up?'

'No, I didn't. Considering my money has never gone up, I presume he is keeping the rest to himself. Creaming it off the top.' Sick to his stomach, Ralph listened. It seemed Paddy was living the high life on his money. He could kick himself for taking his eye off the ball and giving Paddy a free hand. Bloody foolish.

'That brother of his is a right bastard. Always starting fights and Paddy encourages him.' Raising his voice and almost shouting over to the back seat where Ralph and Julie were sitting, Billy filled them in on all of the bad news. 'Believe me, I am so pleased to see you. Some of the guys are ready for a mutiny. He owes them wages.' Everything Billy had bottled up came spewing out as soon as he saw Ralph.

Angrily listening to Billy describe the chaos Paddy was creating in Ralph's wake, Julie sat forward. 'Ralph,' she instructed, 'while you're still in a good mood and before you see that two-faced shit-stirrer, we're going to see your mum. Give us time to drop our suit-cases off at the hotel and let me go to the loo, Billy, but we're going to the care home first. Another couple of hours isn't going to make much difference, is it?'

'I suppose so.' Ralph let out a huge sigh. He was good at throwing money at his mother for her care and wellbeing, but seeing her was another matter. She didn't know him any more and that cut deep.

'Let's get the hard part over with first. And then we go and visit these pubs you bought and listen to the landlords' grievances. After all, it's your name Paddy's trashing and soon it's going to be mine.'

'For God's sake, Julie, we've only just got here. Have you got an itinerary?' Frustrated and nervous at the prospect of visiting his mum, Ralph couldn't help snapping at her.

Raising her voice, her face flushed with anger. 'Well, yes, I have. I want to visit these pubs and tenants before Paddy can lie his fucking head off or threaten them to tell you a pack of lies. Oy, you, Billy. Tell me more about this brother of Paddy's.' Julie sat back with her cigarette and soaked up every piece of information Billy could give her.

* * *

Approaching the residential home, Ralph cringed inside. He could already feel his stomach doing somersaults. It was a lovely place: large, modern and airy. The gardens at the back and front were well maintained and were bordered with rose bushes. Following Julie's lead, Ralph walked down the corridor to the reception desk and signed in. They were greeted by the manageress and the staff, who told them Ralph's mum was in the lounge area.

'Hi, Diana.' Julie waltzed in full of smiles and headed towards her. 'How are you today?' Sitting beside her, Julie held her hand and nodded her head towards Ralph to sit down. Seeing no recognition in Diana's eyes, Julie carried on. 'I'm Julie and this is Ralph. Do you remember Ralph?'

'I have a little boy called Ralph. He'll be at school now; I'd better get his dinner ready.' Ralph's mother, lost in her own bubble and only remembering the past, was about to stand up when Julie stopped her.

'Oh, that's not for a while yet. I think he's got football or something after school.' Looking up at Ralph, Julie felt sad for him. Maybe this wasn't a good idea. Dementia, one of the worst illnesses ever. Not just for the person suffering with it, but for the families, too, watching the person they love disappear before their eyes.

'You mean he's probably in detention again.' Diana laughed, patting Julie's hand.

'I thought you might like to hear my good news. We're getting married. Say something, Ralph,' Julie prompted him. She could see Ralph was lost for words, choked up. But this was a demon he had to face before he moved on. He could see Diana looked as well as possible and her hair had been done. This made him feel better, because the manageress hadn't known they would be visiting and hadn't had time to make his mum look her best for appearance's sake.

'It's good to see you, Ma.' Leaning forward, Ralph kissed her.

Holding up her hand, Diana stroked Ralph's face. 'I know you, don't I?' A fleeting look of recognition flashed in her eyes and then died again.

'It's me, Ma, Ralph. I wanted to tell you I'm getting married again... to Julie.'

There was no reply. Diana turned towards Julie and gripped her hand. 'What's he saying? And why is he calling me Ma?'

Julie shook her head at Ralph. 'Oh, he's just messing. You know what men are. They think every woman is Ma to them.' She nudged Diana's shoulder gently with her own. Julie shot Ralph a look and shook her head, not wanting him to press the matter further. This would only distress Diana.

'Will you be staying for tea?' a staff member asked.

'No,' Ralph replied. Standing up, he walked away. He'd seen enough. He couldn't bear it any more.

The manageress met them as they were leaving. 'Are you okay, Mr Gold? I'm sorry; as you can see, things are not getting any better. If it helps, she's always telling everyone her little stories about her son Ralph. Always in and out of trouble.' The manageress laughed. 'We'll look after her, rest assured.' Shaking her hand, Ralph swiftly headed for the door without a backward glance with Julie running after him.

'Never again, Julie. Never again, do you hear me!' Tears rolled down his face as he tried to compose himself.

'I'm sorry, Ralph, but you had to come and see her sometime. You would regret it if anything happened to her and you hadn't come.' Moving closer, Julie put her arms around him. She could feel him shaking. It nearly broke her heart to see him crushed like this. She felt guilty forcing him to come, but he had to face this and get it over with. All the same, she hated seeing him in such despair.

'Promise me something – if I ever get as weak and feeble as that, you will help me end it. Put a bullet through my brain or something. Promise me, Julie.' Standing back, Ralph took hold of her shoulders and shook her, trying to stress his point. 'I can't end up like that.'

'It won't come to that, but I will make you the promise if it makes you feel better.'

'Yes, yes. Promise me you won't let me end my days not knowing who you are. That's all I ask.' Distraught and upset, he fell into Julie's arms for comfort.

'Anything. I swear.' Julie crossed her heart. 'I will always look after you and if it comes to it, I will make sure it won't happen to you. Even if I have to pull the trigger myself. Okay?'

Hugging her so tight that Julie could hardly breathe, Ralph burst into tears.

Although Julie held him and comforted him at the roadside, she felt satisfied. Finally, Ralph had let all those pent-up feelings out. He needed to grieve, even though his mum wasn't dead. Ralph would be pleased he'd seen her this one last time and she had looked well. But that would be his last image of her. Her hair done and looking well. That was all he needed to know. He had his other childhood memories that would keep her alive in his heart.

* * *

Trouble and revenge brewed in London as Norman's anger reached boiling point. Standing at the bar, all the worse for drink, he couldn't help but vent his anger out. 'I know it was one of Charlie Jenkins' men that killed Johnny, the bastards!'

'You know shit. And if that is the case, what are you going to do about it? Keep your voice down. You have nothing to say and you're saying it too loud.' Mick looked furtively around the pub to see who might be in there listening. It was like walking on eggshells sometimes.

'Oy, what's this, a lover tiff? What's the gossip, boys? You look pretty worked up.' Waltzing up to them in a carefree manner, Jason couldn't help but laugh at Norman's fighting spirit. It was the drink talking, he knew that.

'Jason!' Mick put his arms around his friend and hugged him. 'When did you get back from wherever Ralph sent you last? Good to see you, mate.' Mick was pleased to see a friendly face that wasn't spewing venom. Jason was an older, carefree ex-army guy who did a lot of work for Ralph, mostly collecting. This time he had been away and, as he never spoke about his dealings for Ralph, there was no point in asking.

'It's Johnny,' Norman spat out. 'You know he's dead, don't you, and that Charlie Jenkins and his two fucking monkeys did it? I had no great love for Johnny. But he was our mate, we worked together, and no one is doing anything about it. It is like no one cares what happened to him. That could have been any of us!'

Jason laughed. 'Charlie Jenkins? I know his wife. Not a bad shag.'

Mick couldn't help but laugh. That was Jason – he lived life for today. After being sent all over the place in the army, taking his life in his hands, he had lost all sense of fear and didn't care any more.

'You've been to bed with his wife?' Norman was amazed.

'No, I said I have shagged his wife. I didn't mention a bedroom. Usually a quickie on a Friday night in the back alley at that club-cum-restaurant in Dagenham. Everyone uses it. Bloody hell, sometimes you are fighting for a space. Charlie takes his wife there once a week for her outing. Still has his two idiots with him to fetch and carry the drinks, and the wife likes smoking weed and I can always get my hands on it. So there you are.'

'Well, that's it, then. If he goes there every week, that's where we're going. We're going to rough those two bastards up.'

'You do realise Ralph will go bonkers if he finds out? You're taking the law into your own hands.'

'Well, Ralph's away and he isn't going to find out, is he?' The icy glare Norman threw at Mick made his blood run cold.

The club Charlie went to on a regular basis was basic. It was an old-fashioned disco with chicken in a basket or a steak and chips with a morsel of salad on the side to make it look fancy. As Friday night rolled around, Norman, Mick and Jason walked into the club, looking for Charlie Jenkins. Mick didn't like being dragged along, but felt he had no choice. Jason had tagged along for the fun of it. He was going to have a few drinks, sell and smoke some of his marijuana and hopefully end the night in the back alley with some willing female. More to the point, he wanted to see Norman lose his bravado once faced with it.

Pushing their way past the people dancing, they headed for the bar. Jason pointed up towards a balcony away from the dancefloor. 'There you go, just as I said. Jenkins and his wife. God, she looks spaced out already.'

'Get the drinks in, Mick; we need to wait until those two hard men of his decide to go to the loo, and then we'll make our move.' Norman was all fired up. He hated what had happened to Johnny and hated Ralph for not doing anything about it.

After surveying their surroundings, Jason patted Norman on the back. 'You know where I will be if you need me, but there she goes on the dance floor with her tits half out of that dress. That's me sorted for the night, boys.'

Rubbing his hands together and picking up his drink, Mick looked over to the woman dancing around to the music on the dance floor, half spilling her drink on the floor.

'I don't think her husband has even noticed she's disappeared.' Norman was shocked to see this was Charlie Jenkins' wife. She looked no better than the prostitutes in his pub did.

Jason laughed again and slapped Norman on the back. 'Good, because I have something to get her in the mood. Nothing like a good smoke to get the party started.' Jason tapped his pocket, indicating the small packet of marijuana he had stashed away.

Walking onto the dance floor, Jason made a beeline for her as she swayed her head in time with the music, her eyes half closed and mouthing the words to the song playing. Norman and Mick looked on as Jason started dancing before her. Instantly her eyes opened and she started erotically dancing around him, without a care in the world or a care for what Charlie thought, who wasn't playing a blind bit of notice.

As predicted, Charlie's wife walked away from the dance floor towards the back entrance and, after a glance around to see if anyone was watching, Jason followed her.

'Look, Jenkins has just whispered into one of his mates' ears. He's spotted Jason following that old tart. Come on, this is our chance to show them they can't mess with us.' Norman pulled at Mick's sleeve to follow him.

Putting down their drinks and making their way to the back exit, they pushed the door open. Already, Charlie's men had Jason up against the wall and were punching him in the face. Blood spurted from his nose as he tried fighting back and pushing them off. They kneed him in the crotch, making him double over, and were taking it in turns kicking and punching him. They had jumped him from behind, taking him off guard while he had been undoing his trousers to have sex with Charlie's wife.

She looked on in panic and ran past them, back into the club, leaving Jason at the mercy of the two thugs. Grabbing hold of one of them, Norman threw a punch directly into his stomach, making him bend over and nearly fall to his knees. Norman kicked him backwards and started kicking him in the head, kick after kick. The howling from the man pierced their ears as he curled up into a ball to try to protect himself. It was useless as Norman slammed his foot down on his head, shouting and swearing at him in the process. Other people who were in the alley quickly adjusted their clothing and ran past them back into the club, not wanting to get involved.

'Grab hold of that bastard's arms and put them behind his back,' Jason shouted to Mick. Not being much of a fighter but doing as he was told, Mick wrestled with him, trying to avoid the flying punches. Suddenly, there was a bang and Mick fell to the floor, clutching his stomach as the small crimson stain on the front of his shirt quickly spread into a pool of blood. Mick's eyes were wide open and a groaning sound left his mouth as his body became still and lifeless.

Norman turned and looked up at one of Charlie's men holding the gun. He stood in shock, still pointing it at Mick as the realisation of what he'd done slowly seeped into his brain. It seemed for a moment time stood still. They were all hot, sweaty and bloodstained from the brawl, panting and breathing hard. Jason threw himself on Mick's body, trying to shake some life back into him while shouting his name in panic as tears of shock and disbelief rolled down his face.

'You've killed him, you bastard!' Norman flew towards the man holding the gun and grabbed it out of his limp, shaky hand. He was obviously still in shock at what he had done as he and his friend looked down at Mick's lifeless body. It had all been in the heat of the moment.

Hearing laughter, each of them looked up at the fire exit door, which was still ajar. Someone was coming. Thinking quickly, Norman grabbed Jason by the shirt, so hard it ripped as he dragged him off his knees away from Mick's body. There was nothing they could do now; Mick was dead. They had to get out of there. Norman and Jason fled down the back alley, leaving the two men with Mick's dead body behind them.

Reaching the top of the alley, they were breathless and stood for a moment trying to catch their breath. Jason looked around at the main road, where cars drove past them, their headlights illuminating them in the darkness of the street, as the cold night air cooled their sweaty bodies. Everything seemed normal. Except they were covered in blood. Some their own, but most of it Mick's where Jason had bent over him and held him.

'What are we going to do?' panted Norman in between breaths.

'You're asking me? I only went for a fuck; you were the one determined to cause a fight. We have to get out of here and fast before the coppers turn up. Try to keep off the main road. We don't want to get stopped looking like this.'

'What about Mick?' Norman looked at Jason, hoping for answers. His heart was thumping in his chest so hard he could hardly breathe. He was frightened and visibly shaken.

Jason wiped the sweat and blood from his face and nose with his shirtsleeve. His body ached from the beating he had taken. 'There's nothing we can do about him, is there? He's bloody dead. Now come on, Norman, run! We have to get as far away from here as possible and clean up. This was your idea and now your mate's dead, so don't start shitting your pants now!'

'My fingerprints! My fingerprints will be on the gun from where I grabbed it out of his hand. Shit! I need to go back and get it.'

'You can't go back; you're not thinking straight. His fingerprints are on it too. If the coppers find you with a gun on you, and looking the way you do, you'll do a longer stretch in prison. Guilty as charged. There's no point in arguing now; we have to hide. That guy back there is going to point the finger at us, trying to save his own neck. He shot Mick, not us. Remember that.'

'Do you think we should tell Ralph what happened?'

'For Christ's sake.' Jason was tired, his head ached and for all of Norman's bravado he was now acting like some pathetic schoolgirl.

'I can hardly breathe, my ribs are aching and you want to bother Ralph and tell him what you've started. Good luck with that!' Keeping his head down and avoiding people, Jason started running. Turning his head, he saw that Norman was running down the street behind him.

12

PADDY AND LIAM

'Well, that's been one sob story after another. All this traipsing around Ireland to find out Paddy is a lowlife, cheating bastard. I could have told you that and saved you the journey.'

'Just get off my back, eh? I've had enough today. It hasn't made it any better with them thinking I was there to cause trouble.'

Realising she had said more than enough, Julie sat back in the car and lit up two cigarettes, passing one to Ralph. He never snapped at her intentionally, so she knew now was not the time to press the matter.

Today had been fraught. They had gone to a couple of the pubs Ralph owned to say hello but the worried look on people's faces said more than words ever could. Some of the pubs barely had any customers, which had made Julie wonder how the landlords were paying protection money when they were not earning anything. On their way to another pub, Julie had mentioned it to Billy.

'They can't afford it. That's how he's got that lock-up selling second-hand furniture. What they cannot pay, he is taking in goods. He's got a girlfriend; she belongs to an Irish Traveller family and they go around with their van and pick up furniture and stuff. That lock-up of his is fit to bursting, and then the bastard sells it at twice the price. Usually to the same people who want their stuff back, but this time it's on credit with high interest rates. We've tried our best to stop them but what can we do?'

Ralph was seething inside. This was his fault. He had taken his eye off the ball and expected others to do his dirty work for him. He had fallen in love and his mind had been elsewhere. He was angry with himself for being so foolish.

Reaching forward, Julie squeezed Ralph's shoulder. Ireland was nothing but trouble. She had sensed the tenseness in Ralph's body as soon as they got off the aeroplane. He was a different man here, irritable and snappy, which wasn't like him at all.

Billy drove them to the next pub and the more Ralph heard about Paddy's antics, the worse he felt. He'd never had the best of reputations in Ireland, always in and out of prison. But the one thing he had held on to was his 'good name'. If nothing else, people had felt they could trust his word and he had treated them fairly. Now, all of this trouble had caused him to lose his reputation, all because of Paddy.

'One of the things we need to do is find out who the sagamore is. If all these Irish Travellers are on Paddy's side, it could be one hell of a fight. How many men do we have here?'

'About ten or so. They are really a nasty bunch. Paddy's woman lives in one of your houses. Some of the others have their caravans parked in a field not that far from here.'

'What the bloody hell is a sagamore, Ralph?' Confused, Julie looked around the car for answers. It seemed Ralph and Billy knew what they were talking about, but she was totally lost.

'A sagamore is the leader of the tribe. It's actually a Native American word. But they use it and whatever he says as leader of the pack, the others will do. With him on side, Paddy has no back-up. And from my experience of Paddy, if he has no back-up, he has no guts. Show me this Traveller site, Billy.'

'How are you going to know which one he is?' Intrigued, Julie couldn't help firing questions at Ralph.

'The leader's caravan will be the best one. As soon as you step foot on the site, no one will speak to you and they will point in his direction. He looks after them and does all their talking.'

'How do you know this? This sounds crazy!' Amazed at Ralph's knowledge and calmness, Julie listened as Billy drove nearly to the outskirts of town where there were many fields. There must have been around twenty caravans scattered around with horses, dogs and kids running around, makeshift washing lines and women sitting around having a cup of tea. It was like its own village. Julie couldn't believe her eyes. The closest she had ever got to this before was some old woman trying to sell heather at the front door and professing to read her palm, although she had doubted she was the real thing.

As soon as Billy parked the car at the side of the field, they could see the twitching of the net curtains, curious as to who the visitors were. Men were sitting on the steps of their caravans with cans of beer, talking. Each one of them watched the car.

'You two stay here. I'm going alone.' Ralph opened the car door to get out.

'Are you sure you don't want me to come with you?' Worried, Julie looked around as more and more of them started coming out of their caravans to look at the car and the uninvited strangers. It felt like an ambush.

'No, they won't speak to me with a woman in tow. I have to do this.'

'What are you going to say? What if they turn nasty?' Julie felt nervous; this didn't bode well.

Ralph shrugged as he walked towards the field.

Watching Ralph disappear into a sea of unknown faces behind caravans, Julie felt hot and sweaty. God knows what he was facing. Panic started to rise within her and her eyes scanned the field for a mere sight of him. Her heart sank when she couldn't find him and she reached for her cigarettes and tried to light one even though her hands were trembling. 'Do you think it will turn nasty, Billy?'

'I don't know, but I will say Ralph has some balls walking into that lot without an invite.'

The pair of them sat in silence, smoking cigarette after cigarette, waiting for what seemed hours.

'He's been in there for two hours. I think I should go and see if he is okay.' Julie was determined to get out of the car, but Billy stopped her.

'Don't. He told you to wait here. Whatever he is setting up, you could spoil it. Let's be serious – if they didn't want to speak to him, he wouldn't be in there so long, would he?'

'He could be fucking dead on the floor and we're waiting here like a pair of prats.'

'Give it another half an hour and then I'll go. You just stay put,' Billy said, looking at his watch. Julie could tell he was nervous. There was sweat on his brow and it was clear he didn't fancy the idea of walking in there looking for Ralph.

Relief washed over Julie as she saw Ralph in the distance walking towards the car. He was with an elderly man who wore a flat cap and his dark bushy beard was spotted with grey. They were laughing and joking. All seemed well. Other men waved goodbye to Ralph as he walked past them. This all seemed very strange to Julie, but at least Ralph was alive.

Both of them walked up to the car and Ralph opened the door. 'It's been good doing business with you, Tom. We'll speak soon.' Shaking his hand, Ralph was about to get in the car when he saw Tom knock on the car window where Julie was sitting.

Turning her head, she looked towards him and wound down the window.

'You're a fair looking lass.' He winked at her and then looked up at Ralph. 'If you ever get tired, Ralph, send her over.' He laughed.

Wincing at his beer breath, Julie didn't know what to do or say, but she smiled and reached her hand out of the window. 'I'll keep that in mind, Tom.' She smiled again. Her face ached but she felt it was for the best in this situation.

She could smell the beer on Ralph as he got in the car. It seemed as though things had gone well.

'Well, what happened? God, are you drunk?'

'Tipsy, my dear. They brew their own and by God it's strong stuff. Nevertheless, if you don't accept their hospitality, it's offensive.' Taking hold of Julie's hand, Ralph kissed it, and then kissed her engagement rings. 'You know what, I'm going to buy some matching diamonds and put them in your lovely ears.'

'Drive on, Billy – he's pissed.' Julie laughed. 'But I have a witness, Ralph Gold. Diamonds it is.'

'Did everything go okay, Ralph?' Billy asked.

'Better than expected. We'll get no trouble from them. In exchange, I have offered to buy the land as the council want them off it. The council will snap my hands off. It's far too much trouble evicting a load of Travellers in caravans off sites. I've also got Paddy married off to that girlfriend of his. I expressed my concern about what people would say about Paddy living with her and them not being married.' Ralph burst out laughing. His joviality was infectious. And his high spirits warmed Julie's heart. He'd had a bad day and meeting Tom had just turned all of that around.

'You're making Paddy get married?' Billy burst out laughing.

'Absolutely. If he doesn't agree, it will be a shotgun wedding so he has no choice. Now that has totally fucked him, well and truly.' Again, Ralph laughed. He knew that was the last thing Paddy would want, but he'd have no choice if all of his girlfriend's brothers had anything to say about it.

'You're going to buy that field and just give it to them? Why would you do that? Couldn't you charge them rent or something?'

'Loyalty buys loyalty, Julie, and believe me, it will be worth every penny. If we ever need anything, Tom and his men will be there to back us up.'

'I suppose you know what you're doing, love. But it seems a bit of a waste.'

'That is because you don't see the bigger picture. I give Tom the ownership papers and he and his generations to come have a home or land to sell. That means a lot. In exchange, we become honorary family with a lot of back-up.'

What Ralph failed to tell her was that they were also excellent businessmen. They liked gambling, horse racing and made a handsome profit on it. They had their fingers in most pies along with the other families they dealt with. It was a bit like Carlos and his family, just a different set-up. It had been a good business meeting and marked the start of Paddy's downfall.

'Are you going to join us for dinner, Billy?' Ralph enquired. He was sure they were all starving. He knew he was and he needed something to soak up Tom's home brew.

'Not if you don't mind. My girlfriend will have cooked something so I think I will go home for a while.'

'An Irish girlfriend? Well, you kept that quiet.' Ralph winked playfully.

'Well, that is all there is on offer in Ireland. But, yes, she's okay. I like her.' Billy blushed.

'Come back about nine tonight. It's time we went and visited Paddy at his local drinking hole.'

* * *

Later that evening, Ralph tapped Paddy on the shoulder to attract his attention, while he was holding court. This pub used to be one of his favourite drinking holes and Paddy always held his meetings and his fight nights here. That all seemed like a million years ago to Ralph now. The thick cloud of cigarette smoke hung in the air, making his eyes sting a little.

'Ralph! What are you doing here?' Paddy's shock was more than apparent, although Ralph felt it shouldn't have been such a surprise. He'd been in Ireland all day; he was sure someone would have banged the jungle drums to let Paddy know he was here.

Paddy looked almost pleased to see Ralph, but his face dropped when he saw Julie. 'Oh God, what does she want?'

Julie was just about to give Paddy one of her finest retorts when Ralph squeezed her hand.

'Now, Paddy. There's no need for that. Why don't you get some drinks in? I have something to ask you.'

'You mean you've come to check up on me. That's it, isn't it?' Gulping back the last dregs of his Guinness, he handed Ralph his glass.

Ralph walked to the bar and gave his order to the landlord. 'Well, if it isn't our very own Ralph. Good to see you, mate. I hardly recognised you.' The landlord's welcome seemed to be the only warm one Ralph had received all day.

'It's good to see you too.' Reaching over, Ralph shook his hand and then waited for his drinks. While waiting, Ralph leant on the bar and looked over at Paddy and his friends. Considering how much money Paddy had swindled him out of, it hadn't done him any good. He had no real ambition, although he now wore a suit to show off his newly acquired status. It was creased and shabby and even though he had bought himself a new sheepskin overcoat, it did nothing to enhance his appearance. His shoulder-length, mousey brown hair was uncombed and unkempt. Ralph winced; he was going to ask Paddy to be his best man at his wedding, but the very thought made him grimace. Guilt consumed him; this man before him had once been his closest friend and now Ralph felt embarrassed by him.

Handing Paddy and Julie their drinks, Ralph ushered them to a nearby corner booth. 'Let's sit down, shall we? I have something to ask you, Paddy, and while doing that I thought I would come and check up on some of my investments. Any problems?'

'Don't I get a drink?' Liam, Paddy's brother, stuck his head around the corner booth.

'If you want one, then I suggest you buy one.' Ralph's calm exterior was almost frightening. He was ready for war and had put all his strategies in place.

'Just because you're wearing a posh suit doesn't make you better than me. You don't frighten me.'

Not being able to contain herself any more, Julie snapped, 'Just fuck off, will you? We're trying to talk. Here, you can have my drink if you're so thirsty.' Picking up her glass, she threw her drink at his face, showering him in gin and tonic.

'You fucking bitch. Paddy's told me about you, you old slut. You must be desperate, Ralph. All your money and you hang around with an old prostitute,' he spat.

Ralph stood up. He was angry and his face flushed and, within seconds, he had punched Liam, sending him flying across the floor. 'Don't you ever speak to her like that again,' he shouted. The whole pub started clapping and cheering, which surprised Ralph.

'Nice one, Ralph!' shouted the landlord. 'That weasel had it coming. Here you are, love, let me top your glass up. Bloody hell, Paddy. That's the first wash Liam has had since he's been here.' Everyone found it amusing, except Paddy, who went to the aid of his brother.

'There was no need for that, Ralph. She started it. She's the one throwing drinks around. Fucking bitch.'

Julie pulled at Ralph's arm to calm him down. This wasn't the time. They hadn't come here for a brawl; they had business to attend to. 'Leave it. Sit down.'

'I won't have anyone talking to you like that. You're my woman and that's the end of it.'

'Okay, Tarzan. Sit down. You've made your point.' Smiling, she kissed him on the cheek.

Rubbing his jaw, Liam stood up and groggily walked to the door to leave with Paddy's help.

Angry and humiliated, Paddy sat down again.

'So, apart from punching my brother in front of all these arseholes, what do you want?'

Ralph gulped his whisky down and smacked his lips. He was angry, but followed Julie's lead. 'Well, as it happens, I did come to ask you to be my best man.'

This well and truly knocked the wind out of Paddy's sails. He hadn't expected this. It was clear to Julie he had expected more outbursts from Ralph.

'You want me to be your best man?' The mood softened somewhat and Paddy looked down at the table, embarrassed. 'I'd like that, Ralph.'

'We've been friends for a long time. Who else would I ask?' Mentally, Ralph was calculating what Carlos had said. It made good business to have Paddy on his side. This flattery took away all the bad feeling instantly.

'I'm going now, Paddy, but maybe you and I can have a proper talk tomorrow about business and of course the wedding. You're going to need a proper wedding suit.' Ralph's false laughter made Paddy feel more relaxed and easy to deal with. Now he was blinded by the idea of being Ralph's best man, he didn't give a damn about his brother!

'Yes, okay, Ralph mate. Sorry about our Liam. He can be a bit of a prick sometimes. Tomorrow in here about noon, eh?'

'Noon it is. Night.' Ralph took Julie's arm, stood up, waved at the landlord and walked out. He was angry with himself for losing his temper so quickly. Normally he wouldn't have. But when it came to Julie, he couldn't help himself.

* * *

Back in their hotel, Ralph sat on the edge of the bed. He felt worn out. The whole day had been long and draining. Rubbing his face with his hands and accepting the drink, he lay back, resting his head on the headboard. Sweeping back his black hair, which by now had freed itself from its carefully combed style into an array of waviness, made him look even younger.

Julie walked up to him and kissed him on the forehead, taking his glass from his hand. She could see his eyes drooping and his breathing becoming more relaxed as he dozed off. 'I love you, Ralph Gold,' she whispered and carefully laid the bedspread over him before making a telephone call.

13

PAYBACK

'Jason, I need your help. Charlie's beaten me up and I need to get away from here. He knows I've been cheating on him. Help me. Meet me in an hour at the underground car park in town,' Charlie's wife, Caroline, pleaded down the telephone to Jason. It hadn't taken her long to track him down through his dealers.

'Caroline? What's happened? Are you okay?' Jason inwardly sighed as he held the telephone. This was the last thing he needed, Charlie Jenkins' wife begging him for help. He didn't know what to do, but felt he couldn't desert her now. 'Okay, I'll meet you there. Does Charlie know anything else?'

The line suddenly went dead. Jason was surprised that Caroline hadn't mentioned Mick's dead body or the police. But he reasoned with himself she would tell him everything when he met her. She sounded distraught.

'Where are you going in such a hurry?' Watching Jason grab his jacket and car keys, Norman tried to stop him. 'Where are you running to?'

'Business. That's all.' Jason didn't want to tell Norman about his conversation. God knows he was paranoid enough about what had happened the other night. He was jittery and to calm his nerves he'd smoked far too much marijuana, making him even more paranoid.

'Are you setting me up, Jay? Why won't you tell me where you're going?' Angrily barring Jason's way to stop him from leaving, Norman pushed him backwards.

'Look, this has nothing to do with you. A friend needs my help. I'll be back later. Just keep off that bloody stuff while I'm gone, will you?' he shouted. He was sick of Norman's whining. It was all he had done lately. That and reminisce about Mick. There was nothing they could do now, just wait and see what happened. Although even he was surprised none of his friends had mentioned anything about the police sniffing around. It seemed finding a body in the back alley of a pub must be a normal occurrence, because there had been nothing in the newspapers. He was actually glad of an excuse to get out of the flat.

'I'll come with you. You're not leaving me here on my own – what if the police find out we're here?'

Shoving him to one side, Jason walked out and got into the car. 'Well, they're not looking for me, are they?' he spat out.

Parking in the underground car park, Jason waited. Caroline was nowhere to be seen, then suddenly his car door opened and she got in.

As she took off her dark sunglasses, Jason saw the full extent of Charlie's wrath. Her eyes were black and swollen. She tried smiling but her split lip made her wince as she did so.

'Thanks for coming. I'm sorry about this.'

'About what?' Dread filled him as he heard a car door slam shut from behind and three men got out holding baseball bats. It was a trap and he had fallen for it.

'Sorry, Jason, I had no choice.' Caroline got out of the car, leaving the door open, and walked away towards the lift.

Panicking, Jason turned the key in the ignition and pressed his foot hard on the accelerator. He had to get out of there. As he started to drive off, one of the men smashed his baseball bat through the window to stop him, shattering glass all over him. The others hurried to their car and started to drive, speeding in and out of the tall cement pillars that separated the parking spaces. Once they had caught up with him, they drove into the back of the car. Jerking forward, Jason hit his head on the steering wheel as they rammed into the back of his car again. Jason was terrified and his heart was pounding in his chest. Sweat poured down the sides of his face as he tried to control the car as they kept bumping his and trying to steer him into one of the pillars.

Brushing off the glass in blind panic, Jason neared the exit only to be stopped by a car parked sideways, blocking him. Putting his foot down, he drove straight into the side of it, trying to push it out of the way, but it was a much bigger car than his Ford Fiesta. He swerved to a halt and stopped. Looking up at the car that was blocking him, Jason realised it was empty. It had been left there on purpose to stop him. He cursed himself for being so stupid. That bitch Caroline had set him up for a beating to save her own neck. His legs felt weak as, covered in blood and glass, he saw three men jump out of the car that had been chasing him. They dragged him out, onto his knees. One raised his bat and brought it down hard on his back, making him slump to the ground and cry out. His body throbbed with pain and the glass that had stuck to his shirt from the windscreen was now pressing into his body. Again, more blows followed until he passed out into unconsciousness.

* * *

The brilliant sunshine blinded his view as he stirred and tried opening his eyes in the boot of the car. Tape had been wrapped around his mouth so tight he could hardly breathe and his hands and feet were tied together with rope.

'Pull the slimy bastard out, boys.' Jason blinked hard, hearing the familiar voice of Charlie Jenkins. He tried struggling to loosen the ropes on his hands as the men grabbed hold of him and pulled him out of the boot, dumping him onto the ground, but it was met by laughter and insults. 'Who do you think you are – Houdini? You're not going to loosen those ropes, believe me. Do you feel like screwing my wife again? She told me how you pulled her outside and tried raping her.'

Through the swollen slits of his eyes, Jason looked around. He had no idea where he was or how long he had been unconscious in the boot of the car. His body ached and he could hardly breathe. His head was spinning in and out of consciousness as Charlie shouted insults and kicked him in the face. Someone grabbed his hair and turned him around. Facing him was a freshly dug grave. His eyes widened in horror and he looked up at the men.

'You see that spot over there?' Charlie pointed at a mound of soil beside the grave. 'That is where your friend is buried. You and that clown friend of yours didn't think I would involve the police when I could sort it myself, did you?'

Tears rolled down Jason's face as he trembled and shook, throwing himself at Charlie's feet. Now he understood why there had been no reporting of a man being shot. Charlie and his boys had cleared the mess and dumped Mick's body. No one was any wiser. The people in the club had only witnessed a fight and they were so high on drugs they wouldn't remember.

Charlie took out a gun and pointed it at Jason's head, firing one lethal bullet. As the shot rang out, birds flew out of the trees around them and made them all look up at the sky. 'Bury him,' commanded Charlie as he turned and headed back to the car.

* * *

'Ralph, over here – I already got you a drink in.' Paddy grinned. Walking over, Ralph shook his hand, while noticing Paddy was still wearing last night's suit.

'Thanks, Paddy. And on time, I see; that's not like you.'

'I'm in shit.' Leaning closer, Paddy lowered his voice to a whisper. 'That woman I've been seeing. Her family insist I marry her. For God's sake, you've got to help me. I'm not getting married to her or anyone.'

'Married? Why not? You've been seeing her for a while. In fact, I hear you've set her up in one of my houses for your leisure.' Inwardly laughing to himself, Ralph couldn't believe how quickly Tom had started his plans. Apparently, the brothers had gone around to the house that morning, dragged Paddy out of bed and given him an ultimatum – either marry their sister or they'd beat him to a pulp.

'You have to get me out of this, Ralph. I like her but I don't want to marry her. I'm a dead man walking.' Paddy stressed the words. It was as if the end of the world had just been announced.

'Paddy mate, what difference would it make to you? Now drink up and let's talk business.' Steering Paddy to his favourite corner booth and sitting down, Ralph confronted Paddy with all of the rumours he had heard.

'The point is, you've been ripping me off and ripping off other people, although I don't know why. I pay you more than enough; what the hell are you doing with the money?'

'I have expenses. You don't understand. You and that Julie living the life of Riley while I get your leftovers. Those people you sent over, they don't listen to me or do as I say. That's why I need Liam and my mates.' Excuse after pitiful excuse followed as Paddy tried wriggling out of the accusations Ralph threw at him. Like always, it was everyone's fault but his own.

'I don't care about the money, Paddy, but I want my good name back. You've threatened these people when supposedly working for me. As far as they are concerned, you're following my orders. So here goes. I want your notebooks or whatever it is you keep your payments in. I also want the keys to your lock-up.' Ralph wasn't going to string this out any longer. 'I've moved on and I think you should too. I'm putting someone else in charge. You can work for me if you want, but that's it. Your golden goose has just stopped laying.'

Irate and angry, Paddy spewed venom. 'You're nothing, Mr bloody Goldstein. Remember him? Before you became Mr high and mighty Ralph Gold, you were a good-for-nothing who fought for pennies. You would have been nothing without me. I don't want your fucking handouts. Bollocks, Ralph. Who are you putting in charge? Liam won't have this.'

'What the hell has Liam got to do with it?'

'Liam has lots of good ideas about business. He came up with the furniture business. It's lucrative. If they can't pay their rent, they shouldn't be living there!'

'No. You shouldn't be raising their rents without my knowledge and bleeding them dry. I want rent, not empty properties. There's no money in empty houses.' The argument remained heated until Ralph could stand no more. 'Your books and your keys, Paddy, hand them over.'

Seeing that he was beaten, Paddy nodded. 'I will get them to you later.'

'Not good enough. We'll pick them up now. Where are they?'

Although his face was flushed, Paddy blushed slightly. He knew he had been caught out and the only thing he could do now would be to hold his hands up in submission. He'd had a good run and he still had an offer of a job. Something was better than nothing. 'Do you still want me to be your best man or was that a lie?'

'Yes, I meant that, but I want none of your messing around on my big day and for God's sake take a bath.' Finishing his drink, Ralph stood up to leave, with Paddy following reluctantly.

The lock-up-cum-garage was much bigger than Ralph had expected and once the shutters were rolled up, he couldn't believe his eyes. It was packed to the hilt with furniture of all kinds, including racks and racks of clothing on hangers.

Letting out a slow whistle, Ralph looked around. 'This is more like Aladdin's cave. What the hell have you done?'

For a moment, Paddy's bravado came back. He looked quite pleased with himself as he walked around his empire. He didn't see it the same as Ralph did. 'It's great, isn't it? I told you there was money to be made. We could have these all over Ireland.' The cockiness in his tone sickened Ralph. He'd had his fair share of dodgy dealings, but this was against people who Ralph and Paddy had grown up with – families they knew. Ralph thought back to a time when he didn't have a penny to scratch his arse with and would have had to work twice as hard to pay people like Paddy. At least the people Ralph took money off could afford it and got something back in return.

'Where are the books that tell me what everyone owes you?' Raising one eyebrow and doing his best to remain calm, Ralph held out his hand.

'What's going on here? What do you want?' Liam walked inside the lock-up. 'Not got your lady bodyguard with you today? What's he doing here, Paddy? This is our place.' His dislike of Ralph showed clearly on his face. His arrogance had no boundaries. At least Paddy knew when he had been caught out.

'This is mine and Paddy's business. I suggest you leave.' Ralph ignored his remarks about Julie.

'It's mine. I have worked hard filling this place up and you're not taking it away from me. I knew you'd come here. You want everything. Now go back to wherever it is you came from.'

Ralph had prepared himself for this. 'I was leaving anyway. I've seen enough. Are you coming, Paddy?' As an afterthought, Ralph held his hand out. 'Those books we spoke of.'

Nervous and knowing Ralph from the old days, Paddy knew this calm exterior usually spelt trouble. Opening a drawer, Paddy took out a large black ledger. 'Here you go. Come on, let's all go for a drink, shall we?' Trying to ease the situation, Paddy followed Ralph towards Liam at the entrance of the lock-up. 'I'll close the shutters first. Don't want thieves, do we?' Trying his best to crack a joke and make light of it, Paddy laughed and winked at them both.

'Just one more thing,' said Ralph, bending to his knees as the shutters rolled down. Putting his hand in his pocket, Ralph took out a hand grenade and threw it in the lock-up.

'You crazy bastard! What are you doing?' Liam grabbed hold of Ralph's jacket.

'Never mind him. Fucking run!' Paddy shouted as the explosion erupted, nearly blowing off the roof.

All of them were thrown to the ground as the noise of furniture smashing and burning boomed around them. Flames and black smoke flew out of the bottom of the shutters. They were all still lying on the floor, gasping for breath, as people came running forward. Billy jumped out of the waiting car and grabbed Ralph, who looked around for the ledger and then ran towards the car, leaving the mayhem in the distance.

'Bloody hell, you don't do things by halves, do you?' Billy ranted on. He couldn't believe what Ralph had done.

'It needed doing,' Ralph gasped. 'I knew Paddy would have arranged back-up, and they aren't about to give all that stuff back, so it was the only way to stop their little empire.'

'Do you think the coppers will come for you? I think you'd better get out of here and fast!'

'Maybe. More likely, Paddy will spin them some story. I'm leaving today, anyway; I just have something to do first.'

Billy couldn't understand Ralph. Anyone else would have left as soon as possible, but apparently, there was more to come. No wonder Ralph was notorious in these parts.

'Billy, I want you to stay here. Those Irish Travellers I spoke to are going to run the business with your help. They won't fleece me like Paddy, but Paddy will try and worm his way back in because he is marrying into the family, but they and you are in charge, okay? Do not collect any rents for a month. Let the people get back on their feet first. I want you to go to every one of them and give them my apologies.'

'Sure thing. Are you sure you can trust those people? We don't know them, they are Gypsies and they are a pretty mean bunch.'

Ralph's eyes narrowed and a frown crossed his brow. He hated stigma and any form of racism. He had been a part of it all of his life. 'They are travellers Billy, whether they have Romany blood or Irish. Have some respect.', Ralph warned'. Billy's words had touched a raw nerve. 'It's like saying a "Wandering Jew". Well, I'm Jewish and I'm not wandering. We all have our ethnic roots Billy, just like you do. Respect earns respect and yes. As hard as they are, they are honourable men who earn a living. Tom and I have agreed on this. They are fighters so there will be no trouble and their reputation precedes them. They will also keep Paddy in order. But this time, I'll keep my eye on the ball. I need to clean up first and then we need to do the last of my business. Take me to Paddy's mother's house. I can't go to the hotel like this; I can wash up there.'

* * *

'Ralph, where have you been? I went to that pub and they said you had left with Paddy.' Julie's concern warmed him. She was a strange woman. On the outside, she did not give a toss but on the inside, she was warm, loving and loyal.

'I'm okay, love. Get that receptionist to book our flight back this evening. We're leaving. I just have one more thing to do. I've got to go to that pub we were at last night. The landlord there is a good man. I've known him for years.'

'Why? For what? Let's just go. You're not the same when you're here. Let's go home back to our new place and get married.' Julie pleaded. She felt Ralph seemed tense and a different man back here in Ireland. It was a city of ghosts. The man he had once been. He didn't belong here any more. Maybe that's what hurt him most. He'd moved on and in Ireland life had stood still, full of bad memories. Julie desperately wanted to take him home where he could relax.

'I want him to tell the other landlords of the pubs we own that their debts are all cleared and we'll start fresh in a month. Look at this ledger.' Ralph threw it on the bed. Curiously, Julie turned the pages.

'There are hundreds of names in here.' Looking up at Ralph curiously, she didn't understand.

'That is a list of all the people Paddy and Liam have robbed, deceived and frightened in my name. It stops now. Have you seen the rents they've been charging? No wonder the tenants couldn't afford it. One of them is his own mother, the bastard! I've been there and given her the house. I'll get the deeds sorted for her.'

Seeing that this wasn't the time to argue with Ralph, Julie nodded and agreed with him.

* * *

Everyone turned and stared at them as they walked into the pub. Ralph walked up to the bar. 'You serving me, mate?'

'Are you kidding? This one is on the house.' He winked.

'Take this.' Ralph handed over the ledger. 'Sort the other publicans out for me, tell them their debts are cleared. Can you do that for me?'

'Sure thing. We've heard that young Billy here has started going around your houses telling people they don't have to pay their rent for a month. It's a big weight off their shoulders. Word is spreading. Cheers.' He chinked his own glass against Ralph's and nodded at Julie in acknowledgement. Everyone seemed in high spirits.

Billy was grinning like a Cheshire cat. He had already been following Ralph's orders, knowing that it wouldn't take long for word to spread. He liked working for Ralph. Everyone seemed at ease again, drinking and talking. Some came up to shake Ralph's hand and thanked him for his generosity, while others were discussing a massive explosion at Paddy's lock-up. Everyone knew what had happened, but no one was saying anything. Ralph had been like a knight in shining armour, washing all their worries away in a few days. Although ironically, it seemed some were annoyed at Ralph's interference. There were items in the lock up that had been in their family for years. Nothing worth bragging about, but they had been trying their hardest to buy them back and now Ralph had let it all go up in smoke.

'My dad's old war medals were in that lock up, Ralph. Now they are just a melted ball of metal. I can never replace them. He was proud of them', one man at the bar snapped at Ralph. 'You could at least have given us the chance to get some of our stuff back!'

Ralph listened as others spoke up about their irreplaceable possessions.

'I'm sorry everyone. I really am.' Ralph shook his head. He felt remorse, but he also felt these people were not seeing reason.

'Paddy had probably already sold that kind of thing and taken whatever cash he could have got his hands on. And you', Ralph pointed at a woman who was spouting about her silver photo frame that had been in the family for years and still had her grandmother's photo inside it. 'When was the last time you saw that photo frame? Or had Paddy already sold that too? Grandmother and all!' Ralph spat out. Either way he couldn't win.

Suddenly the doors burst open. 'You bastard! You tried to kill me.' Everyone stopped what they were doing and turned to see Liam pointing a gun in Ralph's direction. He was drunk and waving it around aimlessly, shouting out to everyone how Ralph had stolen from him and tried to kill him and Paddy.

Someone threw a chair at him to disarm him, but it only caused the gun to go off, missing Julie by inches as she ducked her head down. That's when she noticed Billy was holding his arm where he had been shot.

'Billy! Billy, are you okay?' she shouted.

'Yes, I'm okay. It's a flesh wound. Take off my belt and wrap it around my arm to stop the bleeding. You need to catch your flight,' he gasped.

Doing as she was told and tying the belt tightly, she looked around the pub. No one was saying anything. They were stunned and in shock. 'No, we're not leaving you like this. Ralph, tell him,' Julie pleaded to Ralph just as another gunshot filled the air and the barmaid who was coming out of the toilets fell to her feet.

'Liam, you've killed her!' The landlord ran around to the other side of the bar and knelt down beside her as she took her last breath. Someone mentioned the police were on their way and it was all a mad panic as people ran for shelter, screaming and shouting.

'Go, Julie. I'll be in touch.' Covered in blood and trying to put a brave face on it, Billy urged them to go. This was now a murder scene.

Drink had gotten the better of Liam. Even though he had just murdered someone, he walked up to Ralph, muscling past Julie. 'The next bullet is yours,' he snarled, and cocked the gun for firing.

'So do it, if you think it will do you any good.' Trying to remain calm, Ralph looked around the pub. Billy was lying on the floor, clutching his arm, the blood running through his fingers. He was soaked in it. Onlookers were crying and panicking at the poor barmaid, who had just been going about her job and was now dead. Thinking quickly, Julie picked up a beer bottle off the bar and hit Liam over the head with it, knocking him clean out.

'Come on, Ralph, Billy's right. Let's get out of here before the police come.' Julie tugged at his arm in panic. This was the last thing they needed and Ralph would be involved somewhere. Even if it was causing the explosion.

Ralph looked down at Billy, who wearily pointed his thumb towards the door. 'Will you both piss off and leave this to the police?' he panted. Reluctantly, Ralph made his way to the back door. The front entrance would soon be swarming with police. He knew they had to leave, but he hated deserting Billy like this. But he also knew he was up to his neck in it. Why did Ireland always spell a prison sentence? he thought to himself as they left.

'We're not going back to the hotel. Let's just make our way to the airport. You have blood on you – are you okay?'

Shaking a little and brushing a tear from her eye, Julie nodded. 'It's Billy's blood. My hands are covered in it. Weren't you frightened? I can't believe what just happened in there. It could have been either of us.' Feeling the need to bend over as the bile rose in her throat, Julie vomited. Standing over her, Ralph held her hair back from her face as she puked. He knew it was shock and, raising an eyebrow, he looked down as Julie's vomit sprayed all over his shoes. Smiling, he shook his head and looked around.

'There's a puddle of water from the rain in the gutter. Go and rinse your hands in that and use this handkerchief until we can find a toilet at the airport.'

'We have to go back to the hotel. I need to change. They won't let me on an aeroplane covered in blood.' Laying her hands in the puddle of dirty rainwater and wiping them, she walked back towards Ralph, who was waiting by the roadside.

'Okay, but quickly does it. We have to get past the receptionist. It might not be our blood but it doesn't look good and the police will want to question everyone in the pub. Everyone knows Liam came looking for me.'

'Yes, and that lot are going to tell the police he never found you. No one is going to listen to Liam. He's a drunken maniac with a grudge to bear. There's a taxi; stick your arm out.'

Ralph ran into the hotel and picked up the bags while Julie waited in the taxi. Fortunately, it was dark and the driver wasn't paying her any attention. Her coat was dark and she had her hands in her pockets.

Once at the airport, Julie grabbed her bag and headed for the toilets. Looking in the mirror, she saw that she had specks of blood on her face and her mascara was smudged from her tears. It had all been such a shock. Her hands were trembling as she ran them under the taps, and she wanted to scrub under her nails where the blood had dried.

The sooner they were out of there, the better she would feel.

14

A FRESH START

On entering the hotel room back in London, Ralph picked up the telephone to call the hospital regarding Billy. His and Julie's conversation had been limited on the short flight from Ireland, both of them letting their minds wander over recent events.

Pouring them each a long-earnt drink, Julie sat on the edge of the bed and waited while Ralph spoke to the hospital. After what seemed like forever convincing doctors and reception staff that he was family, Ralph gave Julie the thumbs up.

'He's alive, and they said he's comfortable but he lost a lot of blood. I feel better now, knowing he's okay. I hated leaving him like that.' The huge sigh of relief from both of them said everything they needed to say to each other. Julie reached out and hugged Ralph tightly.

'I could have lost you if that madman could shoot straight, Ralph. Do not play the hero any more. We need you. I need you.' Tears streamed down Julie's face. She couldn't stop crying.

'Hey, where's my brave Julie? Didn't you know I'm invincible?' Ralph laughed, trying to comfort her. 'You're never getting rid of me.' Although as he held her he looked over her shoulder to the mirror facing him and winced. That had been too close for comfort, even he had to admit that. But he'd sorted his business out in Ireland and now it was time to move forward and leave the past behind him forever.

Julie looked up and forced a smile, running her hand through Ralph's thick, black, wavy hair. 'Do you know those soft brown eyes of yours have specks of green in them? I suppose that's the Irish in you. They shine like emeralds in your eyes when you're angry.' The warm huskiness in her voice filled the air with electricity. They needed each other; they loved each other. They reached out for each other and their lips met. They made love. It wasn't their usual passionate encounter. The ardency of their kisses and the hungry need for each other's bodies was emotional as they were joined together as one with each tender caress. Every unspoken word of love was whispered in between their kisses as they clung to each other.

* * *

'There's a message for you from Liverpool. Is everything all right?' Putting a cup of coffee on the bedside table, Ralph sat beside Julie while she opened it.

Ripping it open, Julie read it and smiled. Lying back on her pillows, she reached for his hand. Today felt different from other mornings. She felt warm and content with the man she loved. 'I have to go to for another fitting for my wedding dress. I think I will go today, if that's okay?'

'Are you up to it?'

'I'm tired but it needs to be done. Especially if I'm going to look like a million dollars for our big day. If I go today then I can get on with the house and stuff.'

'I've got a message from Carlos. He wants to see us both on

Friday before the big last meeting.' Ralph frowned slightly. From previous experience, that usually meant Carlos had something else in mind for him to do, or there was a change of plan. But why did he want to see Julie?

'Well, that's two days from now and whatever it is, he'll tell us. Don't worry about it. I'm going to get showered and catch the train; it's quicker than Chris taking me in the car and I don't want him spying on my dress for you!' She laughed, and flung back the duvet.

'Aren't you going to eat first?'

'No, there is a lot of sorting out to do. I'll be back late this afternoon if I hurry now. What are your plans?'

Pulling his bathrobe around him, Ralph sat down and waited. He didn't know why Julie was asking, because when she did, it usually meant she had an itinerary in mind if he was at a loose end. He went along with her easy line of questioning, which he knew by now was pointless.

'Well, I have a little business to sort...'

'Good. Because you can help Chris with the furniture and get things sorted. Then you can have a look at the unit. I told Chris to sort the sign writers out. I expect to be moving into the house tomorrow. I'm sick of this place.' Leaving the room, she turned on the shower then walked back to where Ralph was sitting. 'And while you're at it, invite some of those lodge mates of yours with their funny handshakes and tell them you're in the import and export business and you expect orders!' She wagged her finger and went back into the bathroom.

Ralph smiled; he loved the way her eyes shone and her face flushed when she was excited about a project. She loved planning things and was like a child on Christmas Eve, all full of expectation of their home together with Josh.

Was this the way life was going to be? Getting up, he walked to the shower and opened the door. The more he thought about Julie, the more his body reacted.

'Don't even think about it! I have a train to catch and you have things to do. I'll leave the shower running when I've finished. I'll also turn it to cold, because, by the look of things, you need one. Now bugger off.' She waved him off with her hand playfully. Her laughter was infectious and, like a naughty schoolboy, Ralph pulled his robe around him again and went to the sink to shave. *Well, it was worth a try*. He shrugged.

A few hours later, Julie was back in Liverpool and, after meeting Sue at the salon, she was whisked off to Maggie's house. Two of the bedrooms of her four-bedroomed house had been made into a workshop. Liverpool was everything Julie expected and more. The party atmosphere, as everyone gathered with their bottles of champagne and glasses, raised the excitement. Everyone's jaw dropped as Maggie and two others carried in the wedding dress. The seamstresses had made the ultimate Cinderella dress.

'Bloody hell, it's heavy.' Julie heaved up the satin dress, which was decorated in diamanté. It had five layers of netting underneath and the bodice had pearls sewn onto it.

'Too right it is, girlie. You're going to look amazing on your wedding day – like a real princess! Do you know how many pounds of diamanté are on that dress? Believe me, our fingers are threadbare sewing all of those on. You are going to need a wire petticoat underneath it all to help hold it up. You can't hold it up on your body for long; you will sag under the weight. The wire petticoat will take the weight; try this.'

'It looks like a wire basket! You want me to wear that under my dress?' Julie burst out laughing as they fitted her into the wire petticoat. All the women were laughing and fussing around as Julie climbed into her wedding dress. It was spectacular.

'Here's the best part, Julie. The train is seven foot long with even more diamanté sewn onto it. Here is your tiara. If you don't like it, we can always change it. How are you having your hair?'

'I'm in charge of hair and make-up.' Sue beamed while stroking down the satin material of the dress. 'You're having it up, Julie; that will make the tiara higher for the veil.'

'Ladies, you have surpassed yourselves. I never expected anything like this. It's amazing.' Hugging Maggie and the others one by one, Julie was in awe of the dress. It was beautiful.

'You had better make sure Ralph wears sunglasses on the big day; all the jewels in that dress are going to blind him!' Everyone was laughing as the champagne was popped and glasses were passed around the fitting room.

Standing before the wall of mirrors in her wedding dress while they attached the train and veil, Julie could feel the tears brimming on her lashes. Never in her wildest dreams had she pictured herself dressed in such a beautiful wedding gown. This was truly what dreams were made of and Ralph was making all of her fantasies come true.

Sadness stabbed her heart. No one had ever thought, including herself, that she would be wearing a dress like this, let alone marrying a man like Ralph. She secretly wished she could be sharing this with her own family. Her mother and sister would love this, and Julie wished that things could have been different. Frankie would be clean from drugs and her mother would have somewhere decent to live and not be in prison. Well, she consoled herself. This was what her mother wanted for her, to go forward and make something of herself. She had kept her promise and that made her feel better. She had risen out of the ashes like a phoenix and life was good.

'Oh, come on, Julie, no tears now. This is a happy time.' Circling around her as close as they possibly could, they gave her a group hug.

'This is the last fitting. I just need to alter a few things and then we're done. And just before this party gets out of control, here is the invoice.' Looking a little sheepish, Maggie handed over the envelope.

'For Christ's sake, she's marrying Ralph Gold. Don't worry about it,' shouted Sue as she turned up the music and drank her champagne out of the bottle.

Opening the envelope, Julie looked at the figure. Surely it couldn't be right? Ten thousand pounds for a dress? The mood became a little sombre as they pensively looked at Julie.

'You're wrong, Sue. I may be marrying Ralph Gold but Don Carlos is paying for the wedding. More rhinestones, Maggie,' she shouted while throwing the invoice into the air. Turning around, she picked up a glass of champagne and raised it. 'To Don Carlos – the sky's the limit!' Everyone burst out laughing.

* * *

Ordering a cup of coffee and lighting a cigarette, Julie sat on a bench and waited for her train back to London. It had been a great day and excitement bubbled in her stomach. Frowning, she looked up again as she thought she spotted a familiar figure. She couldn't believe her eyes. Impulsively, almost spilling her coffee, she stood up and shouted out, 'Captain Roland. Hey, Roland, over here!' Half walking, half-running towards the tall Jamaican figure, the smile spread across her face. Her eyes widened as she strode towards him.

Roland had been her and her sister's saviour when they had escaped from the trafficking camp in Spain. They'd had nothing and nowhere to go and Roland had taken pity on these two scarecrow-looking women, battered and bleeding, and let them stow away on his ship. He'd taken his life in his hands helping them and had been their guardian angel.

Hearing his name, he stood there and looked at her. There was no recognition in his eyes.

'For God's sake, Roland. It hasn't been that long. Do you still pick up strays in Spain? It's only been a few years; have I changed that much?' Seeing his apprehension and confusion, Julie realised why. Yes, she had changed since he last saw her. God only knows what they must have looked like to him after their escape from the camp.

Suddenly the light of recognition shone in his eyes and that warm, familiar smile spread across his face. 'Julie, I hardly recognised you, girl. You look like a woman.' Standing back to admire her, he let a slow whistle out. 'Give us a twirl, Julie baby.'

Without thinking, she flung her arms around his neck and hugged him, remembering how he had saved her and her sister's lives that fateful day in Spain.

'It's so good to see you, Roland. Have you got time for a drink and a catch-up?'

'For you, honey, I got all of the time in the world.' Throwing his kit bag over his shoulder, he held out his arm for her.

Julie noticed a couple of people staring at her. The looks on their faces annoyed her. It was obvious what they were thinking – a well-dressed white woman linking arms and hugging up to a Jamaican seaman in a rollneck sweater.

'You can all piss off, you racist bastards. You make me sick,' she shouted at them.

'Julie girl, you might dress like a lady but you're still my Julie. Come on, let's go to the pub across the road and have some rum.'

Julie couldn't stop talking, she was so happy to see Roland and tell him about her adventures since they had last met. He was laughing aloud and slapping his thigh.

'How is little Frances doing? You haven't mentioned her.'

Roland's genuine enquiry after Frankie's welfare stopped Julie's laughter and sadness crossed her face. 'She's dead, Captain Roland. Now change the subject.'

A moment of silence passed between them. There were questions that Roland knew she would not answer. Frankie had been in a bad way when she was on his ship.

'So who is this lucky man who stole my Julie's heart?'

'Apart from you.' She winked, the smile reappearing on her face. 'He's a businessman and his name is Ralph Gold.'

The smile dropped from Roland's face and his eyes widened. He let out a low whistle, which seemed to be his habit, and pushed his cap back from his forehead.

'You mean the Mafia man? Ralph Gold the Mafia man, Julie?'

Taken aback and confused, Julie shook her head. 'Well, I don't know about that, but yeah, he knows a couple of Italians – why?'

'A few Italians? Are you joking me? Are you wearing rose-coloured glasses or something? His name is always linked with those people. And you know what they say. No one leaves the Mafia unless it's in a body bag or old age. Everyone knows that, Julie.' Roland dropped his voice to a low whisper. Clearly her perception of her husband-to-be was not what the world saw. This man's reputation was rising. He was not a man to be crossed.

'Oh, he's not that bad. Anyway, who believes gossip?'

Her fake laughter didn't convince him. It crossed Julie's mind that she had mentioned Ralph's name twice now to outsiders, once to Sue and now Roland, and each one of them had stared at her in wide-eyed amazement. 'He's a pussycat. How do you know all this gossip anyway? I thought you travelled the high seas like Sinbad.'

'You're right, I travel a lot. And I hear things. He has more high-ranking police in his back pocket than I have loose change. Be careful, Julie.' Concerned for her welfare, he patted her knee.

Reaching out and squeezing his hand, she felt warm and safe by his concern. He was actually worried about her. 'Don't worry about me. I can take care of myself. Anyway, back to my wedding. Will you come? I mean, you and your family – will you come to my wedding?'

'You a real wild child, Julie. Are you kidding? Me at your wedding?' Slapping the table with his hand and nearly spilling the drinks, he creased up with laugher.

'You okay, Roland man?' A group of men sitting opposite them were interrupted by Roland's uncontrollable laughter.

'Yeah, boys. This here is my friend Julie. A crazy woman with crazy ideas. Julie, this is some of my shipmates.'

'Hi, boys.' She waved at them flirtily. 'Roland doesn't know it yet but he's going to give me away at my wedding.'

Instantly, Roland stopped laughing. The smile disappeared from his face while his friends fired jokes across the table about how Roland could give such a beautiful woman away.

'I think you should ask your man first, Julie. I don't fit into your circle of friends.'

Noticing his apprehension, she gave him a reassuring smile. 'Roland, love. It is my big day. Why wouldn't I have the man who saved my life at my side? Hell, there wouldn't be a wedding if it weren't for you. I want my friends around me on my wedding day. Not a load of freeloaders. And you are my friend.' Nodding to him, her eyes softened. 'Please, Roland. Do it for me. You and your family. Make up any story about how we know each other to them. But you are a very dear friend. You were there when I needed someone. When I didn't have a penny to my name and was frightened out of my wits. You know me better than any of them.'

'As always, you make it very hard for a weak man like me to refuse. If you are sure, Julie. But ask your man first. It's not a problem if you change your mind.'

'Whatever you've heard about Ralph, ignore it. Yes, he is mixed up with some people who know people. That's his business, but that's not the man I go to bed with every night. He's a normal man, from a normal background. We all have to do whatever it takes to survive. He's a good man. I wouldn't be marrying him if he wasn't. Here's my telephone number.' Taking out a pen, Julie scribbled her number on a beer mat. 'Order yourself a suit and call me to settle the bill, or just give me the receipt, eh?' Eagerly, Julie waited for his answer and broke out in a beaming smile when he nodded. Looking at the clock on the wall, she jumped up. 'Blimey, Roland, it's time to catch my train.'

'It's been good catching up with you, Julie. You're a fighter; I knew you would do well. If you need me, I'm not always around but I have the ship's radio. They always pass messages on to me from the family. Go to the shipping office or call them and they will pass the message on. Come on, darling girl, I'll walk you across the road to the station.'

On the train home, Julie's mind was working overtime. She knew Ralph had his fingers in a lot of pies, but some people seemed to know more about him than she realised. Thinking about her new home and Ralph's offices, a thought popped into her head. Dear God, Captain Roland imported and exported all kinds of things – they could be a match made in heaven.

15

WEIGHING UP THE ODDS

It may have had a clean-up and a lick of paint but the club still didn't look very inviting to Ralph. It would need a fortune spending on it to tempt the clientele of the West End, but that wasn't his problem. His side of the bargain was to get a front-of-house manager to run the club so he and Carlos could do the money-laundering through it. How it looked and who came was of no consequence to him. 'So, Charlie, when do you open up to the public?'

Charlie put his hands in the pockets of his overcoat and looked at Ralph suspiciously. Nothing seemed untoward. As far as he was concerned, it was ready to open now. It was clean and tidy and had been fully stocked. Walking around the club, Charlie was satisfied with how quickly Ralph had set the wheels in motion. He'd had his reservations when Ralph had turned up unexpectedly and presumed he was looking for trouble. Had he come here for a fight?

'Is something wrong? You seem out of sorts.' Ignorant to all the recent goings-on in his absence, Ralph could sense something was wrong. Charlie was not his usual self. He seemed edgy.

'No, I'm fine. How about you?' The uneasiness in Charlie and the unspoken words between them made Ralph frown. Something was definitely wrong.

'Don't you like the look of the place? You said a clean-up and a lick of paint. Was there anything else?'

'Not, if you're satisfied with the agreement. If you still want things to go ahead, I'm prepared to move in on Monday. I just have some things to sort out at my place and then we're up and running.'

'I've brought you this for your office; I thought you'd like it.' Ralph held out a clock. Just as instructed by Carlos, Ralph had had a small camera fixed into the middle of the hands of the clock so that they could permanently keep an eye on Charlie's activities. This clock was made for flattery. It was in the shape of a capital 'C', with a capital 'J' at the bottom. Ralph knew he wouldn't be able to resist something with his initials on it for his office. It reinforced his boss status and his ego.

The colour drained from Charlie's face. Reluctantly, he reached his hand out to take it, looked at it for a few moments and then looked up at Ralph. It was as though he was waiting for it to blow up in his face. 'That's very nice of you, Ralph. My initials.' He nodded, looking at it more closely. 'I like that.'

'Is something wrong, Charlie? You don't seem very happy with things, not your usual buoyant self. What's the problem?' Fed up with this cat-and-mouse game, Ralph felt it was better to confront the situation rather than let it stew away. He had to report to Carlos on Friday that everything was going as planned. He wanted to clear the air now so that there were no misunderstandings.

'No, nothing, Ralph. Just a few busy days. You know how it is. The clock is great. Come, I'll show you my office and we'll put it up in pride of place behind my chair.' The tension left the air as Charlie strode along to his freshly painted office.

Things couldn't have worked out better for Ralph and it wasn't even his suggestion. Charlie was putting the clock up behind him, which meant they would have a bird's eye view of anyone that came in or out of the room. Brilliant!

'Here, boys, look what Ralph has brought me. One of you go and find a hammer. I want to see how it looks.' More relaxed and at ease, Charlie showed off his present to two of his men that came in to join him. Ralph noticed that they also seemed surprised to see him and on their guard. He couldn't put his finger on it, but there was definitely something in the air.

'Let's have a drink to seal the deal. Oh, by the way, those men that you said might pop in to sort out their side office have been. I think everything is in order, if you know what I mean.' Charlie tapped his nose, indicating to Ralph that he was in the 'know' regarding the money-laundering. Inside, Ralph wanted to laugh, because he knew Charlie was aware of nothing.

After a drink, Charlie walked back out into the club and showed Ralph around and told him of his plans for the place. Ralph felt satisfied at Charlie's easy manner. Whatever was troubling him had clearly been forgotten now. 'Well, I see you have your name above the door already. Good luck, and we'll speak soon.' Ralph stood up and shook hands with him; he couldn't wait to get out of the place.

Getting into his car and putting it into gear, Ralph was shocked when his passenger door opened and Norman almost threw himself on the seat. 'Drive, Ralph. Drive quickly.' Putting his foot down, Ralph drove on. Norman sat up on the seat properly; his hands were shaking as he lit a cigarette.

'What's happened to you? You look awful.' Taking in Norman's unshaven, dishevelled look, Ralph looked around for somewhere to park. 'Have you eaten?' Norman shook his head. He looked like he'd been sleeping on the streets and, to Ralph's astonishment, he smelt like it. 'Let's find a greasy spoon somewhere around here.'

Parking at a local café that only served fried breakfasts all day, Ralph got out of the car. He was curious when Norman pulled up his jacket collar and furtively looked around before running through the doors. Once Norman had sat himself at the back, Ralph walked past him and ordered two coffees and one breakfast.

'Right, Norman. What is with all of the cloak-and-dagger stuff? Who are you expecting?'

'Whoever killed Mick and Jason. That Charlie bloke and his mates you're so friendly with.' Blurting out his words all in one, Norman kept looking around at the other people sitting at their tables.

Ralph's eyes widened; he could not believe what he was hearing and, for a moment, he was silent while he tried taking in what Norman was saying. 'Lower your voice, man. And stop shaking like a leaf. What the hell has been going on?'

Fortunately for Norman, with the radio blaring out and the man behind the counter shouting out to customers to collect their orders, Ralph didn't think anyone had heard him. Hearing his name, Ralph stood up and collected the breakfast.

'Eat first; you look like you need it. We'll talk in the car. Your eyes are red. You look like shit and you're obviously up to your neck in it.'

Norman shovelled the food into his mouth, hardly tasting it. Frowning, Ralph looked on at the pathetic sight before him. He looked like he hadn't eaten for days. Although, he thought curiously, whatever Norman was about to tell him would explain the odd way Charlie Jenkins had been acting when he first saw him.

Within minutes, Norman had wolfed down the breakfast and wiped the plate with his bread. 'You done?' Norman nodded. 'Let's go to the car.' Standing up, Ralph headed for the door, letting it almost shut in Norman's face.

'Ralph, before you start, give us a cigarette, will you? That was my last one.'

Letting out a sigh, Ralph threw his packet and lighter at him. He knew he wasn't going to like this. 'Out with it. I'm in no mood for games. What makes you think Jason and Mick are dead?' Ralph's anger was rising. He'd only been gone for a few days and it seemed all hell had let loose. Norman told him everything about the night at the club. Ralph listened intently without moving his face.

'So what makes you think Jason is dead?'

'It's a feeling. The last time I saw him he was leaving Fat Paulie's flat. He'd just taken a phone call and said he had to leave. He hasn't been in touch since.'

'So? Maybe he's got a woman somewhere. Better still, maybe he thought twice about hiding out with a poisonous snake like you. You've caused all the trouble and you're the only one alive.' Grabbing him by the throat, Ralph shook him.

'Please, Ralph – stop!' Almost choking, Norman pulled back, banging his head on the car window. 'Jason would have kept in touch given the circumstances. No one has seen him since that day. He's just disappeared off the face of the earth. He had a winning ticket from the horses and he hasn't even been to cash it in. I'm telling you, he's dead. That Charlie and his boys have killed him.'

Ralph slapped him hard around the face. Norman was becoming hysterical. 'Why did you decide to take the law into your own hands?'

'Well, you never did anything to revenge Johnny's death. Someone had to,' he snapped. Again, Ralph grabbed him by the scruff of his collar and shook him. 'Don't get clever, sonny – believe me, you're not up to it. And it's "avenge", not "revenge", you ignorant sod. So, let me get this straight. You cause a whole heap of trouble and now you have come whining to me. How did you know where I would be?'

'I've been hanging around there. Slept across the road. I knew you would go there eventually. Then I hid in the alley at the side until I saw you come out. I need money; I need to get out of here.

That Charlie will come for me next.' Norman was now pleading with Ralph, frightened for his life.

'Didn't I tell you to keep your head down and your eyes open? Jesus Christ, you have opened a can of worms!' Ralph shouted angrily. All his hard work with Charlie Jenkins over the last few months could easily blow up in his face because of a couple of morons thinking they knew better.

'Why didn't you just call the police when they shot Mick? Poor bastard, why take him with you? He was never a fighter. Was that the best you could do? You took a kid and a weed-smoking addict with you. For God's sake, Norman, grow up. We are not playing cops and robbers here. For all of Charlie's faults, he still knows people who know people. He is feared in his own way; of course he wasn't going to let you get away with it.' Disgusted and angry, Ralph turned his head and looked out of the window, opening it slightly so that he could let some of Norman's cloud of nicotine out.

'My prints are on the gun from where I picked it up. I just panicked and ran for it. I don't know what they have done with Mick; there have been no reports about a shooting or anything. They have got rid of the body, I know they have, and covered their tracks. I can feel it. You have to do something, Ralph.'

'Me?' Astonished, Ralph let out a belly laugh. It was the first time during this confession he'd actually found something funny. 'Why do I have to do something? You started it, and now you have to man up and face the consequences… what has it got to do with me?' Once he'd said this, Ralph's conscience pricked him slightly. He had been responsible for Johnny's demise, but Johnny had caused the bad feeling in the beginning with his surly attitude towards Charlie.

Norman started begging a stony-faced Ralph. 'You could talk to him, tell him to back off me and leave me alone. He'll listen to you. Or you could give me some money. I need to get away from here, or

I will end up in a body bag like Mick and Jason.' Fear getting the better of him, Norman threw himself onto Ralph's lap and burst into tears, much to Ralph's distaste.

'To start with, if I did what you're asking, that means admitting I know about it. Which I don't. Secondly, get your snotty nose off my trousers.' Ralph thought about it for a moment. This whole situation needed sorting out carefully. Norman was like loose cannon now. He was frightened and in hiding; who knew what he would do or who he would tell this story to. The police? He might think they were his last option for protection. It was better to get him out of harm's way. He also knew of some of Ralph's dealings and that was the last thing Ralph wanted known to anyone else. He knew Norman would feel like Ralph was betraying him, so there would be no loyalty. There was only one thing to do.

'I tell you what I think, Norman. You know I have businesses in Ireland? Maybe you could go there. At least until things calm down and Charlie has other things to worry about. What do you say to that?'

Raising his head, relief shone in Norman's eyes and he wiped his face with his shirtsleeve. 'Yes, that would be great. Thanks, Ralph, I knew you wouldn't let me down.'

Looking at Norman's pathetic face, Ralph felt satisfied that the matter was dealt with. Norman would be well and truly out of the way; Ralph would have Tom and his men watch him closely. *And who knows? Accidents do happen!*

'I'll sort you out somewhere to live, and here.' Ralph took out his wallet and started counting out a roll of bills. 'There's enough money there for your flight and a little extra to get you back on your feet again. Let's hear no more about it. In fact, I will drive you to the airport now and as you have nothing better to do you can leave straight away.' As he started the engine, Ralph was amazed how quickly things returned to normal. He had just taken the weight of the world off Norman's shoulders and here he was sitting up on the seat and talking normally about day-to-day things.

* * *

Driving up to the units, Ralph was amazed. Julie had said she'd given Chris instructions, but he hadn't imagined so much could be done in such a short space of time. His name was signposted above the unit and as you drove up there were huge billboards with the names of himself and the other offices.

As he walked in, the first person he saw was Chris. 'How are you doing? You've been busy.'

'Ralph!' Chris faltered slightly then nodded towards the back room, indicating they were not alone. 'Mr Gold. How nice to see you. Everything is shaping up here for your inspection.' Chris winked at him and as Ralph looked past him, he saw two cleaners going about their business. They quickly glanced up at Ralph and then started polishing all the woodwork with a little extra vigour.

'Morning, ladies,' Ralph acknowledged them.

'Morning, Mr Gold.' Pleased that they had not been invisible to the boss as most cleaners were, they exchanged glances and smiled at each other while taking in this wealthy, well-dressed, handsome man.

The place was immaculate. Julie had ordered computers, paper and a fax machine, none of which Ralph had ever used. This was all unfamiliar territory to him. Workers were fitting everything up in working order. The icing on the cake was seeing his nameplate on the office door. And when Chris asked him to approve the business cards he'd ordered, Ralph felt a strange stirring in his stomach as he looked at the card. It was just a small piece of cardboard with his name on, but for him it was a huge step towards a new future.

Composing himself, Ralph chuckled. 'Do you work for me, Chris, or for Julie?'

'You of course, Ralph.' Eager to win Ralph's approval, Chris grinned and showed him around.

'Don't worry; I know Julie is a force to be reckoned with. Christ, even I daren't say no when she starts barking orders. You've done a good job here. Well done.'

'The furniture is being delivered today at your flat. I was on my way there after letting the cleaners in here. Do you want to come with me?'

Ralph could not help laughing. 'Bloody hell, imagine if I went away for a month.' Happy, and amazed at what Chris and Julie had achieved, Ralph looked around the office. All of this was real. He felt like pinching himself. He was now the owner of his own company. How crazy was that?

Handing Ralph some letters, Chris continued. 'Here are some. CVs from the agency for secretaries. Julie said she would interview them.'

Raising his eyebrows, Ralph smiled. 'I bet she did. That means I'm going to end up with some old bag in knitted tights.' Ralph secretly wondered how Julie would interview secretaries. What did she know about office work? That would definitely be something to sit in on. 'Who is letting the furniture men into the apartment?'

'The nanny. She moves in today and Josh comes home tomorrow.'

Walking around the room, surveying the desks and front reception area, Ralph listened to Chris. It seemed like everything was in order and Chris knew more about his personal life than he did himself. 'Have you heard from Julie?'

'Not yet; she said she'll give me a ring when she's getting on the train back from Liverpool. Having her fitting for her wedding dress today, isn't she?' Chris followed Ralph around, showing him inside all of the now full cabinets and the new telephone system.

Exasperated, Ralph shook his head. 'Is there anything you don't know, Chris? For crying out loud, does she tell you everything?'

Blushing slightly and looking a little sheepish, Chris looked down at the floor.

'No need to look like that; I'm not angry.' Ralph slapped him on the shoulders. 'You've done an amazing job and there will definitely be a cash bonus in it for you. Now, shall we see what Julie has picked for our new home?'

16

A SURPRISE IN STORE

'Ralph, Julie. It's good to see you again. I take it you enjoyed your time in Ireland – or not, as the case may be. Get them some drinks, Marco; they look like they need them. It's good to see you both.' Carlos welcomed Ralph with the usual Italian style of a hug and a kiss on both cheeks. Julie just got a kiss.

'Don't ask about Ireland; it's a long, sorry story. Another time.' Looking around the hotel suite, Ralph was surprised that Carlos was alone with only Marco at his side. Usually his hotel suite was filled with other suits discussing business. 'Where is everyone, Carlos?' Ralph's brow creased. This kind of thing, with no witnesses, was usually a bad sign.

'Ralph, I know what you're thinking, but I just wanted to speak to you and Julie alone. We have our own business to attend to. Apart from the heist, I want to do an inner jewel pick-up.'

Turning to look at each other, Julie and Ralph were speechless. 'You want to do another robbery while we're also doing one?' Amazed at Carlos's revelation, Ralph stared open-mouthed and, with a nudge from Julie, took a drink.

'I love surprising you; you always make me laugh. Of course. We get a cut of the robbery and we both get a major cut from the inside one. This includes you, of course, Julie.' Carlos's Italian charm floated around the room. Everyone was intrigued, even Marco.

'Why do you want to do that?' Ralph's disbelief came pouring out in a scramble. He couldn't believe what he was hearing.

'I have it all planned and your back is already covered, Julie. You see, everyone at that meeting will think it's you on top of that helipad, but it won't be. I said you were the master of disguise and you're going to prove it.' Carlos's enthusiasm at his new idea became infectious and they all sat forward on the sofa, waiting for the next stage of his plan.

Julie was about to butt in but Carlos raised his hand to stop her. 'Let me finish first. I can see you're all dying to hear this.' Carlos chuckled to himself like a young schoolboy with a secret, the excitement bubbling up inside of him like a champagne bottle about to burst its cork. The surprised look on Marco's face was enough to tell Ralph he had no idea about this new plan of Carlos's either.

The moment Carlos got an idea into his head, he put all his plans into action without telling anyone they would be a part of it until afterwards. He just presumed everyone would agree to his plans. 'A famous auctioneers, whom we all know, are having an auction. Not just any auction, but an exclusive one indeed. They are auctioning off the engagement ring of the Arab prince's mother. It is enormous, a hundred-carat flawless diamond worth between eleven and thirty million pounds.' Carlos paused, waiting for the information to sink in, watching their eyes widen with amazement. Only Julie had something to say to break the ice.

'Well, that makes mine look like something out of a cracker, Ralph!' Blowing on her own rings and polishing them on her jacket, her red, glossy lips parted into a wide grin. 'And you think you can walk into this well-guarded auction house, with a million cameras and security men, and just slip it into your pocket. Yeah, right.'

Reaching over to the silver cigarette box Carlos had in the middle of the coffee table, she took a cigarette and lit it, blowing the smoke into the air.

'Yes, Julie. And why not? Nothing is impossible if it is planned properly. I have to say, for all of this Arab prince's pomp and ceremony, he must be completely broke to sell his mother's ring. Personally, I think it's disgusting.' Carlos spat. It wasn't the family way. 'Now it's your turn, Julie. You're the cleaner. Our inside man - sorry, woman. I apologise.' Even though Carlos was deadly serious, everyone's surprise showed in their faces and Ralph laughed aloud.

'I'm no bloody cleaner, Don Carlos!'

His temper slowly rising at Julie's objections, Carlos glared at her from across the room.

'You are now. All the cleaners have their own entrance and you will already have been police-checked. I have already sorted that.' Carlos waved his hand in the air nonchalantly. He couldn't be bothered with trivia. 'You are given a trolley with the usual mop and cleaning fluids, and my instructions. No one will give you a second glance. There is one hitch I presume you will argue about. I need you to dye your hair.' Carlos waited for the outburst he knew would follow, he was prepared for that.

'You've got to be fucking joking! Dye my hair! No way. I will sit here and listen to your mad schemes, but dying my hair isn't one of them. Can't I just wear a wig?'.

'Your hair is your signature tune Julie. Everyone will notice how beautiful you are', Carlos tried easing this revelation with flattery but, he could see it wasn't going down too well. 'You're easily recognised, Julie, and I want you to look almost dowdy. When the diamond goes missing, everyone will be searched and the first thing security and the police will do is run their fingers through your hair. Diamonds are small and can be hidden,' he paused, almost biting his tongue on the next sentence. 'Well, anywhere, if you know what I mean? If it were a wig that wouldn't look good. So, it has to be your own hair and not the blonde Julie we all know and love. When all of this is over, I don't want anyone putting two and two together. Dye it Julie. I don't care what colour. It's a little inconvenience for a lot of money!' Carlos's anger was rising.

Gobsmacked, Julie looked around the room. She knew she had a million questions to ask, but her mind was spinning. She looked at Ralph and then back at Carlos. The bombshell Carlos had just dropped on them all was struggling to seep into their brains. Ignoring his anger, Julie took a huge drag on her cigarette, and angrily blew the smoke into the air.

'Why would the police search me? Are you using me as bait? You're long gone and I'm left holding the baby. Is that what you're saying?' Suddenly, the penny dropped and Julie's jaw dropped. 'Oh fuck, you mean they are going to strip search me, don't you! No way Carlos, this is one step too far.' She shook her head defiantly to make her point, although she could see it was useless and Carlos was ignoring her. She wanted to give him a good kick in the balls to wipe that smarmy look off his face but thought better of it and decided to listen to the rest of this psychopath's stupid scheme. Mentally, through her fog of anger, Julie decided he was just a greedy bastard. How much jewellery did someone need in one day?

'Is she right, Carlos? Are you using Julie as bait? I don't like the sound of that either. Can't we just cut and run with what we have?' Ralph wasn't happy. He took hold of Julie's hand and squeezed it.

Carlos threw his hands up into the air angrily, 'For goodness sake, you English are so impatient. Let me finish before making judgement. Calm down everyone. Marco, pour some drinks. All of this arguing is making me thirsty.'

Doing as he was told, Marco filled their glasses.

'Now, when you are ready, I will continue.' Carlos paused, waiting for another onslaught from Julie, but it didn't come. 'It has come to my attention that the chief auctioneer who will be in charge of this great coup is someone known to me. He is a gambler at many casinos, and also private poker games. He borrows money all of the time which means he has a lot of debts. He is also a heavy drinker. I have instructed my associates to call the debts in, which of course he cannot pay. He will do anything to clear them. And I mean anything. After all, he knows eventually they will take their payment in some other form and dispose of him.' Again, this meant nothing to Carlos. He called this kind of thing collateral damage. They all listened intently, not knowing what to make of it all.

Julie couldn't help but interrupt. 'Tell me Carlos, is there anyone you don't know?' Sarcasm dripped from her lips and she could feel Ralph's eyes burning into the side of her face.

Ralph glared at Julie. He knew better than to upset Carlos while he was in the middle of something. He didn't like the idea of himself or Julie being easily disposed of because of one of her quips. And Julie's flippancy was annoying Carlos, he could tell. 'Stop it Julie.' He barked more for Carlos's satisfaction than his own. 'Just listen to what Don Carlos has to say before you interrupt him any more. Remember who you are speaking to.'

Seeing the smile appear on Carlos's face, Ralph felt he had done the right thing. He had shown Don Carlos that he was the man of the house, put Julie in her place, although Ralph knew that he'd pay for it later. But at least he had stopped the argument getting out of hand.

'Ralph, you will go in with myself and Marco as a security guards. There will be no more than ten buyers in that auction room and they are from all corners of the world. Argentina, Japan, Texas. You name it. It's an exclusive auction. Marco, you will already be one of the security guards in there at the side of the auctioneer with one of his own security guards. I will get you the badge etc. All that will be taken care of. You and I, Ralph, are going to burst in dressed as security guards and take the lot. I will fill you in on the minor details later and give you all instructions.'

Taking a break from his speech, Carlos picked up his whisky and gulped it back. The silence in the room as they hung on to his every word was deafening, and so he carried on. 'Are you all with me so far? Any questions?' Looking at the three of them, sitting side by side on the sofa, nodding their heads, reminded Carlos of the three wise monkeys. 'Okay, I will carry on. We will only have minutes to perform this miracle and so everyone has to be sure of what they have to do. Julie will pave the way for us by tampering with the cameras but first she has to be there for a couple of weeks cleaning and getting to know everyone beforehand to strengthen her alibi. Ralph, supposedly you will be in Ireland the day before. That is all arranged and Marco and I will be back in Italy.'

Clearing her throat and trying to muster up some kind of respect, Julie raised her hand like a schoolchild to ask a question.

'What is it Julie?' Pleased at her show of respect, Carlos smiled and nodded his appreciation.

'Well, Don Carlos. You all have your alibis – you're in Italy with Marco. Ralph is in Ireland. Where will I be?'

Carlos sighed. 'Obviously, Julie, you will be questioned by the police and be taken to their station. You will have to make a statement of what you know. I'm sure you can deal with that. They won't hold you for long, because I have already planned it that the auctioneer is going to take the full blame for this and then you will be sorting out your wedding plans and dying your hair back to blonde.' Carlos couldn't resist this last snipe at Julie. He too wanted to put her in her place. 'Once they release you, you can go home, Julie. Go to Liverpool. It won't matter. On the big scale of things, you will be insignificant, like all of the other workers there.'

Carlos stood up and walked around the room, waiting for some kind of feedback. Even Julie seemed at a loss for words. 'Okay, you boring bastards, I'll carry on then, shall I? We will attempt to steal the ring; it will set off the alarms, which is why we won't have a second to lose. And we all get out of there as quickly as possible. It's as simple as that!' Carlos laughed at his own joke. He made it sound so simple, while skirting over the risks they were all taking. 'Ralph, Marco and I will run for it, and as security, we will be on our radios and will be shouting for help as we run upstairs. We will have just a few minutes. Julie, you need to be in that auction room cleaning it before we arrive. You will put in place the things we need.'

'What if I can't get in there? What if they choose another cleaner to go in there?'

'Good question. And simply, Julie, it will be your shift and your domain. Cleaners are invisible to people like that. The auction house will be far too busy to pay you any attention. This is a grand affair. The staff will be excited.' Incidental details bored Carlos. Didn't they all realise he'd already looked into all of this? He was giving them the outline of the plan only once he'd sorted every possible option.

Daring to burst Carlos's bubble, Ralph spoke up. 'It seems like a lot could go wrong, Carlos. Julie's shift, but mainly us only having a few minutes to run like hell out of there.'

'All sorted, if you have the balls.' Ralph knew it was more of a statement than a question. Carlos was challenging him.

'When do you intend to do this?' Ralph couldn't help wondering; after all, he was supposed to be at the museum, Julie was supposed to be on the helipad and Carlos was supposed to be flying the helicopter.

'The same day. We can't do it afterwards, can we? Not with the police sniffing all over the place. Our friendly Arab prince won't be at the auction; he will be making his way to the hotel. He will have already given the auctioneers all of the information needed. Why would he sit in a room full of strangers who are bidding on his mother's ring?'

'What?! You must be fucking joking!' Not able to control her outburst any longer, Julie blurted out what they were all thinking. 'Are you crazy, Carlos? So just when do you get to be this security officer with Ralph if you're in a helicopter? Tell me that.' Angry and red-faced, she stood up with her hands on her hips. This was a bloody stupid plan and they were all going to end up in jail! 'Do you really think I want to spend my married life waving from a cell window to Ralph? Bollocks – I'm not doing it and neither is he!'

'Control your fiancée, Ralph, or I will.' Carlos's dark-eyed glare sent shivers down Ralph's spine. He knew she had gone too far.

'Sit down, Julie! And shut that runaway mouth of yours.' Trying to calm the situation between Carlos and Julie was a task in itself. She had already blown a fuse and Carlos was smouldering, the anger rising in him. Ralph knew what he was capable of and now was not the time.

'Don't tell me you're going to go along with this stupid idea, Ralph? Well, I'm not. I'm out of here. See you in court, guys!' Picking up her bag, Julie marched to the door.

'And just how many years do you think you would get for the murder of a policeman, Julie? You could still be spending your life waving to Ralph from a prison cell.'

Stunned, Julie paled at his words; her mind was racing. So that was the deal, was it? Carlos would hand Julie over to the police for killing the detective who had killed her friend. What's more, she had also killed the witness who had been in a witness protection programme in order to prevent Ralph from being sent to prison. She felt sick to the pit of her stomach and the bile was beginning to rise. Slowly turning, the cold stare she gave Carlos matched his own. She could hardly find the words. 'You call yourself a friend, Don Carlos, and yet you would turn on us all like a scorpion and spit out your venom.' This time her voice was low and calm; he'd shocked her to the core, making her voice tremble slightly.

'I'm a businessman. And you have a lot to lose, or a lot to gain if you do this.' The crisp, articulate words that left his mouth dripped with sarcasm. He picked up his cigar and lit it. Lounging back into the armchair, he waited. This was checkmate. He liked insurance on the people that worked for him, and this was his trump card.

Looking across the room at this stand-off between Carlos and Julie, Ralph couldn't believe his ears. 'This job means that much to you, Carlos? You're willing to put us all behind bars?' The disbelief in his voice made them all turn towards him. His brow was creased and he was shaking his head; this was unbelievable.

No one moved; everyone just looked around the room at each other. The silence was deafening.

'All you have to do is clean a few toilets and pick up a few rubbish bags, Julie. Is that really a problem? Is that why you turn on me when I have been so good to you in the past?' Carlos was now turning the tables on Julie. He made it sound like it was she who was betraying him. Defeated, Julie walked back to the sofa and sat beside Ralph.

'We need to know more,' was all she could whisper. Her throat was dry and she avoided Ralph's face. She knew he was angry – she could tell by his mannerisms – but they both had a lot to lose.

Clapping his hands together and rubbing them, like a spoilt child who had his own way, Carlos looked up at Marco. 'Time to pour some more drinks. I think we all need to calm down.'

Ralph could feel the sweat running down his back; he felt uncomfortable and helpless. Numbly, they reached out their hands to accept Marco's large whisky tumblers. Julie gulped hers back in one and handed the glass back for Marco to fill up again.

'Now we have all refreshed ourselves, let me point out to you all: if you do this, Julie, you will have approximately five million pounds to call your own. You, Ralph, will get a bigger share; you're taking a bigger risk. The same goes for you, Marco. None of the others know about this. I have kept this for my closest friends – or so I thought.' His voice trailed off and he took a sip of his drink, looking over the top of the glass at them all. His large brown eyes surveyed them all. He had half expected this outburst. After all, he had just dropped one hell of a bombshell. But this was to be his last big job that he would be involved with. He was Don Carlos now, soon to be married and head of the two families. As much as he loved the adrenalin of the 'jobs', the families didn't approve of him doing them any more. That was what the others were for. He now had to sit back and just give the orders. That was why he wanted to go out with a bang. He wanted to be the biggest and the best. People would talk about this for years!

Pondering for a moment, Ralph spoke up. Everyone had their doubts, but somewhere in the midst of all this, Ralph felt he was protecting them. Carlos's well-planned job had been a close guarded secret to those who were involved and, after all of the time and effort he had put into it, he wanted it to go ahead, but from a different angle. Everyone expected Ralph, Marco and Julie to be at one place. With this new plan, none of them would be where they were supposed to be and Carlos would fly off into the wide blue yonder. 'Outline the plan for me once more. I need to know more. As for Julie, if she doesn't want to do it, she doesn't have to, whether you threaten her or not. We have been through a lot of experiences together, Carlos, but blackmail isn't one of them.' Ralph couldn't resist saying his piece. More than anything, he wanted to protect Julie.

'Fair point, I understand your misgivings. So let's start again. Julie will not be on the helipad, unlike everyone else thinks. Instead, she will be cleaning the corridors and sweeping up. I already have her pass clearance and references from other agencies.

You will already be at the auction, Ralph. Security – we can't go in together. I will follow my part of the plan, pick up the Arab and fly him to the helipad as arranged. I will fly directly over the Thames to a waiting speedboat, drop the jewels off, switch pilots and then I will meet you, Ralph. The rest you know.'

'Who is the other pilot?' Ralph asked, still not feeling totally at ease.

'Dimitri is the other pilot. He will fly the helicopter off into the sunset and yes, I am not stupid – it will blow up mid-flight. I will set the timer when I get out of the helicopter. It is also a good ruse. If the helicopter blows up over the river, people will presume all those precious jewels are at the bottom of the Thames.' Carlos laughed aloud. 'Yes! They will be sleeping with the fishes, as my family say... Dimitri is my ace card and is one of our Arab friend's bodyguards. He is also very greedy. His sexual preferences would get him killed in his own country and I have promised him twenty thousand pounds and a way out, so his family are not disgraced. Always good to have someone on the inside.'

'You really do like squeezing people by the balls, don't you, Carlos?' Julie shook her head in disbelief. This handsome, charming man with his Italian ways was the very devil himself. He cared for no one.

'Better their balls than mine. There is no room for sentiment in business. If you have nothing to hide, you have nothing to fear. Is everyone happy with that?'

'Would you get to the auction house in time?' Ralph asked.

'Already timed it. I have been up and down the Thames more times than you can imagine. I will be there as planned. The waiting car we get into will take us back to the harbour where the speedboat will be waiting. We're gone, Ralph. Home and dry. The next time we all meet is at Ralph and Julie's wedding.'

17

THE COLD LIGHT OF DAY

Carlos had given them all a lot to think about. It seemed to take the shine off moving into their new home with Josh. Although life carried on as normal, it wasn't normal. There was a huge cloud hanging over them. They were in it up to their necks, one way or another.

Sleep became a thing of the past. Julie tossed and turned until in the end she got up and took Josh out of the nanny's room and sat holding him close to her on the sofa, watching him sleep. It was the first time she had been able to hold him properly since he had been born. Now, he was thriving and putting on weight. Julie was afraid; either way she could lose all of this and who would look after Josh? Maybe Carlos was bluffing about informing on her to the police. But maybe not.

For the last couple of days since their meeting with Carlos, Ralph had been out a lot having meetings with fellow lodge members to build his new export business. Many heavy goods vehicle drivers wanted the work. Julie knew they were avoiding each other because to speak to each other meant they had to deal with the problem in hand and make a decision. This whole situation was putting a strain on their relationship and there was only one thing for it.

'Ralph! Get your arse home. I don't care what you're doing or who you're doing it with. Come home,' Julie shouted down the phone. Sending the nanny out for a walk around the private grounds with Josh, she waited for Ralph to get home.

The door flew open and Ralph rushed in. 'What's wrong? What's the matter?' He was flustered and panicking at Julie's urgency to have him home.

'At last! Where the hell have you been? I rang you an hour ago!' She was edgy and worried, taking it out on Ralph. He got it with both barrels.

'Have you seen London traffic? So, what is the emergency? Is it Josh? Where is he?' Concerned, Ralph looked around the room.

'He's getting some fresh air with the nanny and we need to speak before she gets back. Sit down; we can't avoid this any more. In two days' time, I start work as a cleaner. Now, do we do this job or not? I'm prepared to give it a go if only to prove that mad Italian wrong. What have we got to lose?'

'A lot, if you think about it. But if you want to go ahead with it, then I am with you all of the way. I know Carlos and I know he will have covered everything. He doesn't have loose ends. They are having another meeting today with everyone else. Do you want to go to that?' Deflated and confused, Ralph sat down.

'I suppose we should show our faces. After all, everyone believes things are going as planned. He still wants you to put explosives in the museum to cause a diversion, doesn't he?'

'Yes, but I can do all of that on a timer. It's not a problem. The problem is "us", Julie. Don't let this tear us apart.' Reaching out for her hand, he squeezed it. It expressed more than words.

'We're going to do it. What did he say? Five million quid. I can clean a few toilets for that. Christ, I will be the highest-paid cleaner in the world! We're going to do it. So we will go and see him and go through this plan again. And then once this job is done we can get back to living our life, our way. How are the orders going for the import-export business?'

'We've actually got quite a full list. Even furniture removals for people moving to other countries. I've been offered a good contract with the army. That could be a real money-spinner. And it's legal. Old Mrs Meadows, the secretary you approve of, is just what I expected.' For what seemed like the first time in days, he laughed and shook his head. 'Dull as dishwater, an ex-accountant and sixty, so no surprises there.' He liked the way Julie was jealous. She rarely showed her emotions, having trained herself to hide them for so long. However, this was just an insight as to how she felt about him. She was possessive. 'Mrs Meadows has already taken over and is sorting out filing cabinets and checking the drivers' licences to see if they have had their medicals. She's thorough, I'll give you that.'

'I liked her when I met her.' Julie looked under her lashes at him and pouted. She didn't want some young woman flirting around the office, distracting him.

'She could be a world-winning model but she wouldn't be you. You are my Julie and I only have eyes for you. Get that through your brain. You are never getting rid of me, Mrs Gold!'

'Just tell me one thing. If we weren't together, would you have done this job with Carlos?'

'Yes, I would. But I have more to lose now and I don't want it to interfere with us. It's your decision, Julie.'

Julie was perturbed. It seemed now life was like a poker game. No one knew what the next card held. Between herself and Ralph, they were juggling so many balls in the air, they were running out of hands.

Gently kissing her on the lips, Ralph stroked her hair.

Pulling back before things went too far, Julie went back into business mode. 'No time for that. Oh well, we'd better go and see Carlos and collect my tabard, then. Come on, let's go. Incidentally, tell that Carlos he owes me a bloody manicure after all of this cleaning. Christ, I don't even clean my own toilet!'

Ralph laughed aloud as he slipped her coat over her shoulders. Julie was back on form again. 'Done. I'm sure he will go with that, or you could just put it on the ever-growing bill of yours for the wedding. How much did you say that cake cost?'

'Three thousand pounds. There's a tasting next week. Tell you what – let's get Mrs Meadows to sort out the invitations and the wedding presents. Oh, the list is at Harrods. Anyone who wants to buy us something will know where to go.'

'You've sent a wedding list to Harrods? Is that allowed?' Dumbfounded, Ralph's eyes widened. 'How do you know all of this?'

'Chris. He knows all these things and I watch a lot of television. There is loads of information on there. I even know what knife and fork to use!' Julie was like a Duracell Bunny – she just didn't stop. With a little help from her friends in Liverpool, she had organised all of this, even the church. They didn't have any spare dates and at St Pancras church, you had to attend regularly for six months beforehand. That was until Julie had offered twice the usual amount and a lot of bribery, including Don Carlos, and then they had found a cancellation. It was a beautiful church and was central and easy for people to get to.

'You need to get your suit sorted out, because after all this stuff we're going through I want you to look your best on our wedding day. Move your arse, Ralph!' She slapped his bottom and gave him a wink.

The solemn atmosphere seemed to lighten instantly; all was well again, and Ralph was relieved.

'You haven't mentioned the venue for the reception yet. Where is that going to be?' Encouraging her enthusiasm, Ralph knew better than to ask, but he felt he should anyway.

'At the Hilton – where else?' Kissing him on the cheek, Julie got in the car. Yes, she felt better now that they had talked. There were always going to be a few bumps and scrapes along the way. But if you never took a gamble, you would never know what life held for you. And Julie had been a gambler all of her life.

* * *

Over the next two weeks, Julie was exhausted. She was turning up for work at dawn, mopping floors and carrying rubbish out. She had a trolley full of cleaning fluids, which she pushed around with gritted teeth.

As much as she hated admitting it to Ralph, Carlos had been thorough. No one paid attention to just another member of staff from the cleaning agency. They were chopping and changing staff all of the time, apparently, and everyone was used to it. As long as you had the correct credentials, no one took any notice. She had made a point of wearing a headscarf over her now mousey brown hair. It saddened her when she looked in the mirror. The nanny had been shocked, but Julie had said she was just trying out different styles and colours for her wedding. Ralph had looked at her with surprise, and she had stood there stubbornly pouting, with her hand on her hips waiting for his comments and so like the good man he was Ralph had decided to say nothing for fear of getting his head bitten off. She wore no make-up and removed all of her jewellery. Her shapeless blue tabard still outlined her voluptuous figure, which was greatly admired by the security men who checked her security log in and tediously looked through the rubbish bags at the end of the shift. Carlos had been right about one thing: wherever you went in the world, men were men and they enjoyed a little banter with the ladies. She was also instructed to look around for any cameras or exits Ralph and Carlos didn't know about.

The cleaners were put into twos and she had been teamed up with a woman called Madge, who was in her late forties. She had been a cleaner most of her life and had a lot of funny stories who never stopped talking. She would spray polish into the air so that it smelt as if they had polished all the tables. Their cigarette breaks were longer than the norm and Madge had a nosy through everything. She was a real character, with her dyed black hair in a ponytail. It looked like it had never been washed and with her white face and pencilled black eyebrows, Julie thought she looked like Morticia Addams! As much as Julie complained to Ralph, she actually enjoyed hearing about Madge's ex-husband and her lazy son, who seemed to be glued to the mattress and hardly got out of bed.

Every day, Julie took some time to look around the auction house. It was all very different behind the scenes and was mainly offices. They were not allowed near the front of house. That was a different set of cleaners. According to Madge, only the elite cleaners were able to hoover the red carpet of the auction room. 'They've worked here for years, Julie. They're not agency staff like us. We are the peasants of cleaners. Personally, I don't care as long as they pay me,' Madge sneered.

'Don't you think it's a bit silly having two sets of cleaners?' Probing for information, Julie pushed Madge for more.

'Not really. They possibly think we're going to steal something. It's a load of crap they sell anyway. Personally, I prefer John Lewis. They have some good stuff in there. Why would you want to buy something that you wouldn't dare wear in public in case it was stolen?' Madge was like a walking billboard for the famous department store, which she obviously loved. 'Jools, love, give me a sale at

John Lewis and I'm at the front of the queue. The stuff they sell here is all second-hand and overpriced if you ask me.'

The very thought made Julie laugh as she sat on the shelf beside the washbasins in the toilet during their smoke break. Madge clearly didn't see the value in antiques. As far as she was concerned, it was all second-hand crap.

'Keep spraying the polish; it not only hides the smell of the smoke but it stops the smoke alarms from going off.' Turning on the tap, Madge put the stub of her cigarette under the cold water to make sure it was out.

'Aren't you bothered that the security cameras will see us and we could get the sack?' As tactfully as she could without creating suspicion, Julie continued questioning Madge. Now that she had won her confidence a little, Madge was more free with her information.

'Ah, no, don't worry about them.' Madge fluttered her hand in the air and shook her head. 'They only have them on in the main auction rooms when there is an auction. I doubt the ones back here even have tapes in them. God, if they did, I would have been sacked months ago. The security guards who check our bags are as bored as we are but they are constantly on their radios talking to each other and it's usually the football scores.'

Madge smoothed out her tabard and pushed up her breasts in a sort of statement. It was clear to Julie that Madge didn't care a fig about the job. All she was interested in was payday. She thoroughly enjoyed having a novice under her wing and apart from the odd question to Julie such as 'Are you married?' and 'Do you have kids?', Madge wasn't really interested in Julie's personal business. As far as Julie was concerned, Madge had a boring home life and work was the only place she could express herself with her worldly knowledge to new agency staff.

Soaking up as much information as possible, Julie made mental notes. And every bit of information she had she passed on to Ralph, who in due course would pass it on to Carlos.

Life was good. It felt good. For the first time, Julie felt content. Her and Ralph's new home together and its new expensive furniture made her smile each time she sat on the sofa. The fitted kitchen was something she had only ever seen in magazines. This was the stuff dreams were made of and with little Josh settling in nicely, Julie felt like part of a family for the first time in a long time. Sophie, the nanny-cum-nurse, was worth her weight in gold and did more than her fair share for Josh and around the house.

She knew Sophie wondered where she disappeared to every morning, but she never asked questions and Julie never told her. Julie and Ralph had both done as instructed and made a last will and testament and handed it over to Carlos. Suddenly it all seemed real. There was only a couple of days before the job and Julie wanted it over as soon as possible, no matter what happened. The very thought of something going wrong made her cringe inside. She would be going full circle and treading in her mother's footsteps and that was the last thing she wanted to do. Julie had plans for the future and that didn't include dying or spending her last days in prison.

18

THE JOB

Today was the day they had planned for what seemed forever. Parking his car a few streets away, Ralph visited the private viewing at the museum. People were milling around, eager to feast their eyes on the exhibition that had come straight from Las Vegas. It had a celebrity status of its own, full of glamour.

It was busier than he had expected considering it was ticket-only. The Arab prince was charging them to view all of his precious goods. Carlos had got him a VIP ticket, which meant he didn't have to stand in the queue with the others, but could walk straight in once he'd shown his ticket to the doormen. They did the usual searches, although nothing invasive. Ralph had smuggled putty explosives in his socks and was going to use his watch as the timer. It didn't have to be precise, as long as it went off and caused the diversion Carlos wanted.

Champagne was being passed around on silver trays to the VIP visitors; although Ralph took one, he discreetly left it on a shelf without drinking it. Everyone walked around to the glass cases and admired the jewels and sculptures, in awe of their beauty. Tuxedos and mink coats seemed to be the order of the day for the visitors present and there seemed to be as many jewels on the outside of the glass cases walking around as there were inside. Women were adorned in them especially for tonight to add glamour to the proceedings.

After an hour, Ralph went to the toilet to change and set up his explosives. Years of experience had prepared him for this and, removing the wire for the detonator that was attached to his watch, he set the timer for three minutes.

Ralph had also hidden some tear gas in plastic canisters in his underwear, which hadn't made it easy to walk, but had been worth it. He'd decided he would set off two explosives, which would cause panic and fear amongst the guests and hopefully give him the chance to grab the item Carlos most wanted from its glass case.

Ralph couldn't understand why Carlos had asked him to get the large blue marble egg draped in rubies and sapphires. But Carlos had specifically expressed to Ralph and Ralph alone that the egg was what he wanted and Ralph had given his word to Carlos to steal this object he so greatly desired.

Splitting the wire and putty into two pieces and attaching it to the detonator, Ralph then proceeded to do the same again, although on the second one he would set the timer for ten minutes. Now he felt more prepared. Two explosives should be enough to cause a diversion. Taking off his own watch, he used that as the second timer switch. Julie could never understand why he always wore two watches. But as an explosives man, he had learnt this was the most effective way to have a timer on hand should one be needed. Old habits die hard. And there was a lot to be said about an old-fashioned watch that you had to wind up. 'Be prepared' was his motto. Either that or 'KISS – keep it simple, stupid'. He could feel the sweat running down his back as he worked quickly, while keeping his ears open to hear anyone come into the toilets.

Opening the door slightly, Ralph could see the cameras and

security guards walking around the room outside and quickly joined them in his museum security uniform. He'd worn the jacket underneath his tuxedo and overcoat and was already wearing black trousers. The peaked hat, security badge and plastic goggles, as promised by one of his Jewish friends, were wrapped in layers of plastic in the toilet cistern. With his security pass clipped to his breast pocket, he walked out. Taking out the tear gas pellet, he lit it with his lighter and it began to fizz like an aspirin, slowly letting out gas. Pulling the peaked hat down over his forehead, he continued looking around for a diversion of his own so that he could push the putty explosive somewhere discreet without the cameras detecting him. He doubted they would even notice, considering the panic he would create. There was no way he could get to the vault, even in this crowd. But as he paced the room, he spotted the marble egg. He needed that to appease Carlos.

Spying the staircase to the next floor, Ralph smiled. The wide bannister would be somewhere he could innocently put his hand without suspicion. Everyone else was holding on to it. It would be full of fingerprints. Walking up the staircase, he held on tightly as he walked to the top of it. With his left hand, he held on to the wide bannister and pushed the putty explosive underneath it and pressed the winder button, which was used to wind the watch up. Quickly looking around for a minute at the paintings on the wall as though carrying out an inspection, he calmly walked down the staircase again.

Hurrying his steps, he went and stood beside the glass case containing the blue marble egg and waited. No one took any notice of him standing near the glass case in his uniform; if anything, they ignored him. Waiting for what seemed an age, he glanced up the staircase at the bannister. Surely it should have gone off by now? Maybe in his panic he hadn't set it properly or there was something wrong with the timer. Just as he was about to go back to the staircase, an almighty bang erupted. He'd used more than intended. People fell down the stairs, while others fell over the ones lying on the stairs in their panic to get out.

The alarms went off instantly; half the staircase and inside wall was missing. Brickwork and plaster covered people as they ran for the doors. The security guards tried shouting to everyone to remain calm and leave in an orderly fashion, but it was a stupid thing to shout to a panic-stricken crowd in the middle of an explosion. It was mayhem. People were running for safety as paintings fell off the walls, and sculptures tumbled. People ran around in panic and Ralph put on his goggles before rolling a gas canister on the floor, causing even more mayhem. Instantly the tear gas did its job and created even more confusion and fear.

People were rubbing their eyes; they could hardly see as they stumbled and clawed their way to the exits. There was the sound of broken glass as the windows shattered and as Ralph turned, there was the beloved marble egg. His eyes stung a little and felt itchy beneath his goggles. Reaching out, he quickly grabbed the egg from its broken glass case. The alarms started going off, but no one was paying any attention. Ralph recognised it as a weight alarm. It only went off if the weight of the egg was removed from the case. It was heavier than he had imagined and barely fitted his pocket, but he held on to it tightly. The managers of the museum appeared and were trying to stop people pushing past them to leave. They were trying their best in the smoke-filled room to stop people stealing anything. 'The police and fire brigade are on their way,' they shouted to the crowd, to no avail. They were almost trampled as people pushed them out of the way. They could hardly breathe and wanted fresh air. Ralph pulled down his hat, put his handkerchief over his face, and headed for the doors. Looking down, he saw a three-tier diamond necklace and picked it up, slipping it into his pocket. Among the commotion and crowds of people, Ralph took another gas canister and rolled it along the floor. Instantly, the gas sprayed from it, creating a smokescreen. People screamed and shouted, rubbing their eyes to see in the gas-filled room.

Suddenly the ceiling sprinklers came on, drenching everyone. It was time to leave. People were crying and injured. Others were lying on the floor, knocked out from the blast. Ralph stepped past them towards the doors. Some were holding out their arms and shouting to him to help them - their heads were bleeding and they were half-conscious - but still he strode on to the doors, ignoring them. Ralph made his way to the exit, pushing past people. He was a man on a mission; he needed to get out of there.

Once outside on the pavement, he staggered and breathed in some air. Passers-by had stopped and were helping people on the pavement. Taking his goggles off, Ralph looked around at the mayhem he had caused. 'Hey, you,' another security guard shouted to him. 'Come over here and help these people.' Ralph nodded. He felt trapped. Suddenly the police sirens sounded around the corner, followed by fire engines. Soaking wet people were laid on the pavements, holding their faces and being comforted by strangers off the street.

Cupping his hands around his mouth, he shouted above the noise of the crowds. 'I'll go to the police cars and tell them we need ambulances.' Suddenly there was another blast. It was the second explosion. This was what he needed to make his getaway. Shaken, and finding it hard to breathe as the gas stung his eyes, he mustered up all his strength and ran down a side street as fast as he could. He didn't know where he was and couldn't get his bearings. But he soldiered on. People were far too busy running away from the scene of the explosion to give a damn about him.

He was filthy, his eyes stung and his head was banging. Soaked in water from the sprinklers, he wasn't sure what to do next, but his only objective was to get to the auction house to meet Carlos. His car wasn't too far away and, now he could see a little more clearly, that was his aim. Running through back streets, he ignored onlookers and headed for his car. Relief washed over him at the sight of it and he almost fell inside it.

* * *

Carlos leant forward and looked closer out of the window of the helicopter. It was late afternoon and getting darker by the minute. The private aeroplane was lit up, as were the runway lights. The Arab prince and his bodyguards each walked down the steps of the aeroplane in their *thawbs*, the traditional Arabic dress; they looked quite the authoritative figures. The two bodyguards behind struggled to carry the battered trunk containing the jewels between them. Turning, Carlos looked towards Dimitri and smiled, giving him the thumbs up. The noise of the helicopter blades drowned out any whispered conversation and this definitely wasn't the time to shout.

The helicopter was still running, making them all rush forward, billowing out the white material of their robes as they walked across the private runway towards them. Still wearing his headset and dark glasses, Carlos looked over his shoulder at them all and smiled at their stony faces. Thankfully, the noisy blades of the helicopter drowned out any unsavoury comments they made about him as he saw them muttering to each other.

It wasn't a long flight to the hotel helipad but, as he approached, Carlos felt a feeling of doom. His gut instinct had been right. The dusky early evening blurred his vision a little but he could see there were far too many people up on the roof to greet them all.

There should have been three men and a woman, but instead there were six. Only a couple of them wore the hotel uniforms, including the woman. The other men waiting for them were wearing their normal suits. Carlos only recognised two of them and his first thought was to fly away. But he knew he couldn't, not with a group of Arabs in the back. He had to see this through no matter what, but he felt as though he was flying into an ambush.

Everyone stood back and tried shielding themselves from the wind as he landed, but he kept the motor running. Carlos had thought the prince would get out of the helicopter last but, instead, he went ahead and got out first. 'I hate these things,' he barked at the others. Carlos looked at Dimitri and raised his eyebrows. It had never occurred to him the Arab prince didn't like helicopters and couldn't wait to get out. Travel sickness? He looked slightly pale, almost sickly as he got out. Once he was on firm ground, he then beckoned to the others to follow his lead.

Sitting in the helicopter, Carlos surveyed the scene before him. Something was not right. Already this plan was going wrong and he needed to keep those jewels on the helicopter. Looking over to where the private lift was that took them down from the helipad into the hotel, Carlos spotted people behind the cage door of the lift. As he tried to see more clearly, he thought he could see bodies in the lift. The gate was half-open, but they weren't shouting or waving and so he surmised they were either unconscious or dead. Poor bastards – they had obviously gone up there to do their job and this lot had been waiting for them.

A man Carlos vaguely recognised stepped forward, grabbed the prince, and held a gun to his head. The unexpected surprise of it all rooted him to the spot. 'Fly,' the prince shouted towards Carlos. But he ignored him and shrugged, pretending not to hear. Carlos knew what he meant. He wanted him to fly away with the jewels so there would be no bounty for these murdering thieves.

There was a struggle and a lot of shouting, mainly in their own language, as the bodyguards of the prince jumped out of the helicopter. One of the waiting men on the helipad took out a gun and shot one of the prince's bodyguards as he ran towards him. The blood from the gunshot in his chest seeped through his white robe, turning it crimson.

This all seemed to happen in seconds, and Carlos was shocked that his plan had gone so badly wrong. From behind him, the last two bodyguards on the helicopter pulled out sub-machine guns from beneath their *thawbs*. Carlos knew they were not only bodyguards but also assassins of the Arab prince. Their duty was to serve and risk their life for the prince and they jumped out, firing at the waiting men on the ground. The round of bullets shot them instantly. Even though they were dead, the bodyguards carried on firing; bullet after bullet riddled the men on the helipad, making their dead bodies almost dance in the air with each round.

Swallowing hard, Carlos sat open-mouthed at the massacre before him. He had not expected this. The ground was crimson with blood. Holding their fire for a moment, the bodyguards' first thought was to run towards the prince to make sure he was all right, forgetting all about Carlos for a moment. It was all over in an instant.

No one from the hotel would hear the gunshots, because the noise from the helicopter drowned it out. Everyone was out of the helicopter; only the jewels were in the back and Carlos knew this was his only chance to escape. Quickly putting the helicopter into gear, he started to fly off, but one of the Arab bodyguards turned and shot at the side of the helicopter, making it swerve slightly. In panic, Carlos put it in full throttle and flew as they all fired more gunshots at the helicopter. Sweating and struggling to control it, Carlos flew off into the skies, leaving the mayhem and the scene of dead bodies behind him. He was sweating and Dimitri was crying and shouting at him to hurry up. Panic consumed him as he looked out of the window behind them as the Arabs stood there with their machine guns in the air, firing at the helicopter. The window of the helicopter was smashed and Carlos could see where the bullets had hit from the dents in the door. They had aimed for the blades so that it couldn't fly, but thankfully, he was now out of reach of their gunshots. Carlos knew time was now even shorter. The hotel would be informed immediately and the police would be called, though what would be said and done with all those bodies on the ground was anyone's guess. Carlos had what he'd come for and now it was time to get to Ralph. Inwardly shaking, he knew he had to compose himself. Even the best-laid plans went wrong sometimes.

* * *

'Hey, mate, what's your problem? You look like shit!' Ralph staggered to the staff entrance for the security guards and was met by a couple of the others who had sneaked out to have a crafty cigarette. By the looks on their shocked faces, he knew he must have looked a sight. He'd tried cleaning himself up in the car and put the heaters on full blast to try to dry some of his wet clothing.

'There's been a bombing; I've been helping some of the people on my way here. Am I late?'

'Blimey, mate, no. We've heard about it. It's all over the news. Are you okay? You shouldn't have come to work.' Concerned, they flocked towards him to see if he needed any assistance.

'Are you agency staff?' another one enquired while stamping out his cigarette on the floor and walking towards him.

'Yes.' Ralph forced a smile. 'Who would imagine that on my first day on the job I would get caught up in a bombing?'

'Probably some terrorist thing. It's always happening around here.' Another one spoke up.

A thought then occurred to Ralph. If they had heard it on the news, they would know what had happened. 'I didn't see much, just helped people on the pavements. Did anyone get killed from it?' He wanted to know, because that hadn't been his intention.

'Not as far as we know. There were a few casualties but the news hasn't mentioned any deaths yet. I think most of them got out by the skin of their teeth.'

Breathing a sigh of relief, Ralph felt grateful. The explosions were meant to cause a diversion, not a killing spree.

'Come on, mate, let us get you dried off a bit. There are some spare clothes in the lockers.' Leading the way, they walked ahead of him, continuously talking about the bombing and what a hero he was.

No sooner was he taken inside than they all proceeded to open their lockers to find a clean set of clothes for him. This was easier than expected, no questions asked. As he knew where the staff entrance was, they automatically presumed he had been sent by some agency. And to turn up as a hero while they talked of the bombing, he merely blended right in.

Now wearing a clean shirt and trousers, with a tight-fitting jacket, he felt better. He was handed his badge and a radio headset. That was it, it was all over. Once he had his instructions to patrol the corridors, all he had to do was wait for Carlos to turn up and the auction to finish.

Permanently looking at the clock as he patrolled the corridors because he didn't have his watch, Ralph felt nervous. Where was Carlos?

* * *

Over the last couple of weeks, Julie had made it her job to befriend as many people in the building as she could, and by getting supposedly 'lost' had found her way to the security office where all the CCTV monitors were. There were two guards in there. Once she had been spotted by them through the pane of glass in their door, one had jumped out of his seat to see who she was and what she was doing there. In old time tradition, Julie had looked sorrowful and beamed a charming smile at this overweight, aging guard. He was a far cry from her Ralph, with his flexed muscles and flat stomach.

She had flirted and batted her eyelashes and he had been flattered. Now both men looked forward to Julie popping down there for a quick chat to break the monotony of the day. Madge had been in her element when Julie told her. This was the perfect place to have a cigarette without being seen. Each morning, Julie and Madge had visited the security men, drank their coffee and gossiped. All the while, Julie was taking mental notes. She discovered that they weren't that bothered about the job and were bored to death, which is why they had a portable television in the room to watch the football to pass the time. Discreetly, she had asked questions about the equipment. They even told her sometimes they brought their own video tapes and used the machines to watch them. 'Nothing exciting ever happens here'. They had said, much to Julie's amusement.

On the morning of the robbery, Julie had busied herself hoovering everywhere. Keeping on her marigold rubber gloves, she had done as instructed and pulled the telephones out of their sockets in each office she went into. Carlos had said this would delay things a little longer as they wouldn't be able to telephone the police as quickly as normal. Even a second was a second longer to get out safely.

After the regular cleaners for the auction room had left, Julie had sneaked into the now empty auction room. Carlos was right, there were only ten chairs in the room. Under each chair she placed a red hood, which Carlos had had specially made to match the colour of the carpet. From a distance you couldn't distinguish them from the carpet itself. Looking down in her cleaning trolley, she picked up the last and most important item. Ralph had given her a tear gas canister to put at the far side of the room and three gas masks. After careful planning, Ralph had told her where to leave them so they would be easily accessible. Last but not least, she had to get the CCTV tape out of the machine. Although the guards would still see what was going on, on their monitors, there would be no recording of the robbery at all.

* * *

Surprisingly, the helicopter flew, but only just. It had lost some power and, looking at the dials before him, Carlos could tell it was leaking fuel. In the darkness, he hovered over the Thames. When he saw a light flash and someone waving a white flag, he knew that was it – the speedboat waiting for him. The boat had no lights on and so it was awkward to see properly, but gently Carlos flew over the top of it, lowering the helicopter as close as possible to the boat. 'Get in the back and put those harnesses on the trunk and while you're at it, see if there is anything that will help it float if I miss,' he barked at Dimitri, who was still in a state of panic.

'What if it's another ambush? We could both be killed. Let's just go somewhere else.'

Carlos reached out and slapped him across the face. 'Go where, you whimpering fool? Now do your job and let's get out of here.' Carlos failed to mention that the fuel tank was leaking and he doubted that they would make it much further. But then he never intended for Dimitri to get much further anyway.

Doing as he was told, Dimitri pushed the trunk to the open door of the helicopter and slowly eased it down to the waiting boat. Carlos saw the white flag wave again and he knew they had received it. 'You can unclip the ropes now. They have it safe and sound. You take over the helicopter for a while. Let's get out of here now we've dropped the stuff.'

Shaking, Dimitri did as he was told and didn't notice when Carlos sat back and put a hand grenade by the side of his seat. As they flew away from the boat, Carlos gripped the pin of the hand grenade. 'Sorry, Dimitri, but you had it coming.' He threw himself out of the helicopter. The dark water hit Carlos like a brick. 'Follow the bubbles,' his scuba diving instructor had always told him, and now he knew what he meant. Kicking his legs and pushing himself further to the top of the water, he gasped for air as he surfaced.

There was no sign of the helicopter, only a burning wreck in the distance, lighting up the river. Looking around him, he searched for the boat, but the men were already on hand and had thrown a lifebelt for him to grab on to. As he swam towards it and grabbed the side, he was still gasping for air; the water was freezing cold and he shivered as he clung on with all his might.

Once on the boat, he was wrapped in a blanket as everyone scrambled around to help him.

'Get me some clean clothes; I need to get to Ralph. You had better go; the coastguards will be here soon to investigate that helicopter crash.' Although shivering, he still found his tongue to bark instructions at them all. They needed to get out of here and fast. The biggest part of the job was yet to come. The thoughts that warmed him most as he looked into the far-off distance as the flames from the helicopter burnt was that the trunk with the jewels was safety on board and would be smuggled out of the country in minutes, on its way to France to their waiting buyer. The helicopter would sink into oblivion with no trace. If they sent the divers down to see if anyone needed rescuing, they would find the helicopter and a dead pilot.

Realising the time, he knew it would be tight to get to Ralph. Carlos hoped he was okay and hadn't encountered any problems.

All of his best-laid plans had blown up in his face and he had only escaped by chance. It had been an ambush. A disaster waiting to happen. If any of his plans had leaked out to his enemies, what would become of Julie and Ralph? They were his only hope now and he felt responsible for them. The heist had been his idea and he had planned it with precision, or so he had thought.

Reaching for his necklace with a cross on it, he kissed it for good luck. For all of his dealings he was still a devout Catholic and secretly prayed that Julie, Ralph and Marco were all safe. He needed to get to Ralph quickly; he would be waiting for him and if he was too late, God knows what might happen. This whole affair had become a nightmare. A total catastrophe and he needed to make it right. He had caused enough misery in Ralph's life since he had known him; he would never forgive himself if anything happened to Julie. More to the point, neither would Ralph. Carlos knew she was a tough cookie and could stand up for herself, but not if there was an ambush waiting for her. They were relying on him and he had to be there no matter what.

'Can't you go any bloody faster?' he shouted. Panic was rising in him and he was itching to get to Ralph. He had escaped by the skin of his teeth and God only knows what was waiting for him at the other end of this trip. Everything had gone wrong, but he had got what he came for: the jewels. It was of little consolation if it meant he had put his friends in jeopardy. A prison sentence at worst, possibly death. All he could do was put his trust in God to keep them all safe.

19

DIAMONDS ARE FOREVER

The nervous auctioneer who had met Marco and let him in the building walked beside him into the room. There was another guard at the entrance, but he ignored Marco and the auctioneer completely. Marco breathed a sigh of relief; he had two guns in the waist of his trousers at the back. The walls of the auction room were covered with blown-up black-and-white photos of the diamond ring they were all here to bid on. They showed a beautiful woman with her hand out, displaying the priceless gem. Puzzled, Marco looked up at the pictures again. Some of them were displaying a bracelet and earrings. The auctioneer pointed to him and Marco took his place at the back of the auctioneer's desk, keeping his peaked cap as low as humanly possible, avoiding the cameras in the far corners.

At last, the auctioneer took centre stage and introduced himself. His first speech was about the history of the ring and the other accessories the prince had agreed to auction. The next was about the amount of carats to whet everyone's appetites. With a large projector behind him, his colleague he held up the ring and showed it to the waiting crowd. A collective intake of breath seemed to fill the room, followed by an applause. The ring was enormous and Marco's jaw nearly dropped when he saw it.

The auctioneer told them of the highest price that had been offered and so the bidding had to start from there. Much to Marco's surprise, considering the bid already made, the buyers in the room were still raising their paddles with the numbers on to bid higher. He couldn't believe it.

* * *

'Where the hell have you been?' Relieved, Ralph lowered his voice as he saw Carlos walking down the corridor.

'I had a little trouble, but enough about that. All is well now, apart from that nosy security guard who was not going to let me in. They are changing shifts now so everything is okay. I'm here, aren't I? Have you seen anything of Marco?'

'Quick, come with me; the other guards will be here soon.' Pushing open a door, Carlos was almost running up a staircase that Ralph had not noticed. The door looked like any other of the office doors. It was well disguised. There was no one else around. The floor to the auction room was completely empty of people.

Carlos leaned forward and whispered into Ralphs ear. 'Do you think Julie will be in the security office by now? Christ, I hope so because now is the time.' Carlos made the sign of the cross across his chest and handed a gun with a silencer on it to Ralph's gloved hand.

'She knows what to do and what time to do it. You're the one who is late Carlos.' Ralph reminded him. Ralphs's mind was with Julie. He was worried about her. He was wondering what she was doing now.

Each in turn they took off their hats and rolled black balaclavas down over their faces before putting their hats back on. Standing in front of the double doors, they each turned a handle to open them before quietly closing them again behind them. Everyone had their backs to them facing the auctioneer.

'No one turn around. This is a hold up. Put your hands on your heads. Do as you're told and you will not be harmed. We're not here for you,' shouted Carlos. He pointed his gun at the camera opposite him and shot at it. Everyone in the room screamed and bent over in their seats for fear of being shot at.

The auctioneer spoke to the frightened crowd. 'Everyone. Do as this madman asks.' Doing his best to keep their attention towards him, he tried to calm them down and reassure them. Again Carlos gave his instructions. 'Under your seats you will find a hood. Put it over your heads.'

Frightened, they felt under their seats for the hoods Julie had put there earlier and did as they were told. There were a few abusive comments from a couple of the men in the crowd, but Carlos fired his gun at the chandelier, shattering it. Remnants of glass fell onto the crowd. Their muffled screams filled the room. 'Does anyone else in here want to be a hero? Good, then be quiet and we will be gone before you know it.'

* * *

Julie had made her excuses to Madge about going down to the security office. 'You're not really going out with that fat bastard, are you? Bloody hell, I bet he hasn't seen his dick in years!' laughed Madge.

'Love is in the eye of the beholder Madge. He's a nice guy.'

'Yes and he's also married. Don't say I didn't warn you. He's full of shit!'

'Married?' Julie was suddenly more determined than ever to get one over on this cheating bastard!

'Yes, didn't he mention it?' Madge shook her head. 'No of course he didn't. sorry to shatter your dreams love.'

'Well, I'll just pop down anyway. Maybe he's separated from his wife?' Julie knew she sounded pathetic, but it was her only chance to retrieve the tape and the clock was ticking. She made her way to the office, pushing her cleaning trolley before her. She had learned early on that no matter what, you took your trolley with you, and then if anyone saw you idling around, you could always say you were cleaning.

As she opened the door, she was greeted by a welcome smile from the security guard. She thought how pathetic he looked. He was fat enough already and yet he was sat there stuffing his face full of crisps. There were already a few empty wrappers from chocolate bars beside him.

'Hi Pete, how are you today?' Planting a kiss on his cheek, Julie was all smiles, even though it made her feel sick inside.

'All the better for seeing you love.' He smiled back.

'Oh sorry, Pete. I didn't have any change for the vending machine and I'm dying for a coffee. Have you got any?'

Putting his hand in his pocket he pulled out a handful of change. Julie sat at the seat beside him and put her feet up. 'Oh god my feet hurt. Are you going to rub them better for me?' she giggled.

Seeing him moisten his lips with his tongue disgusted her. 'I'll go and get us a couple of coffees love. You rest your feet.' No sooner did he wander off up the corridor, Julie jumped up and pressed the eject button on the recorder for the tape and put it on the back shelf with numerous others. Then she thought better of it. Suppose Ralph and Carlos had already been caught on it? Quickly looking over the monitors, she could see people milling around in the room. She knew it was the right one, because she saw Marco, but, where the hell was Ralph and Carlos? Picking the tape up again, she decided to hide it in her trolley.

Pete and another security guard both walked in carrying their coffees. Julie was sat rubbing her feet and complaining. Once Pete had sat down she put her feet on his knees and wiggled them around near his crotch. His hands rubbed her feet and slid up to her ankles - as far as he could go, with his stomach in the way. The other security guard took the hint and left them to it.

Julie went over and sat on his knee. Suddenly his hands were all over her, but she bit her bottom lip and looked at the clock above his head. Carlos had said they would be finished by quarter past the hour. Although it was past that now, she wanted to give them more time just in case something had gone wrong. She wasn't doing this for Carlos or his money. She was doing it so that Ralph would be safe. She was playing for time and had no option but to let this overgrown elephant slobber all over her; shoving his hand up her tabard to grope her breasts, while she feigned pleasure and gritted her teeth.

* * *

Marco pulled his own balaclava down, walked up to the auctioneer, and handed him a gun out of his waistband. 'Do it,' he whispered.

Shaking, the auctioneer looked at the gun, then back at Marco. Spit dribbled down the side of the auctioneer's pale face and he was sweating profusely. 'I know 200,000 reasons why you should do it and so do you. All your troubles will be over,' Marco angrily whispered in his ear. Trembling, the auctioneer picked up the gun and looked at Marco. It was obvious he didn't know how to use it, especially with a silencer on it. 'Just point and fire you sleazy shit or my friends will do the same to you.' Nodding, the auctioneer raised the gun, pointed it at his colleague, and squeezed the trigger, shooting him in the back. As he fell to the ground, the auctioneer burst into tears, making his face even more wet, besides the snot and the sweat.

Marco looked over the desk and saw the motionless man lying on the floor. His shirt was now crimson with blood. A few people in the crowd fell off their chair onto their knees after hearing the faint gunshot. and started praying. They were crying and begging for mercy.

Carlos and Ralph jumped on to the podium and took the ring. Puzzled, they looked at each other and then back down at the auctioneer's desk. Not only was the ring there but, there was an assortment of earrings, bracelets and even a necklace. Scooping them up, Carlos put them in a small, cloth bag and down inside his shirt, covering it with his jacket. He looked over at the man lying dead on the floor, gave the 'thumbs up' to Marco, and waved at him to leave.

Suddenly the auctioneer leaned forward, almost falling onto Carlos, and grabbed his arm for support. A groaning noise escaped from his mouth as he gripped his chest and fell to the floor. Looking at Ralph in amazement, Carlos's eyes widened and he shrugged his shoulders. The auctioneer was having a heart attack!

Running back down the aisle past the group of people, Ralph looked in the corner where he had instructed Julie to put the tear gas cannisters. Indicating to Carlos to roll their balaclavas back under their caps, they quietly turned the door handles and looked out. There was no one about. Beckoning Carlos, they both stepped out and rolled the cannisters into the room filling it with gas.

* * *

Julie had given them another fifteen minutes on top of the estimated time and she'd had enough. The monitor no longer showed the room; she presumed Carlos had broken the camera as he said he would. That put her mind at rest. At least they were there.

Suddenly the other security guard burst back into the room. 'For fuck's sake, put her down. Something is going on. Everyone is running to the private auction room and gas is coming from under the door and people are screaming! What's on the monitor?' They both froze as they saw it was just a blank screen. Eric tried pressing all kinds of buttons to make it spring into life, but nothing happened. Pete jumped up so quickly Julie nearly fell to the ground. Grabbing their hats, the two men ran down the corridor, leaving her there. Straightening her clothing up, Julie put her rubber gloves back on and reached in her trolley for the video tape, pulling all the ribbon with the recording out of the cassette. She could hear screams and shouts from security guards and it sounded like mayhem up there. Pushing her trolley quickly she followed the noise and hoped to find Madge. As she ran down the corridor, she saw one of the other cleaner's trolleys standing idly on its own. It had obviously been abandoned during the chaos. Taking the cassette out of her own trolley, she looked around to check no one was around and dropped it inside.

* * *

Beckoning Ralph, Carlos pointed. There were two security guards about to make their way down the other staircase. 'Hey, you two, where are you going? We've been told to patrol this floor. Why are you here?' Carlos asked as he casually walked up to them. Puzzled, the other two guards looked at each other. 'I'll find out.' One of them was about to press the button on his radio to speak when Carlos threw a punch. Immediately, Ralph did the same. The men tried fighting back and it turned into quite a struggle but Carlos and Ralph rained blow after blow down on them until they fell to the floor, their noses covered in blood, unconscious.

Carlos dragged one of the men by his feet into a nearby office. Following his lead Ralph did the same with the other man. Taking off their belts, they tied the men's wrists together. Carlos ripped the sleeve off one of the guards' shirts and ripped it in half, stuffing the pieces in their mouths.

'We need something to bar the door. Get that chair; that will do for now.' Carlos and Ralph's gloves were leather. Carlos insisted they wore them always. He did not like the idea of leaving any trace behind.

Hearing noises from downstairs, they ran out of the room, barred the door with the chair, and ran down the stairs. Suddenly they heard the alarms going off. Everyone seemed to be running in different directions, panicking and shouting.

When they reached the top of the stairs, there were two more security guards. The security guards started running down the stairs. 'Where are you going?' one of them shouted after Carlos and Ralph.

'To get more help.' Carlos was swinging open security doors and running down corridors. Ralph was amazed how he knew the way so well. In this maze of corridors, he felt lost, but not Carlos. He knew exactly where he was going.

Just before they reached the staff exit, they bumped into two more security guards. 'You two lazy bastards, don't you listen to your radio? John Squires the senior auctioneer is half dead. There's been a robbery. Go and help some of the people!'

Breathing heavily and angry, the security guards looked at Ralph and Carlos's dilapidated state. Pressing the button on his radio, he was about to speak when Carlos took off his hat and head-butted him. Ralph kicked the other one in the crotch, making him bend over and cry out.

'Hats back on and pull it down over your face!' shouted Carlos at Ralph.

Pulling Ralph by his sleeve, Carlos continued to run. 'That is the best we can do for now. Run, Ralph!' The alarms were now at full volume and doors were automatically locking themselves.

'Shit, the doors are controlled with the alarm. This whole place will close down. How far away from the exit are we?' Ralph shouted at Carlos between gasps of breath. His heart was pounding in his chest like a hammer. They needed to get out of there.

Carlos raised his leg and threw out a kick towards a metal bar across the door. 'Here!' Before them was the open yard and Ralph had never been so pleased to see the dark night sky. As they looked up at the building, they could see shutters coming down all over the place. Already police sirens could be heard getting closer.

'Where are the cars?' asked Ralph and Carlos pointed to the right.

'The police will go that way. Mine is this way. Come on – we will get to my car quicker.' Carlos started running, but Ralph stopped him.

'Carlos, wait. How long is it since you've ridden a bike?'

'Years – why?' Following Ralph's eyes to the row of bicycles in a covered shed, he shook his head. 'You've got to be kidding me?'

'No! Now is the time to bloody learn again. I can't run any more and they never lock them all up. Come and see.'

Ralph was right and as they walked into the shed and pulled at a couple that were not padlocked, they came away from the metal bars that held them up. Pulling them out, they both mounted the bicycles and, after a wobbly start, they pedalled as fast as their legs would let them.

Ralph had a pain in his side and he hurt from running. In and out of streets and across roads they cycled, until finally Ralph stopped. He dismounted and leant his bike against a wall near the Tube station. 'Walk, Carlos, walk slowly.'

There, as if by magic, was Ralph's car just in front of them. It was an amazing sight. Together, they opened the car doors and got in.

'For fuck's sake, Ralph, drive – drive anywhere; just get me away from here.'

Police cars passed them as they drove through the streets. They both sat in silence, trying to catch their breath while Ralph composed himself and slowed down, sticking to the speed limit. Stopping at the traffic lights didn't help their panicked state, but the only thing to do was to act normally. The last thing they needed now was to look suspicious by speeding through the streets of London. They took off their hats and threw them in the back of the car.

At last, Ralph spoke. 'Are you okay?'

'Yes. It's up to Julie now. Fingers crossed she's okay.' Carlos didn't sound so sure. It was mayhem back there!

Ralph looked out of the window. He hoped so too. He'd almost forgotten about Julie. What the hell was happening to her right now? She was in the thick of it, trapped in that building surrounded by police and security. Would she think he had deserted her? He needed to know that she was okay and instinctively wanted to turn back, but he knew he couldn't. For all of her bravado, he knew she would feel frightened and helpless. He hated himself for letting her agree to this. Trying to concentrate on driving, he could hear Carlos talking but he wasn't taking it in. His troubled mind was with Julie. How he longed to hear her voice and just one more word of sarcasm drip from her mouth. He didn't care if she shouted and screamed at him for this mess. He just longed to see and hear her again.

Carlos broke his train of thought. His mind was still on the job in hand.

'By the way, Ralph, do you have something for me?'

Knowing exactly what he meant, Ralph nodded. 'Under the car seat. God help the chicken that laid an egg that size!'

They both burst out laughing, whether it was the craziness of the situation or just plain hysterics. They had pulled it off and they were both alive. Now they just had to wait for Julie to do her thing...

* * *

Julie made her way back to Madge as a piercing sound filled the building. Everyone came out of their offices at the sound of the alarms.

'What's that?' Julie looked towards Madge. She knew what it was but had to play the game.

'Oh, don't worry; it's probably one of those fire alarm trials. They are supposed to warn us, but they rarely do and we can't hear them if they do try and tell us with that racket going on.' Madge nonchalantly carried on with her dusting as people ran down the corridors past the office. It was bedlam.

'Yes, but, Pete and Eric were panicking, too. What's going on'? Julie portrayed innocence.

'Have you been down there all of this time with him? For God's sake girl, wake up and smell the coffee. He's a loser. They'll turn it off in a minute.' Madge seemed very oblivious to the shouts of panic down the corridors. Then they heard the shutters bang down against the windows. 'Jesus, something's wrong; come on, Jools.' Even Madge now realised the seriousness of the situation.

'Everyone, stay where you are! Stand still and put your backs to the wall.'

Julie turned and saw half a dozen police officers running down the corridor. Two men in suits walked slowly behind them. As Julie spied them from the doorway, she realised these were the detectives.

'Will everyone stand still – there is no fire!' the police shouted.

Everyone was confused and did as they were told. They stood with their backs to the walls, turning towards each other for answers and muttering in puzzlement. Although Julie had been expecting this, now was the moment of truth. She felt nervous and her palms were sweaty as she watched the proceedings. She felt as though there was a beacon above her head saying 'Guilty'. Now was the time for her to do her side of the job. It seemed the others had done theirs. Mentally, she scolded herself. This was the time to man up and do what she'd come to do. *For fuck's sake, Julie*, she thought to herself. All of this time, she had mopped floors and been up at the crack of dawn for this very moment. Biting her bottom lip, she did her best to hear what the police were saying. There was no mention of arrests, but she couldn't be sure. The police were all whispering to each other as they surveyed the line of employees standing with their backs against the wall.

'Who is searching the building?' the plain-clothes detective asked one of the police officers.

A police officer came forward and answered them. 'There's another crew upstairs, sir. They are searching the floors.'

Julie watched him, inwardly praying Ralph and Carlos had got out in time. There was no sign of them and no one mentioned them. Adrenalin seared through her veins. She felt sick to the stomach; whether it was excitement or fear, it all amounted to the same thing. The pensive look on her face as she watched the police must have shown clearly to Madge.

'Don't worry, Jools.' Madge took her hand and held it, reassuring her. 'It will be okay, we've got nothing to hide; don't worry, love. You watch, it will be a big fuss about nothing. Anyway, the longer they make us stand here the more we can claim the overtime. Might as well bide our time and hang around for a bit.' Madge nonchalantly watched the police with great interest, mentally noting all of it so that she could tell all her friends about her narrow escape at the robbery. Julie felt sure she would add a little more on to make it more interesting. Her tale would get much longer and embellished until she wouldn't know herself what the truth was any more.

Weakly smiling at her, Julie couldn't take her eyes off the detectives walking down the stairs with the police following them. She could hear them talking but couldn't make out what they were saying. Everyone was making their own assumptions and, feeling a little safer with the police there, they relaxed. They knew there had been a robbery, but to what extent?

* * *

'Two men are dead, and a group of people are gasping for breath.' Inspector Linley shouted at the top of his voice. 'Did anyone see or hear anything?' he shouted, trying his hardest to get through to them. Everyone looked at each other, hoping someone would answer. There were gasps and shocked looks as the detective's words sunk in - people were dead? Numbed and stunned by the horror of it all, some women even started to cry. Even Julie felt herself tremble and shudder slightly. Two men were dead? Surely not Ralph and Carlos. From where they were standing, Julie could see nothing.

The silence and the tension in the air as the detectives tried to make sense of all of this was puzzling.

'I heard a loud crash'. One of the female staff spoke up, her nervousness making her voice wobbly. Looking her up and down, the detective walked over to her.

'What kind of crash'?

Some other people from the offices nodded and mumbled, that they had also heard a loud crashing sound from the room.

'Did you report it or go and see what it was?' Incredulously, Inspector Linley looked around the line of people. 'Did everyone ignore what was going on in a place like this?' Clearly, nothing like this had ever happened before.

'We'd been told by the auctioneer that under no circumstances were we to go into the room.' She said and turned to her colleagues, who nodded their heads and agreed with her. The detective found all of this very suspicious. Everyone heard a crashing noise but had been told to stay well clear of the room earlier by the auctioneer? No one knew what to do next. There were dead men and casualties. But this had to be an inside job. Both detectives agreed on that.

'Get forensics down here. We need fingerprints and I want every one of the staff questioned. Take their names and addresses. Someone has to know something. Can you see anything in that room yet?'

A police woman stepped forward. 'Nearly sir. The fire brigade have arrived. They suggested we open the shutters to let some air in. They are bringing the people out now.'

The police officers were swarming the building, taking the names and addresses of everyone there. Everyone would be called to make a statement. Other managers and auctioneers ran down the corridor towards them to see what had happened, and paled. They all seemed more interested in what was missing than the casualties in the room. 'The ring! Has the ring been stolen?'

'What ring? What are you talking about?' Inspector Linley was slowly losing his patience. No one knew anything and yet gunshots had been fired and people were dead. He desperately wanted to get into that room to see it for himself. These gunmen knew what they were coming for. It was definitely an inside job because he had been assured by the other auctioneers that the auction was a strictly private affair.

'It seems that now we know what they came for,' said the detective. 'Who else knew about this auction?' He wanted to know more about the ring. None of the safes had been blown and there was no mess in any of the other rooms. The manager turned, walking away, ignoring everyone else, and waited for the detectives to follow him. Upstairs, people were moaning about how long they were going to be kept there. Everyone had their excuses for having to leave.

'This is a crime scene. Touch nothing,' he barked at everyone. 'No one is going anywhere. I want statements from the lot of you.' Turning to the police officers, he asked, 'Has anyone looked at the CCTV cameras? That will tell us everything we need to know. There are enough cameras around this place.' Looking up, he could see them all over the corridors.

A police woman walked up to the detective and whispered in his ear. The detective rolled his eyes and shook his head.

In the privacy of the corridor, the detective looked at his sergeant. 'What a fucking mess and no one knows anything. These were professionals.' His only hope was the cameras and the remaining people left inside the private auction room. Just then, a member of the fire brigade told him it was now safe to go into the room, but they would need to cover their faces.

Julie couldn't take her eyes off the detectives. The police started to usher people out as all the shutters were rolled up again. Everything was suddenly turning back to normal. Men and women were going back into their offices to collect their coats and bags. The corridors were a hive of gossip as people made their way out, each in turn having their own versions of what they thought had happened.

Looking inside the room from the doorway, both detectives surveyed the scene. They were given cloths to cover their face by a police woman. The smell was overpowering and made them cough and their eyes sting, even though the gas in the room was clearing. The sergeant pointed to the glass on the floor and looked up.

'There is your crashing sound, guv. The chandelier has been shot at.' Peering in, the detective nodded. His sergeant was right; the long stem of the chandelier hung there emptily swaying around. It must have made one hell of a racket, given the size of it. Glass was everywhere, but they had all ignored it. He'd already been informed that the people in the room had been wearing hoods. So that was a dead end. Other security officers had said they had seen security officers who they didn't know running around the building, but as for descriptions, they couldn't remember. They hadn't taken a lot of notice once the alarms started ringing and everyone was panicking.

Leaving the crime scene because of the still-overpowering smell, Inspector Linley swiftly walked to the security room. This was his big clue. 'Okay, put the recording on from inside the room – let's see exactly what happened here.' Rubbing his hands together, for the first time that day he half smiled. Both security guards looked at the ground, red-faced, and said nothing.

'What's the problem?' Confused, Inspector Linley looked around at the blank faces.

'There isn't a recording, sir' stammered an officer to break the silence in the room. 'It seems there is no tape in the machine and these two didn't see anything.'

'Why not? You must have seen them entering the room. Why didn't you blow the whistle earlier?' Putting his hands in the pockets of his coat, he waited. Mentally toying with his questions, the detective knew there was more to this. Maybe they were the insiders and that's why they hadn't reported it to other security guards to check up on.

Again, there was a red-faced silence. Then one of the men, whose name badge read Pete, spoke up; his voice was low, almost a whisper. 'Eric had gone to the toilet and I was distracted by one of the cleaners. We were messing around... if you know what I mean.'

His chin was almost on his chest as he spoke. He knew he was in grave trouble.

'Distracted? How?' A puzzled frown crossed the detective's brow. He thought he knew what he meant but looking at the man in front of him, he couldn't be sure.

'Please don't tell my wife. I've been married for fifteen years.' He started to cry, but the detective wasn't interested. In fact, he was angry. All of this could have been solved if it wasn't for him neglecting his duties. 'It was just a bit of flirting that got out of hand, that's all. I didn't notice the monitors weren't working. It's all my fault. Sorry'.

Stunned by this revelation, the detective turned to the police officer. 'Take him down to the station. I want a full statement from him.' Turning back to Pete, he asked who the woman was. The detective shouted out of the door to another officer to go and fetch the cleaner Pete had been messing around with.

Police walked down the corridors shouting out Julie's name. She was shocked; this was unexpected. Raising her hand and avoiding the many stares from everyone around her, she stepped forward.

'Would you come with me, please?' asked an officer.

The detective she had seen was sitting in the security office. Looking her up and down in disbelief ,he asked her what she was doing when the alarms went off.

'I was messing around with Pete the security guard', she admitted. She felt embarrassed about it, but it was the truth.

Didn't you notice the screen was blank?' He knew that was a stupid question but, for the moment, it was all he could think of.

Shyly looking down, Julie shook her head in shame. 'I wasn't looking, and I don't know how those things work'. Mentally, even though she was scared, she thought she should get an Oscar for this acting performance.

'Take her to the station. I want a full statement to see if it backs up his story'. Julie was led away. She felt helpless and alone and suddenly needed Ralph desperately.

* * *

Realising there was nothing else he could do, the detective and his sergeant went back to the station. They were preparing themselves for the interview with the security guard when an officer ran towards them.

'Guv! The other guy that was shot in the room. He's alive! Barely, but he has a pulse. The ambulance have just informed us.'

Inspector Linley put his coffee cup down. Raising his hand, he did a 'high five' with the officer. This was good news indeed. 'Thank fuck they didn't bury him already', he laughed. 'Are you going to tell me that the auctioneer is alive and well now?' Raising one eyebrow, the inspector couldn't resist his sarcasm.

The detective's face dropped. 'No guv, but we have checked him out and it doesn't look good. He has a history of angina, he's in debt up to his eyeballs and he had a diamond bracelet in his pocket. Personally, I think he's your man. Here's the report'.

'Yes, I agree, but we need to make sure he wasn't working with anyone else. I want you to get it all over the news that the witness is still alive and get a round the clock guard in the hospital. If he is working with someone then those bastards will want to come and finish the job. Also, check out any old criminals that have done this kind of thing before. Get the word out to any informers we have. See what information they can find out on the streets. This is a big case and it needs sorting, otherwise the boss is going to have our guts for garters. Come on, let's see what lover boy has to say.'

* * *

Although he sat there with his head in his hands, crying, Pete told them the whole story again and again in between the questions they fired at him.

Standing up, they left him there and went into the other room where Julie was sitting, smoking a well-earned cigarette. Her hands were trembling and her mouth was dry, which made her lick her lips, trying to moisten them, but instead it made them feel sore.

Inspector Linley questioned her and again the same story that verified Pete's unfolded.

'Did you clean the auction room? Who cleans in there?' he asked.

'Me and Madge are just agency staff; we only clean around the offices, toilets and corridors. The regular cleaners, the ones employed by the auction house themselves, are the only ones allowed to go in there. Me and Madge always work together,' Julie continued. She knew what she was telling them was the truth and could be verified.

The sergeant stood up and went to the door, whispering to someone behind it. The inspector continued his questioning and the sergeant came back. All of Julie's credentials from the agency were confirmed; she even had references from other agencies. Carlos had been very thorough.

'Well, you weren't working together while you were screwing Pete the guard, were you? I bet his wife has something to say about that.' Inspector Linley threw the fact that he was married in for good measure.

'Married?' Julie looked surprised and disgusted. 'Madge mentioned something earlier but he gave me the impression he was separated. The low life!' Julie turned on her hurt female act and cursed Pete for lying to her.

Before it could go any further, Inspector Linley ended the interview. The last thing he needed was a hysterical woman on his hands. 'I'll check out your story, but for now your free to go.'

Julie breathed a sigh of relief. She was free to go home.

* * *

Sitting on the bus, Julie was nervous. The journey seemed to take forever and, after four stops, she got off. The Barbican wasn't the address the police had and so she knew that if anyone was watching, she had to make a diversion. Now she desperately wanted to get back to the sanctuary of her own home. The only way she could be quick was by hailing a taxi. Asking him to take her to Liverpool Street Station, she got the underground tube to the Barbican. She felt like she was being watched all of the time. She was becoming paranoid. Once she was at her station she pulled off her tabard, dumped it into the bin, and walked the rest of the way home. She felt dirty and tired. She needed a shower. Most of all, she knew she wasn't out of the water yet.

Opening the door as quietly as possible so as not to wake Josh or the nanny, Julie didn't turn the lights on and so walked and felt her way to her bedroom and straight into the en-suite bathroom, stripping off all of her clothes instantly. This was her time to take a breath. Standing with her back against the door, she felt the bile rise in her throat. The adrenalin was dying down and allowing the fear to kick in. She had been afraid and still was. Although she knew the noise of the shower might wake the nanny, Julie didn't care. She needed to wash the events of the day off her body.

Coming out of the bathroom, she was startled to see Ralph sitting on the edge of the bed, waiting for her. 'Ralph!' Instantly she ran to him. Their embrace seemed to last a lifetime as they clung to each other. Julie could feel tears of relief pour down her cheeks as she held him.

Breaking away from her, Ralph put his finger to his lips. 'If anyone asks, I'm not here,' he whispered. 'I've been waiting for you. I needed to see you before I go. I'm in Ireland; I went yesterday. How Carlos manages this is beyond me, but who cares.' Ralph opened the French windows that led out onto the balcony. Once they were both outside, he closed them. 'We can talk here.' He then reached out and held Julie. 'I have been so worried about you. This whole job has been one catastrophe after another. Carlos was nearly killed. It seems he had the worst of it, but I hated leaving you there. I wanted to come back. I didn't want you thinking I had deserted you.'

Still holding him close, she whispered in his ear, 'I was afraid I would never see you again.' Relief washed over her as they held each other. She needed to feel the warmth and strength of his arms around her to reassure her; she never knew how much until now. His calming presence against her feisty ways and brash manner made her feel at ease. This was the man she loved. Diamonds or no diamonds. He was good for her.

'You're never getting rid of me. Even when I die I'm going to come back and haunt you!'

He laughed. He could see she had been frightened. This job was too much for her to handle and the fact that nothing had gone as planned didn't make it any easier. They had all been frightened. It had been far too close for comfort. But Ralph's admiration for Julie had escalated. She had kept her head and carried on with the job in hand, no matter what. This strong, single-minded woman standing in her bare feet, wearing only a towelling bath robe, was his whole world.

Suddenly, their lips met. No words were needed. The passion of their kisses became more ardent with each one. This bond between them could never be broken. Ralph never wanted Julie to be frightened again. He would always protect her, but he also knew that whatever happened in the grand scheme of things, Julie would always be at his side. His wing woman. She had proved that. She had seen the job through, not knowing whether he and Carlos were dead. She must have had doubts, but she was as strong as she was beautiful. And she was going to be Mrs Gold. God help anyone who tried to come between them.

Their lovemaking was silent but frenzied as they clung to each other with all of their might. It was all over too soon and, still panting and trying to catch his breath, Ralph whispered, 'I have to go, Julie. We all need to have separate strong alibis.'

'Do you have to go so soon?' Julie desperately didn't want him to go, although she knew he had to. Her alibi was irrelevant. But Ralph and Carlos's had to be rock solid. Carlos had covered their tracks completely, it seemed, but it didn't stop her worrying. This could be the last time she ever saw Ralph and she wanted to make it last forever. Seeing the concern on his face, she didn't want to worry him any more. He was between a rock and a hard place and she didn't want to make it any harder. 'So that's it then.' She grinned. 'A quick shag on the balcony. Bloody hell, Ralph, who said romance was dead!' Seeing the smile on his face made her feel better. The last thing he needed was a guilt trip. He'd taken his life in his hands coming here tonight.

'You know me – cut and run. That's my motto.' Tucking his shirt into his trousers and getting himself properly dressed again, Ralph laughed. Julie always made him laugh. At least now he felt better, knowing she was okay. They had seen each other and neither of them were left wondering if the other was alive or arrested. All was well in the Gold household. Now it was just a case of sitting it out and letting the dust settle.

Guilt overwhelmed her. 'Ralph there is something I need to tell you. To get the tape from the security guards office I had to...' Ralph put up his hand and stopped her. 'I don't want to know Julie. Whatever you did, you did because you had to.' It felt like knives in his body thinking about what Julie had been forced to do. She was his woman, and no one was allowed to touch her but him.

'It wasn't sex Ralph, I swear. And I did it to protect you,' she pleaded. 'Do you still want to marry me?' she asked sheepishly.

Trying to make light of the situation, he laughed. 'What? After Carlos has paid three thousand pounds for a cake? I think I better had,' he winked. 'I don't want to know what happened, Julie. The only thing I will say is, never again, do you hear me? You're mine, Julie, and you most definitely are going to be my wife whether you like it or not.' He smiled and then kissed her.

The waiting was always the worst part of these jobs. Ralph was loath to leave her, but he knew he had to. Business was business. Julie could feel his apprehension. Putting on a brave face and her biggest smile, she waved her hand at him nonchalantly. 'Bugger off, Ralph. I need my beauty sleep.' Now she was back into Julie mode. Standing up and wrapping her robe around her, she shivered slightly. 'Thanks for the shag, Ralphy love, but you must try harder.' Winking at him in her usual style with a large grin across her face, she opened the French windows and looked around the room before waving Ralph back into the room. Opening the front door, she put her finger to Ralph's lips. 'Don't say goodbye; it's bad luck,' she whispered, then pushed him out of the door.

'See you later, alligator.' Ralph winked, bringing the smile to Julie's face. This had become their tag line.

'In a while, crocodile,' she whispered back as she shut the door. Rubbing her face with her hands, she felt sad, drained and tired. She needed to sleep. And now she could sleep; she had been sick with worry.

Julie trudged to her bedroom and threw herself on the bed with one big leap. What a bloody day! She was shattered and mentally exhausted. Thank God it was over.

20

FALLOUT

Over the next few days, the tabloids were full of news. They were spoilt for choice, but the police had their connection. This all had something to do with the Arab prince, and he and his men were the only ones surrounded by dead bodies and machine guns. No one knew what to make of it. Every newspaper had a different angle but mainly the focus was on the events that had taken place at the auction house. Their biggest bombshell was that the witness was still alive although not conscious. People were amazed at how clever these Robin Hood characters were, who had stolen a priceless ring and just walked out undetected.

Each time the television was on, Julie picked up the remote control to try to find something else to watch, but if it wasn't on the news, it was on talk shows. Victims from the museum were reliving their horror for the cameras. The whole thing seemed like some nightmare circus.

Carlos had left England with Marco hot on his heels. Their men left at the hotel had cleared everything away and paid the bill. There was nothing suspicious there; Carlos and his men came back and forth all of the time and the hotel even kept his suite on hold for him.

Ralph had gone to Ireland. His alibi was solid. He had gone home to see his best man and sort out his wedding arrangements. A chauffeur had checked Ralph in at the hotel and so the staff never saw him. Room service was ordered but with the 'Do not disturb' sign on the door the waiters had knocked and left the trolley outside for him.

Julie was at home. She had worried a little when she didn't turn up for work the next day, but they had no contact telephone number for her and the address that had been given was phoney. Carlos was right: the auction house had more to care about than an agency cleaner. They would possibly presume that after all that had happened, she would be too frightened to return to work.

Chain-smoking and pushing Josh's pram in the private gardens for hours on end, Julie felt she was going stir crazy. There was only one thing for it – she needed to get away. No one would find it suspicious if she went to Liverpool to check on her wedding dress and catch up with her friends. It made sense and it would give her something to do. She bleached her hair back to its blondeness. Although it wasn't as good as Sue's had been, it would do and made her feel like her old self again.

First, she went with Chris to see Mrs Meadows, the matriarch of the export business. She'd been given a free hand to get the business up and running, which included staffing. When Chris and Julie walked through the door, they were greeted by young receptionist wearing a black blouse with a large gold 'G' embroidered on the breast pocket. Even Julie had to admit, everything looked impressive.

Mrs Meadows soon rushed forward and greeted them; she had given herself the office next to Ralph's. 'This is Emma, one of the part-time receptionists. The other girl, Lucy, is not here today – they job-share. That way if one is taken sick there is always another on hand,' explained Mrs Meadows. Her sensible flat shoes and her tweed suit reminded Julie of an old headteacher she had once had. She glanced sideways at Chris, who was looking down at the floor like a naughty schoolboy. 'May in the small office over there is our finance lady. Wages and suchlike, but now she is sorting out your wedding invitations too. Everything is in hand for the big day, Ms... erm...' Mrs Meadows faltered, not knowing what to call Julie.

'Julie, Mrs Meadows. Just call me Julie. I must say you're doing a sterling job. Well done.' Julie's charm and flattery pleased Mrs Meadows and the smile that crossed her face showed a pleasure all of its own.

'I keep all the files and folders containing passport updates and insurance papers in my room, and of course the door is always locked in my absence. Emma, bring Julie and young Chris here some coffee in my office.' Her authoritative voice instantly made Emma jump out of her seat.

'Passports, Mrs Meadows? I don't understand.'

'For the overseas drivers. All the paperwork has to be correct and in order. All passports and medicals are in those folders for inspection.'

'Of course.' Not wanting to sound stupid, Julie nodded and went along with it. Of course Mrs Meadows, being thorough, was checking everyone's credentials should they need to drive overseas on the ferries.

'I won't be staying, Mrs Meadows. I only popped in to tell you that I will be going to Liverpool for another dress fitting and to make any last arrangements. This is your baby now, and I trust you implicitly to handle the business as you see fit whilst we are away. I know Mr Gold speaks very highly of you.' Yet again, Julie saw Mrs Meadows beam with pride at her words.

'Some of the jobs were halted for a couple of days. The police have stopped anyone going out of the country in a lorry now. Possibly thinking we're going to smuggle those burglars out the same way!' Annoyed at the police's interference in her work over a silly burglary, she tutted and continued to do so as she explained to Julie how she hated anything disrupting her routine.

Feeling the laughter bubbling up inside her, Julie felt she needed to leave. Straight-laced Mrs Meadows was funnier than she realised and already Julie had warmed to her. Everything was going to be safe in her hands. 'You will be coming to the wedding won't you, Mrs Meadows? I know Ralph would like his right-hand woman there on the big day. Here, organise some drinks and food for everyone and a little bonus for all of their hard work, and this is for you. Treat yourself. Buy something nice for the wedding.' Julie opened her bag and counted out four hundred pounds.

Mrs Meadows' eyes widened and her jaw almost dropped at Julie's generosity. Graciously taking the money, she couldn't thank Julie enough. She was indeed going to enjoy working for the Golds.

'I will sort everything out. You go and sort your wedding plans out, Julie. I have your mobile number if I need you. And of course, there is always Chris here on hand if I need him.'

After a little more chatter, Julie left and waited until Chris had driven further up the road before she burst out laughing. 'For God's sake, that Mrs Meadows is made of stern stuff. God help any of those drivers if they cross her. She will have their balls on toast!'

'I know, she scares the shit out of me.' They both started laughing. Mrs Meadows was a law unto herself, but she would be worth every penny they were paying her.

'How come she wasn't working for anyone already? I was surprised she applied for the job with all of her experience.'

'Word is she worked for a big company that dealt with export but they moved premises and gave her redundancy. It's hard for a woman of her age to get another job, even with all of her experience. You and Ralph have given her a new lease of life, which is why she is putting her heart and soul into proving herself.'

'Well, as far as I'm concerned, she has a job for life. Come on, drop me off at the station. Do you have all of my instructions?'

'All in hand, even the colour of the flowers at the church. When you going to do that food tasting?'

'I'm not. Tell that chef to make the biggest and the best. What do I know about starters and hors d'oeuvres? Lots of champagne and there is no budget. That is his job. Give him a free hand because Carlos is paying. If it tastes like shit, I'll send Mrs Meadows around!' Again, they both burst out laughing.

* * *

'Sue! Oh, thanks for picking me up.' It felt good to see a friendly face again and Liverpool seemed like a world away from recent events.

'Oh, Julie, do we have a surprise for you. Although, not as bad as the one you have for me.' Sue lifted a strand of Julie's hair and grimaced.

'My roots needed doing, Sue, and with one thing after another, I couldn't get here. Sorry...' Julie didn't like lying to her friend, but she had to come up with a feasible excuse.

'Never mind. I will sort it, but don't you ever touch them again, do you hear me? If the worst comes to the worst, I will come to you.' Sue laughed. 'Do you want to have something to eat first, or shall we crack on with the excitement? Do not make any plans to go home tonight. It's hen night! We're all going out on the town. Don't argue, it's sorted'! Sue had turned out to be a good friend. Possibly, for all of her antics, maybe she was a little lonely too.

Arriving at Maggie's house nearly brought a lump to Julie's throat. Hanging from the bedroom window was a large, white sheet flapping around in the wind. 'Good luck on your wedding day' had been spray-painted on it. All the women came out to greet her, singing the wedding anthem as she walked up the path. Grinning from ear to ear, Julie gave them all a hug. This was just the pick-me-up she needed.

'As soon as you rang to say you were coming, we had to set something in place. Not long now, love. And you can't have your hen night the night before your big day and look like shit the next morning.'

'You asked me if I wanted to go and eat first, you minx. Why?'

'To give everyone more time. Here, take this.' Handing Julie a glass of champagne, she chinked her glass against theirs as they all circled her, laughing and chatting. Their friendship and enthusiasm humbled her. For once, she was at a loss for words. Wiping away a tear that was brimming on her lashes, she swallowed back the champagne.

'Right, first the dress. Then our amazing idea. Then we're all going to piss off to that bar in town and watch the male strippers!' Sue had taken charge and she was loving it. She clapped her hands together to get everyone's attention and they all ran upstairs. Maggie and her team had done wonders. She had made a beautiful Cinderella dress. Julie was in awe as she looked at the finished dress on its mannequin. 'Oh my God, Maggie, I don't know what to say. I dare not wear it; it is too beautiful.

'But you will, you bolshy cow. They are all going to need sunglasses in that church with all that diamanté walking past them.' Again, they all cheered as Julie tried it on. She didn't care about the weight of it. It was the dress that dreams were made of.

'We were worried how you are going to get into the car with a dress this size. Actually, we were worried about you getting through the doors! So what about this? It's available, we've checked. Bloody expensive, though.' Opening a wedding magazine, Sue showed her a picture of a round, glass carriage, drawn by white horses. 'It's the Cinderella coach'!

'Oh shit! Yes, yes, yes. Book it, hire it, do whatever.' Excited and screaming at Sue, she nodded. That coach would finish off the whole look. 'I didn't know they had such a thing.'

'Sweetheart, if you're willing to pay, they will find whatever you want. But this solves the problem of a car. As I say, I have already enquired about it and they say it's free on your big day. Not cheap, though.'

'Bollocks, I'm not paying for it. Carlos is. I want to ride through the streets in my glass coach waving at everyone like the queen! Why would I want to hide that dress inside of a car! Oh, and Sue, I want gold plumes on the horses. After all, I am going to be Mrs Gold.'

'Don't leave your shoes behind!' They shouted with laughter as Sue disappeared to make the call.

After a few more glasses of champagne and a catch-up with Maggie and the girls, Sue appeared. 'They are going to put wreaths of yellow roses and gold flowers around the horses' necks. Plumes and whatever you want, Julie. For eight thousand pounds, they will put suits on them! Oh, and they are going to spray the horseshoes in gold!'

Everyone burst out laughing; this was crazy. 'Eight thousand for a couple of horses. Shit!' Julie could not believe the price.

'Nope, eight thousand for four white horses. If you are going to do it, do it in style.'

'You know what, I'd actually pay to see this parade – you're going to stop traffic!' shouted Jackie. 'This is going to be amazing. Oh God, I hope they don't shit on the road.' Everyone burst out laughing.

'And you're all coming – right?' Julie's eyes lit up as she watched them all jump up and down with excitement. She couldn't contain her enthusiasm any longer. Oh my God, this was going to be a day and a half. She was going to be Mrs Ralph Gold and he loved her. The very thought of it made her smile, without realising it. She felt very lucky and excited to be marrying him and was desperate to show him off to her friends. He was gorgeously handsome, with muscles to match. She felt like the cat who had just got the cream. *Julie Gold...* she mused to herself as she rolled her eyes to the ceiling. It sounded perfect.

21

A DEAD END

Inspector Linley had wracked his brains and followed every avenue open to him. There was no information on the streets. His usual suspects of a robbery like this were either in prison, dead or had rock solid alibis. His worst news was that the witness hadn't come out of his coma and had subsequently died.

They all agreed there was only one conclusion: the auctioneer had been responsible for the robbery – an inside job gone wrong. Obviously, he hadn't expected to have a heart attack and thought he would be sunning himself by now, but the evidence was stacked against him. It was his fingerprints on the gun. He had shot his colleague. He had also instructed everyone before the auction not to enter the room under any circumstances.

But it seemed justice had taken its own reward and the auctioneer was dead. After looking into his background, the auctioneer had been a desperate man who owed money everywhere as well as being an alcoholic. The forensics confirmed that even the water he had on his desk was vodka. And Inspector Linley knew that desperate men did desperate things. Even murder their own colleagues.

And so with no other leads to go on, and the only witness that could have given him a clue being dead, it was one of those robberies that had to be shelved, unless something else came to light.

* * *

Back in Ireland, Ralph felt more confident. He was interested to know about what was happening and to have a catch-up with Tom.

Three-Fingered Pete, as he was known, came to pick Ralph up and take him to Tom's camp. Pete was ex-army like Billy, and had been in the wrong place when a landmine had gone off. He had some burns on his face and body and had lost a few fingers, but he had survived and been discharged from the army. The pension wasn't much, so Billy had brought him with him, and Ralph liked army men working for him. They were disciplined; they were smart. They knew how to handle themselves. They were also grateful for the opportunity to earn a proper living again. The pensions they got and the accommodation they were offered seemed very meagre considering these men could be called upon any time to fight a war.

Many had mental health problems and couldn't get a job. But working for Ralph was something they could do. And that brought loyalty. That was all Ralph asked for. Each of them had different skills; that was also a bonus.

'How is Billy doing? I'd like to see him first.'

'He's doing okay now, Mr Gold. You know Billy, he always bounces back. That's why everyone calls him Tigger – you know, the bouncy tiger from Winnie the Pooh.'

'Yes, I've heard them call him that.' Ralph laughed. 'Well, we'll pop by and see if he needs anything and then I want to go and see Tom at the camp site, okay?'

'Sure thing, Mr Gold. Whatever you say.'

'Well, if you are doing what I say, call me Ralph, eh?'

A few minutes later, they arrived at Billy's place. 'Ralph, thanks for coming – it's great to see you,' Billy said, flinging the door open for them to walk in. Ralph was satisfied that Billy was his usual self again. He had taken a bullet for Ralph, and Julie and Ralph would never forget that.

'How you doing, Billy? You're looking well.'

'Few pints of new blood and a good seamstress at the hospital and I am on top form again. Just taking it easy and healing properly. Thanks for the private hospital. I appreciated that.'

Ignoring his thanks, more out of embarrassment than anything else, Ralph changed the subject and explained about the export business he had newly acquired. 'Everything is run properly, but now and again something might slip through the net – if you know what I mean.'

'Sounds good to me. Just say the word and I will have a whole truckload of the best guns you can imagine travelling wherever. I'm your man, you know that.'

After a little more light-hearted banter, Ralph asked about Paddy and his brother, Liam. Billy was always the source of information. If you wanted to know something, he was the one to ask.

'Liam, the bastard, is doing a long stretch. Can't believe he killed that poor barmaid. Paddy is still trying to fight his corner but has detached himself a little. Tom has made a point, or so I've heard, of making sure Liam has taken a few good beatings inside prison. Even the warders hate him. The publicans know you have their backs and seem just as happy with everything. You see, I still have my ear to the ground.' Billy laughed.

'Why do you think I came here first, you bloody scallywag? You're better than the newspapers. I'm going to see Paddy now. He's not in a position to haggle. Is he working with Tom or against him?'

'Definitely not against him. That mean bunch would tear him limb from limb. The banns have been read in church. They are marrying him off to that bird of his. Don't think she wants to marry Paddy but neither of them have a choice.'

Once Ralph had been brought up to speed, he was satisfied. 'Right, I will be in touch. You take it easy, Billy.' As an afterthought, Ralph asked. 'By the way, how is Norman settling in?'

'Who?' Now it was Billy's turn to look surprised. 'Who is he?'

'Must be my mistake; I thought someone mentioned a new worker.' Seeing Billy's frown gave Ralph more than enough reason to be happy. It seemed Tom or one of his associates had done what was required with Norman and buried his silence with him.

Walking into the pub where he knew he would find Paddy, Ralph was surprised that Tom was sitting with him. 'Am I interrupting, gentlemen?'

'Ralph, you're here. I knew you would come. I've missed you, mate. Any chance of a drink?'

Raising an eyebrow and walking away, Ralph went to the bar. Tom came and stood beside him.

'Everything okay, Ralph? Things are nice and quiet around here, just as we like it, and everyone is happy with the arrangement. That barmaid who was killed – I told the family you would help them out financially, as a goodwill gesture. That okay with you?'

'Absolutely. We'll sort that later. How come your new drinking partner is Paddy? I'm surprised.'

'Well, don't be. You don't think I'm going to let that little weasel out of my sight until he's married my lass, do you? He'll be out of here faster than a ferret up a drainpipe. No, he's under lock and key until the happy day.' Tom raised one of his black, bushy eyebrows, straightened his flat cap and turned to look at a forlorn Paddy sitting in the corner booth.

Ralph burst out laughing. This was Paddy's pay-up time. He was chained to Tom until the wedding and then he could do what he liked – within reason, of course. It was Paddy's worst nightmare.

'Am I still your best man? That means I'll have to come to London with you, doesn't it?' A hopeful Paddy looked at Ralph with pleading eyes as he returned to the booth.

'That depends. What's happening with Liam? Are you still defending him for killing an innocent woman with kids? All of that was partly your fault, Paddy.'

'He's a dickhead. You know that. He is a hot-head and I just went along with it. No harm done, eh? Pals, Ralph?' Reaching his hand out to shake Ralph's, Paddy knew at this moment Ralph was his only hope.

'You're my best man Paddy, but it depends if Tom needs you here.' Ralph was playing him at his own game, dangling him on a piece of string. He knew Paddy was desperate to have an excuse to leave Ireland.

'I might just come to your wedding myself, Ralph. Not been to London for a while. It would be nice to look around my old stomping ground and see some of the other families,' Tom said, and Paddy's shoulders sagged.

'And you would be most welcome. Have the council sorted the deeds to the land yet?'

'They said it would take about another six weeks, but I'm on it, don't worry. Your word is your bond. Their red tape has nothing to do with you.'

'As long as things are getting sorted, that's okay then. You know the wedding date and where I'll be. If you want to come, you know where to find me.' Standing up, Ralph held his hand out to Tom. 'Nice doing business with you, Tom.'

'What about your best man? Aren't we going to have a few beers and a singalong for your stag night?' Pressing the matter again, Paddy waited.

'Paddy, the only person who is going to see me stripped naked and put in handcuffs is Julie. Definitely not you and a load of jokers, thinking that is what you do on a stag night. By the way, what are you doing on your stag night?' Ralph couldn't resist a sly dig.

'Probably spending it with him and his shotgun.' Deflated and unhappy, Paddy nodded towards Tom. He was beaten and he knew it. It was easier to go along with it all. After all, just because he was married didn't mean he would have to change his lifestyle much. But it would get this lot off his back so he could have some freedom again.

'A word outside, if you don't mind, Tom. Hopefully see you soon, Paddy.'

As Tom joined Ralph on the pavement outside the pub, he felt he needed to ask. 'That problem with Norman I told you about. Did you sort it?'

'All done. He won't give you any more trouble, but I bet he gave my pigs bellyache. We met him off his aeroplane and told him we were dropping him off to his digs. End of story.'

'Thanks, Tom – we'll speak again soon. And that offer stands if you want to put Paddy on a leash and come to the wedding. You would be more than welcome.'

Rubbing his dark beard, with whispers of grey running through it, Tom nodded. 'You have a good trip. Go home to that woman of yours. There is nothing for you to do here; it's all in hand. If I need you, I'll let you know.'

As Ralph got to the airport, he felt this was closure. He knew deep inside that it would be years before he ever stepped on Irish soil again. He had a new future to look forward to now, with Julie.

* * *

The next day, back in London, Ralph decided now was a good time to go and see Charlie Jenkins. It was evening and normally a night-club in the West End would be in full swing. There were a couple of door attendants who greeted them, but the place looked miserable. On entering, Chris, who had driven Ralph there, couldn't believe his eyes, nor could he stop blurting out what was in his mind.

'For fuck's sake, this place could be a goldmine in the right hands. It's right on the corner, taking up both sides of the street. But it's a shithole.' Then he remembered himself and lowered his head. Ralph couldn't agree with him more. It was, as Chris put it, a shit-hole. All Charlie had done was bring his old crowd from his pub into his new empire. Same old overweight prostitutes and scum-bags. The man had no ambition. Painting on a smile, he walked forward to Charlie. 'How's everything going, Charlie?'

'Oh, hi, Ralph. Yes, things are going as planned. Not much custom around here, though. Not even with my strippers. But things will pick up,' he assured Ralph.

Personally, Ralph wasn't sure who he was trying to convince, but he didn't like Charlie's flippancy. He didn't seem to be making an effort in this place and it was time to shake things up a bit.

Walking through the back, Ralph knocked on the door. The spyhole on the door let whoever was inside know who was there, and they opened it.

Ralph was pleased to see that they were surrounded by boxes of money, which would be laundered through one business or another. At least this part of the business was working as it should, even if Charlie was doing a terrible job at running the club. After greeting everyone and making sure they had everything they needed, Ralph left. Waving his goodbyes to Charlie and avoiding another boastful drinking session, he got in the car with Chris.

'Chris, I want you to get one of the boys to go and see Marlon on the south side.' Seeing Chris's face drop, he nodded. 'Take this.'

Ralph took two thousand pounds out of his wallet and gave it to him. 'Give this to Marlon and tell him I want Charlie's pub shaking up a bit. Cause a little trouble to keep Mr Jenkins on his toes. Let's not let him think life is too easy.'

Puzzled and slightly worried, Chris took the money. He didn't ask why, because he knew Ralph would have his reasons. But hell's bells, that Marlon was a nasty person to cross.

* * *

As planned, there was no word from Carlos. The news was still full of the jewel heist. But thankfully, they seemed to concentrate a lot on the Arab prince and his assassins. Their embassy had been informed and they had allowed the prince to be flown back home.

That was when people had started making their own assumptions and stories about what had happened that night. Everyone was saying that the prince had planned the jewel heist and burglary himself. The coastguards had divers go into the Thames, only to find remnants of the helicopter and Dimitri, who had worked for the prince. They had sworn that the pilot flew off with the jewels. But they were nowhere to be found.

The prince had used all of his authority through the embassy until the police had no choice but to release his bodyguards from prison and into the custody of the embassy and flown back home. It all seemed to be brushed under the carpet by the government, which caused another outcry amongst the public.

No one even mentioned Julie. As merely a cleaner, she had been well and truly overlooked. The people at the museum embellished what had happened a little more each time they were interviewed on the television; no one knew what the truth was any more. It seemed that they had gotten away with the heist unscathed.

* * *

Julie's day in Liverpool turned into three. They had gone to a nightclub hosting a troupe of male strippers and Julie had been dressed in a makeshift veil and a pink sash with the words 'The Bride' on the front, which made her a prime target for the men's attention. It was the most fun she had had in years.

She explained to Sue when they were having a quiet moment that she had been in touch with Carrie, her old boss from the brothel, but that she had declined an invitation to the wedding, due to ill health. They had both known what that really meant – Carrie didn't want to look back and remember what had happened that night and seeing Julie would bring it all back.

During her stay, Julie had contacted Roland again and he was due to come in to dock the next day, so she waited for him. Standing at the quayside of Liverpool docks, Julie saw Roland's ship coming in. Cupping her hands around her mouth, she shouted, 'Roland! Captain Roland!' Watching him on board his ship, Julie felt a strange sensation. It was as though there were two ghosts at the side of Roland – one was herself and the other Frankie. Shivering slightly, although it wasn't cold, she almost felt like crying. Those memories of their time in Spain would stay with her forever. She and Frankie would both be dead by now if they hadn't escaped. Worked to death, beaten to death. Buried in some mass grave in the ground amongst strangers. The very thought of it made her blood run cold. Roland had been their saviour. God bless him. Brushing a tear away from her eye, she plastered on her famous smile and waved at Roland. 'Hey, handsome. Looking good, my man.' She laughed, even though her body still felt the pain from the past.

'Ahoy, pretty lady.' He waved from the deck of his ship and with a jaunty swagger, he jumped on dry land while his crew tied the ship up. When he stood up, he still looked like he was aboard ship, swaying back and forward like all seamen do.

'Oh, Roland, are you ready for the wedding? You have remembered, haven't you?' she almost shouted at him.

'Why do you think we've landed today? In three days' time, I am going to be giving you away. And that breaks my heart.' Play-acting the heartbroken lover, he hugged her.

'Well, you and your family have a room booked at the Hilton. It's all paid for and you can order and drink whatever you like. But I do have a favour to ask of you. Only you can carry it off, because everyone is so boring. I wanted to know what you felt about it.'

'You got me curious now. What's on your mind?'

Cupping her hand around her mouth, she whispered in his ear, only to be greeted by a deep, warm laugh, bellowing out across the harbour. 'Julie, my baby girl. If that what you want, then I will do it. You are one crazy woman, which is why that man of yours loves you.' Flicking his hands in the air and laughing some more, he walked with her to the café on the corner.

* * *

'Cor blimey, Julie, you look like you've had a good couple of days.'

Almost falling into the car behind Chris, Julie was exhausted. Although it was a good feeling of exhaustion.

'I'm fine, Chris. Just knackered, that's all. The girls threw a hen party for me. I never expected it.'

'It must have been one hell of a good one!'

'It was. Ten women alone on the town causing havoc with Ralph's money. Dreams are made of that stuff.' She laughed and Chris laughed along with her. 'You only get married once. Might as well make the most of your last night of freedom.'

'Well, in most cases. But I have a good feeling about you and

Ralph. You're soulmates. And for all his talk, he's well under your thumb – sorry.' Chris paused, thinking he had said too much.

'You're absolutely right. The key to a good marriage is letting Ralph think he's in charge and then do what I want anyway, while he thinks it was all of his idea!' They both burst out laughing again and Julie lit them both a cigarette. 'Did you sort the chef out? What did he say?'

'Oh God, Julie, you would think he had just died and gone to heaven! He's doing all kind of dishes and now he's seen that some of your guests are Jewish, he is putting that special kosher stuff and vegetarian dishes on. I told him what you said about having something to eat for everyone all day and he is beside himself. Fucking over the moon, he is. Harrods are putting extra stuff on your wedding list because everything else has been bought. Christ, if you ever get skint you could sell some of it.' Again, they both burst out laughing. The wedding present list was as long as her arm and it had been exhausted already. She couldn't believe it.

'Everything else is in place, even the Rolls-Royce for Ralph and a large coach to take everyone from the wedding to the reception, though I presume a lot will have their own drivers. I'm going to miss this wedding. It's kept me busy for days. It's been great fun.'

'Oh, don't worry, I'll find plenty for you to do. I know I haven't told you before, but you have been brilliant. I couldn't have done half of this without you.'

Looking up into the rear-view mirror, Julie could see him blushing and decided to ease up on the compliments. He was a good kid and pleasant company. That was why she was going to ask Ralph if he could be her driver full-time. She knew that would please him and she also knew Ralph wouldn't say no.

Opening the door to her exclusive apartment, she paused. Many times she'd opened a door to her bedsit and dreaded opening it to a dump with a gas meter in the corner. Everyone in the building used to wait for someone to put some money in the meter and then they would all rush and cook something or have a bath. The money soon ran out.

This time she was opening the door to sheer luxury. This was her home. The first real one she'd had. Suddenly, sadness engulfed her. She would have liked her mum and Frankie, her beloved sister, to be at her side on her wedding day. If only things had turned out differently for them all.

The sight that greeted her warmed her heart even more. Ralph was lying full length on the sofa with little Josh on his chest and stomach, fast asleep. She loved them both so much.

'You okay, Julie?' Reaching for the remote control, Ralph turned the volume down on the television.

'I'm fine. In fact, I couldn't be better. Did you miss me, you old sod? Chris says everything is ready for the wedding. In addition, he told me the chef is delighted that I trust his genius.' Sitting with her legs up on the sofa beside him, Julie rested her head on his chest beside Josh. 'I like your hair when it's all wavy and loose on your head. You have lovely black hair. You're a very handsome man.'

'Oh God, you're throwing out compliments. That means it's going to cost me.'

'No, just a weak moment. I'm tired and you're looking very handsome. Where's Sophie?'

'I told her to take the day off; she's a good woman and deserves some time to herself.'

'Do you want to fool around a little? And have a day off of our own?' Smiling, she winked at him.

'Well, that's a proposal I never expected before the wedding night. But if you're offering…' Reaching out for her, he held her chin and kissed her. Which led to another kiss and then a strong need for each other. Josh was laid gently in his cot, so as not to wake him. It seemed a long time since they had shared each other's bodies, and they revelled in it, slowly caressing each other with words of love as Julie stroked and marvelled at Ralph's strong, muscly arms and bulging biceps. Her body was set on fire while he stroked and manoeuvred above her.

Some time later, they were woken by Josh's cries. Ralph looked at his watch. 'Better get up, Julie, it's 6 p.m. You've used my body long enough.' Throwing back the duvet and putting his dressing gown on, Ralph went to put the kettle on and see to Josh. Turning around, he looked at Julie lying flat on her back with her head resting on her arms. 'Are you sure you are okay?'

'Never better, Ralph. Believe me, never better.' For the first time in her life, she knew what contentment meant and she wanted to savour every moment.

22

WEDDING PLANS

At last, the big day was nearly upon them. Chris had been sent to Liverpool to pick up the dress and accessories and Sue, Maggie and all of the girls had turned up at the Hilton where they were staying with Julie. Everyone was bubbling with excitement. It was to be a real grand affair – no expense spared.

'Come and see the reception hall and dining room, girls, it's fantastic. This lot have worked wonders.' The reception rooms were fitted out in white and gold with long pieces of gold material wrapped in bows around each chair. The staff were still bringing in large vases of flowers and decorating around the room.

'There must be around two hundred chairs in here; this place is enormous.' Sue couldn't believe her eyes. There was a senior waiter or 'butler', as Sue called him, watching everyone put out the cutlery. He measured the distance of each in turn with a long wooden ruler.

'What is he doing?' Jackie whispered.

'It's something about silver service protocol and the distance between the knives and forks. They all have to be in line with each other down the table. He's in charge of all of the staff,' said Maggie, giving them all the benefit of her experience.

They were all in awe; they had never seen anything like it. Looking up and seeing them, the maître d' walked towards them with the black tails of his coat swaying behind him. 'Can I help you, ladies?' His dominant presence made them cast sideways glances at each other. They felt like naughty schoolgirls who shouldn't be here.

'I'm Julie, soon to be Mrs Gold. We just popped down to take a look around if that's okay?' Although hesitant, she held out her hand to shake this tall, greying man's hand. Surprised at her gesture, a frown crossed his brow. Ladies didn't normally shake hands with the staff. To make her feel at her ease, he took her hand and kissed the back of it, making her slightly blush. She felt out of her depth and she realised he knew it. He had worked with the upper classes all of his life; she had barely sniffed the hems of their dresses.

'Let me show you around, ladies. We hope you will like what we have done. Obviously, none of the drinks are out yet. All of the champagne is chilling. The flowers are all in place and will have ice cubes put into them tonight.'

'Ice cubes?' Julie looked around at the others. They all seemed lost for words.

'Yes, ma'am, the ice cubes will slowly melt into the flowers and keep them moist. The air conditioning will be put on tonight to keep everything cool and fresh. We have laid a present on the tables for each of the ladies and the table planner will be at the front of the room. That way everyone knows where to sit. The gold and white helium balloons will have your initials on them and will be central on the tables with a posy for the ladies. Everyone will have a goodie bag.'

'How do you know who is sitting where? I never did a table planner.' Now it was Julie's turned to look confused.

The maître d's gravelly voice seemed to bellow out, full of

authority, 'Well, you and Mr Gold will be on the top table at the front on the stage where everyone can see you and your immediate guests or family. I believe there are no family guests?'

'No. No direct family, just close friends.' This made Julie wince inside. She had no family. She had written to her mother telling her about the wedding but there had been no response. Julie knew her mother couldn't come but it would have been nice for her to wish Julie luck on her big day.

Reaching into his breast pocket, he took out a large piece of paper. 'We were left this at reception when Don Carlos left us.'

Accepting defeat, Julie smiled. Of course, Carlos had decided which of his 'families' would be sitting next to who. After all, half of the people that were invited she did not know. These were Ralph and Carlos's friends and colleagues.

'Come and see the ballroom, ma'am. I hope it is to your liking.' They all followed him as he clicked his fingers at two waiters standing nearby. 'Ballroom,' he instructed. Two men went rushing forward and opened up two double doors.

They all gasped. It was a huge ballroom; in one corner, a small orchestra was set up. The white marble flooring made the room look even bigger. There was a huge bar at the far side of the room and the bartender was behind it cleaning glasses.

'Dear God, Julie, this is something out of this world. I've never seen anything so grand. Look at the size of that piano; it's beautiful,' Maggie said. All of the women split up and were walking in different directions as staff rushed past them with trays of glasses or cutlery. Each of them was mesmerised by the hugeness and glamour of it all. It was all hustle and bustle to get ready for the big day.

'You've done an excellent job – erm, sorry, what was your name again?' Julie almost felt weak at the knees. She had given them a free hand, simply because she didn't know what to choose. But they had taken her at her word and it looked fantastic!

'Henry, ma'am. If there is anything you need changing or adjusting, just let me know.'

'Nothing, Henry. It's perfect just the way it is.' She smiled, looking around the room and then back at him. As they looked at each other, there was appreciation in both of their eyes. Henry was flattered Julie liked his choices and Julie was flattered that he had done such a wonderful job. It was very classy and she knew in her wildest dreams she couldn't have planned this. It was sublime!

Walking out, Julie left Henry and his army of waiters to work their magic. 'I don't think I know two hundred people to invite to my wedding,' mused Lisa. 'Oh God, Julie, are there going to be loads of handsome men here? You know what they say. Everyone meets their future partner at a wedding.'

Although still a little stunned, Julie laughed along with them. 'Well, you'll have a real mixed bunch to feast your eyes on. There's every nation eating at those tables tomorrow. Take your pick.' Encouraging their laughter more, she linked her arms through Sue and Maggie's. 'Time to try the spa, ladies, and get a tan. Come on, I'll race you!'

* * *

The sun was shining as Julie drew back the curtains and filled the room with light. She opened the window and lit a cigarette. Switching on the little kettle, she made herself a coffee, then went and sat by the window looking out at everyone going about their daily routine. She wanted these few minutes to herself.

Finally, it was her wedding day and as sure as she was about marrying Ralph and knew that she loved him deeply, she still felt nervous. Butterflies were in her stomach. What if he changed his mind and didn't turn up? What if he was having second thoughts? All kinds of things were racing through her mind. The morning breeze chilled her somewhat and she pulled her dressing gown around her. She couldn't stand it any more; if Ralph had changed his mind, she wanted to know. She didn't want to be made a fool of at the altar. Picking up her mobile, she rang him. Instantly, he answered. 'Sorry, Ralph, were you asleep?'

'No, I'm always up at the crack of dawn – you know that. Why, what's wrong?'

'I just wondered if you were nervous or getting cold feet.' Her voice was barely above a whisper and her heart was pounding in her chest.

'For God's sake, Julie, I always worry when you're left to your own thoughts. It usually ends up with mischief or you overthink things. I love you; I am the luckiest man alive, even though Carlos thinks you are my penance for all my wrongdoings.' He laughed.

'I just wanted to ask. I would rather you told me now. We don't have to get married; we can stay as we are if you want.'

'You are going to be my wife if I have to handcuff you to the altar. But if you're having second thoughts, say so. Let's not prolong this.' Ralph paused. This was his worst nightmare and would break his heart. He wasn't good with words, he knew that. But Julie was everything to him and he didn't know how to get that through to that crazy head of hers.

'I've no doubts, but I just wanted to give you a get-out clause. I'm a very lucky woman. It's not just the money. I don't want you to think that. It's you, Ralph; you're the only person who has ever cared about me and I know I can be a temperamental pain at times.'

'Well, I love my tempestuous woman. Life is never dull with you around. You keep me on my toes. Now go and have breakfast with the girls and show me this amazing dress you've been going on about. God knows what we we'll have to talk about when we're married. It's all been wedding this and wedding that.' Ralph laughed, trying to soothe her. She was worried and he knew it. She did not want marriage to spoil things between them. They were good together. 'Stop worrying, Julie. It is strange, I know, but this is the commitment I want. The rest is up to you.' They were both nervous, Ralph even more so now that she had brought the subject up. It seemed she was having doubts. 'Will you be there? I mean, is it worth me going to the church?'

'Yes, I will be there; it is just a big step. It's okay for you – you've been here before...'

'No, I haven't. I was married, yes, and she was a decent woman, God rest her soul, but even she would agree we didn't get married out of love for each other. It was just the right thing to do and that is all. This time I'm marrying for love and it feels very strange, I know. Stop worrying. Enjoy your day.'

'Thanks, Ralph. I just needed to hear your voice. Sorry, love. I'll see you soon.' With that, she ended the call, took a deep sigh, threw her cigarette butt out of the window, and closed it. Then she turned and looked towards the window and her jaw dropped. Thank God they were so high up; no one would know it was her, especially if it hit someone.

It was time to get married!

23

CHARLIE'S DEFEAT

'Ralph, you should hear this. That bloke's wetting his pants. Everything all right?'

'Sure, Dennis, just a bit of business, that's all. Now tell me more about Charlie Jenkins' pub. Is it such a bombsite?'

'Worse. That Marlon and his men didn't kill anyone but they shot the place to pieces, scaring the shit out of everyone. He was at the West End club and got there as fast as he could. There are bullet holes in the wall outside. He must be shitting himself. Someone has spray-painted "grass" on the windows.'

'Let's listen to his answerphone message again.' Ralph turned on the answerphone to hear Charlie's shaky, frightened voice shouting down the phone. 'Help me, Ralph mate, that south-east mob are shooting my place up. God knows why. You have to help me. It will be your place next.'

'Is that what you wanted?' Dennis looked up and saw Ralph smile and nod at him.

'Let's go and see Mr Jenkins and then we will go and see Marlon. This is all turning out very nicely. All that has happened and he only has me to turn to. What about his friends in the force?'

'They were swarming all over the place. They know it's a turf war but no one was killed or beaten. Just scared the hell out of them.'

* * *

The door to the club was locked and so Ralph knocked and waited with Dennis. 'Who is it?' a voice shouted through the door.

'It's Ralph; you wanted to see me.'

Ralph and Dennis frowned at each other as they heard furniture moving and bolts being moved from the door. Slowly, it opened slightly and one of Charlie's men popped his head around the door.

'Well, are you going to let me in or what?'

Furtively glancing around, Charlie's minder opened the door wider to let them in, then shut the door behind them, putting the bolts back on the door. Ralph cast a sideways glance at Dennis. This was a frightened man and frightened men did stupid things.

Suddenly, Charlie lunged forward and grabbed Ralph's arm. 'Ralph, in the office now. They are trying to kill me. That fucking Marlon and his lot. They've shot my place up. Next time they will shoot this place to bits. You need to stop them. After all, this is your place.'

'Tut tut, Charlie. This isn't my place. It's yours – your name is above the door. And this sounds like blackmail. I haven't done anything; why do you think this mob are after you?'

'Because they shot my fucking place up, that's why!' Shouting and pacing around his office, Charlie lit a cigarette. 'You can take the heat off, I know you can. We might have sold the odd drugs here and there, but nothing on their turf. I swear. If you don't help me, I'm leaving this place. Fuck you and fuck your deal. I know what's going on around here; I'm not even allowed in my own yard space.'

'So you sell drugs, do you?' Ralph pulled up a wooden chair and sat down. All the curtains were closed and the place was almost dark. The only light in there was the end of Charlie's cigarette burning down by the minute as he inhaled as much as he could.

'Everyone does it. It's spare cash and brings the punters in. But nothing like that Marlon does. I haven't crossed him, Ralph, and I don't know why he's doing this. Maybe it's got something to do with this place and you?'

Angry at this stupid, frightened man, Ralph nodded to Dennis in the darkness, who instantly stepped forward, put a clear plastic bag over Charlie's head, and pulled it tight. Charlie pushed and struggled, almost falling off his chair but Dennis held the bag tightly over his head. The bag inflated and deflated as Charlie panted for breath, and slowly the breathing became slower.

'Take it off.' Standing up, Ralph searched for the light switch and turned on the light. Once the bag was removed, Charlie was on his knees, gasping for air and holding his throat. 'Don't you ever threaten me again, Charlie. You deal in shit, you expect to get shit. But don't bring my name into it again. Do you have a gun in here?'

Still gasping for air and holding his throat, his eyes bulging from near suffocation, he pointed at the drawer in the desk. Walking around the desk, Ralph opened the drawer and, wearing his leather gloves, took out the gun. Checking to see it was loaded, he nodded again at Dennis.

'No, no, God help me,' Charlie shouted as Dennis kicked him and pulled the plastic bag over his head again and held it tight. Ralph knelt down and held the gun in Charlie's hand. Looking up, he saw Charlie's minder, who was standing there, helpless, looking on at the horror before him.

'Were you there the night Mick was shot or when Jason disappeared because Charlie's wife couldn't keep her knickers up?'

'No, boss.' He held his hands up in submission. 'Nothing to do with me; I wasn't there.' He paled as he looked again at the bag over Charlie's head and heard his slow, laboured breathing.

'Oh well, this is going to hurt you more than me.' Placing the gun in Charlie's hand, Ralph pointed the gun at Charlie's minder. He began to run but Ralph pressed Charlie's finger on the trigger. A shot fired and Charlie's minder fell to the ground, shot in the back.

'Take off the bag.' Taking the gun from Charlie's hand, Ralph stood up and watched Charlie gasp for air. His eyes were watering and he was coughing. 'I know you killed Mick and Jason so this is an eye for an eye. Don't ever try and blackmail me, Charlie; it's not good for your health. That's a nasty cough you have there.' Ralph dripped with sarcasm. Charlie was lying flat on his back, gasping for air. 'Help him up, Dennis,' Ralph ordered.

Dennis helped him to his feet and sat him on the chair opposite Ralph. They waited.

'This is insurance. You can get rid of the body; I hear you are good at that. But this gun stays with me. It has your fingerprints all over it and if you ever cross me, this gun will find its way into the local police station. Don't ever fuck with me again. As for Marlon, well, he's a good friend of mine and I will have a quiet chat with him to take the heat off you. But be warned: come after me and my boys and Marlon will put you through the mincer whether I'm dead or not. A friend of mine does meat imports. Lots of cows and sheep hanging in the back of his freezer lorry. He had a body hanging up in there on a meat hook once and it took the police three days to thaw him out before they could identify him.'

Resuming his normal breathing, Charlie's eyes widened with fear. 'Who are you?' His voice was husky and dry.

'I'm your worst nightmare with no conscience. You're going to carry on running this place as agreed. The arrangements are the same, all profits are yours. Everything we launder through this place is ours. Keep your mouth shut and your head down and you will live to fight another day. Find him a drink, Dennis.'

Dennis returned from the bar with a glass of whisky and put it down in front of Charlie, who grabbed it and swallowed it back in one, putting the glass down again and letting out a huge sigh.

'What do you want from me, Ralph? And what about him?'

'I want you to be a good boy, Charlie. Carry on as you are, but don't take me for granted and think I am a fool. The next bullet will be yours. As for him, maybe I will bury him somewhere, but you are coming with us to dig his grave. Possibly alongside Jason's, eh?'

Charlie knew he was beaten; he nodded. This man had him from all angles. If he killed Ralph, the south-east mob would kill him. And if he started a turf war with them, he would be killed without a doubt. It was better having the devil on his side than against him.

'Bring your car around the yard; we'll put his body in the boot with you. Don't try anything, Charlie. It wouldn't look good. A body in the boot of your car and a gun with your fingerprints on.'

'I wasn't going to. Let's just get rid of it, okay?' Still slightly shaky, and hoping his legs wouldn't give way beneath him, Charlie stood up and took his car keys out of his pocket. Dennis escorted him to his car. The two of them picked up the dead man's body and put him in the boot of Charlie's car, while Ralph looked on.

Getting in the car with them, Charlie drove them to a remote woodland. Getting out, he opened the boot and waited for Dennis to help him lift the man's body.

'Is he still breathing?' Charlie looked up at Dennis as they dragged the man through the woods, pulling up leaves and plants along the way. Dennis shrugged and carried on walking.

'Start digging, Charlie.' Ralph took the spade out of the boot of the car and threw it towards him.

'I think he's still breathing, Ralph.' Charlie looked around at a stony-faced Ralph and a bored-looking Dennis, then started to dig into the soft soil. Within half an hour, while Ralph sat on a tree trunk, Charlie had dug a shallow grave.

'Roll him in.'

Hot and sweaty, Charlie wiped his brow with his arm. He was frightened. How did he know they weren't going to put him here? Was he digging his own grave? His shoes were full of mud and his suit was stained with blood and mud. Bending down, he rolled his friend's body into the shallow grave and stood up.

'Okay, you can fill it up now. You're right, I think he is breathing a little.'

Dennis looked at Ralph, puzzled. The dead man wasn't breathing. He was definitely dead, but Charlie's mind was playing games.

'But – we could save him. I swear he's still breathing.' Tears started falling down Charlie's face as he tried wiping them away with his mud-stained hands.

'You either fill it up or we leave you here. That's up to you. I haven't got much longer; I have an important meeting to get to.'

Little by little, Charlie shovelled the soil back into the grave, all the while glancing up at Ralph and Dennis. 'Spread some leaves over it, and then it won't look disturbed.' Ralph waited while he grabbed an armful of leaves and threw them about. 'Time to go. Open up as normal tonight. I'll go and have a word with Marlon. A job well done. Let's go.'

Relieved to be walking out of there in one piece, Charlie got in the car. He couldn't wait to see the back of Ralph. This was a nightmare. As they drove back up to the club, Ralph took a black bin liner out of his pocket. 'I want your clothing, Charlie. Shoes, trousers and jacket. The whole lot. This has his blood and your sweat all over it. That's worth a good twenty years of any prison sentence.' Doing as he was told, Charlie stripped in the yard and put his clothes in the bag. He was beaten.

As they drove home, Ralph felt pleased that he now had Charlie exactly where he wanted him. 'We have so much on that prick; he'll dance to our tune for the rest of his life. You burn your clothing, get rid of everything. You have blood on you, Dennis. Is there anyone at your house?'

'No, the wife and kids will be at her sister's. They go shopping every Saturday together. I'll get rid of everything right away. What about you?'

'I haven't got anything on me apart from a little mud on my shoes. That's easily sorted. Will you come to the reception later and have a drink with me and Julie for our wedding day?'

'Yes, thanks, Ralph. The wife is looking forward to it. That's another thing she will be doing... yes, probably going around the shops with her sister to try and find another dress to wear. Bloody hell, every time she walks through the door she has another outfit. She normally orders them from the catalogue and then sends them back after she's worn them, cheeky cow!' They both burst out laughing.

Ralph took out his wallet as he got out of the car. 'Here, Dennis, put that towards your wife's new outfits.'

'I wasn't hinting, Ralph. Just conversation, that's all.' Humbled by Ralph's gesture, Dennis looked embarrassed.

'Take it. Call it a bonus; you've done good today. See you later.'

Waving Dennis off and waiting for him to leave, Ralph took his own shoes off and put them down the chute to the rubbish bins. His shoe prints were never going to be found in that woodland, he was sure of that. And he always made a point of wearing leather gloves.

He looked at the time and realised he'd better hurry up and get ready. He didn't want to be late for his own wedding. Julie would kill him!

24

MR AND MRS GOLD

Adorned in her beautiful wedding dress, Julie had to stand sideways to get out of the hotel room door. It was beautiful. The tightly fitted bodice was decorated in delicate pearls. The numerous underskirts filled out the satin dress, decorated with diamanté. It was stunning. Sue had curled her blonde hair and put it up, leaving wavy wisps at each side of her face. The huge tiara held a veil trailing down the back of the dress and onto the floor. The front piece of veil went as far as her shoulders. There were yards of netting down her back and it was all full of small diamanté stones.

As the lift opened and Julie stepped out, the entire hotel seemed to stop what they were doing. Reception staff leant over the desk to see this vision in white. Sue and Maggie were holding her train at the back and the dress made her look like she was floating on air.

The manager snapped his fingers and porters came running forward to hold her train up, while others opened the doors for her. Some of the other guests stood up and gave her a round of applause, shouting 'Good luck,' and 'Congratulations.' Julie beamed smiles at them. This was a day that all little girls dreamt of. To feel and look like a princess on their wedding day.

As she walked through reception, Julie caught a glimpse of herself in the mirrors. She couldn't believe the reflection of the woman that stared back at her. Who was this woman? It wasn't Julie from the slum estate. It wasn't the prostitute who did what she could to survive. This blonde woman before her looked healthy and happy. Her face flushed with excitement, highlighting her blondeness. It was a woman she would envy, but it was Julie. The girl that all the teachers from school said would come to nothing. Well, they were all bloody wrong! And she had proved that. Secretly, she wished that they could all see her adorned in this beautiful gown, about to meet her prince. None of them would have a wedding like this in their wildest dreams. This was the icing on the cake. She'd never felt happier. She would remember this moment for the rest of her life. Winking at herself in the mirror, she turned towards the admiring crowd and smiled as they applauded her. She felt like shouting out, *Watch out, world, Julie's here and she is going to be pure gold!*

Sitting in reception, waiting for her, was Roland. His family were at his side but he stood up to take Julie's arm. She almost burst out with laughter.

'Is this what you wanted, golden girl?' Roland did a twirl. He was dressed in his grey morning suit, but instead was wearing a gold jacket with tails. This was what she had asked of him and he loved it. 'You look fantastic, Captain Roland. Thank you.'

'I can't have you outshining me, girl. Look at you, all glittery and white. How many jewels are on that dress, girl? Hell, if they were real, I'd say you'd taken that prince's jewels.'

Julie gave a weak smile; he didn't know how close to the truth he was. After saying hello to his wife and daughters, Julie waited. Roland's daughters were dressed in gold bridesmaid's dresses, which looked beautiful against their ebony skin. 'You look beautiful, ladies. Thank you for loaning Captain Roland to me for the day.'

'I've had him for years, Julie babes, but remember, he's only on loan until you get your own man.' Roland's wife burst out laughing. She was everything Julie would have expected. Her laugh was as warm as Roland's and bellowed out amongst the reception area. That big, warm smile seemed to take over her face.

'Well, Julie, your carriage awaits.' Roland waved his hand towards the open glass doors. Julie looked up to see four white horses and a round glass coach. It was not actually glass but it looked like it and was polished to perfection. The yellow and golden plumes from the horses' heads looked amazing. The coach drivers also had gold plumes in the sides of their top hats. Their red livery and silver buttons as they sat on their seats high up above the horses looked stunning.

Everyone at the hotel craned their necks to see out of the doors. This was a spectacle in itself. Now all it needed was the bride.

'Oh, Sue, thank you. Thank you so much.' Holding out her hand, Julie squeezed Sue's.

'Shut up, you'll make me cry. You look beautiful. And what is more, you deserve this.'

Sue stood there in her bright pink dress suit with the largest round hat. It was almost like a flying saucer.

'Thank you, everyone, you all look great.'

'We better had. We've put all our outfits on Carlos's bill.' Sue laughed. This made Julie laugh aloud even more. It took four of them to help her up the steps into the coach with Roland and, riding through the streets of London, Julie gave her best royal wave as people stood on the pavements watching her pass by.

The limousine with Sue and the girls in drove slowly behind them. It was a grand affair. Nearly all of the London traffic came to a halt.

Considering the morning he had had, Ralph stood outside the church nervously having a cigarette with Carlos.

'Do you think she will come? She seemed a bit weird this morning. It sounded like she was getting cold feet.'

'She'd better; do you know how much this is costing me?' He laughed, trying to make Ralph more relaxed.

'That bad, eh? I'll go halves with you, Carlos.' Ralph felt bad that Carlos was picking up the bill for Julie's extravagance.

'Don't be ridiculous, Ralph. I'm allowed to moan about Julie. She's a pain in the arse, but I like her. And little Josh looks nice in his wedding suit. I like that.' Carlos had seen Sophie with Josh in his buggy. It amazed Ralph how such a man as Carlos would notice a baby's suit. 'Any sign of Paddy?'

'I've heard from him. Their aeroplane was late so they are coming straight from the airport.'

Carlos shook his head in disbelief. 'I need to mingle; there are some families I need to speak to. See you inside.' Carlos was just about to walk away when he looked up and saw the white horses turning down the road.

'What the fuck is that?' Carlos stood there, amazed. They both stood rooted to the spot as they watched the glass coach approaching, being pulled behind the horses. 'Come on, Ralph, we'd better get in; the circus is in town.'

The church was full to capacity with standing room only at the sides. With a little straightening out from Maggie, Sue gave the thumbs up and the wedding anthem was played on the organ. With Roland on her arm, Julie slowly walked down the aisle.

She could hear people gasp when they saw her wedding dress and this was the effect she wanted. Carlos made his excuses and told everyone he was standing in as best man, which the other families accepted. Julie looked through her veil at everyone in the pews. It looked like it was Mafia amnesty day.

Ralph joined Julie at the front. He wanted to laugh when he saw Carlos purposely put his dark sunglasses on, but now wasn't the time. She looked amazing. Beautiful. He wouldn't have expected anything else but glamour and sparkle from Julie, but she had certainly got her pound of flesh out of Carlos and was determined to make this day memorable. People would talk about this wedding for years to come.

All was well until the vicar asked for the rings. Julie turned in horror to Ralph. She had forgotten the most important part of all! With one thing and another, they had totally slipped her mind. She was about to take off one of her engagement rings when Carlos stepped forward and took two ring boxes out of his waistcoat and laid them on the red velvet cushion. 'You missed your chance, Julie; these I haven't paid for.' Pulling his glasses down to the end of his nose, he looked at a horrified Julie and, raising one eyebrow, grinned. Touché; now he had his own back. That horrified look on her face was worth every penny!

Ralph shook his head and smiled. He knew she'd forgotten about the rings when she hadn't marched him to the jeweller's or asked for his ring size. This was his input to the arrangements. He'd gone alone and picked the biggest wedding ring he could for Julie and a standard one for himself. He had been unsure about handing them to Paddy in case he made a hasty retreat and pawned them. Thankfully, Carlos had stepped into the breach and had been delighted to have a little revenge on Julie.

Once they were pronounced man and wife, they kissed and were about to turn around when a rabbi stepped forward. Everyone was confused and started nudging each other. Members of the Jewish mob Ralph associated with had insisted he have a blessing from one of their own. After a few Hebrew words, a glass was wrapped in a white cloth and laid on the floor. Julie looked at Ralph, not sure what to do. Raising his foot, Ralph stamped on it, breaking the glass. 'Mazel tov,' a group of men shouted from behind Ralph and started clapping.

As they walked up the aisle, stopping every now and again to shake hands with people, Paddy ran through the doors. 'Ralph, mate, I'm sorry. Bloody aeroplane. Didn't you wait for me?'

Tom nodded at Ralph and shook his hand while Julie glared at Paddy. Even though he had his wedding suit on, it was clear he'd got quickly dressed in the taxi there. His shirt was still hanging out of his trousers and he was trying to push it in as he spoke. His face was flushed and it looked like he hadn't combed his hair.

'You can fuck off, you scruffy bastard!' Julie snarled. 'Bloody hell, he's always on time when someone else is buying the drinks.'

Ralph reached out to shake Paddy's hand. 'No problem. Come on, let's all have a drink. I've just got married.' Ralph wasn't letting anything spoil his day and this only added to the fun of it. It was true what they said; you couldn't make a silk purse out of a sow's ear. No matter what Paddy wore, he still looked scruffy.

The photographers and the video men taping the wedding followed them every step of the way and as they walked down the steps of the church, everyone threw confetti.

'Can I be in your photos, Ralph? After all, I am the best man,' shouted Paddy.

'Yes, I suppose so. You can stand at the end so we can cut you off.' Julie laughed.

Standing on the steps of the church, everyone posed for their photos and then started making their way to their cars and the coach that had been laid on for them that would take them back to the hotel where they could enjoy a drink at the free bar – thank you, Carlos!

Carlos and Marco stepped forward. They wouldn't miss seeing Ralph climb into that glass coach for anything. The pair of them stood there laughing as he tried to find a space to sit near Julie's dress. Everyone was in high spirits as the sun shone on this glorious day, even though some covered their eyes as the glare of the sun on the diamanté dress dazzled them.

'Well, we've done it, Mrs Gold.' Ralph squeezed her hand and kissed her. He was overjoyed. This beautiful, crazy woman was all his. 'Do you like your wedding ring?'

'Oh, Ralph, it's lovely. I would have picked this exact one myself. It's so wide and big. It will make everyone pea-green with envy.' Her loud cackle filled the coach.

'Don't laugh like that; you'll scare the horses.' They both burst out laughing and Ralph sat back in the coach as Julie waved to people standing on the pavements in awe of this marvellous procession.

As they rode through the busy streets, Ralph looked at his new wife and thought back to a conversation he'd had with Carlos about the wedding rings.

'Well, you can buy those yourself. That's why she isn't bothered. Go to this jeweller, and buy the one you think is the most over-the-top and gaudy. Because you may hate it but Julie will love it.'

'Are you saying she has bad taste?' Ralph had laughed at him. 'After all, she's marrying me.'

'You said it, Ralph. She is like a magpie; the bigger and shinier it is, the more she will love it. Our Julie doesn't do modest. Get her another engagement ring as well; that will keep her sticky fingers busy.' Handing Marco and Ralph a whisky, Carlos had picked up his own and raised his glass in the air. 'To Ralph, the bravest man alive. May you never have a day's peace with our Julie!' They'd all chinked their glasses together and burst out laughing. It was true. Being married to Julie would be anything but boring.

'While you're waving, Julie, don't you think you need some extra sparkle?' Sitting back and seeing her excitement as she waved to everyone filled him with joy.

'What do you mean? Do you think this dress needed a bit more glitz? Some of them stones on the back don't half hurt my arse. They are pressing into me.'

Ralph handed her a box. 'Try this for size. The others were a preliminary offer.' He grinned.

Opening the box, Julie was puzzled. It was a beautiful ring, but the stone was black. 'What is it?'

'That, my lovely wife, is a raw, rough diamond. The darker they are, the more expensive they are. That is what you are, Julie. My rough diamond and priceless to me.' Leaning forward, he kissed her. He couldn't ever remember feeling so happy as he did now.

The horses were nearly at the hotel when Julie shook her head out of the small window. 'Oy, you two up there. Drive around again – I want my money's worth!' Ralph shook his head; he couldn't help smiling. What had he just said about a rough diamond?

By the time they arrived at the reception, everyone else was there. Armies of waiters were walking around with silver trays of champagne and hors d'oeuvres amongst the guests, greeting them as they walked in.

Everyone was ushered into the reception room, each one of them reading the table planner as they walked through the doors. Their nameplates and menus were on the table, just to make it more intimate. Everyone had a choice of dishes. There was no fixed meal. As master of ceremonies as agreed with Ralph, instead of the label of best man, which could cause some resentment amongst other colleagues, Carlos announced the bride and groom – Mr and Mrs Gold. Everyone stood up and gave them a round of applause.

With Julie and Ralph placed in the middle of the top table on the stage, Carlos and Marco followed them and took their places beside Ralph. Sue and Roland sat beside Julie with Josh and Sophie at the end. Poor Paddy was at the end of the table next to Marco, who couldn't hide the distaste he felt.

Paddy stood up to make a speech once everyone had eaten more than enough, and Julie glared at him. 'Well, ladies and gentlemen. What can I say about Ralph and Julie? Believe me, I could tell you a few stories,' he began as he swayed back and forth, having consumed far too much alcohol. Marco pulled his arm sharply and sat him back down in his seat, giving him a slap around the back of the head, much to everyone's amusement.

The sound of the pianist wafted from the next room as background music, so that people could talk without being drowned out, and to prevent any deadly silences while they were eating.

Each in turn, the Italian side of the room stood up and formed a line towards the steps of the stage to greet Julie and Ralph. They shook Ralph's hand and kissed Julie on the cheek, then handed them a bulging envelope.

Taking each one in turn, Julie was puzzled and didn't know what she was supposed to do, so she thanked them and cast a sideways glance at Ralph.

'It's money, Julie. This is their custom to get the newlyweds on their feet with their new home and expenses,' Ralph whispered in her ear.

Trying to stop her jaw from dropping, Julie looked at the mountain of envelopes. She had stopped putting them on the table and Henry had instantly stepped behind her with what looked like a pillowcase. He had obviously seen this kind of thing before and Julie was grateful for his help.

Not wanting to be outdone, the Jewish mob stood up next and did the same. Each envelope seemed fuller than the last one. Ralph leant towards Julie and kissed her cheek. Again, he whispered unnoticed, 'The higher you are, the more you give.' For once, Julie was at a loss for words.

Leaning towards Ralph, she kissed him back, 'if all we needed to do was get married, why rob banks?' She laughed. The atmosphere was electric. Everyone was laughing and joking. The room buzzed with excitement, even beyond her expectations.

Hitting his glass with his spoon, Carlos stood up. His warm, Italian voice stopped everyone. 'Sorry for interrupting you, ladies and gentlemen. If you don't mind, firstly I will speak in Italian.' He then spoke to one side of the room in Italian. It was clear by his body language that he was thanking them for coming to Ralph and Julie's wedding. Then he turned to the other side of the room where the Jewish mob were sitting and spoke in Hebrew to them, doing the same. Each table stood up and cheered. Then he turned to the front of the room and spoke in English. 'Julie and Ralph, what can I say? A beautiful couple with a fantastic journey ahead of them in their married life. Ralph is our brother and so Julie is now our sister. I have a small gift for you both.' Reaching over, he handed a brown A4 envelope to Julie. 'Open it.' He nodded.

Opening it, she saw a glossy portfolio that looked like a holiday brochure. In the bottom of the envelope was a set of keys. Turning to Ralph, Julie looked at Carlos, puzzled. 'Have you booked us a honeymoon, Carlos?'

'No, Julie. I've bought you a holiday villa in Italy. That is the details and the deeds to it.'

Stunned, Julie looked at Ralph and they both walked towards Carlos. 'Thank you, Don Carlos.' Julie could feel the lump in her throat rising and a tear brimming on her eyelashes.

Accepting Julie's thanks, Carlos turned to Ralph and put his arms around him. 'You are not Italian, Ralph, but you are my brother. I love you.' Ralph and Carlos hugged each other for all to see. This was the highest acclaim Carlos could have given Ralph. The Mafia boss of the families had just announced Ralph as his brother. Ralph's heart nearly burst with pride. He could feel his own tears in his eyes and quickly brushed them away.

'Everyone, please join me in a toast to Don Carlos,' Ralph

shouted, raising his glass. The room exploded in applause and noise as everyone chinked their glasses against each other's.

More corks popped from champagne bottles until everyone was asked to go into the ballroom. Huge chandeliers hung from the ceilings, lighting it up, and the orchestra began.

'Who is the man in the gold jacket, Ralph?' Carlos asked once he had made his way to the bar. He liked champagne, but now he wanted a real drink.

'That's Julie's friend Captain Roland. They go back a long way. He has a trawler of his own and does freelance import and export.'

Raising one eyebrow and smiling, Carlos ordered another drink. 'A ship of his own, *comprendi, sì*? Business is business, Ralph, even on your wedding day.' With that, Carlos took both drinks and headed over to Roland. A captain with his own ship was worth knowing.

'Mr and Mrs Gold will now step onto their dance floor for the first dance of the evening,' Henry announced.

Ralph took Julie's hand and led her onto the dance floor. 'I can't even get near you in that dress, let alone dance with you.' He laughed.

'Oh, come on, Ralph honey, it's not the first time you have pushed hard enough until you got were you needed to be.' Slightly tipsy, Julie laughed as Ralph did his best to waltz her around the room to their favourite John Denver song.

Cheek to cheek, Julie whispered in Ralph's ear, 'Your mum was a busy woman, wasn't she? A Jewish, Irish son with an Italian brother!' This only added to their laughter, although at the mention of his mother Ralph looked sad.

Instantly noticing that faraway look in his eyes, Julie apologised. She could have bitten her tongue. 'Sorry, I didn't mean that; it's just me being flippant and my Liverpool sense of humour. We are going to send your mum a video of the wedding and one of the layers of cakes. She'll enjoy that, won't she?' She held him as close as she could, considering the wire basket under her dress made it a little awkward, and saw the smile appear on his face again.

Everyone joined them on the dance floor, and the party went on into the early hours. It had been a fabulous day. Now every morsel of food had been eaten and every champagne bottle had run dry, everyone started saying his or her goodbyes.

'Where is Paddy? I haven't seen him in ages.' Ralph looked around the room but couldn't see him. It wasn't like Paddy to walk away from a free bar.

'Oh, he was getting a little loud earlier so I punched him and knocked him unconscious and then Marco took him up to his room. I have to say, these rings really come in handy. Christ, did he go down on the floor with a bang! Served him right, mouthing off like that.' Julie picked up her drink and chinked her glass against Ralph's, who instantly paled at the thought. On her wedding day, dressed as a princess, she had turned into a boxer and punched Paddy on her way out of the ladies'. Why the hell was he surprised?

'Have you enjoyed your day? Was it what you wanted it to be?' Ralph felt it was time to change the subject.

'Oh, it's been a great day. Everyone is pissed and fed. And we're safe in the knowledge that Paddy has been silenced, thanks to my good right hook.' Kissing her fist, Julie put her arms around Ralph. He wasn't sure whether to dodge her or not! Not when she was in a fighting mood. 'Time for bed, Ralph. If you're hoping for any funny business, I am too knackered. You can consummate the wedding in the morning.'

'Believe me, Mrs Gold, I don't have the energy and I'm too pissed to raise it.'

25

IN-LAWS

'What time is it, for Christ's sake? Do you always have to sound cheerful in the morning? God, have I just signed up for years of you whistling in the bathroom?'

'It's midday, Julie. I've been down and had breakfast with some of our guests before they left. I've taken another shower to sober up a little more and I want you to get up as well. I have an extra surprise for you.'

A smile crossed her face as she plumped the pillows beneath her head. 'Why don't you come and lie beside me and give me my surprise, then?'

'No, not that. Though I will do my husbandly duties later, but first I need you to get up – we're going out.'

Staggering into the bathroom, Julie sat down in the shower with her back against the wall and let the water run over her. God, she felt awful and her head was banging. 'Get me something for this hangover,' she shouted through the door.

Ralph was sitting on the edge of the bed in the honeymoon suite when she emerged and was urging her to hurry up.

'Christ, where's the fire? What's your hurry?'

'Come on, it's now or never. Chris has got the car outside and is waiting for us.'

Getting in the car, Julie put on her dark sunglasses. Today the sun made her feel worse, unlike yesterday. 'So what's the big mystery, Ralph?'

Ralph raised his fingers to his lips and sat there in silence as they drove. He was pleased Julie had fallen asleep again behind her glasses, otherwise she would have been moaning her head off. As they neared the prison gates at Holloway, Ralph told Chris to stop. 'Julie, wake up.' Nudging her gently, he waited until she took the glasses from her eyes.

'Where are we?' Looking around at the huge grey walls, she squinted her eyes to see more clearly out of the car window. 'It's a prison.'

'Come on, this has taken a lot of arranging. We don't have long.'

Following his lead, Julie walked slowly behind him, not knowing what to expect. Holding Ralph's hand, she saw two prison wardens standing to greet them and then they opened a small wooden gate and stepped inside. Unsure of what was happening, Julie sobered up quickly as they seemed to walk forever through gates, being unlocked and locked again. Eventually they were shown into an office.

'Mr Gold, Ralph, may I be one of the many to wish you congratulations on your recent nuptials.' Standing up, the thin, slightly balding man greeted them.

Shaking his hand like an old friend, Ralph turned to Julie. 'This is Gordon Mackintosh, the governor of the prison. He has kindly offered to help me with my request. Is everything in place, Gordon?'

'It is. Everything is in the secretary's room next door. Why don't you and I have a drink in here? I always keep a bottle of good malt in the filing cabinet.'

Ralph turned to Julie and held her by the shoulders. Seeing the perplexed look on her face, he knew it was time to put her out of her misery. 'Julie, your mystery tour is over. I've arranged for your mother to have a day release here. She's in the next room. I thought you would like to see her. I hope I've done the right thing?' Worried, Ralph looked at her as her face paled. She just stood there staring at them both.

'My mother is in the next room?' Julie turned to each of them for confirmation. She couldn't believe her ears. Ralph had brought her mother from a Liverpool prison to see her? Her legs felt weak and she had to sit down and gather her thoughts. She was numb. She had wanted to see her mother and now she could, she felt nervous and the palms of her hands were sweating. Rubbing them together to dry them, she shook Gordon's hand. 'Is it true? You've brought my mother here?'

'Gordon is a member of the masons' lodge I attend. He kindly offered to help me in my plight. I thought it would be a nice surprise for you – did I do wrong, Julie?' Frowning, Ralph felt it maybe wasn't such a good idea now. When he'd spoken to Governor Mackintosh about it, over a few drinks, it had seemed like a good idea. After lining his pocket, the governor had arranged everything, but she had to be back in Liverpool before lights out.

'Do you want me to come with you?' asked Ralph. He could see she was nervous.

'No. I want to go alone first. Maybe later.' Trying to find words, Julie looked towards Gordon. 'How long do we have? Oh, it doesn't matter.' She shook her head. 'Does she know why she is here? I mean,' Julie stammered. 'Does she know I'm coming?' Inside she was freaking out. She had begged her mother to send her a visiting order to no avail and now she was sitting in the next room.

'No. We couldn't take that risk. This is all top secret, you understand?' Gordon looked at Ralph. 'I do hope there won't be any trouble. I've put myself on the line for you.' Gordon felt uneasy. The last thing he needed was some planned escape. Ralph had given his solemn word and a huge pay-off to Gordon and promised that there would be no problems.

Ignoring them both, Julie walked forward and turned the handle of the door and walked in. Her mother was sitting with her back to her and turned slightly as she heard the door.

'Julie? Is that really you?' She squinted, moving closer to see her. 'I hardly recognised you. Did you arrange all of this?'

'Mum,' was all she could say as she stood rooted to the spot for a moment. Julie looked across at this grey-haired, old woman. She wasn't as she remembered her. Many times she had thought about her mother, but she had always pictured her as she was when they were at home together. Here she was wearing the prison-blue uniform and looked thin and pale, and her eyes were dull and empty.

Suddenly, Julie ran forward. With all of her need and love consuming her, she threw her arms about her and hugged her. 'Mum, I've wanted to see you for so long. Oh God, I've missed you.'

They hugged each other tightly; Julie didn't want to let go. That familiar scent of her mother hadn't disappeared through the prison's smell of disinfectant and bleach. She loved her and she knew her mother loved her too. They were both cut from the same cloth. Neither of them wore their hearts on their sleeve, but this was different.

Eventually she let her go and kissed her on the cheek. They both stood and stared at each other. Breaking the moment to stop the tears, Julie's mother changed the subject. 'Do you have any cigarettes? I'm gasping for one.'

Julie took out her packet of cigarettes, sniffed and concentrated on the job in hand. Emotions were running high. 'Here, Mum, I'll pour us some coffee if you want some.' This was Julie's chance to compose herself. It had been so long since they had seen each other and they both had buried their emotions deep within them.

'Why have you done this, Julie? You know I don't want you to see me like this. This is not the place for my little girl.' Lovingly, Anna reached out and ran her fingers through Julie's hair. 'I like the new look. It suits you.' She laughed. 'Maybe I should try it myself. You know what they say, love, gentlemen prefer blondes.' Anna looked at the young woman before her. She hardly recognised her, she looked beautiful and so grown up. She'd come a long way from the old estate, but then she always knew she would. Her Julie was that kind of woman. She could deal with anything you threw at her and come out smelling of roses. She was strong and ambitious.

Julie poured two coffees as tears rolled down her face. This was not the happy reunion she had always pictured, seeing her mother in prison uniform. She didn't know what she'd expected, but the very idea of having to leave her here broke her heart. Now she had a better idea how Ralph had felt when he had visited his own mother. 'Did you get the money I've been sending you? Did Gertie pass on my messages? She didn't want to come to the wedding; she said she was too old to travel.' Nervously, Julie put the cups on the table. There were buns and biscuits, but neither of them felt like eating.

'Yes, thanks. I appreciate it; you're a good girl. And thank you for looking after Frances's troubles. I was never there for her when she was alive; what was the point of visiting her when she was dead? You were her mother, Julie. You always put Frances before yourself, but didn't I tell you that I didn't want you visiting me? I want you to move on with your life; that's why I'm here. It was too late for me to change, but I knew you would make me proud. I have newspaper cuttings of you on my cell wall. They don't believe you're my daughter!'

'Really?' Surprised, Julie beamed a smile. Her mum had pictures of her on her wall. As grim as that sounded, it was music to her ears. They had both moved on and she felt she had done right by her mother. She wanted to prove to her all her sacrifices hadn't been for nothing.

'I'm sorry, Mum. But you'll be out soon. I have money now and I can buy you a home and truly look after you,' Julie pleaded.

The room was filled with silence as they eyed each other up. Eventually Anna spoke. 'This husband of yours – what's he like?'

'He's a good man. He's wealthy, but that's not the point. He looks after me. He's generous with his heart. Granted, his money is a bonus.' Julie laughed. 'But, Mum, he could look after you too. We both could...'

'Does he know about your past?' Anna waved her hand at Julie to stop her from butting in. 'Gertie put me in the picture; I know how you earnt a living to look after yourself and Frances. But it bothers me, because if he doesn't, he will soon find out and then what if he dumps you? Try and be honest with him. If he loves you, he will understand. If he doesn't, well, you can walk away with your head held high without getting in too deep. Don't let him break your heart, Julie. I've been there, got the T-shirt.' Blowing her cigarette smoke into the air, Anna waited. Her voice was low. She didn't mean to sound offensive, but she was the only one who could speak to Julie like this.

Wiping her tears away and sniffing, Julie nodded. 'He knows I'm no virgin. But nobody is at my age, are they – unless they're nuns.' Julie forced a smile. 'Do you want to meet him, Mum?'

Her mother inhaled on her cigarette again and blew the smoke into the air, pausing. Yes, she wanted to meet this man who her daughter obviously loved. God knows, her Julie wouldn't have saddled herself with a has-been – he must have something very special.

Getting up, Julie opened the door and held out her hand. 'Ralph, come in.' She was upset and her eyes were full of tears again. Her face was flushed from the scolding she had just received.

'You'd better go in, Ralph.' Governor Mackintosh gave a weak smile and nodded towards the door.

Taking stock of the situation, Ralph scolded himself. This was a bad idea. He'd thought it would please Julie. He wanted to give her her heart's desire, but all he'd done was stir up demons inside of her and brought all her painful memories back. Painting a smile on his face, he breezed into the room and instantly stopped. He was shocked. Anna, Julie's mother, was the spitting image of Julie, apart from the hair colouring. They looked so alike it was untrue. Maybe that was the problem. They both seemed stubborn in their own ways, but their eyes and the shape of their faces were uncanny.

'You must be Anna, my mother-in-law.' He laughed. 'Well, I've come for your approval. I'm Ralph and it's good to meet you.'

Ralph's cheerful exterior did not impress Anna. Her face didn't move and she ignored the hand he'd held out to shake hers for the moment.

'Save the Irish blarney, mister. I know who you are. We get the newspapers in prison. And it's Mrs Forbes to you until I say so. Got it?' Reaching for another cigarette, she pushed back her chair so she could get an even better look at Ralph.

Mentally, Ralph knew this was the original Mexican stand-off. She was definitely Julie's mother. The cold glare from those eyes sent chills down his spine.

'This was all my idea, Mrs Forbes. I thought it would be nice for you both. Julie talks of you often and has been desperate to see you. Stupidly, I thought I could help. That's my job. To look after my wife and make her happy.' Forlorn and spying across at Julie, he knew he'd lost this battle. It was time to leave.

'All you've done, Mr Gold, is prove just how corrupt and greedy the authorities are. How much did you pay him out there to use his office for my prison visit? He's more corrupt than me and yet I'm the one in prison uniform. Bloody joke, really, isn't it?' The loud cackled laughter she let out was definitely Julie's. Raising one eyebrow, Ralph looked across at them both. 'You'd better sit down now you're here, Ralph. It's cost you enough, I presume. Might as well make the most of it. Julie, pour some more of that coffee and bring it here.' Anna was satisfied with what she saw, but, as the mother-in-law, she wasn't going to let him off too lightly. She may be in prison but she was still Julie's mother.

Wiping her tear-stained face, Julie poured the coffee and put the cups in front of Ralph and her mother.

'So, you got married yesterday.' Reaching out, she picked up Julie's hand and looked at the array of rings on her fingers. 'Nice selection you have there, love. Usually when a man buys a woman so much, it usually means he is making up for his shortcomings.' She winked at Julie and gave that all-familiar laugh. Ralph winced. Now he knew where Julie got her famous sarcasm from.

'Don't you think I deserve it, Mum?' She winked. After a short silence, Julie tried again. 'Josh is doing well. He's living with us.' Eager to please, Julie rambled on. This was a different side of Julie that Ralph had never seen. She desperately wanted her mother's approval and seemed to have reverted back to a schoolgirl.

'Poor little mite, he didn't stand a chance. I'm surprised he survived. Sorry business, Julie. It was a whole horrid affair.'

'Here, Mrs Forbes, I asked the photographer to print out some quick photos for me from the wedding. Maybe you would like to see them.' To Julie and Anna's surprise, Ralph took an envelope out of his jacket pocket and laid it on the table.

Begrudgingly, Anna took them and opened up the envelope. Then she burst out laughing and her whole face lit up. 'Horses! Bloody horses. Oh my God, Julie, who do you think you are – a bloody cowboy? Can I keep them, Ralph?' Holding them to her chest, she smiled. It was the first genuine smile Ralph had seen from her. At least he'd done something right, it seemed.

Now the ice was broken, time passed quickly and then there was a knock at the door. Ralph stood up and opened it. They all knew it was the governor; there was no one else it could be. He whispered to Ralph at the door. They all knew what this meant.

'Our time up Ralph? Has your money run out?' Anna snapped.

'You have a long journey back, Mrs Forbes. You need to leave before you're missed. It's been nice meeting you.' Holding out his hand to shake Anna's, Ralph was surprised when she leant forward and hugged him.

'Take care of my baby. She's all I have left.' Her eyes brimmed with tears but she held them back.

'I will, Anna, and I will take care of you. Send some visiting orders to Julie. I will see that you're comfortable in prison and have everything you need. When you come out, which I believe will be sooner than you thought, we will buy you a home of your own and you don't need to worry about money. Just spend some time with your grandson and daughter. How does that sound?'

'You've done your homework, Ralph.' She winked at Julie. 'Yes, the parole board are coming and there is talk about me being released, but I haven't got my hopes up. It's something you don't want to think about until it happens. Unless you're going to grease a lot of palms.' Giving him that all-familiar Julie wink again, she grinned.

'You're coming home, Mum? When?' Rushing forward, Julie put her arms around Ralph and her mother. 'Group hug, everyone.'

Anna stopped her short. 'Now, don't get excited, Julie. Nothing is certain until I walk through those gates.'

'Yes, but you will have an address and a family. Surely that will go in your favour. It will, won't it, Ralph?' Julie pleaded. She wanted this more than anything. And she would move heaven and earth to make it happen.

'We'll see what happens.' Anna lit another cigarette. 'Tell her, Ralph, nothing is for certain in life but death.'

'We'll see you soon, Mrs Forbes, and you can start thinking about whether you would like to stay in Liverpool or move to London with us. You can count on that.' He smiled and returned her wink.

'I think I would like to try London. Be near my family.' Turning around, she hugged Julie. It was an emotional moment as tears fell from both their eyes. Discreetly, Ralph backstepped out of the room. This was their time and it had been a long time coming.

'Bye, Mum.' Julie kept blowing kisses as she walked out of the door. 'See you soon.' Elated, she left the door ajar and stood beside Ralph.

'Hey, Mr Gold. You can call me Anna now,' she shouted through the gap in the doorway.

This last comment pleased Julie immensely; she squeezed Ralph's hand tightly. Her mother had given her approval and liked Ralph. Everything was coming up roses. After her wedding, this was the second-best day of her life!

'Thanks, Anna, or should I call you Mum!' Ralph shouted and was greeted by a well-worded 'Bollocks!' as they left.

Julie was skipping like a teenage girl. She kept going over the conversation and was discussing where her mother would live and what furniture they would buy for her. She wanted to pinch herself; it felt like a dream and she didn't want to wake up.

26

THE CIRCLE OF LIFE

Running from room to room, Julie looked around their new holiday villa in Italy. It was amazing, more like a mansion than a villa; Carlos had outdone himself with this one. It even had staff to wait on them and cook their meals. Julie was beside herself with happiness and mentally couldn't wait until the time her mum could come and stay with them in this wonderful country. Sun, sea and sand – it would be just the thing to rejuvenate her after her time in prison. 'Oh God, Ralph, I have to try that swimming pool; let me get my costume on. This is living. And it's all ours to come and go when we please. Check those documents again – I want to be sure.'

'Julie love, it's ours, all ours. Although there is one downside to all of this you haven't taken into account. Don't you realise this is Don Carlos country? We're nearby should he ever need us. He's not stupid.'

'Oh, sod him, I don't care. This is fantastic: a honeymoon in our own private villa with that lot in there cooking and cleaning for us. What more could you want?'

Apprehensively, Ralph coughed. 'Well to start with, tonight we are expected to dine with Carlos and his family. You will meet his fiancée and…' Wagging a finger in her face, he laughed. 'Be nice. She has come from a very closely guarded family. She's not up to speed like you.'

'Yeah, I get it: the virgin queen who is going to create the heir and spare and then get packed off while he runs amok with his mistresses,' Julie mocked.

* * *

Soaking up the sun and making love by the pool, she was definitely making hay while the sun shone. But now it was time to get dressed and go to Carlos's family home. Inwardly, Ralph cringed. If Julie thought this place was a mansion, wait until she saw Carlos's house. It looked like a castle. No sooner were they ready than the long black limousine rolled up and parked on the driveway.

This was a whole new way of life, and she knew she had a lot to learn, but learn she would. She was like a sponge and would soak up all this etiquette. Long gone was Julie from Liverpool. This was Julie Gold, property owner and a rich businessman's wife. Time to move on. There was a big world out there and she was determined to make her mark on it.

Greeting them at the doors, which was an honour in itself, Carlos showed a mesmerised Julie around his home. It was very impressive, although she didn't compliment his ego too much. She felt he could do that for himself.

The long, oval table in the dining room hosted a lot of friends and family. This was no intimate dinner as Julie had thought. Don Carlos was introducing her and Ralph to the other families. They were now so deep in with organised crime, there would be no way out. Acceptance was a big honour amongst the families; Ralph already knew that. But during their morning he had warned her repeatedly to keep her big mouth shut and to make no sarcastic retorts. Sitting at the table, he crossed his fingers, hoping that his words had sunk in.

Maria, Carlos's fiancée, was young, petite in frame and very beautiful. Her long hair shone like black ebony down her back. Her simple, blue, chiffon dress only heightened her beauty and small frame even more. She had definitely been cherry-picked from the Sicilian side of the family. This cemented all family business and loyalty.

Julie liked her instantly, simply because there was nothing to dislike about her. She was warm, friendly, and genuine, and her modesty preceded her. She could see why Carlos had chosen her. She would be the home-maker, the wife and the bearer of his children. She would never know any of his business and he would never share it. Julie doubted she would ever step outside of Italy; this was her lot in life and as much as Julie liked her, she didn't envy her – not all prisons had iron gates.

Dinner was a relaxed affair, but finally the evening came to an end. Once everyone had eaten their fill and said their goodbyes, Carlos waved Maria off with her chaperones and gave a sigh of relief. 'Come into the lounge; we can have brandy and cigars in there.' Brushing back his own black hair off his face, he led the way to one of the many rooms and threw himself on the sofa, kicking his shoes off and stretching full-length.

'Now we can relax.' Marco handed the brandies around and, given the nod from Ralph, Julie lit a long-awaited cigarette. She was gasping for one by now, but Ralph had given her firm instructions that you do not light your cigarettes up at the table while you are eating. This was another mental note she made in her head that would set her in good stead for the future.

'Right, let's get to business.' Passing around an envelope each, Carlos commented on the job they had done. 'Here are your payments. The insurance company have paid up with some of the items I offered them. Believe me, they were more than happy to have them back. You will notice, Ralph, your money will be less than we agreed.'

'Why? I did everything I was asked to. Granted, some of it didn't go as planned. So what is the problem?' Ralph paused and waited.

'Mine had better not be short. I was a bloody cleaner putting my hands on shit and narrowly escaping with my freedom,' Julie interrupted. She didn't like the idea of going through all of that and being ripped off, villa or no villa.

Carlos laughed. 'I wouldn't dare cheat you, Julie. You would cut my Italian balls off and I am very fond of them.' Then on a serious note, he looked at her, deciding now she needed to know not to insult him in front of anyone else. 'Have I ever cheated you, Julie?' Carlos's eyes darkened and his mood changed. His carefree laughter and Italian insults stopped and in place was a well-articulated voice, dripping with sarcasm. 'Even though the bill for your wedding seemed to climb higher and higher, did I ever criticise you?'

Ralph looked daggers at her; Carlos's temper was slowly rising. It was always on the surface and just needed the touchpaper lighting.

'No, Don Carlos. Just me joking. Sorry.' Backing down off her high horse, Julie blushed slightly and looked down at the carpet. Satisfied with her respectful apology, Carlos carried on. He liked Julie, but he couldn't have her outbursts in front of his other associates.

'Ralph, I have put some of your money and my own into a casino in Las Vegas. My friends own many casinos out there and they have given us the chance to buy shares into it. Believe me, an opportunity like this doesn't come around too often. But it is a show of good faith on all sides. Casinos are also an excellent place to launder money.' Looking very pleased with himself, Carlos sat back on the sofa again and blew the smoke from his thick Cuban cigar into the air.

'I'm honoured you thought of me with such an offer on the table, Carlos. That was very kind of you.' From experience, Ralph knew how to speak to Carlos. Standing up, he walked forward and kissed the ring on Carlos's hand. '*Grazie*, Don Carlos.'

Flippantly, but grateful for the respect Ralph had shown, Carlos waved his hand in the air. 'It was nothing. We are brothers. Do you remember the marble egg, Ralph? That has set us in good stead for future dealings. We have earnt respect and the world is our oyster.'

'Marble egg?' Confused, Julie couldn't help interrupting. She had heard nothing about this, but seeing Ralph nod and smile intrigued her.

'Yes, the marble egg Ralph stole for me. Above all possessions, our Arab prince valued it the most. It is priceless and a long-standing family heirloom. I flew over there and, once I was granted an audience, I gave it back to him and his family.'

'What?!' they all shouted in unison. Ralph couldn't believe his ears. Marco had to sit down and stared wide-eyed at Carlos. Julie was still puzzled by this revelation. But she knew by Ralph and Marco's faces it was something important.

'I like the bigger picture. We could never have sold it, but to take it back to its rightful owner, saying that it had by fair means or foul come into my possession and I felt it should be given back to him, has opened many doors. He knows we could have done anything with it on the black market. Smashed it, used the jewels, anything.' Carlos shrugged nonchalantly. 'But instead we have shown great loyalty. So much so, we are invited to dine at the palace next month. None of our cargo shipped over there will be checked and he will always be on our side. Granted, he can never come back to England, but he doesn't want to. This has exonerated him with his parents and he is bloody grateful!'

Silence fell as Julie, Ralph and Marco looked at each other. It made good business sense. The marble egg meant nothing to them, but it meant a whole lot to the Arab prince and his family and for that they would be eternally grateful. Carlos was like a cat. Whenever he fell it was always on his feet.

'I know, I'm a genius.' Carlos stood up and took a bow. 'Apart from in return, and as much as I refused, he wanted to give me twelve million dollars to cover my expenses. Okay, not pounds but who the hell cares. It's legal money with the royal crest on the cheque!'

Stunned, the three of them sat there, wide-eyed, as Carlos unfolded his story. They couldn't believe their ears. This just got better and better.

'Last, but not least, my good friends. This also clears us of any blame of the robbery. If we were thieves, would we not take our booty back to the owner and ask for a ransom? As far as the authorities care, we are all friends, all suspicion gone. And he is the only one with blood on his hands.'

Carlos's chest swelled as Ralph stood up and started a round of applause, quickly joined by Marco. This really was a stroke of genius. And to make things even better, it opened up a whole new set of contacts to do business with. No wonder he was Don Carlos and they were plain old Ralph and Marco.

Although Julie was listening to Carlos's ego filling the room, she was too busy opening her own envelope. It was better than expected and her jaw almost dropped, but not wanting to give any more satisfaction to Carlos, who was preening, she just nodded her thanks and put the envelope into her handbag. Inside of her head, the numbers on the cheque spun around. Ten million pounds. Dear God, how much had Carlos got for all of the stuff? This was incredible. And was more money than Julie could ever have hoped to wish for. Finally, she was set for life.

* * *

Their two weeks in Italy flew by and soon they were flying back to their home in London and back to reality.

'We're home,' Julie shouted to Sophie, but there was no reply. 'She must have taken Josh out. I'll see if she's left a note.' Looking at the pile of mail on the side, she found her note from Sophie, but also spotted one with 'HMP' stamped on the front. 'It must be a visiting order from my mum.' Ripping it open to read it, Julie stopped short and burst into tears.

Taking it from her, Ralph read the sympathy letter. It seemed there had been a riot at the prison and, during the scuffle, Anna had fallen down the stairs, breaking her neck. She was dead. Julie was distraught and Ralph didn't know how to comfort her. Immediately, he contacted the telephone number on the letter. Once he had been put through to the governor's office, he was told the same sorry story and asked what arrangements they wanted to make for the funeral.

'At least you got to see her, Julie, and make up your differences.' He was at a loss for words. Tears rolled down her face and she became hysterical, shouting at him that she was due out soon. He knew all of this but there was nothing he could do. She kept reproaching herself that while they were enjoying themselves in Italy, her mother was in the morgue. Eventually, she cried herself to sleep.

* * *

Back in Italy, Carlos and Marco were enjoying a drink. 'Well, Marco, I presume they will know the bad news now. Don't forget to be full of surprise and sympathy if Ralph telephones you. I doubt he will, but you never know.'

'Was it really necessary to have Julie's mother killed?' Marco was saddened by the whole affair. He didn't like it. He could see Carlos's cold, calculating reasoning, but it was heartless nevertheless.

'It was better when they weren't in touch and it should have stayed that way. Ralph and Julie have moved up in society; they can't have a skeleton like her mother in the cupboard. A murderer in prison. Who would accept her at their table? The newspapers would make a meal of it and their reputation would be blemished. No, this was the only way. They have a future ahead of them and nothing can hold them back now. Anna Forbes was just unnecessary baggage. Ralph would have thought so too, once he took off his rose-tinted glasses.'

Dismissing a disgusted Marco from his office, Carlos sat with his head in his hands for a while. Being the head of such an organisation meant making decisions, some good and some not so good. It wasn't the first time he had got rid of the dead wood in Ralph's life and deep down he hated himself for it. But he had set Julie and Ralph on a new path. No one looked backwards, only forwards, and he consoled himself with that.

* * *

Not knowing what else to do to help Julie in her grief, Ralph contacted Sue. She turned up within hours to look after Julie, who was inconsolable. Ralph felt helpless. He had his suspicions about the situation but nothing concrete. Everything just seemed too coincidental. It was better not to air them to Julie, so he was grateful to Sue, who sat holding her hand and giving her support while he arranged the funeral.

It was a sorry affair in a cold draughty church for the cremation. Ralph asked Chris and some of the others along to bump up the numbers. He'd sent a car for Julie's old neighbour and lifelog friend, Gertie, who seemed to howl and cry through the proceedings.

He didn't realise it yet, but the worst was yet to come. As Julie leant on Sue as she came out of the church, Ralph noticed blood on her leg. 'What's that? What have you done?' He pointed. Suddenly Julie paled and then fainted.

Once she had been rushed to the hospital, the doctor eventually came through to Ralph and apologised. 'Why are you apologising? What is wrong with Julie?' Fear gripped him. He thought she had done something stupid and tried ending her own life.

'I'm afraid she's lost the baby, Mr Gold. Didn't you know she was pregnant?' Apologising again, the doctor walked away.

Ralph's head was spinning with this new bombshell. Pregnant? Julie had never said a word. Going into her room, he stood beside her bed and held her hand. 'When were you going to tell me, Julie?' was all he could muster. He felt like crying. This was their baby and they had lost it. His mind wandered over all the stupid things they had done recently and wondered if any of those things were to blame for this mishap.

Julie's wide-eyed, mascara-stained face looked up at him. 'I'm sorry, Ralph. I wanted to wait until after the three months. It was going to be a surprise.' With each sob that wracked her body, there was another apology. Sue was on hand, and comforted them both, saying the usual things people do in these circumstances. But Ralph didn't know what to say. He was beside himself with sadness and anger. He could buy anything he wanted, but he couldn't make this right. Excusing himself from Julie's bedside, he went to the toilets and broke down in tears. They would both remember this day for the rest of their lives.

27

THE UNTOUCHABLES

'Morning, sweetheart.' Bending down, Ralph kissed a hungover Julie at the breakfast table and put down a newspaper.

'What the fuck is this?' Bleary-eyed and with the remnants of last night's make-up still smeared on her face, she picked up the folded newspaper. 'Since when did I read a newspaper in the morning?'

'Happy anniversary, Julie. It's paper. It's the symbol of a year of wedded bliss.' Ralph laughed. His love for her hadn't dwindled one bit. If anything, it had got stronger. Especially now, after partying all night; she was always a grumpy cow in the mornings and that only made him laugh more.

'Do you have to be so cheerful in the mornings? You get on my nerves. Whistling in the shower and down the stairs. Fucking hell, you sound like a budgie on heroin or something. She looked down at the newspaper with disgust. 'So, this is it, all of this time putting up with your whistling and all I get is a fucking newspaper. Oh, I see you have written "happy anniversary" at the top of it. That's big of you. Tight-fisted bastard.' Julie was just about to throw it at him when she saw something fall out from the pages. Even through her drunken stupor, she knew what diamonds looked like. A slow smile spread across her face as she unravelled a three-tiered diamond necklace. Quickly, her mood changed. 'Oh, Ralphy love, this is lovely.'

'I forgot to mention diamonds are also a present given. Are you going to wear it at the party tonight? You do know they are throwing you a surprise party?' Raising one eyebrow mockingly, Ralph waited. He half expected the newspaper to come flying across the table anyway. Ralph looked at the necklace Julie was admiring so much. It was the one he had taken from the robbery and he had kept it hidden long enough for it to be forgotten. But now the time was right. Everyone expected Julie to be wearing diamonds. It looked just like her other necklaces, but he knew different. This was his bonus from the robbery. Everyone likes a bonus!

The butler came forward. 'Very nice, madam, if I may say so.' He stood at Julie's side and handed her the usual paracetamol and liver salts for her hangover. 'Would you like a prairie oyster, madam?'

'No, I fucking wouldn't, not unless it has pearls in it. Why are you so cheerful has he raised your wages?' Julie snapped. She was not a morning person and thankfully all of the staff in their manor house knew this. They still had their apartment in the Barbican; it was handy and local for when they were in London. But they now owned a seventeen-bedroom mansion, with acres of land, complete with butlers, cooks and maids.

'Don't mind her, Jarvis. I'll take my usual breakfast. Just keep pouring coffee down her throat.' Ralph laughed as the butler walked up to his end of the table and handed him the freshly ironed newspapers.

'Why are they throwing a party? They don't give a shit about me. It's all to impress you, Ralph. All the men work for you and I hold court with their fawning wives, who bore me shitless. All the rock stars and would-be entertainers bore me and the police commissioners and MPs are the only funny entertainment there with all of their bullshit. Their pompous ways and their charity nights get on my nerves. You are the police, Ralph. You own them. You are the one that pays their wages. They make me sick!'

'Off you go now, Jarvis, I can see to myself.' Ralph brushed the butler away and gave Julie a harsh look. 'Not in front of the staff. Our friends in high places are respectable men, who I do business with. It's worth the money, believe me. They are so desperate to get their hands on more of it, they will agree and help us with any request I make. I know it's double standards but that is the world over. If you have the power, then use it.'

Folding his own newspaper, Ralph showed Julie a picture of herself entering a club in her designer dress, playing up to the cameras. Everyone loved her and loved reading about her and her witty comments to the press.

'Julie, I don't know what your problem is. You are one of the most photographed women in London. You are the envy of most women in the world, with your designer clothes and jewellery. You treat Asprey like a toy store. You're good friends with all the socialites and you gamble to your heart's desire in Las Vegas. You are always ahead of the game with your clothes; none of them can keep up with you and most try and copy you. But why does it feel like this isn't enough for you?'

Secretly, Ralph knew why. He had been so busy lately, he had been neglecting her. He was now on boards of directors' meetings for large companies and his once tiny unit of import and export was now a worldwide chain, with Mrs Meadows still keeping an eye on things.

Lately, he felt she drank too much to blot out the boredom, but she also seemed to disappear for the odd weekend without anyone knowing where she was. In his heart of hearts, he thought she might be having some kind of affair, but her loyalty and love for him had never changed. But when business starts to rule your life, there is always a side of your life that suffers.

'Boring, boring, boring. I will wear these diamonds tonight, though; they will go perfectly with my new dress Maggie has designed for me. I love how it confuses all those bored housewives when they can't buy or find my dress in any store or magazine. They all try and copy them.' For the first time this morning, Julie laughed out loud.

Years ago, she would have been invisible to them, but now Mrs Gold was waited on hand and foot by the very people that had once turned their noses up at women like her.

'Here, let's get some good English breakfast inside of you. That is always the best thing for a hangover.' Ralph stood up and waved the maid away and started filling a plate.

'I don't have any real friends any more, Ralph. You and Carlos even stole Roland from me. He now has a fleet of cargo trawlers at your beck and call. Get some of your own friends, will you? And I don't mean that imbecile Paddy. Thankfully we haven't heard much of him lately.'

Julie waved the maid in the far corner over to fasten on her new diamond necklace. It looked stunning. The Arab prince they had stolen it from was now a family friend who they visited often at his palaces. Making a mental note, Ralph must remember to tell Julie not to take that necklace on their next trip!

'Where are you going this morning, Ralph?'

'Don't you remember? I told you last night. Don Carlos comes to England today and he has asked to see me. I would usually go to see him anyway, but this sounds like business.'

'Oh God, whose granny does he want us to mug next? I swear to God he's got ants in his pants. He can never sit down without having a hare-brained idea.'

'I think it might have something to do with Charlie Jenkins.

Business has been good at the club. It's proved its worth. The place is an absolute rathole. Shame, really – he could have made something out of it. But now it seems he's going to prison and the club will be left empty again. I presume that's what Carlos wants to discuss. We launder a fortune through that place.'

'Why is Charlie going to prison?' Now Ralph had captured Julie's interest. She didn't like Charlie Jenkins, but Ralph was right. He'd kept out of their business and brought all of his lowlife scum to the West End. It seemed now he had met his match and was paying the price.

'Some clever bugger, Tony something, I can't remember his name.' Ralph shook his head trying to remember. 'Charlie was greedy. The spyhole on the clock had proved that. It also proved that he was indeed a police informer, which I just happened to drop into the conversation with Marlon. They never gave him a day's rest. Just when he thought things had calmed down on their turf war, Marlon started sending his boys around again, causing mayhem at his pub.' This made Ralph laugh. He had become good friends with Marlon and they had already done some good business together.

'So what about the club? Are you going to sell it? It's not exactly a going concern, is it?' Julie scoffed at the idea that anyone would want the club. It was indeed a real shithole and Charlie Jenkins had brought it down to his level.

'I don't know; I presume this is what this meeting is all about. Do you want to come?'

'Not today – I have to go and meet that headmistress of that nursery for Josh. It's a special needs one that helps them mix and feel easy with people. Josh won't feel out of place there. I can't have him laughed at, Ralph.'

'I think you're being a little over protective. He's still a baby. Okay, he's a little behind the other kids and he doesn't socialise well, but he has a lot of growing up to do and he will.'

Julie slammed her fist on the table in anger, making her coffee spill into its saucer. 'They say he has all kinds of problems. It's my job – our job – to protect him, and I won't have him bullied. When the time comes, he will go to the best school your money can buy.'

Raising his hands in submission, Ralph shook his head. He knew this was a sore point. Josh was partially deaf, which would hinder his speech. He was miles behind kids of his own age and had been under the spotlight of the doctors all his little life. But Julie was always way ahead of herself, looking into the future. This nursery was to help children like him socialise early. To get used to different faces and people around them. And Ralph knew Julie needed Josh to feel safe. She didn't want him being bullied or laughed at. After doing her research, Julie had found a beautiful private nursery nearby that helped special needs children and she wanted to send him there, where she felt he would be safe.

'Hey, I am on your side. I understand. Josh will be fine; he's still only a baby, Julie.' Standing up, Ralph walked around to Julie's side of the table and pulled a chair out. 'Do you want me to come with you today? Let's show a united front, eh? We're Josh's parents; we'll go together.' Pulling her head forward to rest on his shoulder, he held her close.

'I'd like that. Thank you. What would I do without you?'

'Well, you'd sleep longer because I wouldn't be whistling in the mornings. But then you would have nothing to complain about. Come here. Happy anniversary, Julie.'

'I got you a card – here.' Julie picked up a red envelope off the table and handed it to him.

Raising both eyebrows, Ralph smiled. 'Wow, a card. I'm impressed.' Opening it up, he read it and he stood the card up on the table. 'That's great, thank you.'

'I wrote it myself; I didn't get the butler to write it for me.' She kissed him on the cheek and smiled.

Ralph was bemused. 'Well, that makes it even more valuable, Julie my love. Never let it be said that you're a spendthrift.' He grinned.

'Well, what do you buy the man who has everything, including me? Anyway, you don't need anything. I can't buy you diamonds, can I?' She laughed.

'Well, Julie my love. I got all I wanted a year ago and that was you. What more could a man ask for?'

'Well, Ralph Gold, if that is all you want on your anniversary, so be it. But I was thinking of giving you something more personal... if you know what I mean. I got the cook to make some chocolate mousse...' Letting her voice trail off, Julie grinned, remembering the night she had put chocolate mousse all over Ralph's naked body. What a night that had been! She had decided that would be the kind of anniversary gift any man would want.

Raising his eyebrows, Ralph looked at her. 'Chocolate mousse, eh? Well, that's my favourite. When did you have this gift in mind for?' Excitement rose inside of him. He also remembered that night only too well.

Julie drummed her fingers on her chin as though deep in thought. She enjoyed dangling the carrot in front of Ralph's libido. He was always up for some fun.

'Now? That is, if you're not busy, Mr Gold?'

Ralph looked around for the butler. 'Jarvis, get me some chocolate mousse out of the fridge and bring it upstairs!' he shouted at the top of his voice. Running around the table, he grabbed Julie's hand. 'You are one present I am going to enjoy unwrapping.' They both laughed like teenagers as they ran for the staircase.

28

CONFESSION TIME

'Ralph, it is so good to see you, my friend. It has been far too long. We have been busy, *sì*?' Carlos pulled Ralph towards him in a brotherly hug and held him tight, kissing him on the cheek, much to everyone's astonishment. Carlos never showed emotion. He was a cold, calculated businessman and was now the head of the families in organised crime. No one moved a muscle without his say-so. And they were all aware of his temper and how quickly his mood could change.

Ralph looked around the familiar penthouse suite that was always at Carlos's disposal. It was full of the usual henchmen in their black suits and ties. After Carlos, Ralph walked over to Marco and was greeted with the same familiarity. They were family and treated each other as such.

'Why are you all standing around? Get Ralph a drink and then you can all leave. You stay, Marco; I want you here.' No sooner said than done, Ralph, Carlos and Marco were handed their whiskies and everyone left the room.

'So, Carlos, what's the big emergency. Is it the club?'

'Don't rush me.' Carlos laughed. His black hair was slicked back with just the odd sign of grey at his temples making him even more distinguished. He indeed did look like the godfather of all the families.

'Sorry, go on.' Taking a sip of his drink, Ralph sat back in his chair and waited for another one of Carlos's ideas. It seemed he never ran out of them, although these days he had to take a back seat and just issue the orders.

'How is Julie? How are you?' Concern washed over Carlos's face for Ralph and Julie's welfare.

Letting out a deep sigh, Ralph sat forward. 'Things are not good, to be honest. I work night and day. It's my way of coping, but I know Julie feels neglected. Life has just got in the way. She has her showbiz friends and parties most of the time. She throws herself into the charities and gives everyone a good time. Personally, I feel it's tears of a clown when no one is around, especially me. But you have been fortunate. Congratulations on your fine son!'

'Maria has been a good wife and now a good mother. She has served her purpose. But we are not as close as you and Julie. You two share everything and in that way you are the lucky one. I only have the men around me to discuss business with. We both have our compensations, Ralph. But Julie must remember that you have lost a baby also.' Seeing the sadness on Ralph's face, Carlos stood up and poured them both another drink. Suddenly the room had become melancholy. Standing in front of Ralph, Carlos gave a deep sigh and looked at Ralph. Running his hands through his black hair, he rolled his eyes up to the ceiling.

'What's troubling you, Carlos? This is something big indeed. I have never seen you like this. You look like you're going to burst into tears.' The man standing before him was not Don Carlos, but a very troubled man. He looked almost in pain.

Going back to his chair, Carlos sat down and took a deep breath. 'I need you to absolve me, Ralph. I have been troubled for many years, but now the time has come. While we're talking about how our lives have changed, I need to do this now while it's fresh in my mind. Don't interrupt me.' Carlos held up his hand. The last thing he needed right now was Ralph's concern for his wellbeing. This would only make matters worse.

'My father told me that it was he who instigated the death of your wife Irene. He and my brother Ricky changed your destiny. He wanted your skills so badly; he knew you would never leave Ireland without good cause. I had nothing to do with it. Yes, I agree I wanted us to work together, you know that.' Carlos stammered as he spoke the words that had troubled him for so long. Even now he knew he was only telling Ralph the half-truth. But a half-truth was better than none, and now his father and brother were dead he could use them and clear himself of all blame.

Some things from the past came back to haunt you and Carlos didn't want this to be one of those things. His father had known about the plot to kill Irene, so that wasn't a lie. Well, not exactly. Carlos knew he was as guilty as hell. It had all been his idea. He had wanted Ralph out of Ireland and away from his clingy wife, who would hold him back from what he had to offer him. But Ralph wouldn't understand that. Even now with Julie as his wife, Carlos knew Ralph would never forgive him if he found out that he was the one who had ordered Irene's death. Ralph was a man of morals; this was an easier way to confess his sins without losing the friendship. He'd never realised that his friendship with Ralph would be a strong bond like it was and now he needed to get it off his chest. 'Sorry isn't enough, Ralph, I know that. But both of them are dead now and you have some kind of consolation that you killed Rico with your own bare hands. Is that some kind of vengeance?' Carlos was almost on his knees, pleading for Ralph's forgiveness.

Stunned at this revelation, Ralph paled and sat rooted to the spot. Words escaped him. What was he supposed to say after all of these years? He felt sick and angry, but still he said nothing. The deafening silence in the room tortured Carlos even more than a mad outburst.

Suddenly the words came to Ralph; his emotions were getting the better of him and he couldn't stop himself. 'You stole my family from me. You and your family killed my wife, my child and our unborn baby and you nearly killed my mother. She died not knowing who I was. You have done the best robbery of your life, Carlos.' His voice was calm as he was still trying to take in what Carlos was saying. The words spun around in his head and he couldn't make sense of them. Why was Carlos telling him this now?

'Those Irish protestors would have killed you and your family with or without our intervention. They were determined. They hated you then and they hate you now. That is one score that will never be settled. I didn't need to tell you this. This is a secret I have buried for a long time and could have carried on doing so. But I can't live with these secrets between us. If you wish us to no longer be friends, I accept that. This is irretrievable damage to our brotherhood. And I'm sorry, Ralph.' For the first time in years, tears poured down Carlos's face. With every fibre in his being, he didn't want Ralph to turn his back on him. He was one of the few people he could talk to and know it wouldn't go any further. 'You can never leave the establishment, you know that. Once you join us, the only way you leave is in a body bag or with permission. That permission is granted. Forgive me and my selfish family. I value your friendship very much.'

'Maybe it's you who should end up in a body bag! You and your fucking Italian family. You two-faced bastard. We are not friends. You have used me all of these years. Knowing your sick sense of humour, you probably laughed about it!' Standing up, Ralph couldn't control his anger any longer. He lashed out and threw a punch in Carlos's face. He wanted to hurt him. He wanted him to feel the anguish and pain he had all those years ago.

Carlos didn't fight back. Although Marco came forward to help him, he brushed him aside and rubbed his jaw. 'I haven't used you; you did what you wanted to do.' Blood poured from his nose and he picked up a handkerchief to stop the flow. 'You wanted out of your old life, Ralph. You knew you were destined for better things. Did you really want to spend the rest of your life working in that quarry? Did you want your son to follow your lead and spend the rest of his life doing that? Always looking over your shoulder, waiting for the bullet to come from one of Paddy's friends. Don't be a hypocrite; you didn't want to stay there. Your wife held you back and she always would and you resented her for it,' Carlos spat at him.

The words cut deep into Ralph. More so because he knew he spoke the truth. He was right; Ralph had resented his wife and the life they had in Ireland. But Ralph didn't want to hear the truth; he was as guilty as they were.

'Why tell me now, Carlos? Is this your sadistic pleasure of the day? Couldn't you find anything else to amuse yourself? And so you attack me when I am at a low ebb. I have been nothing but loyal to you and this is how you treat me. Well, fuck your establishment, and fuck you. I'm out of here.' He stood up to leave.

Carlos shouted him back. 'Stop! Tell me truthfully that you didn't want all of this. You are at the head of your game. My fucking establishment has protected you.' Walking towards him, Carlos pointed his finger in Ralph's face. This heated exchange needed finishing now, one way or another. 'You have a woman you actually love and want to be with now. I gave you that opportunity. Tell me it hasn't all been for nothing.' Carlos was shouting now. He so badly needed Ralph to see his point of view. He wished he hadn't done this, but if Ralph turned his back on him, then so be it.

'I need to get out of here. I can't look at you right now. You make me sick. You bring nothing but death and unhappiness.' Opening the door, Ralph slammed it behind him.

Still rubbing his face, Carlos sat back down on the sofa and accepted the ice wrapped in a napkin Marco offered him. 'That went better than I expected, but the truth is out now. Ralph lies to himself. One way or another, he would have gone his own merry way. He contacted us. He could just have easily not dialled the number on the telegram. But he wanted out.'

'Not at the cost of people's lives. I think Ralph is the kind of guy to stick it out. He's a loyal, good guy.'

'Let's see what happens next. Let's hope Julie will talk some sense into him, Marco. She's our only hope. Ring her; we need to put her on her guard about this.'

* * *

'What's up with you? You've got a face like a slapped arse.' Not being able to avoid Ralph's depressing mood, Julie wanted to get to the bottom of it.

'It's Carlos. I can't believe it, Julie. He told me his father was responsible for killing Irene and my son and injuring my mother too. He has begged me for my forgiveness, but could you forgive him?' Ralph's body shook as the tears ran down his face. He was inconsolable and lost. How could his own selfishness have let this happen?

Lighting two cigarettes, Julie handed him one, already noticing the ashtray was full, and sat beside him. 'Well, I'm surprised and shocked at his confession. God knows what brought that bout of honesty on. But I would be a liar if I told you I didn't suspect it. Come on, Ralph, have you never wondered who was behind their deaths, knowing what you know about Carlos now? He's a ruthless bastard and gets what he wants regardless of the consequences. Tell me everything that he said.'

Julie sat and listened to every word Ralph spilt out. Something had always nagged at her when Ralph had told her how he and Carlos had met. Ralph also admitted that Carlos was right in some ways and that he had resented his wife and the life they'd had – but he would never have wished for her and young Shaun to be killed.

'So you feel guilty? After all of these years, you're having to face your demons and admit the truth. You love this life. You love being Ralph Gold, but you feel guilty because you paid a high price for it. I understand that.' Putting her arms around his shoulders, she held him closer to her.

'We had an argument, Irene and me. The last words I said to her were that I wished we'd never met and got married. Can you believe that? I was angry at being forced to backpedal into a shitty street surrounded by her family. I shouted I wished she was dead. Oh God, Julie, what have I done? I could have left and she would have met someone else like-minded and happily lived the rest of her life out. But instead the poor cow met me.'

Tender and loving, Julie held him against her. 'There, there, Ralph. Julie's here. Sometimes when we shout in anger, we speak the truth. You wouldn't have left; you would have stayed and settled for your lot in life – that is who you are.'

'I suppose so.' Raising his head, Ralph wiped the tears from his face. There was nothing he could do about it now.

'Well, you have three options. Avenge their deaths; kill Carlos and be dead yourself in a couple of hours. Go back to Ireland, get your job back at the quarry and give all your fame and fortune away, or move on. It's your call, but I've lived in shit and had to survive hand-to-mouth and I'm not sure I could do it again. I love you, Ralph; you are my heart and soul and I won't stop you, whatever you want to do.'

Shocked, Ralph pulled away. 'You would leave me? I thought you loved me. Is this all I am to you? Do you only love the wealthy man, not the man beneath the money?'

'I love you, Ralph. I don't say it often enough, but I do. But we have a choice now; we can't change the past.' This life might bore her at times, but she would be damned if she'd give it up. 'I've lost my sister, my mother and nothing is going to change that – do you understand me? Being skint for the rest of our lives isn't going to change it. Give Carlos the absolution he wants and let us get on with our lives together.'

'I just wish he hadn't told me. Why do you think he did?'

'Because at some point in your life, the truth always comes out and bites you on your arse. He wanted to get his side of things in first.'

'You won't leave me, will you? You're the only woman I have ever loved. A big strong guy like me under the thumb of a five-foot blonde with a sassy mouth like you, and I love it.' For the first time, Ralph laughed and hugged her.

'You ain't ever getting rid of me, Mr Gold. I'm your penance in life. Now stop worrying about things you can't change and move on. Carlos has helped you build your empire, taken you under his wing. Shit, he's possibly still paying off what I spent on the wedding! Go and see him. Things don't have to be as they once were between you, but don't end it like this.'

Consoled by the fact that Julie loved him and there was nothing he could do to change the past, he knew she was right, and that he was as much to blame. He could distance himself from Carlos, but what would that do? It would only ostracise him from some of the people he did business with. He would be cutting his nose off to spite his face and all of this would be for nothing. 'Give it a couple of days and I will go and see him. I just need to get my head together first.'

29

A NEW KID ON THE BLOCK

With Julie at his side, Ralph breezed into Carlos's penthouse suite. It made Julie laugh when she saw him in dark glasses trying to hide the black eye and swollen nose Ralph had given him. Instantly, Marco ordered everyone out.

'This is a rewind of what should have been said a few days ago. You have said your piece, Carlos, so we leave it now.' Whatever each of them said would not make it right. Even Ralph blamed himself for what had happened to his family.

Humbled by their presence, Carlos sat down. He felt a hug was inappropriate at the moment, so left his usual greeting aside.

'Drinks first.' Carlos waited until everyone had their drinks. Looking down at the carpet and back up at Ralph, he began. 'Well, it's maybe not the time for me to ask a favour, but I will do as you ask and get to the point. This matter isn't something I can be seen to be involved with. I cannot show favouritism; it's bad for business.' Expressing himself in the usual Italian way, Carlos held his hands out openly for Ralph to understand his predicament.

Raising his eyebrows, Ralph turned towards Julie. They were both unsure of what revelation Carlos was going to come up with next. Julie reached out for his hand and squeezed it. Calmly turning back towards Carlos, Ralph nodded for him to continue. 'Well, it sounds interesting, so let's have it.'

Ralph's cold manner hurt Carlos. But if they were here on business, so be it.

Ralph frowned. 'Do you know anything about this, Marco, or are you as intrigued as me?' Seeing Marco nod his head, Ralph looked at Carlos, took a sip of his drink and waited.

'There is a new kid on the block.' Carlos laughed, trying to break the ice, but he realised it was too soon. Especially when Ralph's face didn't move. It was like a poker game and, at the moment, Ralph had a full hand. 'Anyway, he is an old family friend, but he doesn't know it, which is a good thing. I would like to give him the club to manage.' Again, Carlos paused, waiting for a reaction from Ralph, but there was none. 'I think he will do well; he has ambition and nothing to lose. If we think our pasts are full of sad stories, you need to hear about his.' Carlos put a folder on the table. Julie frowned and looked at Ralph. It was an official document stamped by social services for fostered and adopted children. 'He's a street urchin trying to claw his way up into the world. All he has are his brains and his fists. We could still launder money through the club, and I would like to give him the option of buying it in a year. Of course, Ralph, I will buy and pay you for your half of the club. He's young and needs guidance. A little bit hot-headed, but that is the Italian in him. I think you two could work well together once he's trained.'

'Are you passing some young Italian kid onto me? Suddenly, this man is taking your place in our partnership, is that it? You tell me your family killed my family and then you're the one backing out and giving me an apprentice.'

'No, no, Ralph.' Carlos was shaking his head emphatically. 'You misunderstand me. You and I have worked together for a long time.

We have history. All I am asking is you give this young pup a chance and help him.'

'You make him sound like a dog, Don Carlos.' Although Julie retorted in her usual sarcastic manner, she had made a point of addressing him with his formal title. Carlos peered over his glasses at her and said nothing. He knew the point she was making. This was no longer a couple of friends talking. This was business colleagues, discussing business.

'So how come he doesn't know your family?' Intrigued, Ralph butted in.

'I only found out by chance, but I do know that his family in Italy have searched for him for years. It's all in the folder. Read it at your leisure. His grandparents were very good friends with mine. We go back a long way, but he is not to know this – well, not yet, anyway. I want to see what he makes of the opportunities we throw in his direction. If he fucks up, that is his problem. I can honestly say I have done my best.'

'Antony Perry – is that him?' Ralph picked up the folder and saw the name on the front. 'It doesn't sound very Italian.'

'Sadly, no, Ralph. That is why his family never found him. His name is Antonias Lambrianu; his friends call him Tony.'

'Lambrianu? Isn't that the posh wine company? Is that the guy you mean? He doesn't have a pot to piss in and yet he comes from one of the richest families in Italy. For fuck's sake, how come shit like that never happens to me?' Letting out a sigh, Julie reached for the cigarette case and lit two, handing one to Ralph.

'Do you think he will want to manage the club, Carlos? Or do you already know?' Unlike Julie, Ralph dropped the formality of calling Carlos 'Don'. Over the last couple of days, Ralph had done a lot of soul-searching. What was the point of burning bridges now? There was no turning back. He was as guilty as all of them. He had hated the way he had been trapped into a loveless marriage, even though it was the right thing to do. He had even wondered if that was why he'd gone to prison so often. Had that been his escape from it all?

'Well, yes, I have kind of broached the subject and he seems keen. But it is also your property, Ralph. I cannot do it without your consent. I met him in Italy. He had some unfinished business there. He is very keen and very ambitious. Personally, I think he will do well. But he needs guidance.'

'Are you blinded by family loyalty and the fact that he is Italian, or do you think he could make the place a going concern? Seriously, isn't it you who says there is no sentiment in business?' Opening his hands wide and mimicking Carlos's ways, Ralph stared at him and waited for an answer.

'No. He has already started his own protection racket with his foster brother. He just needs a nudge in the right direction. His next step would be contacting you. Sound him out. Meet him and see for yourself.'

'Well, I hate to admit it, but you have rarely steered me wrong. Take the club; if he does well, I will take my half share out of it with the laundered money. If he falls on his arse and doesn't make a penny, then you pay me. Is that fair?'

'More than fair. That's the deal, then. Just keep a watchful eye on him and report back to me. Any stupidity on his behalf and he has blown his chances. No sentiment, Ralph, just opportunity. As I say, if he fucks it up, that's his problem, *capisce*?'

Ralph stood up to leave. 'Project Tony Lambrianu it is, then.'

Carlos's voice softened somewhat as he stood up and held out his hand. 'Ralph, please shake my hand. Let's not part with unfinished business and bad feeling.'

Ralph turned to Julie, who simply nodded at him, and he held out his hand to shake Carlos's. 'No bad feeling, Carlos. We have work to do and if we can get this young pup to work in our favour, that's fine with me.' Ralph opened his arms and, seeing the wide grin spread across Carlos's face as they hugged each other, he knew he had done the right thing. They both knew everything would be okay. This was just another beginning.

Waiting for the chauffeur to open the car door and taking a cigarette out of her gold cigarette case, Julie lit it. 'Give me that fucking folder, Ralph.' Snatching it out of his hand, she slid into the back seat of their Rolls-Royce.

'What's the rush? For crying out loud, what are you so worked up about now? We'll read it later.' Ralph couldn't understand why Julie was so angry. Her face was flushed and her eyes were full of anger.

'I'll tell you why I'm so pissed off. We work our balls off risking our lives for what we have and some rich kid is just going to waltz in with the blessing of Carlos and take over? Like fucking hell he is. Is that what all of his confession was about? Is this your retirement, Ralph? Well, fuck Carlos and Tony Lambrianu... whoever he is!'

Trying to calm her down and placate her, Ralph pressed the button at the side of him which raised the screen between them and the chauffeur. 'Julie, Carlos never mentioned anything about us being pensioned off. Anyway, we have our own money, our own companies. Who gives a shit!'

'I do. We stop when I say so and not before. I'm not going to be passed over. What is so great about this Tony guy? Have you heard of him before? Who the hell is he?' All fired up and shouting, Julie carried on with her tirade of insults and anger.

'For God's sake, will you be quiet! No one has said we're out. On the contrary. We can read the folder and see what we think. If this guy wants to be our fall guy for money-laundering, then so be it. It's no skin off our noses.'

'I'm not interested in reading sob stories. Who cares about his shitty past; we've all had one of those. If Carlos thinks so much about this Tony Lambrianu, let him set him up by himself. This kid is not our business. I don't babysit!'

It was going to be a long ride home and Ralph sat back and thought it was best that he let Julie rant and rave until she ran out of steam. He took out two whisky miniatures from the bar in the car and handed her one. She looked like she needed it.

All night long, Julie sat and read the folder they had been given by Carlos. Although Ralph was in his study making telephone calls, every now and again he would walk towards the lounge and glance around the corner of the doorway to where she was sitting. She was turning page after page, drinking in every word and making notes. Quietly, Ralph slipped away back to his study. Whatever was going through Julie's head, he knew he would find out at some point when she was ready; all he had to do was wait.

It was the early hours of the morning when she had come to bed and crept in beside him. 'Are you okay?' he asked.

'I am. You go to sleep; sorry to disturb you.'

'Did you find what you were looking for?'

'History, Ralph. How are you supposed to know what the future holds if you don't know the history? Carlos likes insurance and so do I. This young kid steps out of line just once and I want to be the one to bring him down. The poor little rich kid, whose mum was a thief and a heroin addict. I would add "prostitute", but people in glass houses don't throw stones, eh?'

'Come here.' Enveloping her into his arms, Ralph held her tight. 'Don't worry, Julie. Everything will be okay.'

'Oh, I'm not worried. I just need to be up to speed on this guy. Leave no stone unturned. I am going to watch him like a hawk.'

Julie felt better now that she knew all there was to know about Tony Lambrianu. If they were going to do business with this man, she needed to know any skeletons he had in his closet and it seemed like he had a lot of them. What is it they say? Keep your friends close and your enemies closer. Well, for the moment this man was unknown to them. He would share their secrets and that would be enough information to put them away for a long time. No, she wasn't taking any chances.

The next day, with her plan firmly embedded in her brain, she waited until Ralph went to work, then called Chris. They had become even closer over the last year; Chris had quickly become her right-hand man.

'Chris, what do you know about a guy call Tony Lambrianu?'

'I've heard of him. Most of us on the streets have. He's taken over the protection rackets in the East End. He has a reputation, that's for sure. Why don't I show you? But be warned.' Chris laughed and wagged his finger at her. 'He is one handsome guy and the women love him. The angels must have blessed that guy with everything.'

Julie laughed. Now she was intrigued. There were only a couple of passport-sized black-and-white pictures of Tony Lambrianu as a kid in the file. But now she wanted to see for herself. What was it that Carlos saw in him?

Julie knew that Ralph would be working late; he always did these days. There was always some meeting to go to or some police commissioner to meet and have drinks with. So, later that evening, she and Chris went into a pub in the East End. It was a decent-looking place, but she had gone in her usual disguise of a black wig.

She wanted to be on top of the situation; she was still Ralph's eyes and ears, after all.

Looking around the usual crowd of drinkers, Julie didn't see anything unusual. There was no Italian god like Chris had described. Sipping her drink, she looked at Chris. 'Well, where is he? Don't tell me he is one of those deadbeats.'

'Just bide your time. Oh shit, they are coming. Quick, hide behind this pillar.' They both stepped behind the pillars holding up the bar like naughty schoolchildren. 'What the fuck are we hiding for? He doesn't know who I am!' Julie burst out laughing. Suddenly she looked up as two young men walked into the pub.

'The dark-haired one is Jake; that's his brother.'

Julie spied the young men. Chris had been right about one thing. The tall blonde one was pretty, with the bluest eyes she had ever seen. When he smiled, his eyes seemed to smile. The suits they wore were expensive and he had a passion for silk shirts that heightened his blondeness. Tonight he had chosen to wear pink. She smiled. It took a very secure, masculine man to wear that colour. He really did have balls.

And even Julie had to admit that he really did look the part. He wasn't her type, but he was tall, masculine, with perfectly chiselled features and a cleft in his chin that seemed to add that extra something. And he was handsome. No, Julie decided, handsome was an understatement.

The publican seemed to be pleased to see him; he was laughing and talking to him. Mr Charming, as Julie called Tony, was shaking hands like he was everyone's best friend. He seemed normal enough, although a bit false. 'So tell me, Chris. What else does he do apart from charm the pants off people and flash that white smile of his?'

'Looks can be deceiving.' Chris lowered his voice. 'He is one evil bastard when crossed. He actually carved his name into one of

Marlon's men's bodies. He doesn't care. Some of the men around here say he's a psychopath!'

Julie noticed the way that even Chris seemed to fear this man, and as he spoke to her, he didn't take his eyes off Tony Lambrianu. It was obvious he was afraid that he would be overheard.

'If you want the voice of reason, you need to speak to his brother, Jake.'

'So how come you know so much about him? What is he to you? Do you fancy him? You seem to take a great interest in his looks.' Julie started to laugh as she watched Chris blush. This mystery got more intriguing by the minute.

'No, don't be daft, but I do admire him. Just look at him holding court in here. He captures the room and lights it up. Nobody ever notices me.'

'Oh, diddums. Poor Chris – haven't you had a shag in a while, then?'

Knowing how Julie liked to be nosy about his sex life, Chris changed the subject. 'Everyone around here knows him. Apparently, to be fair, they run a good, tight ship. He won't have any messing about on his patch and he's got brains by all accounts. Just don't cross him; that smile soon drops from his face and those blue eyes of his turn a murderous dark colour.'

Julie looked at Chris and then back at the two men at the far end of the bar. She knew Jake wasn't his real brother. They had both been fostered by the same woman. Tony Lambrianu had been orphaned young and had lived on the streets. His carefree manner showed he had nothing in the world to lose. He lived by the seat of his pants.

'Does he have a girlfriend?' Julie knew that Carlos preferred to do business with married men. Wives couldn't testify. It looked respectable. It gave them that edge. Ralph had also followed the same guidelines.

'Why, are you interested? Don't worry, your secret is safe with me.' Chris laughed and nudged her with his elbow. He was enjoying this stake-out, but Julie was Ralph's wife, and she loved him. Confused, Chris wondered what was Julie's interest in Tony, that she would go to so much trouble without even speaking to him? 'Well Julie, Tony Lambrianu might have lots of girlfriends, but he doesn't do commitment. It depends what night of the week it is. But they just fall at his feet. Handsome guy, money to burn. All the girls love a bad guy, eh? But Jake, the dark-headed one, has a regular girlfriend or wife. Not sure, really. He is the calming influence. You rarely see one without the other. Does that satisfy your curiosity?'

Julie smiled, although she had to admit, she was intrigued. It seemed this Jekyll and Hyde who Chris was describing hid behind his charming good looks. And underneath he was the very devil himself. She felt it was time she gave Chris more information. 'They want Tony to run the club in the West End and I just wanted to see him for myself.'

'I think he would do okay, although that place needs one hell of a clean-up. But you can see for yourself, he's got the host appeal. Meeting and greeting everyone around here, and all the time he is ripping them off. Like Robin Hood or something. Taking a percentage out of their cash registers to stop troublemakers when he seems to be the biggest troublemaker of all.'

Julie had seen enough. She had the information she'd come for. Tony Lambrianu and his brother Jake were a double act. Each one bounced off the other's strong points. Personally, Julie found Jake more appealing with his boyish looks and that dark hair of his. But each to their own.

'Come on, time to go. Drink up.' Swallowing the last remnants of her drink, she looked at Chris, who seemed preoccupied. 'What's up?'

'Look at him. The smile is disappearing. Something is definitely wrong. Hang on a minute.'

Curiously, she followed Chris's gaze. Sure enough, the smile had dropped and Tony Lambrianu looked serious. Suddenly the pretty boy had disappeared and this man with his temper rising was taking his place. Tony and Jake put their drinks on the bar and walked out. 'Come on.' Pulling Chris by his jacket sleeve, she discreetly followed them outside.

Tony was opening the boot of his car; Julie couldn't see what he was doing. It was now dark and the street lighting wasn't very good.

'You know the price, mister – pay the full amount or we drive off,' she heard Tony say to the publican, who had been hot on their heels, shouting that he was sorry. There was hardly anyone around, but the few stragglers coming out of the pub paid no attention to this confrontation. Julie looked over as the publican held out an envelope to Tony and then took out his wallet.

'Here, Tony. Take it. Take the lot. I must have miscounted or something. It won't happen again,' he pleaded, while waving money in Tony and Jake's faces.

Surprised, Julie looked on as Tony and Jake reached into the boot and pulled out a man, letting him fall to the floor. The man's hands were tied and he had duct tape across his mouth. Peering closer, without being noticed, Julie's jaw dropped. That guy had been in the boot of the car all of the time they had been in the pub. She couldn't believe it.

Chris let out a slow whistle. 'Bloody hell, Julie. It looks like that publican was going to try and short-change them on their collections. I know that guy on the ground; it's the publican's son. He owes them money and they have just blackmailed him into paying up. Told you he was a mean bastard.'

'Don't ever take me for a fool again. I asked you yesterday for my money and I have had to come back tonight. Do you think I have nothing better to do?' Tony barked.

Straining to hear the muffled argument, Julie didn't want to bring attention to herself, but she was in awe of this. Chris had been right. This man was lethal, with a charming smile on his face.

The publican wasn't listening; he was on his knees, seeing to his injured son and trying to take the tape off his mouth. It was clear to Julie he had been beaten up by the state of his clothes and the clear signs of dried blood down the side of his head.

'Lucky for us, you slimy bastard, we were driving along and who should we bump into and offer a lift to? You got it. Your very own son. Next time I won't bring him back to you. Be warned. It wouldn't be my choice; it's yours. If you want your son to die, then don't pay me.' With that, Tony nodded to Jake and each of them opened the doors of the car and got in, waving as they drove away, leaving the publican and his son on the pavement.

'Come on, Julie, let's get out of here. This is no place for you. Ralph would kill me if he thought I had brought you to a dump like this.'

Satisfied, Julie got into the car and they drove home, her mind whirling at the events she had seen tonight.

* * *

Ralph opened the door before she could put her key in. He had seen the car headlights turn into the drive. 'Where the hell have you been?'

'Why, what's wrong? You never tell me what time you're going to be home,' she snapped. The last thing she needed was a possessive husband.

'I was worried. You understand that, surely. Not a phone call, or even one of your sticky notes.' Relief washed over him. He was so pleased to see her.

'Well, pour me a drink and stop panicking. I can look after myself, you know. Anyway, I have been doing your dirty work for you.' Julie waited while Ralph poured her a drink and sat down.

'What do you mean, my dirty work?'

'I have seen Carlos's new kid on the block.'

'What? Why?' Ralph was confused. 'Julie, why would you go looking for him? I bet it was Chris. Why the hell would he take you there? I will be having words with him.'

'Oh, shut up, Ralph love. Don't you want to know what I saw?' Julie sat there smugly with her drink. She knew Ralph would want to know about Tony. It was human curiosity.

Julie told him the whole story. 'Personally, I think he is a loose cannon. Taking blokes out of the boot of his car in the middle of the street and dropping them on the pavement. That is, of course, after he kidnapped the publican's son. Granted, he's no young kid; he must have been about thirty years old. He is self-centred and in love with himself, which is why he won't have a permanent girlfriend. He is handsome and I agree with Chris he could run the club, probably even make something of it. But he's a playboy. He would bring the wrong kind of attention to us. The last thing we need is the spotlight on our business dealings.'

Letting out a deep sigh, Ralph sat back on the sofa. 'I know. I have made it my business too. And I agree we will give him a wide berth. But I also agree that he is an ambitious man and giving him that club and a place to live in the West End would suit his vanity. I think he would make a go of it. I also agree he loves the limelight. Possibly because he's never had much attention in his life – who knows. But I am prepared to keep an eye on him and launder my money through him. What do you think?'

Begrudgingly, Julie agreed. There were pros and cons to everything. At least if this went wrong, it was down to Don Carlos. 'You know, Carlos's folder on Tony Lambrianu has given me an idea. All those businessmen you know who are on the take, we should start our own folders on them, all their little quirks and backgrounds. It's all evidence for blackmail… shit, with all those respectable MPs and coppers in your pocket, we'd have a library! Let's find out more about the people we're dealing with, Ralph.'

'So that's your new project? Gathering information to blackmail people with?' Ralph couldn't help but laugh. Julie was like a scorpion. Smiling and mingling with these men's wives at charity events and all the time she would be watching them and taking notes. But even he had to agree she had a point. 'It sounds like a good idea. Who are these people? Let's find their skeletons. That gives us the upper hand. Nice one, Julie. Where have you been all my life?'

'Oh, shut up – I wasn't born for half of it!'

Lovingly, she gave him a kiss, but mentally she was already setting her plan into action. There could be no surprises if they already knew them. Team Gold would take a lot of beating.

'Did you think he was handsome?' Ralph suddenly asked, averting his eyes. He had seen Tony was a ladies' man, and younger than him.

Playing along, Julie couldn't help but tease him. 'Yes, I'm not blind, you know. Yes, he's handsome. But not as handsome as you. What bothers me is why it's all the men who think he's handsome. Chris said the same thing.' Julie laughed. She always felt at ease with Ralph. He had that calming influence over her.

'Just me being a jealous husband. Take no notice. So are we agreed – do we join Team Tony Lambrianu? Is it the Golds and Lambrianu? What do you say, because I wouldn't do anything without you.' Reaching out and touching a strand of her hair, Ralph smiled.

Chinking her glass against his, Julie nodded. 'Firstly Ralph, thank you for being a jealous husband. It's flattering and I like it. secondly,' she raised her glass in the air. 'The Golds and the Lambrianus it is. Just don't go near the boot of his car!' Julie laughed. They could both see a long business relationship with this new kid on the block.

Julie raised her glass again. 'To Tony Lambrianu; may he make us a lot of money.' They both laughed and chinked their glasses together. Their future looked better than ever.

What no one realised was that Tony Lambrianu would become the most notorious London gangland boss of their time. But that's another story...

ACKNOWLEDGMENTS

Thanks to Sue and Avril, all my readers, and the UK crime and other book clubs for all of their support and loyalty.

Many thanks to everyone at Boldwood Books and to my editor, Emily, who has turned a writer into an author. Thanks for putting up with me!

MORE FROM GILLIAN GODDEN

We hope you enjoyed reading *Fool's Gold*. If you did, please leave a review.

If you'd like to gift a copy, this book is also available as an ebook, digital audio download and audiobook CD.

Sign up to Gillian Godden's mailing list for news, competitions and updates on future books.

http://bit.ly/GillianGoddenNewsletter

Gold Digger, the first in the series, is available now.

ABOUT THE AUTHOR

Gillian Godden is a Northern-born medical secretary for NHS England. She spent thirty years of her life in the East End of London, hearing stories about the local striptease pubs. Now in Yorkshire, she is an avid reader who lives with her dog, Susie.

Follow Gillian on social media:

facebook.com/gilliangoddenauthor
twitter.com/GGodden

ABOUT BOLDWOOD BOOKS

Boldwood Books is a fiction publishing company seeking out the best stories from around the world.

Find out more at www.boldwoodbooks.com

Sign up to the Book and Tonic newsletter for news, offers and competitions from Boldwood Books!

http://www.bit.ly/bookandtonic

We'd love to hear from you, follow us on social media:

facebook.com/BookandTonic
twitter.com/BoldwoodBooks
instagram.com/BookandTonic

Printed in Great Britain
by Amazon

14872189R00185